The continuing and turbulent epic of a dynasty built on the dream of Bennett Lyon. The dynasty that has survived a generation of relentless hate and passion.

Now, the younger descendants of the gentleman from England have taken over the legacy without shame. From the pirate death-ships that sailed the high seas to the war-torn land of their new Virginia home, this Colonial family will withstand a house divided . . .

Also by Mary Shura Craig from Jove

DUST TO DIAMONDS
LYON'S PRIDE

Pirate's Landing

Mary Shura Craig

A JOVE BOOK

PIRATE'S LANDING

A Jove Book / published by arrangement with
the author

PRINTING HISTORY
Jove edition / June 1983

ISBN: 0-515-05296-5

Jove books are published by Jove Publications, Inc.,
200 Madison Avenue, New York, N.Y. 10016. The words
''A JOVE BOOK'' and the ''J'' with sunburst are trademarks
belonging to Jove Publications, Inc.

PRINTED IN THE UNITED STATES OF AMERICA

*To the shadowy ancestors of my mother,
born Mary Francis Milstead (1889–   ),
whose records and charts blazed the
trail that this fictional family follows.*

CONTENTS

For if the trumpet give an uncertain
sound, who shall prepare himself to the battle?

I Corinthians 14:8

Though a man be wise, it is no shame for him to live
and learn.

Sophocles, *Antigone*

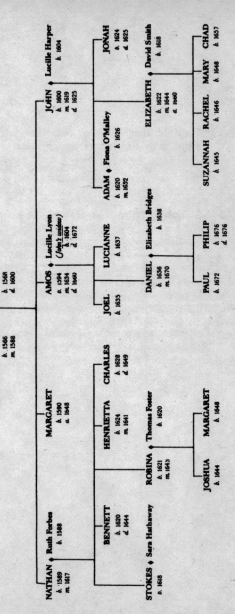

THE DESCENT OF BENNETT LYON,
Gentleman of Somersetshire, England

BENNETT LYON ♦ Anne Stokes
b. 1561
m. 1588
d. 1600

JOHN ♦ Lucille Harper
b. 1600
m. 1619
d. 1625

AMOS ♦ Lucille Lyon
b. 1594   (John's widow)
m. 1634   b. 1604
d. 1660   d. 1672

MARGARET
b. 1590
d. 1648

NATHAN ♦ Rush Forbes
b. 1589
m. 1617

JONAH
b. 1624
d. 1625

ADAM ♦ Fiona O'Malley
b. 1620   b. 1626
m. 1652

LUCIANNE
b. 1637

JOEL
b. 1635

ELIZABETH ♦ David Smith
b. 1622   b. 1618
m. 1644
d. 1660

DANIEL ♦ Elizabeth Bridges
b. 1656   b. 1638
m. 1670

SUZANNAH   MARY   RACHEL   CHAD
b. 1645   b. 1648 b. 1646   b. 1657

PAUL   PHILIP
b. 1672 b. 1676
        d. 1676

BENNETT
b. 1620
d. 1644

HENRIETTA
b. 1624
m. 1641

CHARLES
b. 1628
d. 1649

STOKES ♦ Sara Hathaway
b. 1618

ROBINA ♦ Thomas Foster
b. 1621   b. 1620
m. 1643

JOSHUA   MARGARET
b. 1644   b. 1648

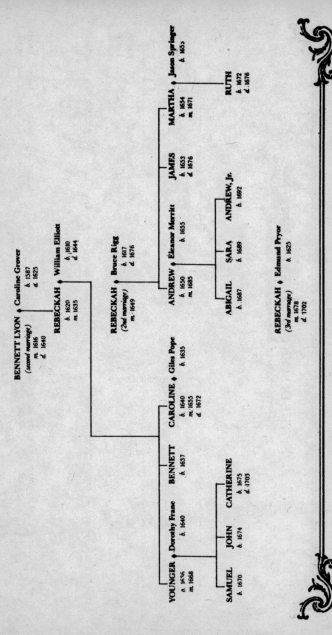

CHRONOLOGY OF DATES
DURING THE LIVES
OF ANDREW RIGG, JR.
AND HIS WIFE,
EMILY FRASER RIGG (1699–1776)

The following monarchs ruled England during this period:
  House of Stuart: William and Mary (1689–1694), William III
  (1689–1702) Queen Anne (1702–1714)
  House of Hanover: George I (1714–1727), George II (1727–1760)
  George III (1760–1820)
Wars During this period that affected the colonies:
  1689–1697 . . . King William's War
  1702–1713 . . . Queen Anne's War
  1739–1741 . . . War of Jenkins's Ear
  1744–1748 . . . King George's War
  1754–1760 . . . French and Indian War

1692	First national debt in England.
1693	College of William and Mary chartered.
1698	Capital at Jamestown destroyed by fire.
1699	Middle Plantation renamed Williamsburg and made capital. Freedom of religion made law in Virginia.
1701	Captain Kidd captured and hanged. Yale College chartered.
1702	England declares war on France.
1704	Marlborough victorious at Blenheim. Indian massacre at Deerfield, Massachusetts. First colonial newspaper, *Boston News-Letter*.
1706	Charleston, South Carolina, defended against the Spanish.
1708	Jacobean attempt to retake England fails.
1709	14,000 Palatinate inhabitants emigrate to North America.
1713	Peace of Utrecht. Carolinas divided into north and south.

1714	G. D. Fahrenheit constructs mercury thermometer. French expand up the Mississippi River.
1715	Jacobite rebellion in England. Vaudeville begins in Paris.
1716	Governor Spotswood leads expedition to Shenandoah Valley.
1717	Inoculation against smallpox introduced into England. Voltaire sent into the Bastille.
1718	New Orleans settled by French. Blackbeard killed. England declares war on Spain. Collegiate School of America renamed Yale University.
1719	France declares war on Spain. Daniel Defoe's *Robinson Crusoe* published.
1720	France bankrupt, (Spain occupies Texas.) South Carolina rebellion results in appointment of a provincial royal governor.
1721	Smallpox epidemic in Boston. Swiss colonists introduce rifles into America.
1726	Stephen Hales measures blood pressure. Jonathan Swift's *Gulliver's Travels* published.
1727	Quakers demand abolition of slavery. War between England and Spain.
1729	Natchez Indians massacre the French at Fort Rosalie, Mississippi. John and Charles Wesley found Methodism at Oxford.
1730	Benjamin Franklin becomes owner and editor of the *Pennsylvania Gazette*.
1732	Only Catholic church in Colonies before revolution built in Philadelphia. James Oglethorpe charters Georgia. Franklin begins publication of *Poor Richard's Almanack*.
1733	Molasses Act forbids American trade with West Indies.
1734	John Peter Zenger arrested for libel. 8,000 Salzburg Protestants settle in Georgia.
1735	Landmark trial for freedom of the press won by John Peter Zenger.
1736	Aymands performs first successful appendectomy.
1737	William Byrd founds Richmond, Virginia, on fall line.
1738	Disputes with Spain bring British troops to Georgia. John Wesley and George Whitefield, leader of the Great Awakening, visits America.
1742	Spanish fleet attacks Georgia.
1744	France declares war on England. George Whitefield visits New England.
1746	Scotch Highland Stuart supporters settle near Cape Fear.
1747	Riots in Boston over British impressment of seamen.
1749	200,000 acres ceded to the Ohio Company for settlement.

1750	Dr. Thomas Walker discovers Cumberland Gap.
1752	British calendar changed; January 1 beings the New Year. Benjamin Franklin invents lightning conductor.
1753	French take Ohio valley, George Washington to negotiate.
1754	Washington builds Fort Necessity. Albany Congress, first Colonial congress, formed for defense of the colonies.
1755	Braddock's army defeated by French.
1756	Britain declares war on France. Seven Years War begins.
1758	British defeated at Ticonderoga.
1759	British take Quebec.
1761	James Otis denies British right to issue writs of assistance.
1762	England declares war on Spain.
1763	Treaty of Paris ends Seven Years War. Ottowa Indians organize revolt. Patrick Henry speaks against Crown's interference in the Colonies. French found St. Louis.
1764	Virginia addresses Crown on taxation without representation. Crown forbids issue of paper money.
1765	Stamp Act passes. Patrick Henry speaks to burgesses. Stamp Act Congress held in New York. Quartering Act passed.
1766	Part of Mason-Dixon line drawn between Maryland and Pennsylvania.
1767	Parliament passes Townshend Acts.
1768	North Carolina Regulators organize. Massachusetts Assembly dissolved. Spanish seize St. Louis from French.
1769	Virginia burgesses adopt Patrick Henry's Resolutions.
1770	Boston Massacre. British cut down Liberty Tree.
1771	Armed clash in North Carolina.
1772	South Adams forms Committee of Correspondence. Revenue Boat *Gaspee* burned.
1773	Boston Tea Party.
1774	Crown closes port of Boston. First Continental Congress meets to plan nonimportation of English goods. Indian war on Virginia border.
1775	Battle of Lexington. Second Continental Congress forms the Continental Army, with George Washington as commander in chief. Battle of Bunker Hill. Governor Dunmore flees Virginia. Virginians battle the British for control of Norfolk.
1776	January 1–2, Norfolk burned.

PROLOGUE

A True-Born Englishman
(1716)

A true-born Englishman's a contradiction,
In speech an irony.
In fact, a fiction.

> Daniel Defoe, *The True-Born Englishman*
> *(1701)*

Boast not thyself of tomorrow; for thou knowest not what
a day may bring forth.

> Proverbs 27:1

1

Guillam the Toad,
Groom to Andrew Rigg, Jr.

GUILLAM JONES WAS called Toad by all who knew him. The
name seemed especially well chosen as he glared at the
passing countryside of Somersetshire with his bulging green
eyes. Even his face seemed less than human, hanging slackly
to hide the turmoil of his thoughts.

No murderer being carted toward his own hanging at Newgate
Prison could have more dread than Guillam the Toad felt at
the journey he was making. He must have been mad to agree
to travel to Virginia with his master, Andrew Rigg. He was
not by nature either a curious man or a brave one. Such flaws
in men's natures naturally led them into danger. Not Toad; he
knew himself to be a man who cherished comfort. The good
life was a foaming jug, a fat hen dripping on the spit and his
feet warmed by a safe fire.

He glared covertly at his companion. Young Rigg clearly
had no doubts of his own. The great buck was staring at the
thatches of the passing cottages as a maiden stares at a full
moon. True, the fields were golden against the harvest, and
the hedge birds sang in air that was scented of cider. It was
also true that the ruts of the road caught at the wheels of the
carriage, sending waves of pain through Toad's gin-soaked
skull.

"A good stout whip across the back of those beasts might
get us there faster," Toad suggested at last.

Andrew Rigg turned to grin at him. "We would only outrun the cart that is rumbling there behind us. We'll be at Plymouth before the *Lark* lifts anchor, even with this stop at my cousin's house. Besides, God only knows when I will see these sweet English fields again."

Toad stifled a groan. God only knew indeed. What a bloody fool he had been to undertake this adventure. For six years he had served Andrew Rigg, as a lad and then a man. Had he ever once had sense enough to wonder how it would end? His master's father was mortal, like other men. Had the young man ever asked himself what would happen when the older one died and the son was called home to the colony?

Now the old man had indeed given up the ghost, and had caught Toad unprepared for his young master's plans. Toad had been quick with comforting words for his grieving young master. He had been brisk in helping young Rigg get his English affairs in order. He had also spoken with great hope of the fine servants whom young Rigg would find to serve him in Virginia.

All to no avail. Rigg had turned on him with astonishment. "Leave you here, Gil? That is madness. I have no intention of giving up such a prize as you. You sail with me, and that's the end of that."

Toad told him solemnly that he had sworn on his mother's grave not to go to sea. This he had done, although he knew no more of that madam than that she had left him on the church steps as a mewling babe. He had pleaded poor health and promises made long ago. The only thing he had not told was the truth. Having once climbed the masts of a pirate ship with a spyglass in his hands and waded in the blood of men on its decks, he wanted no more of sea or sail.

Young Rigg had looked at him only a moment before whooping with laughter. "Indians," he declared with a shout. "My God, I have at last discovered your weakness. You are afraid to find that taffy hair of yours hanging from some savage's belt. What a great joke it is to see you afraid, Toad. I have watched you fight off the vilest highwaymen and tumble the raging Mohawks of London. Forget the gossip of gin mills and coffeehouses. There's a great life waiting for you in Virginia. You have my word on that."

A man could tie himself as tightly in silence as he could by lies, Toad thought bitterly. If his master knew more of Toad's background, he might be inclined to think a little differently. The very secrets he had hidden from his master had brought him at last to this journey. After one brief stop at Lyon Hall, he would be at sea, headed for Virginia.

God help him.

Young Rigg had raved on at length of how it was to travel on the broad sea and how green lay the great land beyond. Little did he know of Toad himself prowling the serpent coves of Okracoke with a knife in his teeth and terror in his belly.

While it was true that he had not become a pirate by choice, the reputation of such men was so vile that no rich colonial would have trusted his son's care to a man who had been hauled to court in chains. And indeed Toad would have hung with the others of his ship if old Captain Owen had not come forward on his behalf and sworn that Toad had been impressed against his will.

Once he was free of the charges, the same old sea dog had obtained this position for him in service to Andrew Rigg, Jr.

"This Zachary Ryder, a friend of mine and a captain like myself, needs a manservant for a sixteen-year-old colonial lad going up to Oxford," the captain had told Toad. "With your quick wit and what I can teach you, you could get a fresh start here."

"He'd take me on, a pirate?" Toad had wondered.

"Never tell a man what he does not ask," the captain had chided him. "Say you're Welsh, since your face claims that. Say your name is Jones, since all Welshman claim that title.

"I can claim to know you from your early youth. I can honestly state that you served me from time to time, with excellence. But keep a sharp sense and a slow tongue. Why should any man know your gory past? Is the chart of any forbidden sea written on your face?"

He had leaned near, his breath rank with claret and time. "A man's past is his own dark sea," he whispered. "Seize the day. Smile that winning way and take comfort in your new life."

Comfort Toad had taken, and some fine entertainment too. He had been more like an uncle than a servant to the young lad, and more like friend than groom to the lusty man who had grown from that youth. They had traveled together from Oxford to Gray's Inn and finally to Rigg's association with

5

his father's London agent. When the closeness between them had been challenged, young Rigg always just laughed. "Thus it is in our land. It is the Virginian's way."

That comfort seemed all in the past, with the sea stretching between them and Virginia, a sea so imperiled by pirates that the bravest captains set forth only with other ships in convoy.

"Come, Gil," his master coaxed from his side, "give us a song to brighten the ride. You wear too dark a face for such a sunny day."

What man smiles and sings as he walks into the jaws of a dragon?

"Come, a chorus," Rigg insisted. "We are within an hour of my cousin's house. There will be little enough merriment in that house when I have delivered the sad news of my father's death to my relatives."

"Death is the curtain on every man's merriment," Toad grumbled.

Rigg shook his head. "My father would not have wished it to be like that. He wore life with a graceful lightness. Look at the manner of his death. He was not a man to grow old on an invalid's couch, taking porridge with a trembling hand. He died as he lived, gallantly, thrown from a blooded horse that he had probably pitted against a flying bird since there was no other wager he could make at the moment."

The rattling of the carriage was soon muffled by the foliage of the yews that lined the approach to Lyon Hall. The green of the orderly garden soothed Toad's road-weary eyes. He remembered rich sauces served in that kitchen, and his mouth was suddenly moist. He wondered if the kitchen maid Bonnie would still be among those who served this great house. Remembering the shortness of her upper lip and the flash of her smile brought him up straighter in the seat with a sudden eagerness.

2

Stokes Lyon of Lyon Hall, Somersetshire

(1716)

AT THE SOUND of his young cousin's carriage in the drive, Stokes Lyon glanced at his clock for the hundredth time. He knew where the hunt would be running now, what fences had been cleared and what groves passed with the dogs swirling like turbulent water and his friends drumming behind. It was bad enough that a man was forced to entertain a colonial cousin whose very face set his teeth on edge without the lout's timing his arrival to spoil the meat of a man's day.

"No doubt he's into some new scrape," his wife had suggested. Though not commonly an adept judge of men, she felt as much distaste for this young man as he did. When Andrew had first appeared as an awkward lad starting up for Oxford, she had called him a pampered fool. More than once since, Andrew's lusty pranks in London society had confirmed her opinion as well as bringing embarrassment to Stokes and his wife.

Flipping the ruffles of his cuffs back from his wrists, Stokes braced himself to heave from his chair. He had not the inkling of the reason for this visit, which had been preceded only by a hastily scrawled note. What curiosity he had was quickly satisfied at the first sight of his guest. Dressed as he was, Riggs could only be coming with tidings of death. Stokes grudgingly admitted that mourning clothes sat as be-

7

comingly on the young man's frame as did a riding coat. But then, he added bitterly to himself, the fabric and tailoring showed that Rigg had spared no cost in this dark tribute.

In truth, the signs of mourning lightened his spirit momentarily. Was it possible that whatever death this costume celebrated could bring some gold into his own hands? The hope was brief. Those of his family who had planted in Virginia had reacted to that sea change by breeding like coneys in a hedge.

"It is my father," Rigg told him quietly. "His mare stumbled and brought him to his death. He would have been sixty-seven on his next birthday."

"And your mother?" Stokes asked, remembering that she had come from the Merritt family and was well connected.

"She lives, and no doubt grieves," Andrew replied, "as do my two older and wedded sisters, Sara and Abigail. The ranks of my father's generation are thinning now. Only my uncle William Elliott, called Younger, and my father's sister, Martha Springer, remain living among all the children born to Rebeckah Lyon, who left here as Bennett Lyon's daughter."

Stokes wanted no more of such talk. It was an irritation that he must share his famous ancestor, Bennett Lyon, with these rude colonials. He pressed wine on the younger mourner and turned the talk to lighter fare.

"You leave England in one of her loveliest seasons," Stokes commented. "She wears October with great beauty."

"As does Virginia," Andrew agreed, "where we also have a later season of warmth and beauty, known as Indian summer."

It was strange that his cousin had never grasped how little interest Stokes had in that savage land. "That is a new expression," he commented, "and is singularly forbidding."

"Forbidding it is," Andrew agreed. "This season bodes trouble for those settlers along the frontier, since the natives make war at their own convenience. In the spring while their women are planting, they go forth to war, and again at this season when the first chill is past and before the onset of deep cold. A warm October sets off wild excesses much like the profligacy of a bridegroom on the eve of his wedding."

Conveying his disapproval of this roguish humour with a frown, Stokes refilled the young man's glass and his own. "It is difficult for us to realize how it must be to live with a constant enemy at one's back. You people have been planted

8

there for a century now. It would seem that you might somehow have subjugated these tribes."

"That land is bigger than you can imagine," Andrew said. "Like foxes that retreat before the pack, the Indians melt into hidden places, to issue forth at will. Even now full war rages along the northern frontiers. There is fighting from Massachusetts to the Carolinas, with the Indians bearing French arms against us."

"French arms?" Stokes asked, interested in spite of himself.

"Aye." Andrew nodded. "The French claim land from their base in New Orleans all the way north. The difficulty is that Virginia's grant extends from sea to sea. But in any case the Indian finds himself between the Englishman on the east and the Frenchman on the west. These people have nothing but fury for those who press them like this."

"The same ship that brought me the sad tidings of my father carried word that Governor Spotswood had led an expedition over the Blue Ridge mountains into a new valley."

"I confess I have barely glanced at that map you brought. The extent of the colony is indeed past my grasp. But the Lyon family seems to have spread far and wide over its face. If this persists, there will be more of Bennett Lyon's blood flowing in colonials than here at home."

"It might even be so now," Andrew agreed. "And all take pride in that sire who visited those shores while good Queen Bess was on the throne."

While Stokes himself was given to mentioning his grandsire's acquaintance with Sir Walter Raleigh and Sir Francis Drake, such talk did not fall so pleasantly from this man's lips. Had he forgotten that his other bloodline was from a clod of a yeoman who had journeyed to America as an indentured servant? His putting on such airs brought a rise of warmth to Stokes's temples.

"So now you return to them," Stokes said, struggling to keep his tone congenial, "to become in truth an American."

His cousin raised those strange eyes, pale in color and ornamented with looped strands of gold.

"A Virginian is only an Englishman abroad," Andrew corrected him. "He is but a citizen with the blackness of coal smoke cleaned from his air. We are Englishmen, the lot of us." The smile that tugged at the young man's mouth was ripe with mischief. "And we are as various as all Englishmen

9

are, claiming in our number planters and papists and even pirates, if the whispers be true. And all with the hot blood of Bennett Lyon pounding against our temples.''

Stokes flushed. Only a peasant could find humor in such a boast. Why could this man ever so easily goad him to fury? Shakespeare had indeed dipped his quill in the color of truth when he wrote that when one takes degree from a man, the string is untuned and only discord can follow.

That discord in Andrew's tone tempted Stokes's tongue. Where had these sturdy sons of England been when the armies of Cromwell had stormed across the land chanting their quavering songs and murdering the true believers? Where had their swords hung while his own father had his land sequestered and laid himself to sleep in a stinking prison?

"English you may call yourself," he told Andrew. "And in this time you may well learn what that estate can mean. This new German king may view you as men to be taxed as we are taxed, controlled as we are controlled. If the day comes that you are no longer supported by this nation's bounty, you may cry to be called American rather than face the levies set against you."

Andrew shook his head. "I am a trueborn Englishman, even as you are, cousin. As God is my witness, such a day can never come." As he swirled the liquid in his glass, a shaft of light touched it, turning the port to the hue of blood.

3

Martha Rigg Springer, Candle Creek, Virginia

(1716)

IT WAS Martha Springer's wish to stay alone with her dead brother Andrew during the night before his burial. His widow, Eleanor, as well as his daughters, Abbie and Sara, accepted this strange request as only one more sign that the strong mind that had powered her life for all the years of their memory was beginning to weaken.

"But she is not very old," Sara Moore protested. "She was the last of Grandma Bek's children. She is only a little over sixty, and Grandma Bek herself lived to be eighty-two."

"More's the wonder that Aunt Martha has lived to see this day," her sister Abbie grumbled, stirring in her chair with discomfort. This latest pregnancy, her fifth in the nine years of her marriage, had rendered her heavy and listless and given to sharpness of tongue. It was not that she did not welcome this blessing of God on her union with Nat Horne. Rather, his living as the rector of a small parish provided only the bare essentials for his thriving family, so that she wakened daily to more tasks than two brisk women could easily perform.

"Why do you say that?" her sister asked in astonishment. "There is more lively mischief in Aunt Martha than in anyone in the family, except our absent brother."

"That's exactly what I refer to," Abbie replied. "It's

common enough to see a half-grown boy so full of deviltry that he starts trouble for the sheer fun of the show, but for an old woman to behave like that flies against nature.''

Sara giggled. ''I am sure you are referring to her getting Uncle Paul started on that wild harangue of his, waving his arms about and describing the devil so that one could barely breathe for the scent of sulphur in the air.''

Abbie smiled in spite of herself. ''What you smelled was probably my poor Nat burning in that silent way of his. Nat would never raise his voice against a man of Uncle Paul's age even if he were not kinsman, but clearly he writhes at this furor. It is a disgrace, a genuine disgrace.''

Sara shrugged. ''It's nothing to make a great fuss over. It is Uncle Paul's great delight to spout his strange beliefs. I think Aunt Martha teases him into it for his pleasure as well as to relieve her own boredom.''

Abbie stared at Sara in amazement. ''What on earth do you mean? Boredom! Why has she cause to be bored?''

''Because of us, for one thing,'' Sara insisted. ''Both of us are always gabbling of children and gardens and little else. You know that she and Mother seldom say five unnecessary words to each other. What has she left? Her servants, her Bible and that grand old journal of Grandma Bek's and her father's that she pores over.''

''Is that cause for boredom?'' Abbie challenged.

''I think so.'' Sara nodded. ''She lived in bolder times. The blood of this family was hotter then.'' She dropped her voice, lest someone overhear. ''Think about it, about her brother Benn, who murdered a girl and then fled the law to become a pirate in Lubberland, of Uncle Younger Elliott, whom none of us have met because he set himself apart from the family in war against Grandma Bek. Then there was James, who was hanged for treason, and her own father, left dumb by his wife's curse.''

Abbie shuddered. ''Stop that talk. Reciting such dreadful things could hurt the child in my womb. Those days are past. A young colony, like a young person, commits excesses. We are settled now, with parishes for all and a college in our midst and a pleasant, sensible governor in Spotswood.''

''That is exactly what I was saying.'' Sara nodded. ''Aunt Martha finds this settled life a little tedious. I would wager that at this moment she sits by our father's bier dreaming of the days when they were young and lively, dreaming with longing."

As she bent to the candle, Abbie paused, staring a long time at the wavering flame. "Have you wondered how it will be with our brother Andrew as head of this family? We know the boy who left. We do not know the man who will return to us."

"He was always Father's child," Sara mused, "more given to laughter than soberness, as Father was. I do hope that he and Mother can be firmer friends than they were before. But in any case, if he has become the man that the boy promised, no one will have a chance to be bored."

With Abbie groaning up the stairs toward her bed, Sara paused in the doorway to look in on her aunt. The candle by the bier cast an angular light across Martha Springer's cheek, catching in the darkness of her winged brow. Even with the curved back of the chair available for her support, the old woman sat perfectly straight. "That is the consequence of growing up on benches," she had told Sara when her niece had complimented her on the beauty of her posture. Sara herself thought this erect attitude more the result of the furnishing of her aunt's mind than the home of her childhood.

Unable to support the flood of love she felt for her aging aunt, Sara walked to her side and took her hand. Martha's flesh was cool and crisp like fine writing paper.

Strangely enough, her aunt's cheeks were dry as she glanced up. An unexpected brightness warmed her face.

"I was thinking, my dear, that your father died as he had lived, astride his life in a joyous and amiable manner."

Sara nodded, unable to respond for the sudden rush of her own tears.

Her aunt's tone turned reflective. "The difference between him and young Andrew, I would wager, is that young Andrew will choose an untamed horse to mount."

Sara, remembering her brother's fierce angers and black stubbornness when crossed, sighed. "Doesn't that frighten you just a little?"

"Frighten?" her aunt repeated. The old woman considered it a moment before smiling. "Not frighten, my dear, but it does fascinate me. Like a swift river that accepts no shore as final, I have watched the Lyon blood run its course through these generations. I will be fascinated to see what path Andrew will take. And in truth, I was even then giving my guilty thanks that I have been spared to watch that show.''

Only when the giggle was halfway from her throat did Sara realize that she was breaking into laughter over the coffin of her dearly adored father. What would her mother say, or even her own children, if they were to hear her thus? She fled from the room into the harsh penitence of prayer.

PART ONE

Behold, This Dreamer Cometh
(1716–1717)

And they said one to another, Behold, this dreamer cometh.

Genesis 37:19

[He seems to be] one (by his own confession to me) that can put on two several faces and look his enemies in the face with as much love as his friends. But good God, what an age is this and what a world is this, that a man cannot live without playing the knave and dissimulation.

The Diary of Samuel Pepys
September 1, 1661

1

A Breach in the Spirit

(1716)

A wholesome tongue is a tree of life: but perversement
therein is a breach in the spirit.

Proverbs 15:4

WHEN ANDREW RIGG had journeyed to England as a lad of
sixteen, he had been assigned, like a prize cargo, into the care
of Captain Zachary Ryder, who had dealt with his father at
the wharf of Candle Creek for all the years that Andrew could
remember. He was to remember that crossing of the sea as
long and tedious, with the foulest food he had ever swallowed.
He was far too full of his own importance, which he felt
it necessary to display, and of his terror at the coming
Oxford experience, which he felt it equally necessary to
conceal, to have more than a hazy blue memory of the entire
passage.

He only vaguely recalled the trip up to Oxford, accompanied by Captain Ryder and a servant named Guillam Jones,
whom the captain had obtained for him. Those first steps
toward his manhood were almost as lost to his memory as the
first years of his steps into childhood.

The death of his father had somehow served to strip layers
of haze from his understanding, exposing him to new levels
of sight. Nothing was as he expected it to be; nothing was as

it had been described to him. These surprises were of such small account singly that he barely acknowledged them to himself. But he found himself growing increasingly wary of, and sometimes even amused by, the petty deceptions of this world of men that he was now entering as a full tithing member.

For indeed he had considered himself a full-grown man all these man years. Didn't he have a man's body and the appetites that went with it? Didn't he have the freedom to come and go, to hear the opinions of other men, study their styles of life and accept or reject them as his spirit prompted? Yet in the aftermath of his father's death he had felt fall upon him something he had not bargained for, the burden of his fellow man in the form of relatives.

The tidings of his father's death in Virginia had come as a giant clap of thunder accompanied by rain. As a coward bolts across open fields with his arms locked tightly across his head, Andrew Rigg had reacted frantically, attacking one task after another, that he need not measure the slow tolling of the death bell in the back of his mind.

God knows there were things enough to do, such as releasing his London lodgings and settling his affairs in that city, equipping himself with mourning clothes and procuring the hastiest passage to Virginia. The visit to his Uncle Stokes at Lyon Hall was the last of this necessary business. There only remained for him to travel with Gil to Plymouth, where the *Lark* would lift anchor on the tenth of October.

The slackened pace after this period of frantic activity forced him to confront the confusion in his own heart. No young boy had ever tried harder to earn the title of master. No man had ever faced the responsibilities of that station with more dread.

The road south from Somersetshire wound through Devon past the moors of that river that had been stained with the blood of human sacrifice when the world was younger. With the waning of day, a mist fingered along the roadside. As busy as he was with his own thoughts, Andrew was conscious of Gil's nervous flinching in the seat beside him.

"That was only a crow," Andrew assured his man as Gil's eyes followed a moving shadow into the darkened trees.

"Aye, but it's legs seemed red in this light," Gil protested.

"In such a bird does the spirit of King Arthur fly since his death at Slaughterbridge."

"Listen to that," Andrew scoffed. "And you on your knees every Sunday in church parading as a Christian."

"And every day at home between," Gil grumbled, "if I must pass the Devil's way at such an hour."

Andrew said no more. Indeed, this was a country whose history made a man's flesh tingle. It was the land of Drake, who was said to be in league with the devil. Who could prove that he and his sorcerer friends on Devil's Point in Plymouth had not conjured the storm that had swept the Spanish Armada into disarray?

But it was not such tales as this, nor even the rumor of Drake's spirit driving a black hearse drawn by headless horses along this very road, that stilled Andrew's tongue. Instead he seemed to see in the shadows of passing trees the forms and faces of those lives now committed into his keeping.

These were shadowy figures from his childhood, his mother, imperious and proud, Sara full of laughter, Abbie deep in thought. The darker shadows of the servants sat also within his keeping. And further still, those relatives who had chosen to become strangers to them all: driven from the family, Adam by a new faith, Joel by bitterness, and William, called Younger, by betrayal. There had always been talk of these men among the talk of storms, pirates and the tobacco crop. But always between him and this hornet's nest of concerns had stood the broad, amiable form of the Andrew Rigg, whose name he bore.

The last breath of his father entered his own lungs with the deepness of a sigh.

The wind rose as they neared Plymouth, rousing him from his sober silence. "Our long journey is nearly through," he assured Gil.

"And none too soon for me," Gil replied.

"There will be taverns with hot food."

"And better ale than the last one, if we be lucky," Gil replied with a faint suggestion of a smile.

Andrew grinned back at him by way of apology. "I have been in a dark, cold place in my mind," he told him.

"Death brings each of us to that place," Gil said. "Any death."

Andrew registered Gil's words against another, more literate voice making the same proposition, but more delicately put. Donne. "Any man's death diminishes me." Andrew stared at Gil. How had this uneducated Welsh peasant's thought come so near to those of the great poet and preacher? Gil's eyes seemed to have abandoned green for gray in such a light. Could a man seem so guileless and yet have secret streams?

He himself had been greatly diminished by his father's death. He wondered if he had enough manhood left for what he must do.

Indeed there was hot food at the tavern, tasty beef for all and a row of hens sending such a drizzle of fat onto the coals that swift jets of flame hissed and flared. The ale had run so freely and the smoke risen in such clouds that Andrew squinted for a view halfway across the room. The serving maid slipped among the tables, moist from her labor. Soiled ruffles fell back from the tray of dripping tankards she carried. Her arms were as round as the breast of a pigeon, and the careless lacing of her bodice provided a satisfying glimpse of damp rosy breasts.

There was dancing toward the back, and a sawing sound that bore the intent of music if not its charm. The briskest dancer swung a tawny-haired girl in a fashion that belied the gray of his closely curled hair. The breathlessness of her laughter testified to the agility of her partner.

"You are travelers, then," the serving girl said, thumping their tankards before them.

"Aye, on the *Lark*," Andrew replied.

The edges of her mouth tightened into a grin as she chuckled softly. "With Fraser, then," she said.

"Fraser it is," Gil agreed, he and Andrew having heard the man described at tedious length when they spoke with Captain Ryder of this passage. "You know him, then?"

"Show me a girl along this coast who doesn't know Fraser." She laughed. "Him with his quick feet, and hands to match." She straightened to look around. "That's him dancing now," she began, only to shake her head. "I spoke too late; by now he has that Bets giggling above the stair. A gay one, that Fraser."

Andrew had followed her glance, only to realize that the fever of the dance had cooled with the disappearance of the

20

gray-haired man and his doxy. A trio of young sailors bounced in a jig in an attempt to lure a terrified maid from between the tables.

"Could she mean the same as our Fraser?" Gil asked, his great eyes rimmed with astonishment.

Andrew shook his head, struggling to recall Captain Ryder's precise words.

"The *Lark* may not be the fanciest thing afloat," he had said. "But she's tight, with a good hull, a solid, square-sterned vessel. Her captain, Robbie Fraser, had her built in Virginia. He shuttles back and forth with tobacco and textiles and what ironmongery he can find to carry. He's a careful man, never venturing out without a companion, with the seas so stiff with pirates. From Norfolk," he added, "a finer Christian never stood under sail."

"He is from Norfolk, then?" Andrew had asked, surprised.

"Aye, and a solid citizen there, a pillar of his church, for all that his own faith be Presbyterian. He's a widower, with a single child left, his son having been lost to pirates some years back. This Scot is heavy in his faith and upright in all his dealings."

"Well." Andrew grinned, meeting the laughter in Gil's eyes. "I would say he was a Scot, by the look of him, and the names do ring the same."

Whatever giggling Bets did above the stairs failed to affect the departure of the *Lark*, which cleared out of Plymouth the next morning, with the *Barbara Lee* readying to lift anchor to follow within the hour.

The staggered windows of the receding town of Plymouth turned the cliff into a tower of mirrored light in the October sun. Yet Andrew knew this to be no tower of light but a ragged old harbor whose filthy streets were busy with beggars and lined by inns where a man was charged twice for stale brew. Neither was the ship moving at a steady six knots beneath his braced feet, the heavily armed hundred pounder that she had appeared to be at his first glimpse of her from the Hoe. On closer view, the ship's gunports were carefully painted circles of black.

"A merchantman does that to fool pirates," Gil explained at Andrew's protest. "From the top of a hundred-foot mast twenty miles away, them ports would make a marauder think twice.''

Andrew studied Gil thoughtfully. What an astonishing bit of information to learn from a Welshman who, for all Andrew knew, had never set foot on board ship before this day.

As for Captain Fraser, Andrew's first word with him came when Land's End was a blurred shadow against the endless line of the sea. He was trimly uniformed and stiff of posture, and his tone veered sickeningly close to reverential.

"Master Andrew, I would extend to you my sincerest sympathies on the loss of your father, whose name has earned praise throughout the colony of Virginia as a man of honor and a servant of our Lord.''

At Andrew's response, he invited him to join in a prayer, "To our heavenly father for the safe passage of this ship and those who bide therein.''

Then the captain invited Andrew to join him for supper in his cabin when the hour came, and left with a sober smile. Andrew found himself controlling a chuckle as the Scot walked away. That smile was considerably less winning than the one the captain had bestowed on the sweating servant spinning in his arms. His departing steps did not even suggest the alacrity with which he had raised the dust in Plymouth Tavern the night before.

---• 2 •---

An Hedge of Thorns

(1716)

The way of the slothful man is as an hedge of thorns: but
the way of the righteous is made plain.

Proverbs 15:19

THE *Lark* WAS eight weeks from Land's End, with a projected
month's sail to Virginia's shores before the weather turned
foul. The *Barbara Lee* still shadowed her wake, disappearing
when the sea becalmed and reappearing when the wind blew
fair. Such rough weather as had come, had only served to
swab the decks and set the immigrants in the hold to grumbling.
The poultry pen on deck was reduced to a single cock, who
cried every morning, and a handful of shrewish hens more
given to ruffled complaint than to the production of eggs for
the cook. One sow remained, having been as canny as her
human counterparts who plead the state of their bellies to save
their skins at Newgate. The cook's mercy had been rewarded
by a row of round piglets that clung to her teats with the roll
of the sea as they fattened for the skewer.

This was not a sea passage that Andrew would forget. His
years as student, both in Virginia and at Oxford, served him
well. The work of a planter was something he had learned at
his father's side. There was no handbook for being the master
of a family unless it was his Bible. Through long hours in his

cabin alone, he mused and searched the scripture for the rules that he should follow to lead his family in peace and good fortune. These rules were simple enough in the end, being formed by reason and informed by prayer.

It was time, he felt, to heal old wounds so that the family might grow together as a fruitful vine, with one branch supporting another when the storms came. It was essential that all tongues and hearts be opened to one another, that nothing remain hidden to fester and damnify the whole. It was proper that the responsibility that he would assume for these lives be endowed with an authority that would be unchallenged, even as God's will with his children was obeyed.

The tedium of this sober study was much relieved by his growing friendship with Captain Robbie Fraser. Pious Presbyterian that he was, Robbie Fraser had a good Virginian's love of gaming. In his cabin when the wind blew chill and on deck when the sky was fair, Andrew and Robbie Fraser endlessly matched wits over cards and dice. Gil the Toad, left to his own resources, ranged the ship like an eager child, ready to lay his hand to a rope or clamber into the crow's nest as lookout when a seaman was felled by the flux.

Accustomed to the accents of Oxford and London, Andrew took great delight in the briar of Scotland on Robbie Fraser's tongue. When he relaxed from his pious, stuffy attitude he became an amiable, almost jolly, companion, full of fine brawling stories of the sea, which he recounted with an applewood pipe tight in his jaws. Unlike most men, Robbie Fraser was quick to tell of other men's lives but wary of sharing his own. Some perversity in Andrew led him to draw out Robbie Fraser's private story in spite of this hesitation. Bit by bit, like a rope stingily let out, Robbie Fraser fed out the lifeline of his own narrow world.

"I was never made to be a shopkeeper," he said. "A shop is like a stone in a meadow, yielding moss one year and nothing the next, or the opposite of that. Give me things that stir and change and grow, something that will struggle against the hand."

"All men cannot be at the helm of a ship," Andrew reminded him.

"Then let them rule families as their nations. What king can sleep easy with that helm tugging in his hand? And a family is cut from the same length of board. If no firm hand be holding it, it be no family at all but a generation wasting away.''

Andrew nodded, adding that weight to his own opinion.

Robbie Fraser at last spoke of his dead wife, Annie.

"From Burnisland she was, the County Fife. Taller than most men but with grace withal. She had been long promised ere we met. Such a shouting her father put up when we spoke of wedding, we two. A stubborn man, that, not any more like to give in than was my Annie's betrothed." Fraser's dark eyes danced from the cloud of fragrant smoke.

"But clearly in time the father yielded," Andrew said, to nudge him to tell more.

"Aye, time indeed." Fraser laughed. "Annie swore she would tumble gray into a grave ere she wed with aught but me. Her father put her on bread and water, only to have her maid smuggle stirabout with cream, so that she stayed rosy. He penned her in the house, and she turned bookish without complaint. Latin she mastered, and the words of the poets. And songs." His voice turned wistful. "There was in her voice a ripple that stilled the birds in trees."

Days were to pass before Andrew broached that subject again.

"You never told me," Andrew reminded Fraser, "how it was that you finally persuaded Annie's father that you two should be wed."

"It was not so much persuading as a slow wearing down," Fraser explained, "like bilge rotting away the wood of the hold or a slow dripping of water on stone. In those days we sailed the southern route, by way of Cape Finistere, the Canaries and the West Indies. Long would I be gone, and each time I returned, the two of them would be barely speaking, with her setting his dish on the table with a crash that would deafen a softer man. She was nearing thirty when her betrothed, despairing of seeing his own self wed, broke the pledge himself.

"By the first bird of that spring we were wed, and she was sweeping the dust from that same humble house I still keep in Norfolk. Such a song fell from her lips, such a spring came to her step, and mischief bubbling from her like a spring freshet." His voice gained a sudden roughness. "Deal up, then, man. Are we here to sport or gabble?"

With no less tenderness he spoke of his son, Philip.

"Never was father so blessed. Light of heart he was, and tall, even as Annie's people were. He and his sister were as close as twined rope as they grew in laughter and loving. That was a merry house while Philip still lived. But he would go to sea when scarce more than a boy, with that stubbornness that came from Annie's blood, only to die at the hands of vile men. Such a sadness. Such a great sadness."

Andrew thought that one day the tale of those pirates might come to Fraser's tongue, but it never did. There was only the glitter of hate at the sound of the word and the high flush of color on his cheeks and such a clamping of teeth on the pipe that it was a wonder that the stem itself didn't shatter.

Piece by piece, shred by shred, Andrew learned the story. Annie did not survive the birth of her second child, a girl named Emily. For all that his words had been so glowing about Philip, Fraser spoke little of the girl.

"Is your daughter, then, married?" Andrew asked.

Fraser's face seemed suddenly closed, like cards held near the chest. "Em? Married?" There was a false robustness to his tone. "She is not of the marrying kind, my Em. She makes do in those humble quarters her father leaves her in, spending her days in good works as the Lord's handmaiden. A good Christian woman, my Em, of the sort who knows when she is being sought for her property and not her person and will not have her head turned."

Andrew studied his cards thoughtfully. When this man spoke of his circumstances, it always seemed that he balanced himself on the edge of disaster. "This poor ship and her fellows," he said in speaking of the *Lark*; "My humble house," "Those humble quarters." Yet he implied that young men sought Em's hand for gain.

"But at least she is still marriageable," Andrew said as he set out his cards carefully, avoiding his companion's eyes.

The words evoked an unreasonable heat. "Marriageable?" Fraser countered hotly. "Such an antique virgin as my Em? She is past the age and softness for marriage. A strong woman, that Em, in ways not often found in women. I know no man who would take the dictates of her stern God, nor do I know such a man as could come between her and that God. Marriageable she is not, and happy she is with me to cherish her and myself for her to cherish."

26

He fixed an angry eye on Andrew, as if to warn him against meddling with such spinsters as "that Em."

"And what great age has she now attained?" Andrew asked.

"What a mouth for clatter you have," Fraser said crossly. "How should I note what age she has, having never been one for counting years? Twenties, maybe; thirties, for all I remember. Once a woman has set herself beyond marriage, age doesn't count."

Andrew smothered his grin. Fraser was no man for numbers, if this was a sample. If he and Annie had been in their thirties when they wed and this Em had been their second child, then his host had himself attained a great age, to have this daughter be in her thirties. The twinkling of those fine firm legs in the tavern at Plymouth was quite a feat for a man of such years as Fraser suggested. Shuffling the cards to deal again, Andrew smiled privately to himself.

Both the gaming and the talk were to end when the weather turned foul in early December. On the third of that month the wind rose so high by midnight that the foremasts must be broken. The next day the *Lark* fared no better. Fraser ordered the foresail lowered, and, with a reef in the mainsail, the ship lay under mizen. So mighty was the storm that the last of the poultry was drowned and two of the shoats cleanly swept away.

From the first of that heavy weather, the Toad worked bravely along with the harried crew.

"God in heaven, I will owe that man a seaman's wage by the time we see port," Fraser told Andrew. "Never have I seen a man take so smartly to the sail. One would swear that he went before the mast as a tad."

Andrew nodded, puzzled himself at Toad's quick grasp of the intricacies of sailing. God knows he had not been that acute in learning the niceties of a man's service.

That night as Andrew and Fraser shared a bottle of Madeira over a hand of cards, an explosion of violent sounds from the deck jerked them to attention. Scraping and loud curses were followed by a strange broken rhythm of footfalls. Fraser was on his feet and half up the stairs within a minute.

Once in view it was clear that their ears had not caught the start of this. On the sodden deck two men circled in combat, their faces gleaming in the light of the lamps. The mate of the

27

Lark, his face twisted in fury, was bleeding from his mouth, and a stain showed along his throat. His opponent, the Toad, crouched in a low swing as he measured his attacker. Toad's vest had been torn away, and his knuckles carried the stain of the mate's blood. The rail was lined with crewmen, whose eyes gloated greedily on this contest.

"You bloody lubber," the mate hissed, daubing his bloody chin with the back of his fist. "I'll kill you for that."

As the seaman lunged for Toad, the blind rage in his face brought a cry of warning to Andrew's lips. There was no need for the warning. Deepening his crouch, Toad slid one foot between the legs of his assailant, seized him about the lower hips and twisted him brutally aside, so that he reeled drunkenly, scattering the men who lined the rail.

"Hold here," Fraser shouted, seizing the mate by the collar and pulling him to his feet. "What goes here?"

"That bloody lubber," the mate spluttered, his tongue wagging along his split lips, "can't keep his nose from another man's affairs, prowling like a hungry Tom, telling a man his business—"

"I'll have some sensible account of this," Fraser ordered, looking from the man in his grip to Toad.

Gil met his gaze firmly and suggested, "Let him recount it, sir. It was him as raised the first hand."

"Telling me my business, he was," the mate protested. "The same as calling me a liar, he was."

"On what account?" Fraser asked.

When the man hesitated, the captain shook him roughly. "On what account, I ask?"

"The *Barbara Lee,*" the man replied.

"And what of the *Barbara Lee?*"

"I say that the ship shadowing is not the same that has followed us since Plymouth," Gil said, when the man only glared in reply.

Fraser frowned, tightening his lips thoughtfully. "And why do you say this?"

"Through the glass she looks to be no merchantman," Toad explained, "but more like a frigate, by her rigging."

"And you, mate?" the captain asked.

The man fell to whining. "There's a great haze there, and it's hard to search through."

Fraser turned from him in impatience. "When do you think this ship to have been changed?"

"This day is the first," Gil replied. "The *Barbara Lee* was lost to view early in the storm. Only today was this craft sighted."

The captain snorted and stared at the sky. A glass would be to small avail in such darkness. But even as he stared, the scudding clouds bared a patch of sky where the moon was rising with a small star trailing close behind. A barely audible sigh passed among the men.

"Move sharp, now," the captain ordered. "To your posts. Fasten the ship for heavy weather. As for you," he said, turning to the mate, "lay but a hand on this man and find yourself in irons. We'll measure the truth by morning."

"Heavy weather?" Andrew asked, watching Fraser's frowning study of the sky.

"Tempest," Fraser grunted. "We'll need more fortune than either of us have drawn this voyage to weather what is promised by that rising moon and star."

As Andrew turned to secure his own quarters, the captain called the quiet question after him.

"This man of yours, he's been a seaman in times before?"

"Not that I knew," Andrew admitted. "I've puzzled it a good bit through the past weeks, though."

"How came you by him?"

"By referral from Zachary Ryder of Gravesend."

"He seemed damned sure of his sighting," the captain mused.

"Is there some reason that a man of the sea would not turn to the service of a gentleman?" Andrew asked.

"Only that it be rare," Fraser replied. "Passing rare."

— • 3 • —

The Whirlwind

THAT VAGRANT GLIMPSE of the star-haunted moon was to be
the last. Within an hour the rain began, a slow drumming that
grew steadily denser, until the decks swirled with water. It
pelted from the sky in gray sheets that thundered against the
ship.

Fraser sent the lookout up even though nothing could be
seen through such a downpour. Finally, with astonishment,
the watch cried, "Ship ahoy."

The sighting was no more than a shadow to the east and
north.

"Three leagues or less," Fraser guessed aloud, taking the
glass. "If your man is wrong, we drown ourselves for nothing."
Lowering the glass, he ordered men to stations of defense.

"And even if she is a frigate, does that necessarily bode
ill?" Andrew asked.

"Pirates like them mighty fine," Fraser replied. "They
handle like a girl for their weight, they arm heavy and can
bear two hundred men."

Andrew watched as the guns were double-loaded and the

30

decks cleared. As crewmen slung the foreyard in chains to keep them from being cut away, two six-pounder guns were run out on the quarter deck and a swivel six-pounder set up in the closed quarters. Two powder chests were rolled to the forecastle and one to the poop.

Even as they labored, by the quarter hour the watch called the progress of the ship nearing. Andrew's watch told him it was ten o'clock when the ship drew near enough that her French flag could be seen dripping from the mast.

"*Joyeuse*," Andrew read through the glass. "Her name is as French as her flag."

"Pray God that her crew be the same, and honest men," Fraser mumbled at his elbow.

The ship moved steadily nearer, until she was ranged on the starboard quarter of the *Lark,* near enough that even through the sheets of thunderous rain they could hear the voice of the man on the bowsprit of the French vessel challenging the captain of the *Lark* to come aboard.

At Fraser's shouted refusal, the seamen opened with a volley of small-arms fire.

"Get under cover," Fraser shouted at Andrew before turning to order a volley from the waist of the *Lark.*

Andrew hesitated. He saw the gunner on the forecastle clutch his chest before falling to roll to the deck with his eyes wide and staring. "God in heaven," he cried as Gil the Toad leaped over his rolling form to take his place at the gun.

"Get your bloody ass below," Fraser shouted furiously to Andrew. "Leave him be, and take your skin away from this."

The gun was in Toad's hand before his slow wit caught up with his swift heels. "Holy Jesus," he whistled between his teeth. "What in the name of the demon himself am I doing here?" Then the terror came, a trembling along his tendons so that his legs jerked as if he were having a fit. He felt the frame of his ribs pressed to the point of pain at the swelling of his heart and wished himself dead now in preference to the death to come.

Not the finest marksman could have scored on such a night. Even as the *Lark*'s big guns opened on the pirate's bow, the tempest caught the two ships in her teeth. One side of the *Lark* after another clapped under water to such a degree that Toad, like the others, clung to his post for dear life.

Toad fought for every firing of his gun against the storm's rise and fall. The fighting went on about him as the bowsprit of the *Joyeuse* became entangled with the rigging of the *Lark*. Toad saw the faces of the first of the pirates to clamber aboard.

No one thing, not the thunder of shot around him or the howling of those vicious men or the stench of exploding powder alone changed the inside of Toad's belly. It was all of them at once, assailing his senses, maddening his brain, that brought him a feeling that was like a memory of a faraway place. He heard his own bloodthirsty yell and felt the cage of his ribs widen with elation and his blood sing for violence. The two ships fired mightily at each other at point range, made wasteful by the heaving of the vessels. As the pirates swarmed toward the *Lark*'s rigging, Toad saw Captain Fraser's fury blaze again and again from the pistol he aimed with a deadly purpose.

"Kill for your life," he kept shouting. With the swivel guns of the *Lark* sweeping the deck of the *Joyeuse*, the brigands directed their attack on the closed quarters.

Prayers and curses mingled as the two ships reeled in their deadly coupling. Toad's ammunition was spent. He cursed the gun and glanced back at the bloody deck. The men in the closed quarters were forcing the retreat of the boarding pirates with their withering fire. Half running, half sliding in the mingled water and gore, Toad zigzagged through the fire to the forecastle and wrenched loose the powder keg from its mooring. He felt his own knees complain in agony as he lifted it above his head, braced by the butts of his hands. A single deep breath of that winy air gave him the impetus. He hurled the keg into the retreating pirates.

The keg had not reached the deck before it exploded, sending a great plume of fire upward and scattering men in all directions. As the mast of the *Joyeuse* rose in a tower of flame, the gunners of the *Lark* raked the deck with partridge and double-chain shot. As a cannonball rent the pirate's second mast, the *Joyeuse* sheered away, the horrifying screams of her wounded and dying shrill above the sounds of storm and shot.

Toad watched her staggered progress as seven-foot waves

swept above her bloody deck, lighting the air with a frail lace of foam.

"God be praised," Fraser muttered. "God be praised."

The firing continued as the crew leaped to cut away the main top mast. It fell, only to butt against the ship, until a sweeping wave made it float free.

Even the shadow of the *Joyeuse* was gone as Toad's master emerged from the closed quarters and made his way to where Toad stood.

"You acquitted yourself with honor, Guillam Jones," Andrew said, his eyes holding Gil's eyes with a question. "No such daring in you was ever guessed at by me."

Gil felt the flesh of his face ache from powder burns as he grinned. "Nor me," Gil confessed. "The air of danger is a heady brew."

"One danger in exchange for another." Captain Fraser nodded, drawing to their side. "There is only left to us to outlast the tempest. For this I ask all men's prayers. For myself, I spare time for prayers of thanks for thee, Gil Jones. If there had been ten of you, we could not have been served better. Would that all my men were trained in your school."

Toad felt himself grow ruddy under the captain's searching eyes. "Not if they were your sons," Toad told him. "Not if they were your sons."

Later Andrew Rigg was to remember that night as the longest darkness since God set his hand to creation. A wave tore away the bowsprit close to the foremast, sending a shudder through the *Lark* like the death throes of a living creature. There was naught to do but cut away the foremast, leaving the *Lark* a headless bird adrift on the rough sea.

At dawn, the ship was drifting under the mizen. Only five men had been lost, though many lay disabled. Although, by God's mercy, the wind calmed, the sea ran rough for three days. On the fourth, the lookout sighted a ship. Birds wheeled about the *Lark,* marlingspikes, rakes and some rake bats. The sail passed along the line of the sky. On the fifth day the lookout cried out that he saw a brigantine, which drew abreast and shared enough provisions to keep the crew alive.

With the whimsey of the wind, the *Lark* made its way west, limping along at four to five knots an hour. On the fifteenth of February, the cry of land brought prayers to every man's lips.

33

"How, then, could we have seen this land again except by the grace of God?" Captain Fraser pondered as the crippled ship was piloted toward Norfolk.

"By no other means than God's favor," Andrew agreed. "God have mercy on those souls lost in this passage."

Andrew had forgotten the passion of Robbie Fraser's hatred.

"The souls of our own men," he corrected Andrew, "the souls of our own men alone."

Andrew studied his companion's face covertly. It was a kindly, even genial face in repose, with fine dark eyes and full, well-formed lips that boded a generosity of spirit as well as a taste for the sweetmeats of life. How complex a man, pious and profligate by turn, with a heart like a budding girl's for those he cherished, and so deep a well of hate that he would restrain another man's blessing from those hundreds of human lives that had been lost with the sinking of the *Joyeuse.*

"I am privileged to know you, Captain Robbie Fraser," Andrew told him.

The man studied Andrew's face a moment before smiling. "And God's blessing on you, Andrew Rigg, and on your man, Gil Jones." He nodded wordlessly a few times, then turned briskly to the dispatch of his cargo.

It was not only his cargo that Captain Fraser was in haste to dispatch. Andrew saw his own possessions being moved, not onto the dock, but into a small vessel lying at anchor near the crippled *Lark.*

"This way you will lose no time in reaching your bereaved family," the captain explained. "With some fair luck, the tide might find you at your own wharf while the sun still rides."

Less than an hour from Norfolk, Andrew roused from his revery to turn to Toad. "Does it strike you that for a man of such noted Christian goodness, the captain showed himself more than a little rude in his haste to be rid of our company?"

Toad nodded with a grin.

"When a man makes so much haste in my cause, I am beset with curiosity to know the reason," Andrew mused.

"What is in your head, then?" Toad asked.

Without replying, Andrew approached the master of their craft.

34

"If I should discover that I left valuables on the *Lark* at Norfolk, what should I do?"

The man shook his head. "Pray or whistle," he counseled. "The world is poor in saints and rich in scoundrels."

"But perhaps we could go back for them and catch the tide with the morning. Would I need to make you much richer to achieve such an end?"

The man laughed. "My hours pass the same here or there," he replied. "It is the captain whose fortune you fatten."

"Captain Robbie Fraser?" Andrew asked.

"Who else?" The man shrugged. "For who else has sloops and scows and ships to spare from this harbor?"

Andrew met Gil's eyes with a grin. "We'll make the poor captain a little richer, then," he decided aloud. "It's back to Norfolk with us, and we will leave with tomorrow's tide."

"Will you have lodgings, then?" the man asked. "I know a widow."

Andrew shook his head. "We will find some humble place, I ween. Some mean quarters here or there."

Andrew felt the man's puzzled eyes on him as he burst into laughter, with Toad joining in his chorus.

4

An Army With Banners

(February 1717)

Who is she that looketh forth as the morning, fair as the moon, clear as the sun, and terrible as an army with banners?

Song of Solomon 6:10

ONCE AT THE harbor, it was a matter of only few minutes to find the home of Captain Robbie Fraser, which was on a narrow street lined with like houses, all trim and smartly painted, with gardens showing the first spring green. Sweet wood smoke from the chimney breathed fragrance on the stoop, where they waited for some response to the pull of the bell. The voice of a hound was raised in alarm within as a flat-faced servant girl opened the door to them.

From the rooms within came the sound of some stringed instrument and a woman's voice in soft accompaniment.

"The captain has just returned to the harbor," the girl told Andrew. "Perhaps you would leave a message against his return."

"Perhaps we could speak with Mistress Emily, then," Andrew suggested. "Tell her Master Andrew Rigg stands without."

The girl left them on the sill, with the door a little ajar. Her plain face was shadowed by doubt.

The music stilled with the murmur of talk down the passage before the girl returned to show them in.

The scene seemed to have been posed for some artist's hand. The light from the fire twinkled on rich appointments of copper and brass. A young man rose at their entry, but the girl only raised her eyes from the lute in her lap, keeping one hand firm on the restless dog at her knee. Her face was half in shadow, but what a face. Her clear dark eyes were set above high, firm cheeks. Beneath a perfect mouth, full and well rounded as her father's, Emily Fraser's shapely chin was indented with a single, deeply cleft dimple. Under the lace of a ruffled cap her hair exploded in a bounty of rich dark curls.

Not until she rose did Andrew realize that this woman reached nearly his own height. With those fine eyes studying his, she dipped the tiniest curtsey before extending her hand to him. Her other hand stayed firm on her dog, whose throat rumbled a warning at his approach.

"Welcome, Master Andrew." Then, with a widening smile, she included Gil the Toad in her greeting. "And to you, Gil Jones. I would know you anywhere, from my father's words of praise."

Andrew was ill-prepared for the beauty and strangeness of her voice. The briar of her father's accent was here transformed into a blossom, a rich sibilant tone that transformed such simple words into something akin to poetry.

At Gil's flustered nod, she moved to lay a slender hand upon his arm. "My tenderest blessing on you, Gil Jones, for your brave service to my father. And to you, Master Andrew, for bringing aboard such a man as this."

The ordinary civil acts were performed with remarkable ease. The young man was introduced as Captain Bruce Forrester. Tea was brought by the flat-faced servant girl, along with fat golden scones and a buttery cake trimmed with brandied fruit.

While the cream still swirled in the cup she insisted that he accept, Toad was beset with a barrage of questions by this young beauty.

"Tell me all about the great battle," she said firmly. "What madness induced those beasts to attack during a tempest? I want to hear every detail."

Andrew swallowed his laughter as Toad, his great eyes glistening from this attention, recounted, blow by blow, the boarding, her own father's daring and the ferocity of the storm. In truth, Toad recounted some blows that Andrew could not recall, but whose tongue would not flower under the sun of such a smile?

It was upon this scene that Captain Robbie Fraser returned home.

"Rigg," he cried, his face grown more ruddy than the wind warranted.

"And our brave Guillam Jones," Emily Fraser added, her glance a little high with challenge.

"I thought it urgent that you be up the James within the day," Captain Robbie said, with a defensive note in his voice.

"So it was," Andrew agreed. "But we had no more than lost the shore when I was overcome with guilt. I realized I had not half thanked you for saving us from an eternal home in the sea, nor praised highly enough your skill in bringing in a vessel so woefully damaged."

"You thanked me quite enough," the captain protested, a sullenness about his mouth.

His daughter was at his side, her arm wound through his. Fraser had said his Annie was a woman of noble height. Emily was clearly her mother's child in this as well as in the sweetness of her voice. The crisp white of her cap stood above his gray curls.

"But what a joy to have them here, Father," she said in her remarkable voice. "I so earnestly yearned to thank Guillam Jones for his service to you. They must dine with us and spend the night, there being no cause to hasten until the morning tide."

Andrew held the captain's eye, giving no quarter.

Having no recourse, Captain Fraser sighed, unwound his muffler and called crossly for wine, that a man might be warmed from the wind. When the girl had brought the tray, he commissioned her to show Andrew and Gil to a guest chamber, "that I may review some affairs of business with Forrester, here."

Once alone, Andrew opened his purse to Gil and gave him some instructions. "These orders may sound strange to you, Gil, but do them all the same. And do hurry back. Unless my

38

memory is gone along with my manners, that smell in the air is a joint of beef roasting."

Andrew spent that hour in merry thought. So this poor Scot had a fleet of sloops and scows as well as the *Lark*. His idea of humble quarters included a tight house richly furnished with the spoils of all the seas. The rug beneath his feet was the finest work of the Orient, and he knew from his mother's weaknesses how great a value was set on such lace as curtained the bed.

Had Fraser said his Em was plain? Not in so many words, but what language he had used to bring her alive had not touched on her beauty or grace. As to her age, if Em was twenty, he himself was a doddering old man at twenty-five without an eye in his head.

Andrew laughed aloud at the expression on Gil's face when he returned with the purchases Andrew had ordered.

"You wear the face of a man who feels he has done a fool's errand," Andrew chided him.

"It's not likely that I would tell you so." Gil grinned. "But indeed, it took awhile to convince the merchant that you wanted his wares without first trying them on for size."

"Fit they will," Andrew assured him, relieving him of the smaller of the packets. "Fit for a jest, at least."

"A costly jest," Gil said, "as was the Madeira."

"This time the captain and I are gambling for very high stakes," he told Gil. "I would be a fool to risk losing such a great prize by guarding my purse in the opening bid."

· 5 ·

A Seal Upon Thine Heart

Set me as a seal upon thine heart, as a seal upon thine arm:
for love is strong as death; jealousy is cruel as the grave:
the coals thereof are coals of fire, which hath a most
vehement flame.

Song of Solomon 8:6

ANDREW HAD BEEN right about the roast of beef. There was
also a platter of red ham and a chicken pie whose crust
concealed thick gravy and tender tidbits. There were more hot
dishes than Andrew could later remember, and such fine
oysters that he had no taste for the cheese with biscuits and
the glowing trifle that followed.

This fine meal was mostly wasted on a man who forgot to
eat, for the distraction caused by Emily Fraser's presence.

Andrew's sisters had wailed to him that he never noticed
what they had on. Emily could make no such complaint.
Although he couldn't name the fabric, he was fascinated that
the rich chestnut color of her gown so perfectly matched her
hair. The lace at her throat was whiter than anything he had
ever seen except her own teeth, which she bared in laughing.
Everything about her was beautiful in a way that brought a
thickness like pain to his throat. It was clear that as a woman
she stood alone. The housekeeper at the table would have

been a fine figure of a dowager in any other company. Beside Emily Fraser she faded to gray sallowness.

During those months at sea Andrew realized that he had turned from prodigal son to patriarch in his own mind. Until he watched Emily Fraser, heard her forthright sayings and shivered at the precise beauty of her laughter, he did not realize that those months had also turned him from bachelor to hopeful husband in his heart. Fury raged in him at the thought that the trim young Bruce Forrester might be suitor as well as associate of the captain. He rued the tales of London adventures he had recounted to Captain Robbie. He mourned that he had retreated to the closed quarters during the battle with the *Joyeuse,* when it was clear that the way to this lovely woman's heart was across a field of dead pirates.

Only when the dinner was over and Andrew and the captain had removed to a private fire did Andrew produce the gifts he had sent Gil scurrying for.

"This is in no wise a proper memento for such gracious hospitality," he told the captain, proffering the Madeira. "I can only plead that it is the best to be obtained."

"Ah, and a good bottle it is." The captain nodded, turning it in the light. "It is too bad we won't have time to enjoy it together."

"I am sorry about that too," Andrew said. "But as you know, I am expected at my grieving mother's side. It is because I have so little time that I have gotten this second gift for you. It isn't a gift at all, but rather something for which you clearly have a need."

The merchant had wrapped his wares in a piece of fine linen. Frowning with puzzlement, the captain laid back the folds, only to stare at his guest with a look of affront.

"Need?" he challenged. "Me, who can spot an errant feather on a gull in the highest mast?"

Andrew lifted his brows in a shrug. "What else could I think? It was you who called this sumptuous home humble. It was you who spoke of your ship as a bare source of meager life, unable to see the other craft that nestled about her. It was you who spoke of your daughter as a woman past prime, unmarriageable and impossible on all counts, an antique virgin to whom no man would pay passing attention. I either had to decide that you were losing your eyesight or face the fact that you were trying to trick a friend."

Andrew caught the captain's eye boldly. "Every man to his own taste," Fraser grumbled.

The spectacles lay discarded on the linen cloth between them as Andrew leaned forward. "My taste is for such fresh, bright wit and beauty as brightens your daughter's eyes. I would like your permission to make suit to her."

Fraser was on his feet in instant fury, pacing back and forth on the glowing rug. "Give suit to my Em? Ridiculous." His tone turned crafty. "But you are a gentleman of rare parts to sweeten your gift with such flattery. It is unnecessary. My Em is content in her state and would not forsake her poor old father for any man's soft words. Be off to your Anglican plantation and save her pure ears from the stain of false flattery."

"So that's it," Andrew challenged. "You object that I am not of the Presbyterian belief."

"That is an insurmountable objection," the captain agreed at once. "No decent Presbyterian maid would have half an eye for a churchman such as you. That is, if she were to have an eye for any man, which my Em does not," he added swiftly.

"Then religion alone is your cause to deny my suit?" Andrew asked meekly. "You have no objection to my family or fortune aside from that?"

Seduced by Andrew's tone, the captain nodded. "It is sufficient in itself."

"I have been led astray," Andrew mused. "It was my understanding that Calvin himself laid upon every Christian the obligation to lead the erring from their ways. What better chance has a good Presbyterian maid of being such a fisher of men than to marry into an errant family and carry her message through the cradle of its generation?"

Fraser's face grew red with annoyance. "Don't you go spouting sacrament and scripture to me, Andrew Rigg. Grander men than you has she turned away, and will again, for all her great age. And good men," he added angrily. "Men not given to whoring and the throwing of dice and sucking at the neck of a bottle until their brains turn to pudding."

Andrew remained motionless a full moment. When he rose, he spoke with an icy tone.

"My dear Captain Fraser," he said quietly, "it is strange to me that you should insult me in soberness with such words as most men would only speak under the influence of strong drink. I thought you enjoyed my company as I did yours. I thought our idle games aboard the *Lark* had passed tedious hours, giving as much pleasure to you as to me. When I first saw you disappearing abovestairs with rosy Bets at Plymouth Tavern, I was misled into thinking you a man of such natural human appetites as myself. I beg forgiveness for this error. And having so insulted you and felt the tongue of insult on my own name, I insist that I remove my man and myself from your house, to wait the tide in other quarters.''

Fraser's face swelled with fury and then pain, only to grow smooth and controlled, even as his voice was. "Come now, Andrew," he coaxed. "Don't carry on so. First you hand me spectacles and accuse me of blindness. Is that less than insulting? Then you threaten to take my Em from me. Is that a threat to make in jest? It was my spleen that spoke, not my sense. But in the end I truly would not have my Em marry any man, no matter how dear he be to me, who has such frivolous tastes as we share and is not a sober Presbyterian. You would ill suit her, and she you. Fair she is, even as her mother was before her. But she is stubborn to a fault. And believe me, Andrew, that soft flesh conceals a will of iron when it comes to service to her God. I admit to having spoiled her past any man's bed by my delight in her company."

"There is a great difference between a husband and a father," Andrew reminded him.

"Aye." Fraser nodded. "And Chaucer himself put his pen to it neatly by saying that a servant in love becomes a master in marriage."

"Those spectacles are still a proper gift, Robbie Fraser. You need to look once more on your own daughter's face. You say she is close to God yet would not care to lead a man to Him. You say she is stubborn and wilful and yet fear that such an amiable man as I could not manage her with love. You insist she is a spoiled woman with her own will but do not give her the chance to state where she herself would stand on a proposal from me."

"Pup," Fraser shouted. "Insolent English pup. You would teach me of Calvin and marriage and the management of my own family when the beard is not ten years set on your jaws?" Striding to the door, he brought the maid scurrying with a bellow.

"Bring your mistress here," he ordered.

"She may have retired," the girl said, backing off.

"Then damn well get her up," he ordered. "She has one simple word to state and she will be free to return to her pillow."

The minutes passed slowly. The fire spit and crackled. The dog by the hearth rose, scratched some nameless tenant and restored his rump to the warmth of the fire. Fraser sucked furiously on his pipe. Andrew, not having been invited to sit again, stood like a dark pillar beside the hearth.

A rustle sounded in the passage, and Emily stood in the doorway. Her hair was caught back with a wide ribbon, and a robe of some deep color covered her garments.

"You asked for me, Father?"

The vibrance of her voice sent a thrill along Andrew's spine. He kept his eyes on the floor, not out of respect for her modesty but out of a sudden terror that indeed the old man might know this blazing creature better than he, that he had misread the warmth and interest in those intelligent eyes.

The captain had not wasted those silent minutes. The phrases he spoke had been carefully tailored in his mind. They fell ponderously, like a verse newly learned by an unsure pupil.

"My dear Emily," he began. "Master Andrew Rigg, late of Oxford and London and heir to Candle Creek on the James, an Anglican and a man of the world, has asked for permission to lay suit to your hand. I have thanked him for this compliment, but in his incivility he has insisted on hearing this refusal from your own lips. Forgive me for submitting you to his ordeal, but it seemed better to have it over and disposed of."

In spite of himself Andrew felt his eyes drawn to hers. There was no change of expression on her face. With no coquetry in her glance, she studied him for a long moment. The echo of her father's pleading was poignant in the air of the room.

"There is nothing to forgive, Father," she said quietly. "Please tell Master Andrew that I am complimented by his interest and would be delighted to entertain his suit according to your pleasure."

The words had barely left her lips before she was gone, with a respectful curtsey.

Fraser was on his feet, livid with fury. He started after her, only to stop at the door and turn in triumph.

"There," he shouted at Andrew. "She has shown you better than I could tell you what a shrew you seek to wife, a disobedient daughter, a woman whose tongue flies like the lash of a harbormaster. Only a madman would take such a woman to wife."

Andrew, exploding with elation, concealed his face with a slight bow.

"At your service, Captain Robbie Fraser," he said solemnly. "Andrew Rigg, Jr., planter and madman."

————— • 6 • —————

A Crucible for Silver

The crucible is for silver, and the furnace for gold: but the Lord trieth the hearts.

Proverbs 17:3

From the journal of Bennett Lyon, Esq. Lyon Hall, Somersetshire, Autumn 1617

God be praised that this day my son Amos Lyon has returned safely again from America. He is leaner and his voice is deepened by this experience with the travails of manhood. When we had greeted him and supped in grateful fellowship, he brought forth a map and showed us where he has obtained land in the new country, that this family might plant there to till and prosper and blossom in spirit, even as has been promised by the new covenant.

He told of resting some days at the mouth of the James River and then traveling upstream with two companions. He speaks of that river as at least half a league wide at its mouth but narrowing as it rises past shores whose trees are melodic with unknown birds. Thirty miles upstream they halted and claimed four hundred acres in the name of the master of the ship. Amos's land runs south into the woods and east along the river adjoining Merchant's Hope.

That afternoon he walked along the bank of a creek that tumbled through his land. Though Amos has never had a tongue for poetry, in this event his words waxed golden. I quote them here, with some possibility of small error, as they clung to my mind.

"The trees devour the sky there, making only small patches of light to glint through. The stream was a bare trickle until I turned the bend to find a pool dammed by beavers, deep and blue and glinting with fish.

"The clearing beyond was matted with leaves, such a clearing as a tired hunter might choose for sleep. Even as I stared at that fair sight, a slight wind stirred the trees and let a single shaft of sunlight pierce that canopy of green. As straight as a candle it came, gleaming into the darkness of that wild, peaceful place."

It was then that he told Carrie and me what name he had given to that land. Remembering the steadfast Bishop Latimer, who was martyred at Oxford for his faith, and with what strength he had even encouraged his companions in distress, he quoted the good bishop's words spoken from the scaffold.

"Be of good comfort, Master Ridley . . . We shall this day light such a candle by God's grace in England, as (I trust) shall never be put out."

God willing, the land that will see the Lyon family thrive in America will ever be called Candle Creek.

February 1717

The season was poised between winter and spring. Tree limbs reddened in preparation for the bursting of leaves, and

46

here and there a prodigal plum floated its cloud of pale blossoms between its darkly clad neighbors. The birds contended in a great commerce of nest building.

Andrew breathed the river's scents with eagerness. To travel upriver with this tide was to ride backward in time, his own time as well as the time of his family, which had committed its fortunes to planting here when James I sat on England's throne. What he did not know by fact he had learned from legend.

"A hundred years," he murmured aloud to himself.

"A hundred years?" Toad asked, turning his gaze from the shoreline to his master's face.

"A hundred years ago this coming autumn my people came to this place. Through famine and pestilence and savage Indian attacks they seeded and tended and harvested this land and that great excess that has been added to it. For one hundred years they have stood at Candle Creek.

"It was not named by whimsey," Andrew continued. "In only a few more miles, you will see the creek itself, where a mill has stood since Amos Lyon first came to this place."

"I see something now," Gil cried after a few moments. "A village of some sort."

Andrew laughed. "No village that, but a plantation. Look sharp, now. That first house, the one in ill repair, belongs to my Uncle Paul, a strange, dour man, like his father before him. That grove shelters the mill, and just beyond lies my father's house."

"So many buildings," Toad said. "And that great wharf."

Andrew studied the scene, his heart suddenly beating faster. "Such a place is its own world, and this river is its life's blood."

Barely visible between the stripped trees, Andrew saw the burying ground. A heaviness flowed into his chest. His father's light stride would not bring him to the wharf in greeting. His fine head would not rise from blessing with that winning smile. They would not walk together, man and man, as they had been wont to do when, man and boy, his father had bid him farewell.

Andrew knew how much it had grieved his father that he and his mother had not gotten along since Andrew was a very young boy. Now he must find a new friendship with her in this shared loss.

As they moved toward the wharf, another ship hung at anchor, heavy laden. "It carries the wheat from last year's crop," he mused as a servant crossing the wharf stopped to stare, threw his burden aside and ran for the house with the clamoring of dogs at his heels.

Home. He was home.

At that moment he felt himself ready for this homecoming. Had he not searched his heart and the scriptures? Had he not set away from himself the unfettered sport of his youth, to face this new responsibility? Almost at once he realized how miserably he had failed at this preparation. He had remembered the wrong things. What he had failed to remember became suddenly vital to him.

He had forgotten his own mother's nature. Instead of flying forth to greet him, as his father would have done after this six-years' absence, he was left to wait downstairs while a great whispering and scurrying of swift feet sounded beyond the stairs. At last he was led to his mother's room.

The room had been his father's room too when he last saw it. The furniture was the same, and the same gold cloth trimmed the canopy and the curtains, which were drawn against the window. Yet this had become a woman's room, with the smell of perfume in the air and his father's guns gone from the shelves by the door.

His mother's style in accepting a compliment had always been to remark that the Merritts, the line she was born to, were slow to age. She fulfilled this claim in the trimness of her figure and the thickness of the gray hair that tendrilled carefully around her face. Her mourning clothes were graceful and becoming. Only a darkness about her eyes and the lines by her mouth revealed her age. At the first touch of his hand on her arm, she bent her head against his chest and fell to helpless weeping.

She cried so long and with such abandon that Andrew felt a sudden terror that she might become ill from it. At last, to his relief, she laid her handkerchief aside, took his hand and began a long recital, which rested mainly on complaint, the weight of the burden of the household and plantation, her loneliness with none to understand her or listen to her thoughts.

"Aye, but, Mother," he replied, "so grand a man you have had for all these years, how could you fail to miss him? It is the very gaiety and tenderness that he brought you which have left you now so desolate. Think on the goodness of those years and be comforted.''

Petulantly she withdrew her hand from his. "Are you to be like the others, Andrew? I need no lectures or admonitions. Is there to be no understanding and comfort from anyone in my declining years?"

His remorse was instant. "I swear to you, Mother, I will do all in my power to lighten your burdens as well as your hours in this time to come.''

Her soft sigh of relief was muffled as she rose. Her eyes were suddenly dry.

"You will want to see the stone I had set," she told him, "while it is still light enough to appreciate its color.''

In the days to follow, Andrew was startled, upon opening familiar doors, to find that time had made strangers of even the lives closest to him.

Sara was grown plump from motherhood. The giddy laughter of her girlhood had settled into an easy geniality that smoothed the faces of her young. The child she had been expecting when he left was a glowing girl, with her father's clear eyes and a face as open as a field flower. While young Joseph was solemn in greeting, the hand be extended bore the scrapes of a rowdy lad.

These same years had laid a differing imprint on his sister Abbie. Perhaps her solemn mein should be laid more to the cares of her growing brood of children than to time. This troop of little girls, five of them, ranged from a shy, gawky girl of nine to a babe of only a few months. There was a stiffness in all their manners, and Andrew was puzzled to see that Abbie's eyes went more often to her mother for reassurance than to the gentle parson she had married.

Only his father's sister, Martha Springer, had stayed unchanged. Her house smelled of rose petals and old books. An assortment of spotted cats fled at his knock, only to file after him into the house at the opening of the door.

Aunt Martha had the fine eyebrows of the Lyon men. She peered out at him from under them with a merry smile.

"Have you, then, braved storm and sinners to come home to us?" she asked, lifting her face for his kiss. At his expression she laughed.

"This colony is a hive for gossip," she reminded him.

"Word passed from a brigantine that had provisioned you that the *Lark* dragged broken wings from tempest and pirates."

"Mother must not know," he remarked. "She made no mention of it, and neither did I."

She grinned, angling her head at him. "One does not prod a drowsing ox to raging. It was soon enough when she saw you well at home."

"Your tongue is no better behaved than when I left you," he chided her, taking the low seat by her chair. "Come, now, my dear, and talk to me of my father."

"It was such a day that comes in late September. The woods were jeweled with late grapes and the sky strung with geese anxious for passage. He had a mare whose speed he had not tested." She shrugged. "A stone? The den of a rodent? We will never know what threw the beast. But death was swift and without pain."

Andrew, listening, felt a smoothness come where there had been discomfort. The flesh of her hand was soft with age and cool against his own.

"I would not want every gossip to know that when we spoke of Andrew's death, I quoted a poet instead of scripture, but some lines of Webster's have kept coming back to my mind. 'Death hath a thousand doors to let out life,' he said. I thank God that our Andrew, having his day at hand, found so pleasant and so swift an exit."

Within days of his arrival, Andrew's mother told him of a gathering she was planning at Candle Creek.

"It will not be a party," she explained soberly. "But all the friends of your father's family and mine are eager to see you and wish you well in your new responsibilities."

Although his instinct was to protest any such event with the shadow of his father's death still upon them, Andrew stayed silent. The most surprising small things were important to his mother, and in the course of a short time he had already inadvertently brought her to tears over many of them. This was obviously important to her, so he shrank from making an issue of it. She was still raw with widowhood, he reminded himself. In time she would remember the same admonitions that she had preached to him as a child, that the management of a family should rest in a man's hands, according to the will of God.

The spring that had hung back so coquettishly at his arrival now came forth boldly. The orchard floated with blooms, and the early planted Indian corn was pricking through the soil. Suckling pigs grunted in their mother's shadow, and a tottering colt tried to fly from the green of the pasture.

Even the sun greeted the guests warmly, and the air in the old rooms grew festive. Andrew needed prompting to recognize many lads who had turned to men and awkward girls made into matrons in his absence. Looking over the well-laid board, Andrew knew that his father would have been gratified at the pleasure of his friends.

Among the guests who were strange to him was a family named Cowper. The heavyset gentleman who was introduced as a planter and merchant was accompanied by a wife and daughter as reed-slim as he was portly. Andrew only slowly realized that each time he turned, the girl, called Nance, seemed to be at one elbow or another. His mother was clearly impressed by this pale child and recounted her skill at housewifery and the spinet at tedious length. He nodded genially at her words, but it was the talk of the men that interested him.

Guesses about the season for tobacco were rampant as always, and there were some heated words on the progress of Governor Spotswood's house, which, one man averred, "bid fair to be a castle befitting a king if we subjects can but survive the taxing that must build it." And as always, there was talk of pirates.

"Those who privateer in war go on their own account in peace," the planter Cowper said. "God help us. Since Queen Anne's war is past, we have been more plagued with these creatures than an ill ox in foul weather."

"And look at the Bahamas," his neighbor chimed in. "Hornigold of the *Mary* and Jennings with the *Bathsheba* have made it a peril to pass from one island to the next."

"But that is far away," Cowper pointed out. "It is commonly guessed that fifteen hundred pirates commonly range off this coast of ours. While they claim to honor an English registry, this courtesy does not extend to our colonial ships."

"There is little that can be done against pirates, with their being so welcome, along with their loot, in the coves to the south of us. But in Spotswood they find an enemy, a mortal enemy."

"As any who have come against them would be," Andrew

agreed, moving away. Every voice turned his thoughts to Emily Fraser—not only the gowns and laughter of the maidens, but even the talk of men when they dwelled thus on pirates. With each day he hoped for a likely time to speak of her to his mother, a time that seemed slow to come, with his thoughts so constantly turning to her.

When the last of the guests had gone, Andrew and his sisters were joined by their mother as they toyed with the remains of the feast. She seemed more voluble than was her wont, and Andrew was glad he had not denied her the pleasure of this event.

She prattled brightly about one family and another before turning her words to the Cowpers. "Tell me, Andrew, didn't you find Nance Cowper an enchanting companion?"

"Cowper," he repeated, trying to fix the name. "Oh, yes, the man who was so full of pirate tales."

"Not him, his daughter," his mother said with some irritation. " 'Tis a pity that we could have no music. She is an angel on the spinet."

"She is very nice." He nodded, setting a thin slice of ham on a biscuit. "Very nice, I am sure."

His mother leaned toward him, her tone lower and fraught with significance. "She finds you appealing too."

He thought he heard a faint chuckle from his sister Sara but was too distracted to take heed. "She knows me not at all," he protested.

"She knows of you," his mother said archly. "I have seen to that for you."

He felt a flag of warning begin to flutter in the back of his mind. "All mothers speak kindly of their children," he said calmly, wishing to God that someone would raise another topic of conversation. Instead he caught an unmistakable look of wariness on his Aunt Martha's face.

"Cowper has made a good thing of himself since coming here," his mother continued. "He has combined the work of planter and merchant, much like Harrison did, and with grand success, I might add. And Nance is his only living child."

Andrew nodded, and Sara's chuckle became a peal of laughter. She leaned over to tap him gently on the hand. "Come, Andy, have you been away so long from the company of women that you do not know when matchmaking is going on?"

"Sara," her mother cried furiously.

Sara sighed. "Mother, Andy is barely home and used to dry land under his feet. Don't be throwing a wife at him until he gets used to being son and brother again."

"Wife." Andrew repeated. He stared from his mother to his sister and back with a dumbfounded air. Wife? Could they be thinking of that spare, pale creature in terms of wifery? It was as if the room faded and he stood in Fraser's room in Norfolk, with Emily's song sweet in his ears and the beauty of that richly toned face half hidden in shadow.

His mother would have railed at Sara, considering his marriage to be her business. But his life must be his own. The deception of the festivities just past rushed in on him. This event had been arranged for his own entrapment. Like the *Lark*, with false gunports painted on her sides, like Robbie Fraser parading as a Presbyterian saint when he was not sowing wild oats in a stinking port tavern, the significance of this "event" had not been what it appeared. Rather, it was intended to snare him as husband for that pale stick of an heiress. A knot was in his throat.

"Mother," Andrew said firmly, breaking in on her rebuke of Sara. "While I am most appreciative of your efforts in my behalf, I should tell you at once that I have already chosen my wife. I have the permission of her father to make suit to Mistress Emily Fraser of Norfolk."

The silence seemed eternal. Then his mother paled and wavered in her seat. Andrew would have reached to support her, but she would have none of it. She rose and left the room on swift, angry feet.

"Now you have done it, sir," his Aunt Martha said quietly. "Let me see how you resolve that one. We have heard nothing but 'Andrew and Nance' since the Cowpers moved here."

"I do not intend to resolve anything," Andrew replied candidly. "I am here because I was summoned. I am prepared to take my father's place at the head of the family, and in the parish and the government. I am not trained to cajole or play with the truth. I love Emily Fraser and want her to wife."

Sara rose and laid her cheek against his. "My prayers are with you, Andy, and with your maiden."

"And mine," his Aunt Martha added. "Though I will add

53

that the quicker you stroke down this fever of your mother's, the easier she will be to handle later.''

He looked at her and rose with a sigh.

"Stroke her I will," he agreed. "Submit to her matchmaking, never."

• 7 •

A Charge of Angels

Spring

He that dwelleth in the secret place of the most High shall
abide under the shadow of the Almighty.
For he shall give his angels charge over thee, to keep thee
in all thy ways.

Psalms 91:1, 11

YOUNGER ELLIOTT was numbered among the ancients. Although he had been christened William after his father, he was never called by this name. William Elliott's name died with him on that black Good Friday when Chief Opechancanough raised his warriors against the Virginians in 1644.

Time had served Younger Elliott as an insect does a leaf. All that was left of him was the veining, with his flesh transparent between. Only the dark eyes that he raised to Andrew showed the vigor of the Lyon blood.

"You, then, are Andrew's son," the old man said, studying Andrew's face. "You bear more the look of your Uncle James."

"So I have been told," Andrew replied.

"Many years have passed since I looked on any of my family from down there," Younger told him. "I pray that you do not bear ill tidings. I have not yet ceased to grieve over the death of your gentle father."

"Nor have I," Andrew replied. "As for tidings, I bring you none at all. I bring only myself."

The girl who served them was a slattern. The food had been indifferently prepared, and the cloth she laid for them was drab with old stains. Somehow, in this place, with the old man's eyes intent upon him, such details were unimportant.

Only when they had finished their meal did the old man return to his questions.

"Since there are no tidings and we have managed all these years without each other, why do you come now?"

Andrew had been so sure of the purpose of this journey, but those searching eyes stripped him of his words.

"I am come into a new estate," he said at last.

"You speak of land and slaves?" Younger asked.

Andrew shook his head. "Those of course, Uncle, but more than that, a responsibility before God for the family my father left . . . my mother, my sisters, even your own sister Martha Springer."

The old man chuckled softly. "Each man that lifts such a mantle to his shoulders finds it of a different cloth. Your father, like Joseph the son of Jacob, wore a bright coat, decorated by many colors of love. I know little of his marriage, but his parents and his brothers and sisters cherished him dearly, especially James."

"I know I am not of his cloth," Andrew told him. "He had a rare skill of taking what card fell to hand and playing it to win. I am a man who must have rules to work by or I falter."

"Rules," the old man repeated, nodding. Then he chuckled again. "How is it that I ask your errand and we end by talking of the role of husbandman?"

Andrew grinned. "Then you have discovered that I also don't have my father's great skill with words. I have come because of my new responsibilities as head of the family. The rules I have spoken of include you."

"The scripture states that a man must be the head of the family and governor of their business even as a king leads and

55

controls his people and our Lord does his flock. Is this among the rules you embrace?"

"Aye." Andrew nodded. "It is the first of them."

"It is well that it be placed first, because it is the hardest," the old man said. "The difficulty comes when a man must choose which business is his and which is God's. Your grandfather Bruce Rigg, God rest his soul, yielded up too much of that authority, and by this he perished. Your great-uncle Amos Lyon, God forgive him, took too much of God's dominion unto himself, and by this he perished."

"Your words carry more wisdom than encouragement," Andrew told him.

"It is the man who knows where the pit has been dug who stays free of the nets," Younger reminded him. "Have you more rules than this one from God?"

Andrew nodded. "I have a great love for openness in any dealing. I would like to see members of this family treat each other in that manner, so that no one is secretive and evasive with any other."

Younger whistled softly between his teeth. "Deception is a tool with more than one use. One day it is used to maim and another to protect. Would you dull both sides of that tool? You cannot dull one without losing the other."

"Honesty among loving souls cannot be that difficult," Andrew protested.

"Only when there is love, is true honesty difficult," the old man corrected him.

Andrew laughed softly. "Do we have a problem in dealing honestly with each other? Yet I love you and have you in my mind from my earliest childhood though I never saw your face."

"Age makes the difference," Younger conceded. "More things leave with time than most men know of. That same failing energy that takes a man's hand from his plow also strips his tongue of deception. Old scars wholly heal, leaving only the love that was their cause. Fury burns itself to ash, enriching the soil where it lies. Great issues are seen in a brighter light and dwindle in size."

Veins, Andrew thought. Not only his flesh but his thinking has been stripped of that puffy corpulence that conceals its structure.

"Your words bring me real hope," Andrew told him. "It

56

has always seemed so sad to me that the Lyon family struggles apart when, by twining in friendship, each branch might be strengthened.''

To Andrew's astonishment, the old man bent in laughter.

''My son, my son, how you delight me by reminding me of the amazement of old Bennett Lyon's heritage. What deep color that Lyon blood has, that it still stains to the fourth generation. My mother, Rebeckah, lost that name into Elliott by marrying when she was only a girl. Twice more she laid new names onto it, and yet all who came from that blood are called Lyon, no matter what name they bear. But this is a great endeavor you set for yourself. What of Joel Lyon and his generations? I thought myself ill-used. Joel knew himself to be, even as his brother Daniel was.''

''Daniel was Uncle Paul's father?'' Andrew asked.

''Aye. And I have it on account that the bitter grapes his father ate have put Paul's teeth on edge for the whole of his life.''

''That may well be,'' Andrew agreed. ''He is strange of faith and manners and desolate of friends.''

''Then what of Adam Lyon and his generations, and my brother Benn Elliott's seed, if such persist? Have you room in this proud family for Papists and pirates?''

''Perhaps the passage of time on the race of man works even as it does on one life,'' Andrew suggested. ''Such issues seem diminished in the light of time.''

The old man reached out and laid his hand on Andrew's. ''There is nothing more becoming in a strong man than an innocent heart, especially if he can keep his hands in that same state. This comes as a gift to me, to greet you as kinsman and then to love you as friend. Perhaps in you the Lyon's blood has indeed been tamed by reason. It is high time. And my blessing, Andrew, on this stewardship given you by your father's untimely death. My blessing.''

''You have not seen the last of me.'' Andrew laughed. ''I am different from my father in other ways too, I fear. Where he was content to stay where his father labored, I have a thirst for the land beyond. I was in England when word came that Governor Spotswood and his party had crossed those blue mountains and claimed what lay beyond. It is my dream to marry and set my own family beyond the fall.''

Younger laughed. ''It is good to see some of myself in

you. I could not rest until I moved upriver to this place. After that I could not rest until my name held land in the valley beyond. Even though I have stayed here, I go there in my mind. What began with fifty acres is now a great block. The Rapidan flows into the James with such force that a mill could be set. Valley land, rich land that lies idle except in an old man's dreams.''

"What of your sons?" Andrew asked.

"They married more land and slaves than they have hours for. They show small interest in either my land or the Simms place, over in Henrico, which I bought lest it fall into uncaring hands.''

"The Simms place?" Andrew asked.

"It was the homestead of the girl whom your Uncle James loved. It was when she died at Indian hands that he went to war with Bacon, seeking death. That it came with a rope was a matter of chance.''

"I seek land and you own land," Andrew pointed out. "While I did not come for this, it would be a great joy to me to see these acres for myself.''

"It is as good as done," Younger said. "I will send a guide with you and your man on the morrow if you wish.''

Andrew was seized with an unreasonable excitement. "And if I should want to buy this land?" he asked.

Younger laughed. "Then we would forget we were kinsmen and sit down as men of business.''

The acreage that lay between the James and the Rapidan rivers struck Andrew's eye with a sense of recognition. He knew almost at once that this was the place where he and Emily could fulfill the great promise of his marriage. He would return and sit down with Younger Elliott as businessman on this.

The journey to the Simms place was a pilgrimage. There he found an eyeless hovel squeaking with fugitive life. Where outbuildings had stood, saplings had risen with twisted trunks to accommodate that rubble. Three nameless, ill-carved stones heaved from the weedy turf of the burying ground. The forest had its arms about that clearing, a seemingly endless wilderness haunted by owls and night creatures.

The wind rose after they made camp. It sang in the

saplings. From the river came the swishing of fish. Toad, at Andrew's side, rose on an elbow to whisper into the darkness.

"And what came of this man Simms and his daughter?"

"It is best that we talk of it in the sun of morning," Andrew told him, not eager to dwell on the savagery of those deaths, which had driven his uncle from life.

From his pallet the guide chuckled softly, a sound nearly lost in the cries and the drones of that wild place.

8

Deep Waters

Save me, O God; for the waters are come in unto my soul.
I sink in deep mire, where there is no standing:
I am come into deep waters, where the floods overflow
me. I am weary of my crying: my throat is dried: mine
eyes fail while I wait for my God.

Psalms 69:1–3

BY THE END of March, the feeling of spring was everywhere. What blossoms still hung in the orchard were well past being damaged by the high winds that brought frost along the riverfront. The river ran rich in herring and whitefish, and the rows of peas sowed early rose bravely in the garden.

Andrew nursed his growing exhaustion at the series of campaigns his mother was waging against his betrothal to Emily Fraser.

"The woman has a damnable way of twisting a man's

59

words about, that they explode in his own face,'' Andrew raged to his Aunt Martha.

She was his only ally. Sara had retreated to her home and children, pleading the duties of her housewifery to keep her skirts from being bloodied in this internecine war.

Andrew had discovered that Abbie, for what reason he could not guess, sided with his mother on any issue. Perhaps the fatigue of her constant childbearing and the demands of producing edible meals and keeping a suitable home with her parson husband's pittance had dulled her mind.

"Are you, then, a sugar loaf, to be melted by tears?'' his aunt challenged.

Andrew shook his head. "But neither am I a man of salt, with cruelty enough to bring a fair, trusting girl into a house where she will find neither welcome nor comfort except from me.''

"But you are the master of that house,'' Martha reminded him, "even as your father was before you.''

"My father and I are different men,'' Andrew replied. "With no disrespect intended, I cannot slip from compromise to compromise for the sake of a surface peace that hides boiling waters. I must insist on being honest until there is no air left for subtle lies.''

His aunt sighed. "You will gain many bruises at that game.''

"My mother was wasted on housewifery,'' Andrew commented. "She would have made a notable general.''

"I am sure we have all heard of the Merritt men who acquitted themselves with such honor in that profession,'' Martha Springer said slyly.

It was a long war, and many were the bruises.

"Can you remember any gentleman wedding a ship captain's daughter?'' his mother asked. "What dower would such a match bring to you?''

"I do not marry for station or dower,'' Andrew explained. "I marry for love, a treasure more sought by men than gold.''

"You would need to stand by such a wife against a lifetime of slights in parlors and drawing rooms,'' his mother warned.

"Then I would take care to keep only such company as had the decency to judge a person on her own merit,'' was Andrew's reply.

The campaign his mother waged against the brevity of his

meeting with Emily Fraser offered a challenge. Andrew could either imply that he had lingered idly in courtship on his way to a bereaved mother or admit that his whole exposure to Emily Fraser's charms had been an hour in the parlor, the length of a dinner and that startling moment in which she had defied her father.

"Then you are such a man as can judge a life companion by a song and how delicately she takes food?" his mother asked.

"I knew I loved her the moment I heard her voice. I knew this twice when I looked into her eyes."

"You had been at sea for four long months," she reminded him. "It has ever been noted that such journeys can infect a man with a temporary madness at the sight of the first pretty face after such privation."

The matter of Emily's faith was brought forth only by probing.

"Our rector claims that his fellow in Norfolk knows of no such communicant as this Emily Fraser."

"She is Presbyterian," Andrew said, bracing himself for a storm.

Instead there was silence. After a moment his mother rose and walked to the window to stare out.

"This is your Lyon blood," she said sadly. "No Merritt would ever look outside the church for a mate. It is unseemly. Your father had an uncle named Adam Lyon who went forth to England and warred against Cromwell for the king's cause. Driven into Ireland, he was trapped by a Papist woman into marriage. He has no proper family now, only this woman, who stole him from his hearth and inheritance and, instead of heirs, filled his cradle with priests and nuns."

"Was he a happy man?" Andrew was uncivil enough to ask.

"Was it for happiness that God put man on the earth?" she countered.

When she saw him readying to visit Emily in Norfolk before it was time for the next crop to be put in, his mother asked Andrew quite meekly how he liked the girl's father.

"He's a good sailor," he replied, disarmed by her manner; "a lonely man who lost his wife some nineteen years ago and his only son to pirates only a few years ago. He is well read, as many Scots seem to be, and a jolly fellow in a man's company."

"It is strange to me that a man so bereft would be so eager to rid himself of his only child."

His chuckle had come unbidden. "He is anything but eager," he told her. "He did all he could to prevent my even seeing the girl. He named her as stubborn and overpious and past the age of marrying. All this was to keep a man from seeing what a treasure he had hidden."

"Yet he was quick enough to accept your suit for her hand."

He did not realize how the words would sound until they hung in the air between them. "On the contrary; he made it plain to her that my suit was ridiculous and she was to refuse me at once."

She did not have to feign the amusement in her eyes. "Is it possible that her father spoke the truth when he referred to her lamentable stubbornness?"

The spring that bloomed along the James River also surged in the gardens of Norfolk. Andrew was ill-prepared for the paleness of Emily's complexion and the sadness that darkened her eyes.

"Forgive me," she pleaded, summoning a wistful smile. "The reports of the last two days have kept me sleepless on my pillow."

"Reports?" he asked, knowing that Captain Fraser's *Lark* was still under repair.

"Father took a schooner to Charles Town. It is the ship usually commanded by Captain Bruce Forrester, whom you met here."

"Then it is fear of pirates that holds you sleepless?"

The tenderness about her lips made his arms hunger to comfort her. Such a gentleness in her manner made her words even more startling.

"I loathe pirates," she exclaimed with sudden fury. "I hate them with my heart's blood. Had I the power, I would cut the heart from every pirate alive and toss it into the ravening jaws of sharks."

At Andrew's startled expression, she sighed. "Forgive me. This port is babbling with reports. They say that Captain Bellamy, who served with Benjamin Hornigold is cruising this coast in the *Whido Gallery* with a crew of two hundred and a sloop besides. My father's hatred of pirates is as notorious as any man's. I cannot face his fate if he should fall into Bellamy's hands.''

In time he distracted her from her concern. She was delighted with the gift of a handmade lace bag he had bought for her in Williamsburg and touched by a gift of spiced petals from his sister Sara's own hand. He told her of his visit with Younger Elliott and the two parcels of land he had bought in the valley. She grew thoughtful as he talked to her about the old man.

''A family is a new thing to me,'' Emily explained. ''There has been only my father and me all these years. Your family has so many souls, I may never learn them—your mother, sisters, uncles and aunts!''

''You will be the fairest blossom on that tree, and the most dearly loved,'' he told her, hiding his fears.

As they parted, she had, as always, a special word for Gil the Toad.

''I would that you were riding on the *Swallow* with my father, Guillam Jones. He gives no man a better name for the murdering of human dogs.''

''You have a fair reputation in that place,'' Andrew teased Gil as they traveled home.

''It is one I prefer to rest on,'' Gil admitted.

Having listened to Emily tell him her worries about pirates, Andrew found his own concern was great throughout the following month. The pirate Bellamy took the *Agnes* from Bermuda early on the morning of April first, a few leagues east of Cape Charles. The next day he took the *Anne of Glasgow* and the sloop *Endeavour* from Brighton. Then came the news of the capture of the *Tryall of Brighton*.

''I find myself almost as worried about Captain Robbie Fraser as my lady herself is,'' Andrew confessed to Toad.

''I think I might be riding with him this day if your lady had her way,'' Toad told him.

''I would not part with you lightly, Guillam Jones,'' Andrew assured him, ''even if you were fool enough to seek such a life.''

He did not tell Toad that even so personal a thing as his

own manservant had become a new source of strife between himself and his mother.

"It is strange to a Virginian's eyes to see a gentleman disport himself with a servant, as you do with that Welsh peasant," she remarked.

Coming on top of her other attacks on him, Andrew bridled. "Gil has been friend and defender and loyal champion to me since I was a lad. It would be strange if something more than a passing loyalty had not developed between us."

"Maude has served me personally since she was a girl of twelve," she reminded him, "yet we do not banter as you do."

He turned away. Maude had had no choice, having been bought along with her mother and two others when she was barely old enough to stand.

By the first week of May, the strawberries gleamed scarlet among their tendrils and the garden was crowned with the green of burgeoning melons. With the happy word of Robbie Fraser's safe return to Norfolk, Andrew traveled there to complete his marriage plans.

The old Scot insisted on a marriage contract that caused even his lawyer to raise an eyebrow in surprise. Emily Fraser was not only to keep her entire inheritance from her father under her own control but, "covert of her husband," was to receive a monthly stipend for "such desires as she might have and for the wages of her two servants, Chad and Tansey, that she not be forced to submit to service by any but free men and women."

"Make no mistake, Andrew Rigg," the captain told him, "I like you as well as any man for myself, but as a husband to my Em, I cherish you as dearly as I would the sight of Blackbeard himself hoving over the side of the *Lark* with the flares lit in his demon cap."

Out of consideration for his mother's year of mourning and a failing hope that he might bring that woman to show some gentleness toward his bride, Andrew set the marriage date in late September, just after the anniversary of his father's death.

"You are a good son," Emily told him, her slender hands flat against his chest. "It is an old saying that a good son maketh a gentle husband."

"How could I be otherwise, with such a wife?" he asked, wishing the summer that held them apart might be sped.

Her laugh was soft against him. "I do not even know why I love thee so dearly, and have from the first," she confessed in a surprised tone.

"It was the wave of my own devotion for you striking your heart and washing that bounty back to me," Andrew told her.

The song that he bade her sing each time they were together hung in the air all the way up the James River to Candle Creek.

• 9 •

Awake, O North Wind

> Awake, O north wind; and come, thou south; blow upon
> my garden, that the spices thereof may flow out. Let my
> beloved come into his garden, and eat his pleasant fruits.
>
> Song of Solomon 4:16

THE WAR OF THE SPANISH SUCCESSION, which the colonists called Queen Anne's War, raged for eleven years over four continents. During its progress, the colonists gained in one way, by developing trade with Spain. Their loss involved the Indian attacks on their frontier, spurred on by the French. At the completion of the Peace of Utrecht, in which England gained control of the entire American hemisphere's seas except for the Spanish *flota*, the colonies lost the freedom of their own seas.

As was common in war, open licensing was granted to plunder the ships of the enemy. The British law of 1708 encouraged thousands of men to seek their fortunes by rapacity at sea. With the war over, these same thousands, having no other skills or means of livelihood, turned to piracy.

The attitudes of colonial governors toward piracy ranged from open collusion to righteous fury. Colonel Alexander Spotswood, who had replaced Francis Nicholson as governor of Virginia in 1710, was as zealous in his campaign against these brigands as his predecessor had been.

Except for those Virginians who dabbled in the sport on their own, the colonists stood firm behind Spotswood, conscious that the area's only guard ship had a bottom so fouled that she was useless in pursuit and that the sea was the only highway for the transport of their tobacco.

While talk of pirates was common enough everywhere, Andrew found that Emily was always full of tales of their misdeeds.

"My love, if you know the catalogue of the saints as well as you do the flags of these sinners, you are a pious student."

She flushed and laughed. "That is a fair charge, but you must remember that a woman does not easily forgive what robs her of her near and dear."

Andrew had no intention of throwing those words back at her, but the day came when he had no choice.

When he returned from Norfolk having signed the wedding contract and set the date of his marriage, he found his mother had taken to her bed. The servants were fluttering about her, while the kitchen steamed with special brews designed to give her strength.

"I shall be astonished if any cure be found until your wedding day is past," his sister Sara said with a perfectly calm face.

"You have a slicing tongue, sister."

"You have a short memory. This malady is remarkably like the one that used to strike Mother whenever Father insisted on a course that was displeasing to her."

"And what happened when his deed was done?" he asked.

"Such an event never occurred," she told him. "It was always our father who retreated under the fire of pills and potions."

"I am going to marry Emily Fraser," Andrew insisted.

66

"And I hope you do," Sara said, mocking his assertive tone. "I cannot imagine that in the flesh this maiden of yours would not win Mother's heart. Could she and her father be persuaded to visit here and meet Mother while she is in her bed of pain? Such graciousness might flatter Mother into making peace."

"But Emily hasn't been invited."

Sara shrugged. "They have to meet sometime." Her face brightened. "Perhaps when your Emily hears of Mother's indisposition, she might offer to come herself."

To Andrew's astonishment, Emily took his broad hint readily and planned a visit within the fortnight.

"You are so gracious to make this effort," he told her. "I tremble that I do not deserve such a creature as you."

She flushed. "Don't make of me more than I am, Andrew, lest I fall short of that mark and you turn against me. As to your mother, how could I fail to love one who has such a son as you? I have never known a mother, Andrew, and am childishly eager to have the chance to love and serve yours."

The visit was a disaster from the start. His mother not only stayed invalid for the whole of the time but granted an audience to these guests with a disdain that chilled the summer air. Sara valiantly did her best to make Emily and her father comfortable. At Andrew's request, his Aunt Martha had come for those brief and unhappy days.

As loath as he was to part from her, Andrew was relieved to see the change of tide that would bear his guests back to Norfolk. Captain Fraser held Gil the Toad in conversation, which granted Andrew a brief moment alone with Emily at the wharf. She made a beautiful picture. Her skin glowed with the heat of the day, and the basket of fruit Sara had pressed on her was not more rosy than her lips. Yet those same lips held a sober line. Andrew knew from her appearance that a lesser woman would have been in tears. Instead, she had the strength and honesty to put the truth into words.

"She hates me," she said with disbelief. "Do not protest, Andrew. I am not oversensitive, but neither am I blind. Your mother hates me with a brooding passion."

"My mother is not a woman easily read," he told her, wishing his own words were more candid.

Her eyes snapped with annoyance at his dissimulation. "On the contrary, she is a primer writ in bold letters. You heard her talk of the splendid blood of the Merritt family that beats in her own pulse and yours. You heard her careful cataloguing of the powerful church posts that have resided in your family. She hates my source and my faith and me and considers all of them beneath her station.''

When he hesitated, she sighed. ''Do not try to deny it, my love. We have had no half-truths between us, and I want none now. It is only that I wonder . . .''

He could see her pulling away from their marriage in her mind. With every word she had deepened his love for her even as she explored the thought of pulling away from him.

It was then that he threw her own words back at her.

''Aye, Emily,'' he said quietly. ''I do admit that she hates you, in the same degree and for the same reason that you hold such a loathing of pirates.''

Her eyes widened in surprise. He took the basket and set it down to take both her hands.

''A woman does not lightly forgive what has robbed her of her near and dear,'' he quoted.

She paused, catching her lip between her teeth. ''But sons have married since the dawn of time.''

''And mothers have rued this and been won by such wives as you will be.''

''Oh, Andrew,'' she sighed, her eyes on his face. ''I wish this were not so public a place.''

But public it was, with Captain Robbie bearing down on them, his eyes angry at their joined hands, and his voice gruff with haste. ''Quick, now,'' he told Emily. ''Get thee aboard and do not stand mooning like a struck calf, for all the world to see.''

With a heavy heart, Andrew watched until the sails were out of sight.

That night in his mother's room, his Aunt Martha suggested, in the calmest possible way, that Andrew and Emily make their home with her after their marriage.

''There is room here and to spare,'' Andrew's mother said in an affronted tone.

''Space is not the issue,'' Martha replied. ''A young marriage should have its own walls. Lacking that, it should be in some situation where the bride could seize the reins of the household from the first. My own strength fails for such a task. If Emily and Andrew were there, I would be free to putter in my garden and pore over my books like the idle creature I would like to be. It is not a grand house, you must remember, Andrew, but it would be like your own until such time as you wished to raise your own walls."

Andrew did not meet his mother's eyes. "Emily and I would find it grand enough and more."

"But Andrew has this plantation to run, and the books to take care of," his mother protested.

"Many a man rides farther to his acres than this," Martha said lightly, "and finds his health and disposition improved by the canter."

Andrew could not meet his aunt's eyes, for he saw by the twist of her lips that she was perilously close to a chuckle.

In August as Andrew oversaw the sowing of the second crop of wheat, two well-equipped frigates arrived in Virginia. The *Lyme* and the *Pearl* held full complements of men. It was said in the weeks following that not a pirate ship was sighted in the bay.

"They would not be here in this season anyway," Toad said acidly. "They would be off before the storms of this season, and working in warmer air."

"You and my Emily," Andrew said, laughing, "you might both be pirates yourselves, for the knowledge you show of them."

To placate his mother, Andrew and Emily Fraser were married twice, once in Norfolk, in the church of the bride's childhood, and then blessed again, by the rector of Andrew's own parish.

When he stood at last in the flower-decked room they would share at his aunt's home, Andrew found himself trembling as if with cold.

Emily smiled at him, her head cocked a little to the side and her lashes half closed.

"Are you afraid, then, of being a husband?"

"Aye," he admitted, drawing her close. "I have such love for you that I am stiff with fear that you don't love me, even so painfully, in return. And I am afraid of not succeeding in keeping that flush of joy on your face, as well as that we both will not live as many years as I hunger for. I cannot even now believe the chance of that day that turned the boat on the river so that I went back and met you. I cannot believe that you defied your father and my mother's ill grace to wed with me.''

"It was to be," she told him quietly. "Only know that it was long meant to be, or it never would have been.''

Emily's hair against his face smelled of spice. Her lips under his were not moist like the mouth of a strumpet but were of a cool softness into which Andrew thought he might happily sink forever.

PART TWO

A Price Above Rubies
(1717–1719)

Who can find a virtuous woman? for her price is far above rubies. The heart of her husband doth safely trust in her, so that he shall have no need of spoil. She will do him good and not evil all the days of her life. Favour is deceitful, and beauty is vain: but a woman that feareth the Lord, she shall be praised.

Proberbs 31:10, 12, 30

Nothing is more gratifying to the mind of man than power or dominion . . . I look upon my family as a patriarchal sovereignty, in which I am myself both King and Priest.

Spectator, 1712

1

The Sower

(1717)

Be not deceived: God is not mocked: for whatsoever a man soweth, that shall he also reap.
Let us not be weary in well doing: for in due season we shall reap, if we faint not.

Galations 6:7, 9

WITHIN HER FAMILY Martha Springer had a reputation for being a quiet woman in spite of the mischief that shone in her eyes. She was said to resemble her father, Bruce Rigg, of whom it was said that he never spoke ten words if three would suffice— and if only three were needed, Bruce would merely nod.

Martha was also pitied for being so nearly barren that the only child she bore had died young. She was considered strange because, like her mother Bek before her, she was fonder of reading and writing than of the company of most people.

Quiet and strange she might have been in that autumn of 1717, but she was no longer a woman to be pitied. In Andrew's young Presbyterian wife, Martha Springer found herself a daughter.

And Emily Fraser, in spite of the hurt that darkened her eyes, found a mother in Andrew's aging aunt.

Jason Springer had built her house for Martha in 1670. It was as solid and attractive as Jason had been. A wide passage

73

admitted the breezes that came from the walnut trees he placed in the dooryard. The rooms were generous and well lit for the comfort of the children that never came. Into these rooms and the maze garden came Andrew and Emily, along with Gil the Toad, Tansey, Emily's handmaid, and Chad.

The love that blossomed at once between Emily and Martha Springer was Emily's salvation. Unwittingly her father had spoiled her about the company of men. Although she was used to her father's long absences while he was at sea, she was also used to his undivided time when he was in port. Robbie Fraser gloried in her company, walking the streets and markets of the city, proud of this fair daughter he wore on his arm. It had not occurred to Emily that she could have so little time with Andrew.

Pressed by the management of his big plantation, Andrew left home with Toad after an early breakfast each morning. He dined at his mother's house for convenience and only returned when the lamps were lit for evening, to have a bite of supper and a glass of wine with Emily and his aunt.

That much she could understand. But as autumn lengthened, Andrew began to be absent in the evenings, either at the homes of friends or off in the smoky taverns of Williamsburg, where he stayed until what seemed to her a scandalously late hour.

"What do you do?" she asked, incredulous that a man would spend that much time in a smoky tavern by choice.

He laughed. "Wager and pass the news about and visit with travelers who bring fresh tidings. With the governor's not having called an assembly all this time, the air is stiff with complaint. I feel I must stand for my father's seat in the Assembly, and to do that, I must be more Virginian than Londoner in my knowledge, current on all that I have missed these six years."

"And you must drink," she added, wrinkling her nose and pulling away from him.

"Yes, drink." He laughed, tugging her near again. "Fine toasts and laughter and pirate tales and bad music. Williamsburg gets to be a fair town as it grows."

Except for an occasional turn through the shops with Sara, who was amusing company, Emily seldom went to Williamsburg. While it was a bare village compared to Norfolk, the houses were pleasant, set along a wide street, with the capitol building facing the college in a graceful confrontation. She liked to kneel for silent prayer in Bruton Church, for all that it was in the poorest of condition, with a vicarage barely fit as a dependency house.

Most of the time Emily simply stayed at home, where she was now prey to strange fits of giddiness that had come soon after her marriage. She spent much time in prayer, puzzling a way to make friends with Andrew's mother, for his sake and her own.

With her mourning at end, Eleanor Merritt Rigg resumed her social pattern of making calls or receiving guests almost every afternoon.

"I have set aside one day each fortnight when I call on Mother," Sara told her. "You might make your own call on that day with me. I would much enjoy having you."

Emily became thoughtful. "I have no skill at deceiving, Sara," she said carefully. "If I plan to win your mother to my case, I cannot travel in the shadow of your gown but must do it on my own."

Sara sighed. "I will tell you what I tell my son Joseph. Bravery earns more bruises than blossoms."

Emily smiled at her. "Like your son, I must do it my own way. Have you any ideas?"

Sara shrugged. "Even more than most women, my mother thrives on compliments and gifts, if they are not pretentious. And even a mother-in-law likes something to boast of in her children."

For Emily's first call, Martha Springer went along. Emily carried a gift of pale jelly she had made from the wild grapes that grew in the garden. Eleanor Rigg offered her a cool cheek to embrace and thanked her coldly before having a servant set the jelly on a shelf by the hearth.

The talk swirled around Emily as she bent to her needle. She knew her work to be as fine as that of the neighbor who sat beside her, but it was the neighbor's stitches that Andrew's mother called attention to for their fineness. There was talk of "my son Andrew" and the cleverness with which he had turned from London agent to Virginia planter with none to guide him. Her own name never passed Mother Rigg's lips. Now and then Martha began a sentence with, "Our Emily, here . . ." only to have the words cut off in her mouth by some exclamation or other.

Andrew's sister Abbie was there, hanging on her mother's every word in a way that irritated Emily. Later she asked forgiveness for this, since she assumed her irritation must be jealousy that she had not a mother of her own to be intimate with.

But as they left, she was nearer fury than prayer.

"My dear child," Martha said, taking her hand. "You must not let so small-minded a performance as that upset you."

Emily drew in her breath sharply. "I am strangely weak now. I turn to anger when I should be strong. Later I will handle this better. But as for now," she burst out, "I call it rudeness. I would scarcely treat a pirate in my home with such incivility."

Martha's peal of laughter dried Emily's tears. "Knowing you as I do, my love, a pirate in your house is so unlikely as to be hilarious."

By the end of October, a jar of brandied fruit and a nut cake had taken their place beside the grape jelly on Eleanor Rigg's shelf by the fire. None had been moved since they were set there. Emily, feeling a little nauseated after a jolting ride to Candle Creek, stared at them dully until she could gracefully take her leave.

"With winter coming on, we shall all see less of each other, I suppose," Andrew's mother said as Emily rose.

"She clearly wants me to stay away," she told Martha when she reported this comment to her.

"The greater her loss, then. I will send a note that I have chosen that same day to receive and have asked you to share the burden of being hostess with me."

"One more time," Emily promised herself. "I will make that effort one more time."

As she saw her jar of spiced rose petals take their place on the shelf with her other gifts, Emily felt herself grow limp with despair. Almost every morning now she wakened and got up with difficulty. Calling on her mother-in-law was one burden she could lift from herself.

The gentlewomen who called on Martha Springer could not have been more various. The sisters Dillon were near to Martha's age, rosy puddings of women who tended to laugh in concert. A planter's wife called Cece seemed scarcely old enough to bear the child that made her gown billow. Still they all clattered together in the merriest of talk, until Emily felt her own sides ache from it.

Emily's friendship with Cece was immediate. Cece grinned from a pointed face rimmed all about with carroty red hair. "Why they call this condition delicate is beyond my ken," she confessed as she awkwardly took her chair. "I feel as graceful and delicate as an ox, although, in truth, this is my favorite state."

"This is not your first, then?" Emily asked, noting the childish appearance of Cece's hands.

"Lor', no." The girl giggled. "We have nine, and three of them be from me." As she spoke she pulled out her work, a satin panel on which a trailing of woven birds was forming. "Jacob has six from his first wife, rest her soul, the oldest coming on thirteen." She nipped a thread with her teeth and grinned wickedly at Em. "Can you wonder that I love to get away to this quiet place with Granny Springer?"

The shorter days of winter found Andrew gone before full light. He had long since insisted that Emily need not rise to sit at breakfast with him. Finally she took his advice. Each day found her carefully poised at the bedside, groggy and nauseated, moving with great care lest she have to bend over the chamber of nightsoil to retch.

Tansey turned traitor and reported her illness in the kitchen.

That next morning she was wakened by Andrew, trimly dressed for his day, coming to sit by her side.

"I have brought you a bite to eat before breakfast," he said his tone teasing and sly.

She rose on her elbows to stare at the stand by the bed, where a plate held two buttered biscuits crowned by a fat ladeling of scarlet jelly.

At her confusion, he burst into laughter and caught her into his arms.

"My Em, God help me, I had no idea that you were with child. These come on Aunt Martha's word that a sweet buttered biscuit on the belly of a coming mother will save her from sickness. Why had you chosen to hide this joyous news from me?"

Em burrowed her head in his chest. "I wanted to be sure, absolutely sure."

"Every one of the servants is smilingly sure." He chuckled. "God be praised, Em, that we are so soon blessed. Come, now, tuck those away before you rise."

At the door, he paused. "Gil and I are on our way now. May I break this glad news to my mother?"

"No, no," she cried without thinking, then added, "Give us another month, Andrew. We would not want to raise a false hope in her."

—— • 2 • ——

A Garden Enclosed

A garden enclosed is my sister, my spouse; a spring shut up, a fountain sealed.

Song of Solomon 4:12

SHE HAD HAD enough false hopes, Emily decided in the days following. For so long she had hoped that Eleanor Rigg would soften toward her and find something in her daughter-in-law that she could love. For so long she had wistfully hoped that Andrew would realize that it was not his drinking and gambling that upset her, but rather that he seemed to have so little desire for her company.

She had even hoped that by listening and watching, she could learn to be more like the women who visited her mother-in-law and Martha Springer's homes. This was not to be. Emily loved Cece dearly and was equally fond of Andrew's sister Sara, but she simply didn't share their interests in clothing and jewels and the management of children. It was strange to her that such bright women would amuse them-

78

selves with idle chatter, when there were good books to be read or a productive task to do. It was worse than strange; it was ridiculous. Emily's only hope was to compromise. She would act like the others when it seemed to matter a great deal to Andrew, even if she found herself bored and disgruntled by such a waste of time. Only when she felt that these customs violated her relationship with God would she behave in the manner that Andrew had begun to call "Presbyterian hardheadedness."

The Governor's Ball was clearly important to Andrew. Because of this, Em found herself turning and bowing before Aunt Martha and Cece in an elaborate costume assembled for this affair.

"Vanity of vanities," Emily quoted with a smile, "all is vanity."

Cece giggled. "Would that I had such a form to be vain of. They will clear the floor for you and your Andrew because of your handsomeness."

"I have never danced with Andrew," Emily admitted. "I may shame him."

"Of course you won't," Cece assured her. "But I warn you that my Jacob will dance you off your feet if you give him but a chance. He is such a man for dancing that not even his great belly slows his steps."

"And yourself?" Emily chuckled.

"Give yourself time to join me," Cece warned with a wink. Cece's open delight in Em's coming child brought Emily such a rush of joy. Sometimes she was tempted to let Andrew tell his mother the news but could not bring herself to speak the words.

In the end, the Governor's Ball, which glittered like something precious at that moment, was to become fool's gold, with Emily herself playing the embittered fool.

The lights and the music and the din of chatter and laughter made her giddy from the first, after the quiet of her staid life with Aunt Martha. For the first and second dance, Andrew led her out with such flair that she was deeply grateful for the hours she had spent with her dancing tutor in Norfolk. But then Cece's Jacob was nodding and bowing and Andrew was off and gone. After Jacob came an old friend of Andrew's, who was gallant and flattering but awkward. Emily had no lack of partners, but her eyes followed Andrew moving among the dancers, leaning over the punch bowl and talking with his friends. He was laughing, always laughing in that bright boyish way that had won her heart from the first. When he bowed over the hand of another maiden, her heart plunged, and she was fortunate not to lose the step of her dance.

By the time of her second turn with Jacob, she might have turned surly if the jollity and gentleness that marked his face had not been so soothing to her. Shorter than herself by a good ten inches, he steered her about, smiling up into her face like a delighted child, for all the gray in his hair.

"My Cecilia joys in your company," he told her.

"And I in hers," Emily told him. The light in his face at her words made it plain that Cece was no less treasured by this marvelous portly little pixie of a man than he was by her.

The dancers thinned. Emily and Andrew had no sooner than taken a table, when he excused himself at the summons of a friend. The couple at their side lingered awhile and wandered off too, the woman to a table of cards, the husband into a room beyond, from which could be heard the laughter of men and sounds of drinking.

Emily wondered if Mother Riggs was responsible for the coolness she felt from the women at this gathering. These elegantly dressed creatures gathered into knots and games, leaving her quite alone. Cece and her Jacob remained at the dance together, with the music still rising and falling in the festive rooms.

When she had been alone for a long time, Emily saw Gil passing and hailed him with her fan.

"Where is your master?" she asked, her face flushing at the necessity of asking.

"Beyond"—he motioned—"gaming with the gentlemen."

"Would you convey to him that I am fatigued and would like to return home?"

Gil returned within moments, his broad face carefully arranged to show no expression. "He bade me tell you he would be with you when the game was through."

An hour passed as she grew stiff in her chair. Sounds of laughter continued from the gaming room as uniformed waiters passed to and fro with laden trays. Her discomfort was nearing a definition of pain, and still she caught no glimpse of Gil. Then the music faltered and the stands were folded away and Cece and Jacob came to bid her farewell.

"You look like you don't feel very well," Cece said.

"It grows late," Emily replied, attempting a smile.

Exchanging a quick glance with his wife, Jacob leaned toward her. "If you would like to be taken to Granny Springer's, we would gladly oblige. Those men could carouse till dawn over their cards. Perhaps your servant could take Master Andrew word that you are retiring."

Emily rose at his words. She would have sent Andrew word, as Jacob suggested, but she could not see Gil anywhere. As Tansey fastened her cloak, Emily felt a sudden annoyance. Why should she make an effort to let him know? She had asked him to come once, without result. Let him ask himself when and why she had abandoned this fruitless vigil.

The Springer house lay in darkness. Even as she stood at the door, where Jacob had gallantly led her, a cock warned of morning from Aunt Martha's poultry yard. A slender line of color was staining the eastern sky. Emily's decision was sudden, and born of humiliation and pain.

"Tansey," she ordered briskly. "Waken Chad and have my chaise brought around. Tell him that if he wakes everyone up with his clatter, I shall be very angry with him."

"But mistress," Tansey protested.

"I do not wish to sleep in this house tonight," Em told her with a brisk finality that the girl knew better than to combat.

Her packing was the affair of a moment. She took nothing that had come from Andrew's hand but left nothing that she might need if she stayed away for a long time.

Tansey and Chad exchanged dark glances as they set her possessions aboard and clucked the sleepy mare into progress along the lane but dimly lit with the promise of the day's light.

Andrew Rigg wakened fully clothed. He shook his aching head and stared at the bed beside him. The angle of the light in the room and the emptiness of the bed indicated the day was well started. The pounding in his head and the foulness of his mouth contradicted that observation. Having Emily gone was the worst. There was not even the imprint of her head left on the pillow. There would be the devil to pay if she were angry. In truth, he could not even remember their journey home. From the feel of his body, he might have been flown home from the governor's house by witches wearing sharply pointed boots.

With Gil's assistance he managed to put on his clothing. The sound of his own voice set up such a rumble in his head that he barely grunted to his man.

"I did manage to overdo it, didn't I?" he asked.

"That you did," Gil agreed without meeting his master's eyes. Andrew groaned inwardly. Son of God, he must have been a boar. But what was done was done. The smell of hot corn bread and smoked meat hastened his steps downstairs.

His aunt was pouring a stream of fragrant coffee into her cup as he entered. Her smile was replaced by a look of surprise.

"Good morning, my dear," she said with her usual warmth.

"And good morning to you," he replied, touching her hair with his cheek. He knew the day must be cold, from the shawl the wench Mattie wore over her usual shift. When she lifted the cover from the platter, the room was flooded with the rich scent of ham.

"And is Em coming along soon?" his aunt asked.

He stared at her stupidly, then realized the import of her words. The moment froze in the cool room. He was conscious of Mattie's serving his aunt. He watched a trail of steam rise from the hot meat. At his silence, his aunt looked up at him. He glanced at Mattie, stilling her question. Only with the door closed behind the girl did he lean toward her.

"She was gone when I wakened. Haven't you seen her?"

She shook her head. He paused only the barest moment before shouting for Gil.

"Where's your mistress?" he asked.

"I don't rightly know," Gil confessed.

"Don't know! She came home with us last night, didn't she?"

"No, she did not."

The blind rage that had presaged some of his uglier adventures in his London days brought him to his feet. "Speak up, man. What madness is this? What do you mean, she didn't come home with us?"

Gil seemed to be breathing more deeply than usual. "By the time you were ready to leave, she was already gone. The governor's man said she had left earlier, in a carriage, with her maid and some others."

"Why in the name of God didn't you tell me that?"

"Last night you couldn't have heard it, and this morning you didn't ask," Gil said stolidly. "If I had pressed it on you, you would have been in no condition to listen."

"Leave him be," his aunt ordered Andrew quietly. "He's not the one who poured your throat too full. Tell me, then, Guillam, did the governor's man say whose carriage she rode in?"

Gil's breath was coming easier now. "I made the best inquiry I could, mistress. He kept saying there were too many gentry there for him to count, much less call names for."

"Jesus Christ," Andrew groaned, sinking back into his chair.

Only Martha was unperturbed. "Gil, please go ask cook to prepare a large flagon of very strong coffee for Master Andrew and stir into it all the sugar it will bear."

Andrew stared at her, and she explained, "This often helped your father after such a night. Now, think: who was there with whom she might have gone off? Your sister Sara? Abbie?"

Andrew shook his head. "Abbie was not invited, and Sara was kept at home because her Sally has a fever."

"Then who was visiting with Em when you men went off to your gambling tables?"

He could not meet her eyes. "I did not notice."

She needed no words, her glance being rebuke enough. "Then was my friend Cece there?"

He brightened at once. "The redheaded one with the big belly and the husband shaped the same? Indeed they were."

"Andrew," she commanded, "send Gil to inquire if Em is there with her friend."

He rose. "I'll go myself. Damn that woman anyway: What kind of a wife leaves in the midst of a party without a fare-you-well?"

"You might have had a fare-you-well that you failed to remember," his aunt replied tartly. "And you might well ask what kind of a husband leaves a young bride among strangers who have, like as not, been turned against her by a gossip's tongue?"

He stared at her. "Damn it, Aunt Martha, I am new to this role of husband and may manage badly. But in any case, one who claims such piety must know that a man must be lord of his dominion or the whole marriage be askew."

"She has had no more practice at being a wife than you have had at being a husband," she reminded him quietly.

Cece met him in a dimity wrapper that flared from her chin like a great bell, with her slippered feet for clappers.

"Aye," she told Andrew, smiling. "Emily grew tired, and we took her home—a little before dawn, it was." She paused for a moment. "Oh, my God, is she all right? Jacob himself said she looked very wan when he left her at your door."

Andrew nodded, hating himself for the half truth that sprang to his tongue. "I only wanted you thanked for your kindness to her," he said, backing away precipitously. He cursed to himself as he felt her thoughtful stare follow him to his saddle.

Martha's face was uncommonly long at his return. "Her servants are gone too," she told him, "and her chaise and mare and a trunk with her clothes."

"That woman is mad," he shouted. "Candle Creek. Perhaps she has hied herself off to Candle Creek."

"You might do better to see what ship hangs at wharf," Martha advised. "The child wouldn't lightly seek more of your mother's welcome."

"Child she is not," he replied angrily. "She is full woman, and as iron stubborn as her father. Aunt Martha, I know full well how you cherish my Em, but I warn you that when I find her—"

"*If* you find her," his aunt interrupted tartly. "You cannot choose a horse for the smartness of its canter and then beat it for choosing that pace."

"She can't have left me," he decided, struck by a sudden realization of what could have happened.

Martha merely shrugged.

"You've no suggestion for me, then?"

"The poor girl has no friends except Cece and your sisters," Martha replied.

He met her eyes with remorse. "I see her doing this and that for Abbie and her brood but I do not see them in an easy friendship. And Sara has a child with fever. Surely Em would not dare her own health in this condition in a house where there is fever . . ."

His aunt raised her shoulders again in a helpless shrug.

The day now rose toward noon. His mother and her overseer would have been watching the road for hours. He scrawled a note to his mother saying only that he was delayed and would be along when he could. More than anything he did not want this latest act of his stubborn wife's falling on his mother's ears, to slide gleefully from her tongue the moment he was apart from her.

"Damn them all," he told Gil as he dispatched him with the note. "Damn this whole race of women and their teasing, deceitful ways."

Driving to Williamsburg, he discreetly made the rounds of the town, starting up conversations about the festive night just past, mentioning how his own wife had enjoyed the music and the dance. All to no avail.

He checked the wharves along the river. The *Tryall of Southampton* had left with the early tide for the Bahamas, with a full load of oxen and woven cloth. There was no ship bound for Norfolk.

When the sun rose the next morning, Andrew heard the first crow from his side of the quiet bed. His anger had left with the pounding in his head. All that remained was a sick despair. He tried to remember when he had seen Emily last. She had been at the table they shared and she had smiled as he left with his friend, smiled with her fan slowly moving in her hand. She had been the loveliest creature there, with a jewel in her hair catching the candlelight, and the warmth of her complexion paling that of the women who had gathered at tables with their games.

He had been called away on a wager, and from that came the toasts to the winner and another wager and a challenge at dice. He groaned. She had sent for him; that much he remembered. Gil's message had been quietly relayed, but the laughter of old friends had made it into a great jest.

"God in heaven, Andrew," his friend Jeremy had cried. "Are you so quick to the marriage halter that you be summoned from a winning hand at the whimsey of your maiden?"

Marriage was not as he had pictured it. Indeed, it was hard for a man to hold his temper while his mother's vicious tongue sliced away at his wife. His mother always couched her criticisms in the words of others: "Abbie feels that Emily . . ." "Is it true, as my friend Dolly states, that your Emily . . . ?" This hate had eroded his own disposition, set up a rawness in his nerves that even Emily's gentleness could not heal. It was true that Emily was a woman of great stature, but she was not ungainly, as his mother suggested. It was true that she held control of her own servants and took no service even from the slaves of his aunt's household. It was true that while she knelt at his side in church, she took no communion from the rector, saving that sacrament for the pastor of her own faith.

He was startled from this reverie by the sound of horses in the drive and Gil's feet urgent on the stairs.

"Em?" Andrew asked as Gil burst into the room.

Gil shook his head.

"Who is it, then? Speak up," Andrew ordered, hastily dressing.

"The old one," Gil finally got out. "Your mother, I mean."

"Why is she here?" Andrew pressed.

"She seems in great despair," Gil reported, "asking your aunt, Mistress Springer, what this great hubbub is about Emily Fraser's being spirited away."

Andrew felt his insides begin to curl with anger. He had been married for three months now; it was time his wife ceased being called by her unmarried name.

"And Aunt Martha, what is she responding?"

"She is paying small heed and even laughing in protest that your wife is visiting with friends."

"Pray God that she be right, Gil. But now what am I to do? I cannot stand and lie in my mother's face."

Gil shuffled his feet uneasily. "You'll think of something," he promised. "God willing, something will come to mind."

If his mother showed even the slightest concern, Andrew might have been able to control himself. Instead she poised stiffly on his aunt's chair with such a look of self-righteous triumph on her face that bile rose in his throat.

"Your Aunt Martha tells me that Emily Fraser is spending some days visiting a friend. Is this, then, the reason that you have not been at the plantation?" Her tone was mocking.

"I have been absent these days, as I told you in the note I sent with my man Gil," he told her calmly, "because I had business in Williamsburg and along the river. Have you had word from Sara? I understand that your granddaughter has a bad fever."

His mother had the grace to flush. "I have sent jellies and a tart," she told him shortly. "With my own health so uncertain, I was sure she would not want me about. But do tell me about Emily Fraser."

"As my aunt has told you, she is with friends." He forced his eyes to meet hers. Pray God these words be true, he repeated in his own mind as he spoke. Pray God these words be true.

Triumph rose with her fan, stirring the ruffles at the neck of her morning dress. "It is a shame that such a different tale is current everywhere. It is said that the girl left you in a fit of temper and disappeared like a puff of smoke." She smiled archly. "Come, now, Andrew, do not hide your annoyance at me or make a show of false pride for your own mother. This is not the first time that a headstrong woman has set off in a fit of unholy disobedience at the chafing of the marriage state. The woods are full of runaway wives."

The fury. He would not let the fury seize his tongue. He gripped the back of the chair and seated himself carefully. Gil had said that something would come to mind. Let it come now. Pray God, let it come now.

When the idea struck, it brought such a smile to his lips that even his mother, for all her suspicion, could not take it for less than genuine.

"Come, Mother." His tone turned bantering. "Your tongue lays harsh words upon my wife. Like many a bride swelling with her first child, she has strange desires. Surely even you must agree that a few days of quiet respite with a friend is little enough of a demand. I would be a poor father to risk damaging my child with my selfish insistence that she not be apart from me for a few days now and then."

He saw her face grow slack before the fan rose to hide it from his view. He heard the hoarse whisper, "Child. Child," as if it were a slow knelling of doom in her life.

"Child indeed," Martha said briskly. "The only reason you have not been told before is that Em did not wish your hopes unfairly raised for the first child to bear the Rigg name."

As always during a time of stress, Eleanor Rigg burst into tears and had to be comforted and petted a great deal before she regained her presence. Somehow Martha restored her

87

voice and her shawl and got her packed into her carriage and off down the road.

"Now what should I do?" Andrew asked dully.

"Wait and pray," his aunt said. "Wait and pray soberly that our desperate words be transformed into truth."

— · 3 · —

Obscure Darkness

Whoso curseth his father or mother, his lamp shall be put out in obscure darkness.

Proverbs 20:20

THE LAST THING Andrew expected to hear from his Aunt Martha was a plea that he forgive his mother for the open delight she had shown from the first with the smallest thing that went awry in his marriage. Now, with his distress so acute, her triumph had kept his fury boiling. He stared at his aunt in disbelief.

"Think of her pride as an impediment," she urged him. "Grieve for her that she must bear it."

"Grieve for her?" he exclaimed angrily.

She nodded. "If she had been born with a crossed eye or a leg that had to be dragged behind her with every step she took, if she had been born mute, as my Aunt Lucianne was, or had a cleft lip, like many unfortunates you see, then you would be quick enough to pity her. Yet this overweening pride of her Merritt blood, which she suckled with her mother's milk, is a hidden impediment. She is a lonely, bitter woman and not much loved, and all for a fault for which she cannot be fairly blamed.''

"She has wit enough in other concerns," Andrew protested. "Can she not see that she behaves with arrogance?"

"Can a man see the mote in his own eye?" she countered.

Five days had passed since the Governor's Ball. For five days he had alternately flamed with fury and trembled with terror at Em's absence. For five nights he had twisted on their bed, visited by such terrible dreams that he wakened more exhausted than when he had lay down. For the story was as widespread as his mother had said. Shame and embarrassment were added to his fear. No man wished to be marked as one who could not control his own household, his own wife.

But the fear was the worst. He had returned to a colony changed since the time of his youth. The population had grown by such numbers that the old timers shook their heads in dismay. The importation of black slaves was a flood that brought with it dark fears of rebellion and violence. His country's Acts of Grace, which forgave pirates past misdeeds if they promised to reform, had loosed in the colony crews of men whose dark pasts and vicious tastes ill-suited them for civil life. The emptying of England's prisons onto Virginia's wharves had set in the citizenry a wariness as in the old days when the Indians still battled among them.

Andrew returned to his duties at Candle Creek, in part because he had nothing else to turn his hand to, and also to support his own words to his mother about Em's absence. He had just seen his horse to its grooming, when his aunt launched into her great sermon about gentleness toward his mother.

"And what is the source of this fine lecture?" Andrew asked, half teasing.

She tightened her shoulders. "Your mother was here today," she replied.

He frowned. He had left her within the hour, and she had made no mention of her visit.

"And so?"

His aunt sighed. "Now, Andrew, please be calm. It was just in passing that she mentioned what great friends our Em and your sister Sara have become."

"Sara?" he asked. "But they have been great friends since their first meeting."

She sighed. "Only much later did she mention how helpful it had been for Sara to have another woman's hands in the nursing of her little Sally in this fever just passing."

He had not meant his voice to come forth in a bellow, but it apparently did not surprise his aunt. He was instantly on his feet and shouting for Gil, even as she stayed him with a hand.

"Carefully, now," she cautioned. "Go carefully. Look at what boils already in Em's heart, before you add the venom of your tongue to that brew."

Gil came, only to be dismissed. After all, Em had taken her servants and her own chaise, which would serve to bring a runaway wife home. If she were not with child, she should be made to walk that path back as an exercise in humility, to clear her mind of rebellion.

Only with great effort did Andrew restrain himself from making the trip at a dead gallop. Such an arrival could only show Emily his concern. His sister Sara greeted him with eyes gaunt from exhaustion, but her smile was swift with welcome.

"Oh, I had not expected you, brother. Come and sit. Em is with little Joseph. I'll tell her you are here."

"I would prefer to tell her myself," he growled, a little put off by the lightness of her tone.

"Then come along." She smiled. "How fortunate your children will be, Andrew. Em has a great gift for teaching."

As was the whole of Sara's house, the room set aside for Joseph was tastefully furnished. Em was in a low chair, with the boy and his dog on the rug at her feet. She was reading aloud. The soft rise of her voice ceased when Andrew stood in the door.

Joseph leaped to his feet, shamefaced at the absorption with which he had been listening to his aunt's story.

"I would speak with your aunt," he told Joseph without meeting Em's eyes.

"Joshua is at a vestry meeting," Sara said. "His room is free for your use." A note of doubt had crept into her voice.

Andrew saw a warning in the straightness of Em's back as she preceded him into his brother-in-law's library. When she sat like that, with her eyes full on him and her graceful hands at ease in her lap, he found his words slow in coming.

"I have been sorely concerned for your welfare," he began.

"After the liquor finally left your brain," she amended.

"Now, Em." Her words pricked his fury to life. "What madness seized you, to leave the festivities without cause? Was it your intent to make of me a laughingstock? Have you no decent sense of how a wife is to behave?"

Her quiet voice broke into his tirade. "Was I, then, missed?"

"So that is it." He seized on her words. "Because a roomful of addled crones did not flock to amuse you, you left in a petty huff?"

"I did not go there with any crones," she reminded him.

"No—with me, and with me you were obliged to return."

"And did you seek me?" she asked slyly.

"Stop that," he ordered, struggling to keep his voice low against the treachery of frail walls making their private matters the gossip of servants. "I did not marry you to become a priest and forego the fellowship of men."

"And I, sir, did not marry you to be abandoned with broad-bellied old men and crones while you gamble and drink, with less thought of me than of the next roll of dice."

Although her voice was tense, there was no sign of weakness in her face. She was strong. God in heaven, she was strong for a woman. Where were her tears? He had long known that tears could be stopped by pressing them against his chest as he stroked her hair. But this face, calm and beautiful and locked against him, was beyond his ken. He rose and paced, his hands joined beneath his coattails.

"Then what would you have me do?" he asked in a mocking tone. "Foreswear all manhood and become eunuch for you? Restrict my tastes to tea? Carry a holy book to the taverns for entertainment and look away at the passing of a comely wench?"

Her calm tone made his mocking posture ridiculous in his own ears. "I would have you treat me as you yourself would like to be treated."

He sighed. "Now she misquotes scripture," he told Joshua's wall angrily. "She makes free with the holy word to defend her own mad jealousy."

"Aye," she told him calmly. "Indeed I am jealous, and have no fear to admit this. I have heard your voice raised against duplicity too many times. I have accepted your dictum that ours should be a marriage where honesty ever reigned. I will be honest with you, Andrew Rigg, as I have been from the first. I am jealous when you look lustfully on other women. And I think you would feel the same if the situation were reversed. I am jealous and saddened that you prefer the company of tavern transients to my own. I am repulsed when you tumble into bed a slobbering drunk instead of a gentleman. But most of all I am pained that my happiness is of such small account to you, when yours is of such great import to me."

He stared at her in disbelief. "What upbringing does a Presbyterian maiden receive that she is so presumptuous about her husband's habits? What spiritual training does she receive that she does not honor the man who is lord of her household? Show me a man . . ."

She shook her head, her eyes holding his. "Do not prate on to me of other men. I have no interest in other men. I did not venture forth in ribbons and furbelows to seek you out. I was content to be a virgin in my father's house rather than be chattel to such men as you would tell me of. Since I did not train myself as wife, it is a small astonishment that you find me deficient in these skills."

Her father's words came to his mind: "an ancient virgin," "comfortable in that estate," "many supplicants she has turned away." "Yet you were quick enough to battle your father to accept my suit," he reminded her.

"That indeed was my error," she conceded quietly.

He stared at her. "You are saying that our marriage was a mistake? You say this even as our child grows in you?"

"What of you?" she challenged. "You have named me as madwoman, jailer, heretic, presumptuous and deficient in wifely skills. And jealous," she added. "What man would not regret such a joining? Surely you must be now as jealously yearning for the freedom of your unmarried state as I am for the serenity of mine."

How could a man be furious and fearful at once? She had taught him this, first with her disappearance and now with the coldness of her words. Which did he fear most, losing her or losing what small control he had over this family of difficult women?

"I cherish you as my wife," he told her quietly, "but only as a wife to myself as a man. Gaming is as natural a heritage to me as my breath. My very blood would run cold at the thought that no fine wine would ever course along its channels.

And if my pulse should cease to rise at a beautiful woman, what kind of a bedfellow would I be for such a wife as you?''

An instant flush stained her face as she rose.

"Then, we have at last been honest with each other. Even as God sets the blossom on the limb to be blasted by wind, all things that are made can also be unmade. My father's ship is due in Norfolk within a fortnight. He will not grieve to find me again as mistress of his house.''

The plunging in his belly made him unsteady on his feet. Yet he wavered. What sort of a life would he lead after this hour if he submitted to her unreasonable demands?

"How would you choose to be treated, so that your father might not find you resident on his return?'' he asked. His tone was icy, but his heart thundered as he awaited her reply.

She smiled.

God in heaven, she smiled. This was no smile of triumph, such as his mother affected, nor one of fawning servility, such as his sister Abbie so often wore. This was the level smile of friendship that had represented the richest of their times of sharing.

"I would choose to be treated with the same consideration that you would cede to a good friend who happened, by the prattling of a parson, also to be your bedfellow.''

"And the gaming and the wine and . . . the warm glances?''

"I would hate to strip joy from your life. I only wish that my own pleasure and happiness be given equal measure in your consideration.''

"If that were true, would you return with me in peace and friendship?''

"If you would take me thus,'' she said.

Only as he stood with her pressed warm against his breast did he note the silence of the house. The very beetles were sounding in its wall in that depth of silence. He cursed silently and drew away.

He needed to know one more thing from her before they went forth to say goodbye to Sara and her family. He asked this in a whisper. "Tell me, Em, how is it that my sister and Joshua, with whom I have always enjoyed great closeness, have hidden you here without a word to me all this time?''

She looked startled and then amused. "There was no hiding in it, I think. Sally was so very sick that there was simply nothing else to be concerned about. As for my coming, I am somewhat confused on that score myself. Upon finding me on her doorstep with the day just born, Sara looked a question. I merely told her that I had no wish to be at Aunt Martha's house anymore for a while.

"She laughed merrily, brought me in, and made us all at home at the same time that she was telling me how, when Joseph was yet unborn, she had such a frantic desire for muskmelons that her poor husband met every ship from the islands in hopes of sating her craving." She paused, turning thoughtful. "If you have just discovered where I was biding, it must have been from Abbie, who was here a day or so ago for the first time since the child fell ill."

He only nodded and led her toward the door.

Martha's words returned to Andrew's mind the next day when he greeted his mother at Candle Creek. Indeed, her pride was an impediment that had sharpened her tongue and her spirit past comfort for herself or others. He resolved not to let her goad him to fury but to cling to sympathy for her plight. His resolve melted at her infernal habit of referring to his wife by her unmarried name.

"Until Abbie told me where Emily Fraser was biding, I had no idea that such an intimate friendship had grown between the two."

"Indeed, yes, Mother," he told her. "You must know that it is possible to be linked by marriage and still be friends."

Even as he spoke, he saw the words of the Proverbs rebuking him, and he was struck with contrition and self-loathing.

God in heaven, how far he had fallen from his own high ideals of what his family should be. Not only were these wilful women running beyond his control, but he had sunk to the double tongue of sarcasm with his own mother.

But he had kept his Em. At a great price to his own pride, he had kept his Em.

4

The Greatest of These

(1717–1718)

> Though I speak with the tongues of men and of angels,
> and have not charity, I am becoming as sounding brass, or
> a tinkling cymbal. . . . And now abideth faith, hope, and
> charity, these three; but the greatest of these is charity.
>
> I Corinthians 13:1,13

As CHRISTMAS NEARED, a good tide brought Captain Robbie Fraser, browned by the sun of the islands.

"God's blessing on your coming child," he told Emily with moist eyes. "A greater joy man never had than I when your letter with this good tiding arrived. Even now a new ship is being built. It will go unnamed until you choose it."

"Can the naming wait till June?" Em asked. "Perhaps it could bear the same name as our babe."

"That is an excellent idea," he agreed. Then he sobered. "In that same letter you asked for your mother's childbed linen. Forgive me, Em, it is long gone."

"Gone?" she cried with surprise.

He flushed at her question. "I was so heartbroken at the loss of your mother during your birthing that I ordered it burned, lest it bring such grief to another house." He sought her eyes with eagerness. "But look at what I have brought in their stead. You have only to ply the needle in your clever way."

When he was gone, Emily lifted again the lengths of fine fabrics, the bolts of lace. She shook her head at the bounty of fruit and sugar and rum her father had left them.

"You must help me think of a way to share these with Abbie and her family," she told Aunt Martha. "Even with her eldest child now living with her grandmother, there are still too many mouths in that house to feed. It is shocking that Nat's parish provides him with such a small pittance."

"It is the law that they need pay him only a fixed stipend in tobacco. The land of Nat's parish yields the meanest sort of crop, so that even with every bale sold, he gains little."

"It distresses me to have so much when they have so little."

"That speaks eloquently of your charity, Em," Martha said bluntly. "You have less to thank Abbie for than many women I know."

Em could not meet her aunt's eyes. In truth, it had not been easy for her to think anything good about Abbie. Only after much thought did she decide that the woman behaved the way she did out of desperation. Abbie had her mother's Merritt pride, even as Andrew was said to have his grandmother's hot temper. All the mean things Abbie did, running to tattle with all the gossip, letting Em's name be ridiculed (which Sara would not permit), these were acts of desperation. Given Nat's poverty and his own stiff-necked pride about accepting gifts, the only relief Abbie had was her mother's private dole. Such gifts were small but steady, a length of fabric for a gown, fresh fruit from the orchard, a ham from her mother's smokehouse. Now her mother, pleading poor health and loneliness, had taken Ruthie, the oldest, and was feeding and clothing her like a little princess as she grew into the age to marry. God only knew how Abbie would be if she carried her husband's pride instead of her mother's.

"In the name of Christmas," Em decided. "These great pineapples from the Bahamas, the fine Carolina rice, even the smoked beef from the boucans of the Indies will make gifts for Andrew to carry there in our name."

It was clear that Em herself need not make these Christmas calls, either to Abbie's or Sara's or to Candle Creek. Her newly increased bulk gave her such a discomfort in traveling that they kept Christmas at home, with massed greens and scented candles and ribbons wound in profusion.

Andrew was perversely glad that the child had gained its bulk so quickly, thus keeping his wife at home, for, while it was not in his mind to deceive Em, yet neither would it profit her to hear what dire events were being reported about the colony.

After surrendering to Governor Charles Eden and Tobias Knight, in North Carolina the January before, Edward Teach, known to all as Blackbeard, began at once to violate the pledge he had made by submitting to the Acts of Grace. Resuming his career in piracy with brutal dispatch, he had seized the *Adventurer* in the Bay of Honduras as well as the *Protestant Caesar* out of Boston and four sloops. With her father off again at once to sea, Emily's heart need not be burdened with concern about these doings.

Em cherished the lazy, idle months of that winter. Martha Springer's eyes were failing rapidly, so that the threat of blindness hung over her every wakening. Em watched her peer at her book and close it with a sigh.

"Here," Em insisted, lifting it from her hand. "Tell me what selection you want to hear and I will read to you, as my father did to Philip and me for so many years."

After only a few days, Martha smiled at her with a mischievous twinkle. "Do you know the story of the man who let the camel's head into his tent, only to find that the entire beast followed?"

Em laughed. "It works that way with these cats of yours," she said. "Have you some special camel in mind?"

The old woman nodded. "Your voice is so gentle with the sacred word, I wonder if you would read to me from this journal of my grandfather and my mother's."

"How old and fine it is," Em remarked, turning it in her hand. It was of a remarkable weight and bound in a rich, deep-brown leather, which was darker along the spine. The edges of the pages had been brushed with gold leaf. The handwriting crossed the pages as straight as a surveyor's line. "The journal of Bennett Lyon, Esq. Lyon Hall, Somersetshire," Em read. The first entry was dated, August 1585.

"Just read a little there as it starts," Aunt Martha urged.

"Within this week, God willing, I, Bennett Lyon, the second son of Frederick Lyon of Lyon Hall, Somersetshire, do set forth on the expedition led by Sir Richard Grenville under the charge of Master Ralph Lane to that new paradise beyond the sea that is called Virginia.'' Em fell silent. There followed the kind of testament and will as her father always left when he went to sea.

"If you look at the dates or watch where the script changes, you will see the length of that record,'' Martha suggested.

As she had said, on one page the script became different, an upright, firm hand, graceful without being ornamental. "That is by your mother, Bek,'' Em said with delight.

"Aye,'' Martha said quietly. "And on the page before, you will find my grandfather's last entry, September of 1640. Your Andrew and the child you are carrying are mentioned in those lines.''

"May God shepherd the lives and generations of Amos and John and my own cherished Rebeckah, the new keepers of the covenant. In God's name, Amen.'' Em found that she had a sudden dampness in her eyes.

"The others jest that this journal is my second Bible. And in truth, I cherish it only a little less,'' Martha told her.

In the weeks following, Em read deeply of both books to her contented aunt, whose cat purred in harmony with Em's voice.

This was richer than any history to Em's mind, more filled with excitement than any novel or story. Em found herself holding that story to her heart as she did her unborn child, cherishing those long-dead lives, grieving for their anguish and rejoicing in their triumphs.

Spring surprised her as from a reverie. The child was strong enough to bounce the book out of her lap as it kicked, and Andrew, successfully elected Burgess in his father's place, went off to Williamsburg to fulfill this citizen's duty.

From the twenty-third of April until the last of May, the Assembly sat in session. Andrew leased a tenement in the capital, where he stayed, except on those weekends when he came riding in to fill their ears with the doings of government.

He was careful to keep his talk to laws and discussions of the colony's affairs. He didn't want Em to hear that Stede Bonnet, now a cohort of Blackbeard's, had seized three rich cargoes off Charles Town and held the city hostage with eight or nine ships penned in the harbor out of fear of venturing onto the open sea. Even the hint of a pirate atrocity raised such a fury in Em, that Andrew felt it must be dangerous for their unborn child.

On the second weekend in May, when Andrew was there, his mother came from Candle Creek to have dinner with them, at her own suggestion.

The meal was a tense one, not because of dissension but from a lack of it. Her mother-in-law's compliments to Em fell on astonished ears. She remarked on the elegance of the linen in Em's sewing basket. "It is lovely," she said, sliding it between her fingers, "simply lovely. Is it from New England?"

Martha was quick to explain that Captain Robbie had brought it from Ireland for Em to make her childbed linens.

A wariness hung in Em's mind as Eleanor Rigg waxed effusive over the delicacy of her stitches. Em felt guilty about her wariness but found herself waiting for something to happen. "There could not be this much ripe peach without a stone," she told herself, quoting one of Aunt Martha's sayings.

And stone it was, when it fell.

"I have been giving much thought to your coming child," she told Andrew, her fan moving almost seductively. "I have wondered if your thoughts have followed mine as to its naming."

Em kept her eyes down. What parents, wakeful in their bed, have not sounded a hundred and one names on their tongues for their firstborn?

"My mother was called Tabitha, which is charming for a girl as well as being quite elegant. A boy might be named Andrew Merritt and called Merritt, so that he would not be mistaken for his father, as you so often were, my son."

Em realized she was holding her breath. Tabitha was a loathsome name, and she could not bear to think of a child being given the name Merritt, which seemed to be bloated with self-esteem.

"Em and I have talked a great deal of the naming," Andrew replied. "But we will add those suggestions to our list."

She was dauntless. Her tone turned suddenly arch. "I daresay a handsome gift would be forthcoming for a child who bore those names."

Em let out her breath in a long slow venting but kept her eyes on her bulging lap.

"Are you going to let her buy the naming of our child?" Em asked directly when they were alone.

99

"It is the first child to bear the Rigg name," he reminded her. "At least she finally shows some interest." He smiled and drew her close. "The names we have chosen are fine, Em. Let us not worry until it is time."

She was little mollified. Indeed the names were fine. If the babe were a son, he would be named for her dead brother, Philip. If indeed it was a girl, it would be called Anne, after her dead mother. And as for Mother Rigg's showing interest, had she once offered the childbed linen that had been used for Andrew and his sisters? Had she shown a moment's concern over Em during the long winter?

The ripe cherries were gone from the trees in the orchard when the assembly finally adjourned until the tenth of July.

"What sweet relief I feel," Andrew told Em. "I was in deathly fear lest we be apart when the babe came. Have you thought more of what Mother suggested as names?"

"Aye," she replied. "And I still prefer our choices."

He frowned. "I hadn't considered it as settled as all that. It does seem that giving in on this point might make some healing between our houses."

"But all its life," Em told him, "a child is known by its name."

He said nothing more then, but the subject kept coming up as the days passed.

"My mother is eager to hear what names we have selected."

"And what was your reply?"

"I told her we were considering her choices among others."

Em wondered from Andrew's sheepish expression if he had traded these words for some necessary peace in his dealings with her.

"Would Andrew do that?" she asked Aunt Martha.

"A man will say unwonted things when his ears are being scalded," Martha replied.

It was Sara's boy, Joseph, who planted the idea in her mind. She was showing him the melons that had sprung from the seeds she had helped him to plant.

"I wager that mine will grow faster than those in the garden," he said.

"Are you wagering already?" she asked with mock alarm.

His pale freckles were radiant in the sunlight. "It is a man's way, Aunt Em," he told her.

That night she put it to Andrew that she should choose the names once and for all by throwing the dice.

He laughed uproariously.

"Listen to me," she insisted. "There are the two names for a boy, Philip and Merritt, and two for the girl, Anne and Tabitha. Let us toss and see which names win."

There on the smooth coverlet of their bed Philip came up seven times and Merritt eight.

"Two out of three?" he asked at the sight of her face.

Philip came up six and Merrit five, and she was heartened. On the last toss she almost prayed, barely stopping in time at the thought of such sacrilege.

Philip came once and Merritt three times.

She had less heart to wager with the girls' names, but the game was on and Andrew was clearly enjoying it. Em swallowed her heartsickness when Tabitha came up, not twice, but three times, over the gentle Anne.

Martha was sympathetic when Emily confessed her gamble. "Wagers, like prayers, can be dangerous, child. One must not wager unless one is ready to lose. One must not pray unless one can live with God's answer."

At Em's puzzled look, the old woman nodded. "I see this as my mother's life. God so loved her that He answered her prayers, and each one turned to a chastisement of her. But this you must allow her: she was never known to whimper of loss."

"And neither will I," Em promised herself, although the names caught at her craw. Tabitha and Merritt. She imagined that the child within her writhed at that repetition.

The letter from Younger Elliott arrived on the third of June. Martha took the letter from Andrew's hand with wonder.

"I have never even seen his handwriting before," she confessed. "What great emergency moves him to send for you?"

"He gives no hint," Andrew admitted. "But he is of such great age—and such a fine man, Auntie. I would go to him even though he asked merely from whimsey."

"Your child is very near," she warned.

"Em has you and Tansey, and the midwife besides. Younger has no one, and he would not lightly call anyone of this family, even me."

She nodded. "But only you," she added, still amazed and warmed that Andrew had healed this old rupture between her half-brother and the family.

Em was sitting quietly. "A babe comes in its own time," she told Andrew. "A man of great age has not this leisure. You could be gone and return and still the midwife might not be called," she went on at his thoughtful look. "That is the way of the firstborn, they tell me," she added with a grin.

Only his mother was to challenge this journey.

"What is there for you at that place?" she asked.

"My uncle's need," he told her.

She turned her head away. "If you must follow your father's ways, there is nothing I can do to stop you."

• 5 •

A Glass Darkly

For now we see through a glass, darkly; but then face to face: now I know in part; but then shall I know even as I am known.

I Corinthians 13:12

THE OLD MAN sitting in the darkened room did not rise as Andrew entered.

"Come in, come in," Younger urged. "With your indulgence, we'll keep the lamp unlit."

"It is cooling," Andrew told him.

"And there's fresh cider beside you," Younger offered,

"cold from the well." He paused. "My great thanks, Andrew. You were not obliged to come, you know, there having been so little time passed between us."

"I do not breathe but that more than time passes between us."

The old man chuckled. "Sometimes you are like your father, Andrew, sometimes like his brother, James. Such words make you like Benn. Have you a wife by now?"

"Aye. And a child coming this summer."

Younger nodded. "I wouldn't have taken you from your family if I could have solved my problem myself. It needs time, Andrew, and I have little of that left to me."

At a loss to guess what troubled the old man, Andrew waited in silence.

"There were three of us born to Bek Lyon by William Elliott. You know that?"

"It is written thus in the great Bible at Candle Creek."

"Aye, so it is. There was myself, and Benn, a year later, and then dear Carrie, who was not to see a great age. Benn was all that I was not, clever and swift of tongue, with the kind of charm that all men and women cherish. But he was like a comely tree whose hollow heart is only exposed by an ill wind. Benn was my mother's madness, and it was for him that she cut me from her heart and cursed Bruce Rigg to his death."

The light had gone from the sky as he spoke, silvering the trees beyond the window. A slow seesawing of insects began in the brush. From the dependency houses came the slow thrum of stringed instruments and mournful voices in song. How long would Andrew be in this country before he heard those slave songs without astonishment?

"Benn was to be hanged for a most foul murder, you know," Younger went on slowly. His was a singsong not unlike the rhythm that came from beyond the window. Andrew could imagine the old man waiting out those days in his chair, perfecting the order of these words, pruning them to these bare limbs of truth, stripped of his agony.

"He got away. Benn always got away, and in truth, I rejoiced for it. Benn was what my mother made of him. A bad wheel should not be burned for the errors of the wright. These were stories—that he was in Lubberland and dealing with pirates, that he was killed in a set-to and his head was set on a stake to caution other men. But these were stories, only stories, with never the thread of truth to catch about your finger.

"He was my brother and my friend." Younger's tone suddenly changed. He had lost the rhythm of this recital, and his emotion seeped weakly through his words.

After a long silence, he said simply, "Help me, Andrew."

"Have you heard of your brother, then?" Andrew asked.

"Aye."

"And does he yet live?"

There was only the numb shaking of his head.

"His children perhaps?" Andrew probed.

"A grandchild." Younger cleared his throat, and with it his voice. "A girl. I have it all on paper, but I think I'll tell it right without that. Benn married one Annie Steele and had three children, two boys and a girl. Of them, only Bartholomew lived to marry, a girl called Roma, as she was from Romany and had no other name. The wife was already dead when this Bartholomew went down in a great tempest in the sea this autumn past. His child is here."

This autumn past. Andrew felt his flesh creep. It was a wide sea and beset by tempests, yet he saw the deck of the *Joyeuse* raked by gunfire and the screams of the dying as she sheered into the maw of the deep.

"What can I do?" Andrew asked.

"Look at these papers and then counsel me."

At Younger's call, the slattern came with a light. As the old man groped for the paper, Andrew swallowed a gasp. The old man's body was still a slab against his chair, but his neck had grown to such great bulk that his shirt lay open about the growth.

Younger smiled at him. "I have no lease on time."

The paper he extended was addressed to "Younger Elliott, Near the Fall Line on the James River."

"I, Bartholomew Elliott, legal son to Bennett Lyon Elliott, being of uncertain fortune in my trade, do beseech that if death befall me, you take into your care this girl Magda, since there is none other I can trust."

The letters had been written smoothly in the hand of a public scribe. The signature could have been scrawled by an untutored child.

"I think I might have liked the lad, for all his fiendish trade," Younger said quietly. The lamp betrayed a glitter in his eyes.

"Then she is here?" Andrew asked.

When the slattern responded to Younger's call, the old man spoke almost haughtily.

"Please tell Mistress Magda that Master Andrew Rigg would be pleased to receive her."

How strange it seemed—the dying old man, the sullen maid slouching in her soiled linen and then this courtly phrase echoing in the steaming heat of that primitive room.

But Magda herself was the strangest of all.

While she was scarcely taller than a child, the dignity of her bearing made her dark eyes seem almost level with Andrew's own. Her eyebrows were dark wings above an impassive face. She rested so lightly on her feet that it seemed the most casual draft might bear her away. But Romany she looked, with that darkness of flesh and eyes as intense as wet coal. She was garbed in bright colors.

"Greetings, my cousin," he said bending over her hand.

Her curtsey was brief, before her eyes rose to his with interest.

"My Uncle Younger says you might help me find employment."

There was a strangeness to her voice, almost an accent. There was no diffidence in her tone.

"And what work can you do, Magda?"

She gave a quick smile and a shrug. "What falls to hand. I can cook in some fashion, and dance and strum a lute, and read the hands of wanderers." Her face lit suddenly. "Most of all I love to sew. Fine things," she added hastily. "Hats for ladies or gentlemen, fine stomachers wreathed with designs." Her eyes sparkled as she spoke, and Andrew caught Younger's gaze tender upon her. She had won his heart, and by God, it was no wonder.

"Have you dreams, Magda?" Andrew asked suddenly.

She glanced at Younger for reassurance before smiling up at him. "What maiden does not?"

"Gold and jewels and a husband for your hearth?" he asked.

Her eyes darkened. "Not those," she said as if in rebuke.

"Tell him," Younger urged. "This is the man who might help us make them come true."

"A warm house," she began timidly, "work for my hours, and . . ." Again there was that sidelong glance at Younger.

"Tell him," the old man insisted.

"A shop," she spilled out. "A shop of my own, with my own name on it. I would sell laces and ribbons and other fancy gewgaws for ladies. I would make dresses and sacques and such glories that women buy."

"How old are you, Magda?" Andrew asked, a little surprised that such a young maiden held such industrious and unsentimental dreams.

"I will be twenty-one on All Souls Day," she replied.

My God, she was within months of Em's nineteen years.

"Thank you for joining us," Younger said quietly. "Now we men will talk on these things."

"I ask you, Andrew Rigg, did you mean those fine words about this family's holding as one, as it did in the old days?" Younger asked when she had left. At Andrew's nod, he spoke again. "Then she shall have her shop, and in Williamsburg. I have ample credit for the shop and such supplies as will start her toward profit. Time is what I lack." He touched his swollen throat with a fingertip. "She needs a protector, Andrew, to watch over her and be her champion. Are you that man?"

Before Andrew could reply, Younger went on. "I do not expect that she will be drawn into the life of the family. Given the past, I cannot fault any Virginian who fails to welcome a pirate's child into his gatherings. But I refer to guardianship, Andrew. With such a shop in Williamsburg, would you fend for her?"

"God in heaven, yes," Andrew exploded. "As I would for my own family."

"Make no careless promises," Younger cautioned. "We take but one careful step at a time. I know your mother only by public account," he added.

"But not my wife."

"I know young wives burdened by young and tamed to a hearth. Magda is more Romany than English. She is more wild than tamed."

"But she could keep a shop in Williamsburg?" Andrew asked.

"She is more actress than anything else." Younger laughed.

106

"She will be such a fine seamstress and shopkeeper that others will ask to be apprenticed. She has been with me for two weeks, Andrew. She speaks humbly of her singing and dancing. She has been the unexpected star of my twilight. Each day could be my last and I would have no complaint for its perfection. Now, do you remember the Simms Plantation, which you saw when you traveled to the bigger plantation you bought from me?"

"Aye." Andrew nodded, suddenly confused.

"It is yours on paper, only needing to be sealed by law if you take over this trust of Magda for me."

"That is not right," Andrew protested.

"It is the seller's privilege to name the price." Younger reminded him. "Can you spare me another day?"

"Aye." Andrew nodded, thinking of Em as the great moon rose beyond the window.

"God's blessing on you, Andrew Rigg, and mine along-side."

The exchange of the Simms property was sealed and entered in the records on the following day. Four days had elapsed when Gil and Andrew started back downriver together.

"He's a very ill man, your uncle," Gil the Toad said quietly.

"He is that," Andrew agreed, "and a fine one."

"He wanted to see you that one last time," Gil said thoughtfully.

"Pray it may not be the last time." Only then did Andrew realize that Toad had shied away from asking anything about the girl who was new to that place. Perhaps Younger was right. Perhaps it was best that all be done privately for Magda, at least in the beginning. If she were anything but a pirate's daughter, Em might be quick to take her cause. What had Younger said on that first visit? Only when there is love is true honesty difficult. Andrew sighed and cursed and set his face toward home.

6

The Hour

A woman when she is in travail hath sorrow, because her hour is come: but as soon as she is delivered of the child, she remembereth no more the anguish, for joy that a man is born into the world.

John 16:21

WITH THE CHILD so near its time, it was easy for Em to imagine fleeting pains in her great awkward body. To escape from these fantasies, she and Martha, by mutual consent, dined early and tumbled into bed right after prayers.

Em wakened to the cry of an owl in the walnut trees. She heard his mate answer and then a farther voice, until this colloquy faded from hearing in the distance. Insects droned, and she knew the lights of fireflies rose and fell in the grasses cooled by evening.

The first pain shivered almost delicately down her frame. Those that followed gained assurance and strength until she finally sat up and called Tansey from beyond the wall.

"It's nothing," she assured Tansey, "nothing at all, I am sure. But with the master gone, I am nervous. Still, just in case . . ."

She heard the rattle of hooves in the drive as Chad left to fetch the midwife. While Em did not dread her coming, the woman had so bold a tongue and was such a lively gossip, that Em wanted her in the house for as short a time as possible.

By the time Chad returned with Dame Bray, Em was more than grateful for her knowledgeable hands.

Martha whispered gently as she left them alone. "Pray," she urged. "Forget all that you have heard and pray to keep the terrors from flooding your mind."

And indeed there were terrors. The ghosts of all the mothers lost in childbed haunted Em, especially that of her own mother, whom she remembered as a hand-sketched face whose lineaments had faded from the weak tincture of the wandering painter who had limned them.

It was Em's own will that no messenger be sent upriver to tell Andrew of the onset of her labor. Neither did she permit a message to be taken to Candle Creek. "Soon enough this business will be done, and then there can be notice," she said, her eyes pleading that Dame Bray agree with her. Instead the woman frowned and sent to the kitchen for more strengthening teas. The day failed, and Em's strength with it.

Martha wore the day like a cross. The agony had gone on too long. There was too great a profusion of blood. The paleness in Em's face was that of fine paper. At twilight she could bear it no longer. She sent a lad for Abbie's husband, Nat. If there be no other need of a man of God, he might at least add his prayers to hers. To her astonishment, Abbie came along. Too weak from her hours of concern to seek her knees, Martha pressed her head against folded hands and echoed his words with streaming eyes.

The sun was gone and the moon halfway up to its heaven when a high, thin wail sounded from down the hall, followed by silence.

"Go, child," Martha urged, breaking the prayer in mid-sentence. "Go and ask of my Em."

Abbie returned with streaming eyes. "She lives," she assured her aunt. "She lives but barely. As for the child . . ."

"Does it breathe?" Nat asked her.

"Aye, Nat," Abbie sobbed. "But it is so weak and small."

"Then it must be baptized," he said swiftly.

"Is it the same with Presbyterians?" she asked doubtfully.

His eyes blazed at her. "It is Andrew's child, and no Presbyterian. Would you condemn his seed to eternal hopelessness?"

Em herself lay gape-mouthed with exhaustion, her breath coming labored and weak. Nat leaned close, forcing her to harken to him. "Baptize," he repeated. "To save this soul."

Em's eyes fixed only hazily on his face; then the slow comprehension came, and she nodded.

Her words came painfully through cracked lips. "Oh, God, yes," she whispered hollowly. "The name is Merritt. Merritt Lyon Rigg."

• 7 •

Old Leaven

Therefore let us keep the feast, not with the old leaven, neither with the leaven of malice and wickedness; but with the unleavened bread of sincerity and truth.

I Corinthians 5:7

ANDREW SENSED SOMETHING was wrong even as Gil brought the craft to the wharf. He had barely started toward the house before he saw his mother standing stiffly at the door.

"You have missed the coming of your child," she said coldly. "Emily Fraser has given birth and named the child Merritt."

He stared in amazement. "My God, a child. A son. How is my Em?"

Her anger fairly blazed forth. "There is no son, only a weak, puling girl whom Dame Bray doubts will survive a fortnight. But Emily Fraser has named this creature Merritt all the same."

"How could it be named so soon?"

"Nat was there and found it likely to die. The baptism was for the saving of its soul. But there must be something you could do even now, Andrew. A proud name like Merritt cannot be carried by a sniveling girl. Can a christening be voided?"

He had traveled too swiftly between worlds. Only lately he had left a dying old man twisting his property this way and that to succor one who was barely of his blood. Andrew felt a stone form in his chest. Where were his mother's comforting words on the weakness of his child? Where were her prayers of concern over his wife's health? Where was the fond hope that gentle care might yet wrest this life from death?

"I am going to my family," he said, brushing past her.

Her hands were swift on his clothing, her voice supplicating. "Stay with me, Andrew. I have been sore beset with all of this."

He shook his head. "I go to my wife and child."

"Where are the obligations of son to mother?" she challenged. "Where are your fine words of being my support and pleasure? The name, Andrew. You must do something about the child's name."

He caught a deep breath of the hot air that was fouled by the stench of the stables beyond. The words came from nowhere into his mind, and he repeated them in a firm tone.

"For all the pomp that is attached to your name, Mother, the word itself suggests a more general and felicitous galaxy of virtues than any term I know. Women have been named for prudence and charity and hope. I think that Merritt Rigg rings well among them."

The childbed linen given by Robbie Fraser had been sewn with bands of lace and ribbons drawn here and there. The angled light from the half-shaded window caught the rich lights that Andrew cherished in Em's hair. He would not let her be wakened. The exhaustion of her labor still made her sleep heavy. The full lips were a little apart, and the dark lashes stirred on her cheek from the chimera of her dreams. She had labored too long. While no judge of the newly born, he had found the small face in the crib too pinched under its cap and too short of breath.

"Every day's breath is a battle won," Dame Bray whispered as he studied the child.

"Then pray that there be long years of such victories." The child had stirred and pursed its lips. The hand that rose from the sleeve was a veined claw.

Emily was a long time wordless in Andrew's clasp when she wakened. Once they pulled apart, she unburdened herself of her great concern.

"I did not know whether it was lad or lass when I gave the name," she told him. "I only knew that death hung near."

"It doesn't matter," he assured her, summoning the gayest smile he could muster. "In less than an hour I have grown to cherish my daughter with that fine name."

"But your mother?"

"She wanted a Merritt," he reminded her, "and a Merritt she has gained."

Her face softened with relief. "Tell me, Andrew, do you find our daughter pretty?"

"She needs more time before she can challenge her mother on that," he told her. "But with you as a pattern, how could she be otherwise?"

By the time the Assembly was to meet again, on July tenth, the child was fuller of face and suckled with some strength. Em, enthralled by the babe at her side, did not even realize that a messenger had come.

"The Assembly has been prorogued," Andrew told his aunt. "I have some commerce to do for Uncle Younger, and will go and attend to it. I should be absent only a few days."

"You will not tell Em that you are not going to the Assembly?" his aunt asked.

"I would rather surprise her with a swift return than burden her mind with talk of business."

In those three days Andrew found a house that Magda could use for living quarters and a shop. In truth it was only half a house, but it was available for buying and using at once. There were rooms below for sewing, and a shop on the street, and ample sleeping rooms above. The kitchen house stood apart as did the necessary. While neither was in the best condition, only some small repairs would be needed to set them right.

By now it was clear that Gil must be party to all this scheming or the man's damnable curiosity would drive him berserk.

"You noticed the girl at my uncle's house?"

"Aye," Gil replied. "And handsome she is, in a strange, foreign style."

"This is to be her lodging and her shop," Andrew explained. "We arrange this for Uncle Younger, as she is his niece."

"And so your cousin," Gil added thoughtfully. "But a woman here alone?"

"So she would live if she were widowed," Andrew reminded him. "No doubt she will swiftly find a maid to attend her. With all that is afoot in my own house, I am sending you upriver to take this word to my uncle and bring the girl here."

"And none is to be the wiser?" Gil asked.

"This is my uncle's business," Andrew explained.

At Gil's summons, Andrew traveled again to Williamsburg.

Magda seemed different as she faced him in the rooms of her own shop. A new assurance stiffened her posture, and her dark eyes met his with delight.

"That was grand news that awaited your return," she told him.

Startled at her joyful noting of his daughter's birth, he nodded his thanks.

"Her years will be long upon this earth," Magda told him.

He knew it as a blessing but thought it sounded more like a foretelling.

"Then you are pleased with this place?"

Her face lit with joy. "Oh, cousin, I have walked from dark to light." Then, as if she sensed his confusion, she asked, "This house, then, is in Uncle Younger's name?"

"Aye," Andrew replied. "I made it plain that he leased it to another for shopkeeping. I did not name you."

She studied him soberly. "Would it be easier if I used some other name than my uncle's and mine?"

"I hadn't thought of that," he admitted. "What name would you use?"

"I never knew my mother's name," she said, her eyes

113

leaving his to study the fire. "But my grandmother was called Annie Steele."

"Steele it could be, then." Sensing a sudden strangeness in the room, he asked, "Do you fear this new life, Magda?"

Her eyes were puzzled. "Fear?" she repeated. Then she shook her head. "The fear was left in the darkness, cousin. I have only the sense one has of wakening in a dream. I must set my foot with care lest the sleep be rent and I awaken falling."

<hr />

8

A Stumbling Block

(August–November 1718)

So then every one of us shall give account of himself to God.
Let us not therefore judge one another any more: but judge this rather, that no man put a stumbling-block or an occasion to fall in his brother's way.

Romans 14:12–13

IT WAS NO easy task to select an overseer whom Andrew could trust to take a dozen slaves, including some artisans, up beyond the fall line to build a shelter and clear the fields for the spring planting. By August he had found such a man and was readying to go upstream with him after Captain Robbie Fraser's impending visit.

This was to be no ordinary visit from Em's father. The new ship *Merit* (for so had they fixed the spelling of the child's name) was being brought for Emily's blessing before it faced the sea. "I myself will take the *Lark* and leave the new ship to the mastery of Captain Bruce Forrester." Her father grinned at Emily. "As fair and tight as this ship be, she is no match for that launching of yours." His face softened like butter in the sun at the sight of the baby, grown rosy and bright-eyed from tender nursing.

Only when they were apart from the new mother did Andrew and his father-in-law discuss the crisis with Blackbeard in North Carolina.

"Governor Eden is openly in league with that scoundrel, as is his secretary, Tobias Knight," the captain told him. "That old pirate has married again for the fourteenth time, with a dozen of those wives still living. He has got himself a great house in Bath, and it is rumored that he is fortifying the Okracoke inlet as a pirate's rendezvous."

"Can nothing be done by decent folk?" Andrew asked.

Captain Fraser shrugged. "Some of those are said to have sent appeals to our Governor Spotswood for assistance, though what he could do, God alone knows. He has war enough with his own House of Burgesses."

Talk of the pirate threat lingered in Andrew's mind as he made preparations to go to his new land. With the coming of the child, he found himself increasingly wary of leaving his household of women undefended. These restless men, carrying their Acts of Grace like a universal absolution, ranged through the colony along with the felons sent from British prisons. Andrew did not doubt Chad's valor in a fight, but the servant was of such an age that no rogue would hesitate to cross him.

In the end Andrew left Gil the Toad behind for the good of his household, though he sorely missed the companionship of his servant and friend.

The slattern at his uncle's house met him with wide, shocked eyes. " 'E's dying," she told him in a shocked whisper, without the civility of a greeting.

Dying Younger Elliott was, with his head thrust wholly aside by the great growth, but his grateful eyes rested on Andrew.

"I don't want a surgeon," he rasped. "I've no intention of giving a man both blood and gold for doing the Lord's work. Only sit, son, and speak of home."

Fighting his own grief, Andrew sat and talked of the stream that still chimed into the mill pool at Candle Creek, how his Aunt Martha's voice still rang with laughter. He did not add that the mill stayed silent and the wheat unground, with so few ships daring to go out on that pirated sea, or that Martha's laughter had survived the darkness of blindness, so that Em read to her each word that came from the Bible and the old Lyon journal. He told of his babe and her growing beauty and Magda's joy and success in her neat, bright shop. "She has a maid with her now," Andrew reported, "a young widow by the name of Mollie Plum, who has a child barely on its feet."

Sometimes the old man slept and sometimes he waked, and Andrew was only sure which he did when Younger spoke. At last the old man smiled and reached for Andrew's hand. "I go to join Benn," he said. A shudder passed through him with the yielding of his spirit. Andrew held Younger's hand in his own until the flesh cooled in his grasp, loath to release this man into the long stream of eternity. The minutes hung dreamily in the quiet room, minutes doomed to fall outside the life of his uncle.

This deformed shell, stripped of its agonies and transient joys, had so long been a shepherd of hours. Andrew groped in his memory for the long catalogue of this man's years.

William Elliott, called Younger, had been born in 1636 as a subject of the Stuart King James I. He had lost his father to Indian attack in 1644, severed his life from his mother in 1667. He had survived the reigns of seven monarchs and two Lord Protectors, and died under the dominion of George I of Hanover, having achieved the great age of eighty-two years. At the end of this, Andrew found himself overcome, not with grief, but with prayers of praise and thanksgiving.

Only when Younger lay by his beloved brother, James, and the girl, Doll Simms, whom James had cherished, did Andrew proceed upriver with his overseer, James Ward, and the coffle of slaves. The land had begun to color sweetly against autumn. Nut trees still held their burden, and the wild grapes tangled on the vine.

Andrew grieved that Em could not see the bounty of this place, the clear river and the forest variously colored against the blue of sky. The time would come for her to be here, he knew that. In the meantime he carried home some grapes from his own forest along with a handful of smooth stones from the river's bed.

That November when the Assembly was called again, Andrew denied himself the company of Gil the Toad and took instead his father's man, Cyrus, off to Williamsburg with him.

"The ladies will find some way to occupy you, I am sure," he told Gil. "And I will feel that much more secure having you here."

Em credited Gil's obvious disappointment to his love of the ordinaries of the capital. A high excitement of song and celebration was known to accompany these public times.

Tansey disabused her of this thought.

"They say he has a girl there now," she told Em, "a young widow with a child."

"But how would he meet such a person?" Em wondered aloud.

"She works as maid and housekeeper in a shop. He might have just passed while she was sweeping."

"She is not a slave, then?"

Tansey shook her head. "Irish, they say, red-topped, with that mess of freckles they sometimes wear."

The Assembly had barely begun its sessions when the messenger came for Gil. He rode no common horse, this man who stood at the fence talking earnestly to Gil. Smartly attired, he cantered away with an air of authority that intrigued Em. As Gil watched the horseman depart, Em felt a rush of affection for this little Welshman. Though she was careful to call him by his Christian name, she couldn't help that his nickname, Toad, leaped to her mind. He was only a shade from being comical, so short of stature and slender of frame, except for the round belly that surprised the eye above such remarkably thin legs. As she watched, he scuffed his shoe on the ground and threw back his head to breathe as if gasping, froglike, for a great swallow of air. When he turned toward the house she realized his face was screwed tight with torment.

She was not surprised that he asked for an immediate and private audience with her.

Em had observed that her aunt's slaves, when face to face

117

with their mistress, often lost their grip on their tongues and fell to stammering. But Gil was a proper paid servant, even as Tansey and Chad were. Yet he reddened before her, his words coming this way and that, without sense.

"I can make no sense of this," she admitted directly. "Sit you down, Guillam, and breathe quietly a bit. You received a message. That much I saw."

"I am to go," he got out, "on a bit of service of which I can tell no one."

"Andrew has sent for you, then?" she asked, not understanding.

When he shook his head, she sighed. "No man except Andrew can command you."

The color of his face deepened. "There be such, mistress, though I cannot name him."

She studied him. "He must be in the government," she decided. "Since you are not a slave but a freedman, you owe allegiance there."

After a fierce grimace he nodded. "Then you must ride off to Williamsburg and tell Andrew what you are about and then do what is legally required of you."

"I was most particularly told not to speak to any member of the Assembly on this," he told her.

"But that is ridiculous."

"Aye," he nodded.

"Just tell that man that you are not free for just any mischief that is afoot."

His great green eyes held hers imploringly. "For such words I could be clapped in irons by he who summoned me. Besides there is a good deal of money to be made from it. Not tobacco, mind you, but good English pounds."

"And what do you need money for?" she teased. "You are fed and clothed and get your wages besides."

This brought a wave of high color to his face. "Someday," he began. "One day, I've been thinking . . ."

She grinned at him. "There's a girl, then."

He nodded with relief. "Aye, and there is always land to be had. One day . . ."

She had set her work aside to contemplate him. Although he had ceased to stir under her glance, his face was unreadable. This man had been friend as well as servant to Andrew since he was only a lad. He had left his own country's shores for

Andrew's sake. He grew no younger with each year than any man did. Why should he not wish to have a wife at his side, and perhaps babies, like any man?

"You are a man of faith?" she asked, rising.

"Aye," he stammered, stumbling to his feet.

"Then lay your hand on this Holy book," she ordered. "I want an oath from you. Repeat after me as if you stood before a judge."

His voice echoed her words without hesitation.

"I, Guillam Jones, being conscious of the great sin of perjury if I lie in this state, do solemnly vow that what I have been asked to do has been required by an authority that holds dominion over me as an Englishman and a freedman of this colony."

His eyes met hers levelly.

"Wait," she cried. "There is more. And that what I set out to do is not in violation of the King's law or the laws of Virginia or my Almighty God."

She set the book aside and smiled at him. "I cannot imagine that Andrew would do other than give you his blessing. When do you leave? How long will you be gone?"

"Tomorrow," he replied. "As to my return, God alone knows when it will be."

"My blessing, Guillam," she told him. "And know that I am accountable to Andrew for your absence from here, and you are not to worry about this."

There was little else on Em's mind for the rest of that day. In spite of everything, she kept hearing the words that Andrew had hurled at her in their days of great anger. Had she presumed too much? Yet how could she act otherwise without risking great trouble for Toad, caught between the two masters of employer and crown? She had finished reading the evening prayers to Aunt Martha when Tansey reported that Toad was below, wishing to have a word with her.

If possible, he was more flustered than he had been earlier.

"I have a great favor to ask of you," he blurted out. "Mind you, I can read and cipher and make my own name, but as for writing things out in plain English . . ."

She drew a sheet from her desk and dipped her pen in the inkwell. "Now, what would you have me write?"

He breathed deeply. The candle light gleamed on an entire circle of white rimming those great green eyes.

"I, Guillam Jones, previously of Cardiff, now manservant to Andrew Rigg, Jr., being in sound mind and body"—Em felt her own heart plunge at these words, but she wrote dutifully—"do solemnly bequeath all I own, along with wages due and unpaid, to the widow Mollie Plum, for her to do with as she sees best, with no man to say her nay. And my soul to Christ. Amen."

When the scratching of her pen ceased, Toad took the paper awkwardly and signed next to the date Em had written, November 15, 1718. Emily signed below, though she wondered if the witness of a woman would bear any weight if the matter were challenged.

"Would you have me keep this for you?" she asked. After sealing it with her own mark, she locked it in an inner drawer. "So you fear danger," she said, suddenly humbled.

She knew the will had raised a weight from him by seeing his smile, which had regained its old cockiness. "What man knows which breath be his last?" he countered.

As she suckled the child Merit and saw her wrapped up for sleep, Toad's words hung tenderly in Em's mind.

". . . the widow Mollie Plum, for her to do with as she sees best, with no man to say her nay."

This would be the gentlest of love stories to report to Andrew on his return from the Assembly.

— • 9 • —

A Trial By Fire

Every man's work shall be made manifest: for the day
shall declare it, because it shall be revealed by fire; and the
fire shall try every man's work of what sort it is.

I Corinthians 3:13

TOAD WAS NO sooner at the bank of the James River than he
wished himself back in his bed again.

A dawn mist had draped the guard ships, the *Lyme* and the
Pearl, with phantom rigging, specter ships tugging at a slate-
dark river. He recalled a saying of Captain Owen's that the
Lord Himself couldn't tell a brave man from a fool by
candle light. Even in such a haze, Toad saw himself as a fool.
And a sinner as well, if it came to that. Hadn't he puffed up
with pride to receive a summons from Governor Spotswood
himself? Hadn't his greed for gold and his lust to have Mollie
Plum to wife blinded him to the folly of this venture?

He listened with his heart in his throat as the scheme
unfolded. Didn't these glib fools know that Blackbeard commanded such a fleet that four hundred cutthroats served as its
crew? Hadn't they learned that both Governor Eden and his
secretary, Tobias Knight, were tongue in groove with the
scoundrel in his doings?

Yet they proposed that sixty men in two shallow-keeled
sloops might seize this great pirate from his own coves. Of

the men in the party, many were known to him by face or by account. Captain Ellis Brand of the *Lyme* was setting out overland in hopes of arresting the demon Teach ashore. The sloop Toad was assigned to was under the command of Robert Maynard, first lieutenant of the *Pearl,* a brisk and canny fellow, for all his great age. Maynard had a force of thirty-five, while a small sloop, the *Ranger,* held twenty-five men, under the command of Midshipman George Baker of the *Lyme.* The captain of the *Pearl* had remained with the now-desperately undermanned guard ships.

Toad kept thinking of that will he'd had Mistress Emily write for him, as the sloops moved down the James River. That afternoon and in the days following, he kept seeing sweet Mollie's face when she heard of his death by pirates.

Toad knew himself to be a fool from the fear that grew greater with each day's sailing. For three days this natural and healthy terror festered in his soul, giving him no peace. When at last they entered the narrows of the Roanoke, the first news of Blackbeard's whereabouts almost brought relief. If a man was to die, let it be quick, and not dragged out forever, like a mouth's being emptied of teeth one at a time.

The master of a merchant sloop told Maynard that Teach himself had his sloop *Adventurer* aground on Brant's Shoals, with another sloop laboring to get him off again.

Something about the feel of his own sloop changed with this information. Voices were held lower, and the hollowness of waiting began to be felt. The shoals were searched in vain as the hours lengthened. Only late in the day following, with twilight already hazing the view, did Maynard take the sloop into Okracoke Inlet, there to see two sloops riding at anchor, Blackbeard's *Adventurer* and a merchant prize.

At least there was no time left for Gil to score himself with fear. He and his shipmates were set briskly to work preparing their craft for battle. As the stars began to prick out, the wind calmed. From across the water came strident sounds, the breaking out of casks and screeching of music and roars of men reveling as Teach and his crew made merry with the master of the captured sloop.

This clamor rent the air the whole of the night, and would have disturbed any man able to sleep. For himself, Toad found small comfort in his bed, and even less taste to the food he dropped into his roiling belly that next morning. Clearly the *Adventurer* was stoutly armed, and their only hope lay in outmaneuvering her. At nine that morning, Toad, along with some others, was dispatched in a small boat to plumb for that full fathom that the sloop must have beneath her keel. When they wandered into range of the *Adventurer*, a round of shot bent Toad and his companions swiftly to their oars.

At least the waiting was through. That same round of shot that sent them scurrying out of range signaled the beginning of Maynard's offensive.

Because of its shallower draft, the *Ranger* was sent forward first, with Toad's own vessel following. God help a man who feared omens! They had no more than begun, when the *Ranger* ran aground, and they were forced to pitch ballast. Once free, they found themselves immediately on a sand bar, from which they could only move when the water casts were emptied. As Maynard maneuvered towards the *Adventurer*, he was hailed across the water by Blackbeard himself. Damning the lot of them as villains, the pirate asked where they hailed from and who they were.

With the British ensign fluttering over the sloop, Maynard shouted back that any man could see that they were not pirates. This earned him the invitation to come aboard the *Adventurer* and be recognized.

"I cannot spare my boat," Maynard shouted at him. "But I will come aboard you with my sloop."

Still swigging at the mug of rum in his hand, Teach leaped to the top of the roundhouse and shouted in anger.

"Damnation seize my soul if I give you quarters or take any from you."

"I expect no quarter from you," Maynard replied. "Nor would I yield it."

As they spoke, Teach's black ensign fluttered upward, so that the death's head grinned down at them from the mast. Cutting his cable and unfurling his sails, the pirate made ready to run for the open sea.

At Maynard's shouted order, Midshipman Baker threw the helm of the *Ranger* over to block the *Adventurer*'s passage. The pirate sloop bore down to a pistol-shot range before swinging around and delivering a broadside. Toad felt his belly heave as Midshipman Baker and two of his command as well as several seamen were rent in sudden death in that explosion of shot and bone and blood. Though the master mate, Thomas, leaped to command, the *Ranger* began to drift helplessly, with her jibe and foremast shot cleanly away.

The breeze that had favored the pirates' sails died as it had risen. Maynard shouted them to the sweeps, and the sloop moved towards the *Adventurer*. Although the fire from the damaged *Ranger* was all they had covering them, Toad realized that Blackbeard had not come from that encounter unscathed.

Even as they manned the sweeps, the pirate, cursing to split the air, sent a broadside across the deck. Cries and curses rose all about Toad as the Swan and Patridge and such killing small shot took their toll of his shipmates. Then Toad himself realized that the heat against his head was the creasing of his own skull, and it was the spouting of his own blood that was suddenly awash in his shoe.

Even as the letting of blood is designed to ease fever, the hot flow of his own life juices cleansed Toad of fear. It was again as it had been that night when the winds of the Lord had swept so fiercely on the *Lark* and the *Joyeuse* in deadly combat. A fine flood of air swelled Toad's lungs, and he felt, as much as heard, the vibration of the growl rising in his throat.

Time, which had filled him with panic during the maneuvering of the sloops and the crippling of the *Ranger*, seemed to grow smooth in his understanding. Minutes that had passed as fleetingly as bullets passed slowly, almost leisurely, giving him time to aim and fire and aim again with deadly intent.

When Captain Maynard ordered the decks cleared, Toad wanted to scream his protest. His hands ached for combat, the buck of the gun in his hand, the sleek polished grip of a cutlass. Maynard would have none of it, but forced them below except for one midshipman and a pilot named Butler.

Toad, restrained among the others, knew himself to be a grenade ready to explode even as the pirate grenades burst on the deck above, turning it to a gory hell. No man's voice could stop this fever to battle. Even as Toad and some others leaped from the quarters, Teach came aboard with his rope to lash the sloops together.

With that horde of fiends scrambling over the gunwales, Maynard kept shouting, shouting. Cutlass in hand, Toad leaped into the thick of that fray. One after another pirate fell screaming at his hand. The din was like the heart of a great storm, pistol shots and mortal screams and the whine of cutlasses. Face to face with a scowling giant, Toad brought him to his knees with a slash across the belly, only to see Captain Maynard and Blackbeard, face to face, both firing their pistols at point-blank range.

The rum that had tainted the pirate's blood ruined his aim. As Blackbeard's shot went wild, Maynard's ball struck the giant before him without seeming damage. The pirate lunged with his cutlass, snapping off Maynard's sword as if it were paper. Toad felt the scream of warning rising in his own throat as he saw Maynard's death written on the pirate's distorted countenance. The scream was to turn to one of pain. With a hiss of fury, his assailant raised his knife and plunged it into Toad's side. With his last surge of strength, Toad lunged free of the man, only to have his own eyes betray him with giddy waves of darkness folding themselves before him. The sun seemed darkened like the soot-filled sky of London, and his head, once the province of his own thoughts, was wholly filled with a painful slow rhythm. He felt himself falling.

Toad's wakening was to searing pain and the heaving of his belly at the movement of the sloop. He came into a different darkness, spattered with clear cold stars. Forcing himself up on his elbow, he looked along a deck lined with injured men. Some slept, and others, like himself, groaned softly in pain. The voice at his side came weakly, as if from a man of great age. "You live, then."

"Aye," Toad replied. "But I am much the worse for it."

"Many died," his informant reported. "Ten, they say, but all that matters is him."

Toad stirred to follow his gaze. The moon that had emptied half the sky of stars with its brightness shed a glaze on the bowsprit. Toad only slowly realized that what swung there was the head of that giant. Blackbeard, Edward Teach himself, his evil eyes blinded by death and his braided beard stirred by night wind.

"Twenty-five great wounds it took to bring him down," the man whispered in awe, "five of them pistol shots. He was not a man to let death have him with ease."

"He knew the devil to be long waiting," Toad told him.

Letting himself gingerly back down, Toad stared at the moon, crossed now and then by a night flying bird. He had cursed himself as sinner and fool, but God had spared him this far. With Blackbeard dead on that bowsprit, they would all have gold, and he would have Mollie Plum.

He wondered if the Lord, having seen him that hazy morning on the James, had mistaken him for a brave man instead of a fool and spared him. For this he gave thanks, most fervent thanks.

· 10 ·

A City Without Walls

> He that hath no rule over his own spirit is like a city that is broken down, and without walls.
>
> Proverbs 25:28

THE SCARS OF Em's old wounds throbbed painfully in the days following Gil the Toad's departure. Nearly a year had passed since she and Andrew had forged the delicate truce that had held their marriage together. Frail as it was, it had survived the birth of young Merit and Andrew's growing realization that, because of her devotion to Martha, Em would not be ready to follow him to his new plantation west of the fall line as long as the old woman needed her. As for herself, burdened with the care of both the child and Aunt Martha, there was little time in her life, nor did she have the strength, to bemoan how few of his hours she shared.

But neither of them had come through this without loss. The pride he despaired of in his mother grew in Andrew in a different style. He was sensitive to his station and conscious that he neither controlled, nor publicly seemed to control, his family with the force that society expected or he himself deemed proper. As for Em, she walked that careful line between her two masters, her husband and her God, sometimes rebellious that their causes could not be the same.

Had it been presumptuous for her to permit Gil to leave with Andrew's permission? Had it been arrogance on her part to make this judgment without counsel? At last she took her doubts to Aunt Martha.

"What a puzzling event," the old woman said musingly. "No member of the Assembly to be informed! This smacks of some secret doings by the Council or the Governor himself!"

"But the intent was serious," Em reminded her. "So serious that without hesitation Guillam swore on the Holy book and then asked to have his testament written."

"I cannot imagine that Andrew will object to your doing what he himself would have been obliged by law to do."

Even this assurance was of little help during those long nights that Em lay sleepless, hearing the least sigh from the child in her cradle or the cold creaking in the joints of the old house. Andrew must understand, not only for herself, but for the sake of the sleeping child and the new babe that even now swelled within her. This time it would be a son. This time, pray God.

The puddings were being put down for the coming season and the embroidered vest Em was making for Andrew's Christmas gift was half flowered with careful stitches. Em had sent fine fabric from her father to a nearby seamstress, that a fine French sacque be made for Aunt Martha.

As she and Cece visited over tea, Em wondered aloud if the seamstress would tailor the garment properly for her aunt's flaring proportions.

"I am sure you will be pleased," Cece told her. "But in another such case, you might try this new woman named Steele in Williamsburg. She does most entrancing work."

"Steele?" Em asked. "I can't remember hearing that name."

"She's fairly newly arrived," Cece told her. "I think she came in the late summer, when I was so bound up in the coming of baby Harry's teeth that I thought of little else. But since then, I have visited the shop. She is a strange, dark bird of a woman, and given to silence. But such laces and handiwork you never saw."

Em stared thoughtfully, "Andrew has brought me several

lovely handworked things since Merit came. Do you suppose that is where he got them? He always just says they are from Williamsburg."

"As likely as not." Cece nodded. "There is no one to touch her, short of London." Then she giggled at herself. "Hear me, now, that great tongue clapping away like that. I should say that the sacque Jake had her make for baby Harry is as fine as any I have seen that came from London."

All thoughts of French sacques and puddings, even of the coming of Christmas, were swept away by an unexpected call from Captain Bruce Forrester, master of Em's father's ship the *Merit*.

She knew at first glance that he bore ill tidings.

"I searched my soul a long time before I came," he told her. "God forbid that I should concern you without cause."

"My father," she pressed him. "You bring some news of my father."

At his nod, she tried to hasten his words. "Is he ill? Has something gone wrong with his ship?"

When he stammered in reply, she turned coaxing. "Forgive me, Bruce. Tell me the worst at once, to still this hammering in my heart."

"We know neither the best nor the worst," he admitted. "It is only that twice now the *Lark* has been sighted in strange waters, once carrying a black ensign. There is no word from your father or of what has become of him."

"My father would run up no pirate flag," she said hotly.

"This we know," Bruce said. "But if his ship was taken by such—"

"He is a good master," she said softly, trying to absorb the enormity of his words. "Often pirates will spare a master whose crew speaks well of him."

Raising her eyes to his stilled her voice. Too well she knew that for every pirate who would impress a captain for his skill or free him ashore, there were twenty who would see him dead within an hour of boarding.

She sat so quietly that he spoke again out of pity for her. "There may yet be hope, but it has been two months since that first sighting."

Her grief went past tears, to numbness.

His tone turned brisk. "His legal counselor and I have

spoken about this. We felt you should know of these reports. We thought that we should at once confer with you about the business and its accounts.''

"Business? Accounts?" She looked at him with anger. "How can you talk of business and accounts, when my father is God knows where and in what condition?"

Ignoring her anger, he went on quietly. "The counselor and I agreed that, lacking word from him, his orders should be handled as he directed in such a case: that the house be kept for you until you wished it sold; that the business be run under my management and that of his counselor, with all profits being paid to you; and that all decisions concerning the business be made by you, free of your husband's control, as was written in the marriage contract.''

"I cannot see that it is time for such directives to be considered," she said at last.

"The oldest of the vessels, *The Blessed Annie* is even now careened for her hull to be scraped, leaving only the *Merit* seaworthy, along with the sloops and such small craft as are used for light traffic and ferrying. If we wish to have a new hundred-pounder of the *Lark* class for the harvest of next year, it must be commissioned now." He added, "If God sees our master safely home, he will be raging to have a deck beneath his feet.''

This is an act of faith, Em thought. Such a commission would be an act of faith for her father's return.

"Your reasoning is sound. Be about the plans—and, God willing, my father will be shouting at the workers as it progresses, even as he most surely did when the *Merit* was being built.''

"You remember the building of the *Lark*," he said with a smile. He rose. "My wife, Peggy, sends her tenderest greetings.''

Em was struck with remorse. "Dear Peggy. And convey mine to her. And how is your boy, Asa?"

"He is his mother's delight," Bruce told her, "for all that he is a stubborn little beast, who will soon be tamed by the coming of another.''

As was her father's custom, Captain Forrester had brought rich bounty for Em's kitchen, a great live turtle as well as fresh fruits and Carolina rice. Of these she took a generous share to Abbie and Nat Horne, asking Nat to add her father's name to his special supplications.

"You need not bring gifts for me to pray for your father," he rebuked her.

"I bring gifts for the selfish joy of seeing you and your family enjoy them," she told him. "I ask for your prayers because of my great fear for my father."

That same night she was roused from her troubled sleep by the sound of horses in the drive. Knowing both Gil and Andrew to be gone, she groped for covering with frantic hands, wondering how difficult it would be to rouse old Chad from sleep.

To her relief, the step on the stairs was Andrew's.

He said nothing, but only came swiftly to her to gather her into his arms. Then, to her astonishment, he sat her down on the side of the bed. He was clearly in the grip of strong emotion.

"Ill tidings came to Williamsburg today, my love," he told her. "I came to you directly."

She would have interrupted him, but his words tumbled out at too great a speed. "They say your father is missing, Em. I cannot credit it wholly, but we must face what facts we know." At his words, her first tears began to flow and she clung to him.

"He was my friend as well as father to you, our Robbie Fraser. He was all things that a man should be, blessed in faith and still a lover of life. What games he played with his tongue were simple ones for his own pleasure, and never for malice against any man. I am so grieved, my love, so grieved."

Her tears could not be stayed. "He may yet be found," she insisted. "It might be that he was marooned like that Alexander Selkirk we heard of. He might yet ride on another ship somewhere."

"You had heard, then," he said, staring at her. "By what means?"

"Captain Forrester came just this morning."

"This morning? And you did not send for me?"

"How could I? And what good would it serve?"

"You could have dispatched Gil within the hour. As to the good it might serve, I am hurt by that question. We are one. My joys are your joys, and your sorrows mine." Then he frowned. "As to Gil, where is that lout at this hour, that he did not challenge our entry?"

She felt her heart pound in a way that stripped her voice of its force. "He is not here," she said. "Let me explain."

He was apart from her now, staring. "What is there to explain? I pay that creature and leave him here for your protection. Any rogue might have entered upon you sleeping, even as I did. I can think of no explanation that might fit this misdemeanor."

"He went with my permission freely granted."

"But where? For what reason?" His eyes narrowed as he spoke.

"He was sought for a commission that he was not allowed to explain, and I gave him leave to go."

He was pacing the room in the manner of one struggling for control.

"You gave him leave," he repeated slowly. "God help me, woman if we be wedded a thousand years, I would not be able to read that twisted mind of yours. When did you give him leave? At least be so kind as to report to me of your control over my personal servant."

"A few days had passed," she said. "It was the fifteenth."

"And where was he off to?"

"I do not know."

"And on what man's business?"

"Please, Andrew. He swore—"

He stilled her with a wave of his hand and sank into a chair. "In deference to the child that swells in you and the grief that you have so suddenly gained, I wish to talk no more."

"But Andrew," she pleaded, "please try to understand."

"I already understand far too well," he said dully. "Today that accursed Assembly drew to a close. The House has drawn up an address to the king containing a bill of particulars against Governor Spotswood, with a request for his recall. This is a colony whose arrogance allows no room for proper government. I come to my home to comfort my wife, only to find that she has dealt with my affairs as if she were head of this household. I have been much into forgiveness these past months. When I was informed of your malice in naming our daughter, I held my tongue. But this goes too far.

"Unless you wish to see me drink myself into that sodden

and disgusting state that you so modestly abhor, then you had best remove yourself from my sight. I have seen vanity and deceit and the flaunting of petty pride for the length of this Assembly. I will not look at its face in my own chambers.''

She was halfway down the passage when he went to the door to call after her.

"One other thing," he said quietly. "You have torn Guillam the Toad from my service by your foolish weakness toward him. He is no longer in my employ.''

She turned to stare at him. "But, Andrew," she protested, "do not lay a penalty on Guillam. The fault is entirely mine. To do otherwise is unreasonable and unfair.''

He drew his breath sharply between his teeth. "You may be judge of all reason and fairness only for yourself, madam. Merely mark that I do not wish to see his face or hear his name again for any reason.''

She stood studying him until he turned on his heel and closed the door behind him.

Perhaps the day had held too much grief and pain. She found herself without tears, feeling only a dull wrenching. One can only read a scripture a certain number of times before it is emblazoned in the brain. Now she saw the words clearly, their place on the line, the slender seriphs clinging thereto:

No servant can serve two masters; for either he will hate the one, and love the other; or he will hold to the one and despise the other.

As long as there had been misunderstandings between herself and Andrew, they had been able to be fixed. This was no misunderstanding. In the choice between obeying Andrew's will and obeying God's dictates on such matters, she was obliged to follow the word of God. Could she reject a man to whose cause she was pledged, as she was to Gil? Could she see a man of no property thrown into poverty or want by her own hand without succoring his needs?

Yet, God willing, she prayed that Gil be spared. Like herself, he had been caught between two powers beyond his control, and had been changed into a helpless pawn by those powers.

PART THREE

The Sojourner
(1718–1730)

Hear my prayer, O Lord, and give ear unto my cry; hold not thy peace at my tears: for I am a stranger with thee, and a sojourner, as all my fathers were.

Psalms 39:12

The first string that the musician usually touches is the bass, when he intends to put all in tune. God also plays on this string first, when he sets the soul in tune for himself.

John Bunyan, *Pilgrim's Progress*, Part II (1684)

1

The Crown

(1718)

A virtuous woman is a crown to her husband: but she that
maketh ashamed is as rottenness in his bones.

Proverbs 12:4

As DAYS PASSED, and then weeks, with no word of Guillam
the Toad, Em became steadily more concerned about his
welfare.

She heard a good deal about the campaign against Edward
Teach, the pirate called Blackbeard. She heard accounts of
how the governor's sloops had returned bearing that great
pirate's head on a bowsprit. Those sloops had carried a
fortune in pirate loot along with wounded and dead men. She
could not separate these stories from Gil in her mind.

"My father used to say that in a great battle he would
rather have Gil the Toad at his side than five more solid
men," she told Aunt Martha.

"Why do you mention this?" the old woman asked.

"If the governor heard such talk and believed it, Gil might
have been ordered on that deadly errand."

"Has anything been seen of him since that day?" Martha
asked.

Em shook her head, suddenly near tears. "And how would
I know, trapped here with my baby and a husband who hates
me?"

"He does not hate you, child," Martha assured her. "It was but a vicious chance that you ran afoul of him when he was already worried about your father and in a dreadful mood from the meeting of the burgesses."

"I see no cause why he should vent his anger at burgesses on me," Em told her.

"A man's head is not a hand basket to be filled with a single tart," her aunt told her. "Think of how he has spent these past weeks, battling an assembly where his own cause was lost. He hears of the loss of a dear friend, your father, at sea and rushes to give you comfort, only to find another dear friend off and gone for no cause that he understands."

"He will not let me explain," Em protested.

"He is wrong not to listen, but the man has been carrying burdens past his strength. And now he returns to battle with his creditors over the settlement of debts."

"Debts?" Emily cried. "How can that be? The crops at Candle Creek yielded well, and if there was a cargo lost I did not hear of it."

"Never mind," Martha ordered. "I lost control of my tongue just then, because of your concern over Guillam."

Em studied her a moment. "You do neither of us a favor when you hold things back. I have burdens too—worry about my father and Gil the Toad. I am heartsick about this trouble between Andrew and me. Why add mysteries to this? If what you know would help me understand all this trouble, it would be an act of mercy to tell me."

The old woman shook her head. "I *know* nothing. I have discovered a strange fact in my blindness. Simple people seem to lump all senses into one. Because I cannot see, they shout in my presence as if my hearing were gone from me too. Should I distress you with the false whisperings of slaves?"

"Let me weigh them for myself," Em suggested.

Martha sighed. "You must know that an Englishman doing business from Virginia falls into debt easily. The orders are sent when cargo is shipped, and in time those cargoes are credited against his account. But the accounts are never clear, as new debts are incurred even as the old are being paid off. It was for the watchful management of his father's accounts that Andrew stayed in London until my brother died."

"So it has not always been this way?"

Martha nodded. "But now many ships do not pass, because of the fear of pirates. Also, Eleanor has taken on even more expensive tastes since her husband's death. The slaves whisper that Andrew has secured a section of his newly bought land for the costs of getting his land ready for a harvest this coming summer."

"Not his land beyond the fall?" Em cried in dismay. "He has spoken so happily of building there for me and the children in time."

"Are whispers that precise? I know not. I only hear the deep pain in his voice and your sadness, and weep that I cannot smooth the way between you two."

Em studied her aunt thoughtfully. Though there had been coolness between herself and Andrew's mother from the first, now Andrew and his mother were similarly held apart. For some reason she didn't even know, Andrew was now barely civil to his own sister Abbie. He came and went from the Springer house like an angry stranger. Without warning she found herself overwhelmed with tears.

"This is unlike you," her aunt protested in dismay.

"I am a weed growing in a fruitful field," Em wailed. "I have brought nothing but dissension into this family. Not only does Andrew's mother hate me, and my child for her name, but she even grows cold toward her son. Now I have spoiled that fine bond that time had set between Andrew and the Toad. If Andrew also loses that land that he loves so dearly, I think I will surely perish of remorse."

"Money and land are mended with different coins," Martha replied. "It is your spirit that must not be struck down. As to Guillam, those men who made that journey to Okracoke know who was in that party even if the governor kept all word of it from the Assembly until the deed was done."

Em raised her head to stare at her.

"There is a trial going on," Martha reminded her. "Much testimony has been given, and many have heard those words."

"The trial," Em whispered to herself. "Aye. Even Edward Teach's quartermaster, Israel Hand, is said to have testified to save his miserable skin."

Martha chuckled. "Was a gentlewoman ever so versed in pirates?"

"Gentle does not refer to soft," Em said firmly. "Pirates have been the principal object of my hate since I first recall.

Beasts they are, and barbarians. To them I lost my Philip and, pray God I be wrong, perhaps my own father too. If they have brought an end to Guillam the Toad, I shall wax hotter than the hell they will be consigned to.''

"You will not be alone. When that crew is hanged in Williamsburg, you may be sure there will not be a spare inch on the street from the Capitol to the college grounds.''

"The hanging.'' Em repeated. She had been a child, with her hand tight in her father's grip, when pirates had been walked in chains through Norfolk. In the end he had lifted her to his shoulder, that she not be trampled like grain. All about rang the boasts of men who had known this pirate at such a place or seen him within on a certain day.

"You have turned very quiet,'' Martha remarked. Then, with astonishment, she queried, "You aren't thinking of risking yourself in that unruly mob at the hanging?''

"What an idea!'' Em laughed, but she did not answer the question.

A white dusting of snow still clung to the fences. A chill wind bit Em's face through the shawl she drew about it. Tansey, her nose scarlet from cold and her eyes streaming, whimpered as Em prodded her along the streets of Williamsburg.

"What of the master?'' the girl had dared to ask when she realized where the chaise was taking them.

Em had withered her with a glance. What of the master indeed? Had he exchanged two words with her at a meal since his return from the Assembly? Had he asked how a day had gone or what the next promised? No, he had left for Candle Creek before the breakfast was laid and returned with the moon as his light. Who knows but that she might have told him her destination if he had asked?

The mob was as great as Aunt Martha had predicted. Try as she might, Em was unable to get herself or Tansey within view of the scaffolds that were to dispatch the thirteen murderous pirates to their appointments in hell. But she knew when the first of them died. A stillness like a great indrawn breath stilled the tumult, followed by such an outcry that Em felt her unborn child leap in her belly.

A sudden terror struck her with weakness. God in heaven, how might such a scene mark this unborn babe? Suddenly filled with panick, she tugged Tansey out of the thoroughfare to the edge of the street. There she leaned, gasping, against the wall of a shop. Resting there, her eyes half closed and fighting for her breath, she listened to the clamor of the crowd. "Blackbeard himself was struck twenty-five times, he was," "... hand to hand they stood, with cutlasses swinging," "... and in the nick of time, a seaman caught the giant's neck with the slice of a knife." Clamor and talk but no hard words, no names of the dead or the wounded. No names of heroes or cowards.

So intent was Em in listening that she did not turn as she heard Tansey being engaged in whispered conversation.

"Your mistress," the voice asked, "is she all right?"

"She only needed a breath of air," Tansey replied. "Thank you kindly."

The voice had ceased by the time Em turned. She saw only Tansey, her face twisted with concern. With the last of the pirates dispatched, the crowd was thinning. Men made their raucous way to the ordinaries, and women disappeared down lanes, with shawls tightly closed against cold.

Tansey seemed about to speak. Before the words came forth, her mouth fell open. She paled as if her own throat had been drawn by hemp. Turning, Em followed her glance and felt her own cheeks lose their color.

He was among a crowd of men who were passing in a group, young men, smartly dressed and in jovial company. As he saw her, his own joviality bled from him. She would have fled into the shop behind her, but it was too late. The fury in his stride as he crossed to her caught the interest of the gaping crowd, which stopped to watch. How much larger he seemed in this place, how much more menacing.

"Well, mistress," he said, his voice as low as his fury would allow. "Can you tell me what business you have here?"

She dared not look at him, for the weakening that came in her limbs when he spoke like this. Yet she had sworn to him to be honest and truthful, and she would not be the one to break that oath.

"I came to see the hanging and to find Guillam the Toad."

"The hanging," he said. "Is this the gentle creature whom I brought to bed as mother and nurse to my children, a bloodthirsty harpy who would venture into this unruly crowd on a bitter day to see the death of men?''

She shivered, not from cold but from the humiliation of that crowd of mocking eyes, the eager ears. She had answered him in truth, and that was sufficient. Lifting her head, she turned, and would have walked away. The grasp with which he seized her arm brought unexpected pain. ''Let me see you to your chaise. Now that the spilling of men's blood is past, there is naught here to entertain you.''

A rising laughter followed as he sped her stumbling feet along the street. Chad leaped from his post as they approached.

''Get this baggage home,'' Andrew ordered. ''And if ever you bring her to such an unworthy place again, I will whip you to shreds, though you be a freeman a thousand times over.''

As Chad fumbled at the reins, Andrew leaned close to Em's face. She had not imagined that such hatred for her could exist, and she stared at him in a kind of wonder. ''As for you, madam, let me never hear the name of that worthless servant on your lips again, or your flesh too may feel the bite of correction.''

In all her years, she had never wept before Tansey. Now there was no help for it. The tears scalded her cold face. Tansey began to moan and then to whimper and finally to mumble frantically to herself, as if to shut from her ears the sound of that helpless sobbing.

''He had no call,'' Tansey muttered furiously. ''And what's wrong with a hanging, be it one or thirteen? Was we, then, the only women there, I ask him? It wasn't any hanging at all that fierced him so, it was where we was, that's what it was, where we was, before that woman's shop that himself can't seem to stay away from.''

Em felt her breath stop and then begin shallowly, so that the words could make sense to her. ''Not the hanging, but where we was.''

''What shop?'' she asked Tansey. ''What woman?''

Tansey would not meet her eyes. ''Who knows?'' She shrugged angrily. ''Some millinery woman and seamstress. They say . . .''

Em turned away. It didn't matter. With what lay between herself and Andrew, one woman more or less seemed a paltry thing.

It was at the door of the Springer house, with a chastened Chad helping her from the chaise, that the day changed. Chad, his seamed face still livid from his public dressing-down, held her arm a single minute longer and nodded close to her face.

"There was other drivers about, mistress, and they talked of the battle."

She froze, her eyes intent on his. He nodded, as if with pride.

"They say he was the bravest of the lot, and much killing of pirates he did. Sore injured he was, too, by knife and gun, but still he lives."

"Gil the Toad?" she whispered, her heart almost too wild for her chest to contain.

"The same," he said, "our Gil."

"But where, Chad? Where is he now?"

He shrugged. "With some woman I know nothing of. Plum, they called her. The widow Mollie Plum."

2

The Right Hand and the Left

And though the Lord give you the bread of adversity, and
the water of affliction, yet shall not thy teachers be removed into a corner any more, but thine eyes shall see thy
teachers:
And thine ears shall hear a word behind thee, saying,
This is the way, walk ye in it, when ye turn to the
right hand, and when ye turn to the left.

Isaiah 30:20–21

WHEN EM HAD been a child in Norfolk, with the fire fluting in
the grate and Philip beside her, her father had read to them
for a long time from Scripture. Even now Em could hear the
soft burr of his accent blending with the words of Holy
writ—the story of Jacob, who was left alone and wrestled all
night, until the day broke. How close she felt to that story
during the days following the hanging of Blackbeard's men.
However, it was no angel that she wrestled, but rather the
demon of temptation. Though she had been tired in her life
before, now she knew exhaustion. She had been downcast
before; now she knew despair. Nothing that she did now
would help; any action of hers would only deepen the chasm
that lay between herself and Andrew.

Yet how could she face her God if she abandoned Gil now.
What had Chad said? ''Sore injured he was, by knife and

gun, but still he lives." While Guillam the Toad lived, Em had no choice but to be his champion, even if it meant plunging herself into the kind of deceit that her nature abhorred.

She knew that Chad would not take her to Williamsburg, and she blamed him not at all. Worse than that, if she were to ask him, the old man, out of respect for his own skin, might report this request to Andrew himself.

In the end she turned to Cece. She intended to be direct, to tell Cece plainly why she needed to accompany her friend on her next trip to Williamsburg. But face to face with her friend, her courage failed, and her words turned to fluttering foolishness of other things.

Cece giggled. "You chatter like one who tells everything but what is on your mind," she chided. "If you have something to tell me, speak it directly. Are we not dear enough friends for that?"

Em felt her cheeks flame, and sighed. "I wished to ask to accompany you to Williamsburg the next time you journey there. I simply couldn't find the right words to ask you."

"That is strange," Cece said thoughtfully. "It is such a simple favor, when you know I enjoy your company."

Em felt Cece's waiting but dared not comment.

Cece leaned over to refill Em's cup. "Very well. I am traveling to Williamsburg Tuesday next. Shall I pick you up a little before two?"

"Oh, no," Em protested quickly. "Chad will bring me here and then pick me up later in the day."

Cece's eyes narrowed. "That way, no one would know that you were apart from this place. Come, Emily, I am wary of what secret you are hiding from me."

"Guillam the Toad," Emily blurted. As Cece listened to the whole of the story, her forehead tightened with concern. "But Andrew did not forbid you to see this man, only that he not be mentioned in his presence or appear in his home?"

When Emily nodded, Cece relaxed. "Then I will not feel ill-used. I could not face Jacob if I took part in any unseemly conspiracy against your husband's wishes. A little before two on Tuesday, then. I shall expect you."

As the carriage rolled toward Williamsburg, Cece asked the question whose answer Emily did not know. "How do you propose to find the widow Plum?"

143

"I can only say that there are not so many souls in the town that she might be unknown. She is a housekeeper to some shop owner. I shall simply ask everywhere."

And everywhere it truly seemed, as Emily tagged after Cece on her errands. She went to the harness maker's for some equipment that Jacob had dropped off to be repaired, to Dr. McKenzie's for herbs and powders for the ailments of Cece's various children. At John Brush's, on the east side of the Palace Green, Emily herself was tempted into purchasing a pistol so fine that she couldn't resist its workmanship.

"Are you conversant with pistols?" Cece asked, smiling.

Em flushed and nodded. "My own father taught me to shoot, even as he taught Philip. In such a port as Norfolk, there is such a dread of pirates that one stays armed."

To Emily's dismay, all inquiries yielded nothing.

"Mollie. Mollie Plum," the clerk at Dr. Blair's store repeated. "There is a Mollie who sweeps around the new milliner's shop, but I've no idea if she is the same."

Cece's mood changed darkly as Em insisted on going directly to the millinery of Mistress Steele. The owner herself came from the back to greet them, a small dark woman with haunting eyes and a face shaped rather like a heart.

"Mollie Plum," she repeated, her eyes full on Em's face. "And what business would you have with this Mollie Plum?"

"I have been told that a person I value is in this woman's care," Emily replied. "I seek to know of his well-being."

"And this friend's name?"

"Guillam," Emily said carefully. "Guillam Jones, also known as Guillam the Toad."

The panic that had thundered in Em's breast as she entered the shop had abated. This was the shop where she had leaned that day to catch her breath. This was the shop of the woman whom Tansey had said Andrew was seeing so often. She was small and young, and lovely in spite of a strangeness in her tone and manner. Em could see her Andrew bewitched by such eyes as hers. But strangely, she did not flame with jealousy. Jealousy is for those who share love. Andrew no longer gave her any share of his.

The elegance of the shop astonished her. Carefully arranged on the shelves were such tempting wares that a woman with a covetous heart might lose her mind here.

"And your name, mistress?" the woman asked, those disturbing eyes still full on her face.

"Emily Rigg," Em replied. "Mistress Andrew Rigg."

There was no change in Mistress Steele's face, not the shadow of a change, but Emily saw her hands tighten into small knots, and for the first time her eyes left Em's.

"And Master Andrew sent you?" she asked.

"Quite the contrary," Em said firmly. "It was I who released Guillam Jones to follow the governor. Because of this, he lost his employ. I feel responsible for him." Then, on impulse, she added, "And I care, for he is a fine fellow and undeserving of his fate."

Em heard Cece's small gasp behind her without heeding it.

The woman glanced at Cece and then at Em before nodding to Emily. "Follow me."

The kitchen house was only a few yards to the rear of the shop. From outside Em heard the prattle of a child and a cozy clanging of pot lids. When the door was flung open, a round-faced girl turned, her cheeks aflame from the fire's heat. The prattle stopped as a toddler stared at them open-mouthed. Beyond them, on a cot in the corner, a man struggled as if to rise.

Em crossed to him swiftly. "Don't, don't," she urged. "Lie still. Oh, Guillam, God be praised that I have found you."

Toad's green eyes seemed to have grown in that thin face stripped of color and flesh.

"Are you healing?" she asked in great concern.

"Thanks to them." He nodded. "And yourself? And the old one, Mistress Springer, and Chad?"

She smiled at him. "Well, all are well, but I need to know of your prospects."

He was clearly embarrassed. "Mollie, here—" he began.

Em interrupted to turn to the girl in remorse. She had not even acknowledged her presence. "You must be the widow Mollie Plum. You cannot know how grateful I am to you for what you have done for Guillam."

The girl's sudden smile was radiant.

"She is Mistress Mollie Jones now," he corrected Em. "With the goods I got from Maynard after the battle, I felt I had the case to marry."

The almost childish brightness in his expression cut into

Em's heart. Poor simple Toad. He was clearly badly injured. Who could promise that he would heal? Yet with his uncertain future, he had taken on the support of wife and child.

"Surely there'll be more," she insisted, "more than some pirate goods."

"That rests with the government," he explained. "They say there'll be no pay for killing Blackbeard, his having come home dead instead of alive."

Oh, God, what wouldn't she give to talk to him of Andrew. He must have read it in her eyes.

"I would have gotten in touch with you," he told her, "but there was word in the street that the master wanted no more of me."

She flushed. Word in the street indeed, and Andrew had said that she had shamed him. What greater shame he brought on himself, with his angry tongue.

She fished in her pocket and emptied it in his hands. "This is a wedding gift from me," she said, "to the both of you. With God's blessing on your union. Should the government prize not be enough to start you fairly, I want to hear of it. We are together in this exile, and I don't intend that you should suffer."

The comfort of that kitchen gave the path outside a sudden bleakness. Emily paused outside the shop door.

"Mistress Steele."

The woman turned gracefully, like something caught in flight, her shawl half off her shoulder.

"It is known to me that my husband frequents this place. Yet he nourishes a great anger for Guillam Jones. How can that be?"

"He frequents only the shop."

"If he were to know I came here, dire consequences would occur."

"You are asking for my protection?" the woman asked as if puzzled.

"Only your silence," Emily replied. "It may be a flaw in my understanding that I believe my devotion to my husband does not alter my responsibility for a man injured more by my fault than his own."

Mistress Steele had stared at her soberly through this careful speech. Suddenly that dark face widened into a dazzling smile. Merriment danced in the dark eyes. The hand she

146

extended to touch Emily's arm was no more than the touch of a moth. In that moment Em felt a sense of remarkable intimacy. From other lips the parroting of her own words would have been mocking. "A fine riddle lies between us, Mistress Emily Rigg. It is a flaw in my own understanding that I believe my great obligation to your husband does not alter my concern for a good man injured in a cause he did not seek."

"Obligation?" Em echoed in confusion.

"I have been under your husband's protection, which he did as a service to my uncle, now dead," she explained. "My uncle, William Elliott, called Younger."

With sudden giddiness, Em caught the lintel of the door. The woman's hands were quick to support her.

"I reveal this private truth for three reasons," she told Em quietly. "I do not wish to be judged the cause of what demon troubles your marriage. Nor do I see you as one who would be shamed that one of Romany blood is also a Lyon." The smile blossomed again. "Most of all, I expose myself that you will know to trust my silence as you would a solemn oath."

"Thank you, Mistress Steele," Em began.

"I am called Magda," the woman replied, smiling as she opened the door into the shop.

"I could have robbed her a thousandfold if I had been of a mind to," Cece pointed out in the carriage. "As it was, a woman came in asking for ribbons, and I sold them as if I kept shop from a child. For heaven's sake, tell me now what went on during the time you spent there. You look a cat whose whiskers are dripping with cream."

Emily laughed softly. "Gil the Toad is married to the roundest little partridge of an Irisher that ever a man slept warm with."

"Emily," Cece cried.

"Don't take on so," Em teased. "If I were your Jacob, I would dance all the way home to see that simple Toad so well nested."

Cece giggled in spite of herself. Her glance turned timid. "I thought you were taking advantage of me when we started toward that shop. There has been talk of your Andrew and the seamstress."

Emily shrugged. "Talk is the only thing left untaxed in this colony. Magda Steele is my friend."

"In that brief time?" Cece challenged.

"Indeed she is, though I did not myself know it until the words were out of my mouth."

"There is something strange about her," Cece said musingly.

"Aye." Emily nodded. "Something strange." Lyon and Romany blood mixed and mingled. Why did that bring such a chuckle to her throat?

The place was set for Andrew as usual, and put away unused, as it commonly was. Em felt no distress at this. She was, however, distressed that Aunt Martha seemed pettish and out of sorts.

"Are you in pain?" Em asked as Martha stirred restlessly in her chair.

"I just feel ingratitude," Martha admitted. "I am so pampered by your care, that a day alone turns me sullen."

"I am back now," Em soothed her, "and not likely to stray again for a while."

"Not in body," her aunt agreed. "But your spirit is in some new and happier place."

Emily laughed. "Let me give you a riddle that I myself cannot untangle, yet it makes me want to chuckle to myself."

Martha shifted a little in anticipation.

"Take the case that there is a woman who is Romany and a Lyon at the same time."

"Romany?" Martha asked in astonishment.

"Young and small and brisk of wit, yet gentle."

"These are details only," Martha protested.

"Who claims William Elliott, called Younger, as uncle."

The old woman stiffened, her mouth unconsciously agape.

"A niece of Younger's? My God, Emily. Benn. A child of Benn's? It must be. Where? By what name?"

"I said I could not untangle it. I only know she is a shopkeeper and seamstress. She calls herself Magda Steele, a name that hides this mystery of our kinship."

"How did you learn this?"

"She trusted me," Emily replied, suddenly sobered by that remembrance. "And I her."

Em knew her words could not make the picture glowing enough, of that warm kitchen and the baby and the rosy-cheeked Mollie, but Martha hung on her words with excitement.

"Does Andrew know?" she asked at last.

"Andrew is her protector. Yet she shelters Gil for his innocence in incurring Andrew's rejection."

"I must meet her one day."

"I will see it done," Em promised. "But no word of this to Andrew."

The old woman sighed. "Secrets are dangerous in a marriage bed."

"Not to one as cold as mine," Emily reminded her.

• 3 •

Dreams and Visions

And your sons and your daughters shall prophesy, your old men shall dream dreams, your young men shall see visions.

Joel 2:28

MARTHA SPRINGER HAD never been able to understand why God sent only one child to Jason and her, when all about them were great families. Grief was added to this mystery when the child died at the age of four. During the time that this mystery gave them no peace, they undertook the design and planting of the formal garden west of the house. Jason himself drew the plan for the maze, where the stone benches would be placed and where the false runs would lure a stranger astray. A single path led into this garden, and, in spite of a dozen false promises, a single path led out.

Even in blindness Martha could walk those paths unerringly, with Emily at her side. From her aunt's smile, Em knew she pictured the leaves verdant in the privet, and the tidy shadows of those lanes. Fortunately, Martha could not read the misery in Em's face. And misery it was. What had seemed a choice to Andrew had been no choice at all to her. One simply could not obey temporal authority that was in violation of God's instruction. Gil the Toad was her responsibility even though this burden meant the death of joy in her marriage.

The garden maze became a symbol of Em's own life to her, an endless repetition of seasons from green to sere, with the promise of blossoms falling from the shears while yet in the bud.

Emily was made of frailer stuff than the old woman at her side, who could even summon laughter into the pain of her blindness.

"There is no night," Martha told her, "that is not somewhere visited with stars."

"You are too brave," Em replied.

Martha shook her head, despairing of explaining her blindness to one who could still see. Her sight had faded like twilight after life's long bright day. A general dimness had cut off first the far landscape and then what lay at hand, until the geography of her own rooms was an exercise in memory.

And yet there were stars.

There was Emily's voice reading. She read gracefully, not with the breathless stumbling of the impatient or the tedious drone of the bored. Passages of scripture that Martha could recite by rote took on new meaning in Em's sibilant voice. She heard the journal of her grandfather, Bennett Lyon, and her mother with renewed delight. Emily, having no memory of Bek Elliott's voice, endowed those words with new emphasis, shedding unexpected light on Bek's thought.

The other star was one that Martha could not put a name to. She found a sight beyond seeing, a soft and shapeless glow that seemed to enter the room with any human visitor. These luminous presences differed, one from another, so that she knew without hearing a voice who shared her space.

With the same singleness of mind that she had applied to the small skills of her life, the culture of herbs and flowers, the perfect carving of a joint, the delicacy of an ornamental stitch, she collected a small body of observations about this phenomenon. What could this be but the glimmering of spirit that set man only a little below the angels?

She realized at once that the purer the spirit, the stronger its light. By the summer of 1719, when Emily's second child was born, Merit was on her feet, stumbling around Martha's room, a firefly dance that Martha could follow with delighted eyes.

"You have the ears of an owl," Em teased. "You never miss a move that child makes."

Martha only laughed, fearing to tell of her discovery, lest the words come forth sounding like witchcraft.

She knew by that same glow that that baby, who was christened Philip, after Em's lost brother, was a sturdy child, fit to be Andrew's son.

The only person whose light glimmered as brightly as a child's was Magda Steele, Benn Elliott's granddaughter.

Martha could not find it in her heart to condemn Emily for such diversions as she could find apart from the loneliness of her marriage. The plantation Andrew had settled beyond the fall line often took him away for many days. It was during one of these absences that Magda Steele first came to visit Emily and Martha.

From Em's words, "Romany and Lyon," Martha knew the girl must be of dark complexion. From the fall of her foot, she guessed her to be frail of form. From the richness of her voice, she knew her to be wise and gentle. The glow of her presence startled Martha into silence.

"Do not let us tire you," Magda said with concern.

"Not fatigue, but delight, stops my tongue," Martha confessed. "Having no sight, I must hold your voice in my mind to know you."

Magda laughed softly. "I will spread my life in my mind for your delectation."

"You love your mother deeply," Martha said, with surprise at her sudden certainty of this. "She still lives?"

"In my heart and mind," Magda replied. "There the beloved never die."

"Was she as clever a seamstress as you?" Martha asked.

"Aye, but much more. She had the gift of our people for seeing hidden things."

Martha fell silent, wishing she dared to tell this girl of the luminous glow that even now blazed in her darkness. Instead, she turned to lightness.

"For such time as mine, there is only the matter of record, there being so little left for my use."

"Your time will stretch through generations, even as your ancestor's time has done."

"My dear," Martha rebuked her. "You speak in riddles."

"Perhaps Magda refers to the family journals I have told her about," Emily explained.

"Perhaps," Martha echoed, again distracted by the brilliance of her consciousness of this Magda Steele.

Once this meeting was past, Magda came whenever Andrew was absent. She brought a soft pillow for Martha's back or a special pudding steamed by Gil's wife. Even when she was away, Em often quoted Magda's puzzling words, as if the girl were an oracle.

"Magda says I will have a son who will achieve fame as a great surgeon," she told Martha.

"Young Philip?" Martha laughed,

"Not Philip," Em told her thoughtfully. "A different son."

Martha pondered these words, wishing she dared ask Magda the questions that made her own heart heavy, about Em and Andrew's harried marriage and about the fate of Em's father, still missing at sea. Yet such foreknowledge was forbidden by scripture and not to be sought by one of faith such as herself.

Throughout the year since Robbie Fraser's *Lark* had appeared under a black flag, it had been sighted again and again by other masters. Emily kept her vigil alive with faith and the telling of old tales. She found the story of one Alexander Selkirk so comforting that she repeated it over and over, not realizing that Martha now knew it as well as herself.

"He was a sailing master," Em would say, "a Scot, like my father. Being a man of contentious spirit, he fell out with his master. In a fit of spleen he asked to be set off the ship rather than sail farther in such company.

"His master set him ashore on a small island called Más a Tierra in the Juan Fernández Islands, leaving him there with neither shelter nor supplies." At this point, triumph rose in Em's voice.

"Don't you see, Auntie? The facts of such a tale prove that even a marooned man can be saved. Four years and four months later, the privateer Woodes Rogers was sailing around the world and picked up this Selkirk, returning him safely to England. Such a rescue could come to my father too, any day, any time."

But the seasons turned to years, and no word came. Young Philip drew his bulky body to his feet, and Merit became a babbler and a singer of songs. At last Emily stopped retelling the story of Alexander Selkirk, refusing to read even the story of this man, now printed in a book, with the Scot's name changed to Robinson Crusoe.

Each time the *Merit* returned to Norfolk, Bruce Forrester came with fine gifts and good news of the growth of the Fraser business. Em asked him about his family, which grew apace, and endless questions about the sightings of the *Lark*. Always he was forced to say of her father, "No word. No sign."

In the spring of 1722 the question she put to him was a new one.

"Is it possible that my father's business has need of a man who knows the seas and ships even though he walks with a bad limp?"

"A man of the sea," Forrester mused. "Such a man would be very useful if he could be trusted. With such growth as we see now, the local affairs are shifted from one hand to another in my absence."

"This man has small skill at reading and none at writing," she added.

Forrester shrugged. "If he but knows ships and cargoes and is able to read the souls of men, he would be of value."

"That was my hope," she told him. "I refer to Gil the Toad."

Forrester leaned forward with excitement. "One such as Gil the Toad need not know one end of a quill from another."

Emily smiled. "Then it is as good as done. I will let the house in Norfolk for the use of him and his family if you have such a situation for him."

His eyes asked the question his lips dared not speak.

"If God should spare my father and he returns, he would relish sharing his quarters with Gil and Mollie and their young. But in truth, Bruce, I have at last yielded my hope to time."

Martha rocked silently for a long time after Forrester left.

"Something Magda said turned my mind about," Em told her. "She spoke of Uncle Younger's death with a strange phrase."

"Magda turns strange phrases," Martha agreed.

"He had reaped the whole of his harvest, she told me, and put his last lamb into shelter. As she spoke I remembered my father's last visit and his pride in Andrew and me and this Merit of ours. I was his last lamb, and he thought me in good shelter."

That night the old woman lay wakeful, her clouded eyes searching an inner darkness. "What harvest remains that I should gather?" she asked herself. "What lamb strays out of shelter?" More lives that she loved slept under stones than trod their surface, and yet she wakened daily to darkness, by God's choosing, not her own.

Certainly not by her own choosing. She pressed the backs of her hands against her streaming eyes. "Help me," she prayed. "Guide me. Take me."

Merit was a restless sleeper. Em's last precious task of every day was to untangle her from her linens and lay the rosy arms back under their warmth. She always stood for a moment, studying that face, which had her own mouth but the dark winged brows of her father. This child and Philip were lambs that held her to reluctant life. She sighed as she turned away.

—— • 4 • ——

An Inheritance of Wind

(May 1722)

He that troubleth his own house shall inherit the wind: and
the fool shall be servant to the wise of heart.

Proverbs 11:29

THE SAME DRIZZLING May sky that boded so well for the spring
planting brought a great unhappy outcry from the women of
Candle Creek. Old saws about weddings and weather were
quoted ominously even as the cakes were baked for the
marriage of Ruth Horne, the oldest daughter of Abigail and
Nat Horne.

All concern was in vain, for the day rose in splendor. The
nearest thing to a cloud in that blue-lidded day was the drift
of blossoms decorating the orchard beyond the fence.

Custom dictated that Ruth Horne be married from her own
father's parsonage among a gathering of friends and family
and the communicants of his parish. Eleanor Rigg of Candle
Creek finally prevailed in her insistence that the family home
on the James River be the setting for the first marriage among
her grandchildren.

In truth, Andrew had given scant attention to the plans that
had been unfolding for months. He had been apprised that his
mother had persuaded Nat to accept a modest dower for his
daughter to carry into the marriage. He was painfully aware

that the fabric of his mother's gown had been brought from France at an exorbitant cost. Of the ceremony itself he thought little, until the parson stilled the fluttering crowd with the opening words from *The Book of Common Prayer*. *"Dearly beloved friends, we are gathered together here."*

The afternoon sun smiled on the face of the river beyond the broken line of trees. Such a bright hue had glittered on that river when those same words had been spoken for himself and Emily just five years before.

Five years. Turning his eyes from that remembered brilliance of his hopes, Andrew studied his wife's face.

She was still beautiful. Aye, she was more beautiful than ever. Her flesh glowed with color, and her hair seemed to trap the sun's own richness. Yet it took no more than the sight of that serene face to start the slow boiling of rage inside him. Fairness dictated that he admit that Emily was not the sole cause of his chronic anger. Rather, it was that his hopes in joy with her had been so unreasonably high.

Five years married. This year would see him turn thirty. "The Wednesday of life," his friend Captain Aaron had called it when Andrew had drunk to his friend's own birthday. "The Wednesday of life, with the best of the week just past."

God help him if this were true. The catalogue of his disappointments was the inventory of his life.

"Blessed be they that fear the Lord; and walk in his ways. For thou shalt eat the labor of thy hands: Oh well is thee and happy thou shalt be."

On those ghost-haunted roads of Devon he had faced the task the Lord had laid on him as head and master of this family. Five years later he saw this family rent by discord, his mother miserable in body and spirit, his sister Sara avoiding her own mother with the same civil coldness with which his mother insulted his own wife. Abbie, for all her seeming gentleness, had eyes more servile than any slave's, haunted by need and want. The only lightness among them came from his Aunt Martha, whose blindness saved her the sight of her family's ruin.

Had ever a man fallen further short of his private ideals?

And in the public arena, had he done better? He had stood for his father's seat in the Assembly, hoping that his time in the study of English law as well as his experience with his

London agent might enable him to make sound contributions to the colony's government. Instead he sat among burgesses more qualified by their readiness to buy these posts by meat and drink than to win them on policy and wit, men whose sole appraisal of a cause was made on the basis of self-interest.

And even as burgesses warred against governor, and governor against the crown, the streets and lanes remained clotted with such brutish felons and criminals that a man was left wakeful in his bed. The avarice of slave traders darkened the faces of the land, even as the duties on the tobacco crop gave a man no choice but to buy these lives.

Yet all this and more he could endure if there were somewhere in his life such a warm place of acceptance as had once existed between himself and Emily.

"Thy wife shall be as the fruitful vine upon the walls of thy house. Thy children like the olive branches around thy table."

His own children stood at Emily's side, graceful Merit, soberly absorbed, Philip, gaping and restless under her restraining hand.

Like all of his line, he knew well the dream of their ancestor Bennett Lyon, who had seen this plantation in Virginia as the fulfillment of the second covenant, a land where a man might dwell and thrive, at peace with God and man. This might yet be, at that fairer land beyond the fall. There at least Andrew had not wasted these years.

His well house boasted water as sweet as new wine. The hams from his smokehouse rivaled those from Candle Creek. The ice house, the stables, the barn, even the smithy, which shared a roof with the cooperage, were worthy of any man's pride. The mill house where his own grain was turned to flour provided him serene quarters when he went there on business with his manager. There was only a great house left to build; yet strangely, he could not imagine it, for all that he had studied drawings and pondered every dwelling that had risen along the river. He had even conferred with an artisan who foolishly claimed, "Commonly it is a woman who can picture what is unseen and describe it for the open."

"He that loveth his wife loveth himself. For never did a man hate his own flesh but nourisheth it and cherisheth it."

Emily's head bent in prayer with that uncommon dignity that drew all men's eyes to her. Was his rigidness as stubborn

157

as her own? Was it his dominion or only his pride that she wounded with her strength?

Andrew found himself so touched by her demeanor that he resolved to move to her side when the service was through. In truth, he had been slow to learn to please her, and the two of them, learning at once, had wasted cruel blows on each other. Four years had passed since she had taken that unwomanly authority over his man Guillam Jones. While he still sorely missed Gil, this wound was not one to be healed by coldness between himself and Emily. And in those years, she had played so sweet a role as loving Christian in his own family. Her tenderness to his blind aunt, her charities to that ingrate Abbie, her supportive friendship to his sister Sara . . . even her long-patient endurance of his mother's ill use. Surely all these had earned her some indulgence for that hardheadness that was more a matter of bad upbringing than a native flaw.

In the rustle of the service's close, he drew to her side. Merit smiled up and slid a hand into his own, while Philip lurched against his knee like a delighted hound. Her eyes were watchful on him, and her lips parted a little as if in waiting.

Before he could speak, a hand caught at his own, and the gruff voice of the captain whose sloop stood beyond the wharf hailed the both of them.

"A fine family you have here, Master Andrew, and a fine marrying we have just seen."

Then he turned to Emily. "What good words all of Norfolk has for you, mistress. It gives a man heart to see that fellow swinging off from your father's house, of a morning. A good man, that." He winked broadly. "It is commonly said that no mischief ever escapes the eyes of that Toad Jones."

Andrew felt his smile stiffen on his lips. There were more flattering words, and the man was gone. Emily's eyes had not left his own, yet there was neither fear nor distress in her expression. A rueful passing respect hit him. God damn the wench; she might be a mighty meddler in the affairs of men and as arrogant as the devil on horseback, but she was no coward. The tribute was short-lived. This was the woman who had promised him honesty and forthrightness. What words would have risen to his lips were silenced by his sister Sara, joining them with a more depressed demeanor than was common to a romantic woman at such an event.

"Tears?" he said to her, trying to force some lightness into his tone. "Tears at a wedding?"

"And tears of joy they are not," she replied, pressing her handkerchief beneath one eye and then the other. "Never have I seen so pretty a girl make so plain a bride. And little wonder that she goes in dread to such a mate as she wed. I had no idea. Mother said—"

"That he was a man of healthy property and sober age," Andrew filled in for her.

Sara glared at him. "She did not mention that he is nearer her father's age than her own, and with half the wit. Not to mention that passel of whining young that he brings from his recent bereavement."

"He is said to be a Christian man, and pleased with his choice," Andrew told her.

"He is pleased to have so young a bride along with the dower, which Mother put wholly into his control," Sara snapped. "The true question is whether little Ruthie loves him."

In spite of himself Andrew felt his eyes drawn toward Emily. The tenderness that had infected him during the service had been swept from him by this new evidence of her scheming.

"Are you proposing that a love match guarantees a joyful union?" he asked his sister in a tone that he hoped sounded bantering.

• 5 •

The Heavy Heart

(January 1724)

Give strong drink unto him that is ready to perish, and wine
unto those that be of heavy hearts. Let him drink, and forget
his poverty, and remember his misery no more.

Proverbs 31:6–7

IN THE MONTHS following Ruth's marriage Em found herself
replaying those moments when she had seen Andrew turn
and walk toward her. Some difference in his expression had
brought hope lunging against the stays of her gown. Then,
even as his lips had parted to speak, the captain from Norfolk
had stepped between them, and then Sara with her heartsickness,
and then the question.

"Are you proposing that a love match guarantees a joyful
union?"

In time that memory of hope, being frailer than his bitterness,
ceased to return, leaving only his words engraved in her
heart.

Along with growing fatigue. Aunt Martha, with neither
night nor day in her world, confused one with the other and
was too restless to pass her wakeful hours alone. For days,
sometimes, the old woman carried on soft conversations with
the beloved and dead. Then, without seeming cause, she
returned to her old self, chipper and warm with laughter.

Whatever the nature of her wakefulness, Em answered the small bell she had tied to her aunt's wrist and read or talked until the old woman nodded with sleep again.

She was always the liveliest when a guest was about. Sara, even in the bustle of marrying off her only daughter, Sally, remained a faithful caller. Abbie and Cece also came, as well as a few of her old friends. Then there was Magda.

Martha was always the most anxious in the small hours before dawn, when she complained that the sins of her life had come to sit on her chest and shorten her breath. "Send for Magda," she pleaded. "Send for Magda; I am going to die."

Twice Em was so frightened by these spells that she indeed sent for the pastor and had her aunt shriven, only to have her bounce back as lively as before.

"The poor love," Em told Magda. "She always asks for you when she thinks she is about to die."

Magda raised her remarkable eyes to stare at Em. "It matters to her?"

"Very much," Em told her. "She loves you very dearly."

"Tell her that I shall be here when she dies," Magda ordered. "Tell her this is a sacred promise between us, that she shall not die without me here."

"Magda," Em cried. "How can I promise her such a thing? She gets to this state in the middle of the night, with no warning at all."

Magda's hand touched Em for a moment, as was her want. "I will be here. Believe me, Em, I will be here."

Strangely, Aunt Martha found this assurance so comforting that the midnight terrors ceased to visit her.

Even as Em grew more tired and worn and the old woman weakened, the children waxed in strength. For a while Merit would grow swiftly, leaving Philip behind, only to have the boy make a great spurt of growth, so that Em could lay a board across their shining heads without its tilting.

By January of that year Merit had learned to spell letters out and race a fat pony around the enclosure by the barn. Philip was swifter than she in any task that fell to hand or heel but was a laggard in learning his letters and numbers. Em began to think it time for a tutor to be brought. But like all things that must be discussed with Andrew, she put this off because of the discomfort of their communication.

For if she and Andrew had been enemies before Ruth Horne's wedding, that day turned them into strangers. In a most offhand way, he told her she might feel free to go anywhere she wished, by any means at her command, as long as she did not take along his children without a proper guard.

Aside from this he said less than nothing.

It was Cece who reported the rumors of a slave insurrection. Andrew came home and went to his work at Candle Creek and to his place beyond the fall line without a word.

But Cece told Em that Williamsburg had been chartered a city and that Virginia's new governor, Hugh Drysdale, was a fine and gentle man. There were celebrations and parties, but Andrew did not invite her company. His mother fell ill, and Em learned of it only through his sister Sara.

"She maintains that she is in great pain," Sara told Em. "But she has become such a great creature for nostrums that I wonder that the pain does not come from some war among the physics and squills and opium and bark with which she punishes her poor old body."

Abbie told a different tale. "Our poor mother's strength is waning. Though I am with her as much as I can be, with my other duties, she is very lonesome for her family."

"Sara goes to visit her, and she has many servants," Em reminded her. "Andrew is there every day that he is not beyond the fall line at his other land."

"Andrew is cold and lacking in understanding," Abbie told her. "Sara is not much more gentle, for all that she is a woman and my own sister. Mother needs young lives about to cheer her."

"You have more of those than any of us to share," Em said.

Abbie frowned. "Nat will not let our girls go there. He's afraid Mother will marry them off as she did Ruth." She shrugged. "So they stay about, learning little and caring less."

"I have been intending to speak to Andrew about a tutor for Merit and Philip," Em told her. "It would be so nice if the little ones, at least Dorothy and Lucinda, could come to study with their cousins."

Abbie's face lit with excitement. "Would that be possible? Oh, what a joy it would be to have them read and cipher. Even Nat would agree to that much education for the girls."

"More baskets are discarded for being empty than for being full," Em said. "I will talk to Andrew about it right away."

But as Em feared, the subject brought the swift undercurrent of Andrew's rage boiling into words.

"I suppose you have selected some Calvinist, that they might be indoctrinated with your own stern joylessness."

She breathed deeply and chose her words with care. "My concern is only that he be honest and clean and well versed in classics."

"A Huguenot, then," he suggested. "They are stern bigots, and common in the trade."

"I am only concerned about learning and the happiness of the children," she said, turning away.

Each of these confrontations deepened her despair. Life was indeed the maze garden with a single path in and a single path out and the blossoms shorn off between. She remembered what Magda had said of Younger Elliott's death and thought of her own. Her debt to Gil the Toad was clearly paid, from the glowing reports she received from Bruce Forrester. The children would grow and have small need of her. There was only Aunt Martha left among her lambs before she might be granted the key to the path that led beyond this place to peace.

It was late in January of 1724 when word came that two soul-drivers were to be in Williamsburg with a parcel of indentures, some artisans and educated men among them. Andrew rode to Williamsburg to seek a tutor from among this number.

In spite of herself, Em waited with eagerness for his return. When he did not come at twilight or by the time she had read the evening prayers with Aunt Martha and the children, she made her lonely way to bed. She would have thought that he might share any news he had gathered, when the matter concerned their children.

She had read so deeply in the Lyon journal that passages came back to her mind without her even willing them. Passages from it, quoted by Bek Rigg as spoken by her husband Bruce, caused her pillow to be damp with tears.

"Loving and giving are both curious businesses. For each you must have one to do the act and the other to receive."

She did not know how long she slept before she felt rude

163

hands upon her body. The stench of wine made her gasp. She struggled in terror against those imperative hands, and would have screamed, except for the hand clapped roughly across her face.

"Is this, then, a husband's welcome?" Andrew asked angrily.

He was drunk, painfully, hopelessly drunk. The fury with which he possessed her exhausted even her will. Helpless tears flowed by the time he wrested his weight from her.

"Now, that is a wife," he scoffed, turning away, "soft and loving and bleating." His words fell off into a drunken mutter and the course breath of snoring.

She rose and cleansed herself and curled against the chimney, wrapped in a blanket. With the coming of dawn, she observed her flesh with amazement. How could a soul be so painfully wounded and the flesh not give witness?

He wakened her staring down at her. For a fleeting moment she thought penitence softened his face. He turned away too swiftly for her to be sure.

"Forgive my precipitate invasion of your body, madam," he said. "If memory serves me, it gave me as little pleasure as it did you. Consider it as, not a resumption of our lovemaking, but rather the crazed action of a wounded beast."

At her puzzled glance he began to dress with awkward hands.

"Wounded," he repeated. "I am wounded and you are wounded, and perhaps our children and their blood the most of all. Wounded and outcast. God help us Englishmen who are so far removed from the heartbeat of our prince."

"What has happened?" she asked, stunned to see such fury unleashed on any but herself.

"We have been betrayed by those we trusted. We have been given a stick that breaks in our hand, a gun that is not drilled for powder. What has happened? The House of Burgesses is a farce. A proclamation was being cried in Williamsburg today repealing our law of two years past against the flooding of this land with the offal of English prisons. We are the kennel into which London and Bristol and such hellholes will dump their human slime. Our laws are pieces of paper to tear into shreds at their convenience. God help Virginia. God help America."

Em stared for a long time at the door he closed behind himself. How greatly he loved England, and how sturdily he had defended it against the pratings of self-centered Virginians who had forgotten whose land they tilled.

Poor Andrew, she found herself repeating.

She even forgot the nature of his errand to Williamsburg in her distress over his unhappiness.

• 6 •

Mighty Waters

(1724)

Behold, the Lord hath a mighty and strong one, which as a tempest of hail and a destroying storm, as a flood of mighty waters overflowing, shall cast down to the earth with the hand.

And the glorious beauty, which is on the head of the fat valley, shall be a fading flower.

Isaiah 28:2, 4

BY APRIL EMILY could no longer deny to herself that she was with child. Her first reaction was shame, which came from the manner in which the seed had been set in her body. Then came the harrowing sorrow. Innocent though the soul of this child be, its life was nothing to her but an anchor pinning her to a bleak and joyless existence. She felt none of the tenderness that had surged at the quickening of Merit and Philip, only resentment. She found a guilty comfort in the thought of how many women had found death in childbed. She wondered if God could forgive her for wishing such a fate for herself and this unborn babe.

Once knowing, she carried her secret silently. The burden of nursing Aunt Martha had stripped her to such leanness that it was summer before the child was evident to other eyes.

In spite of her most modest attempts to conceal herself, she felt Andrew's eyes thoughtful on her.

"Well, madam," he said briskly, "let us both pray that this creature is not born with the anger of its begetting."

She turned away, eyes awash with tears.

At least the children were profitably occupied that summer. Within a fortnight of Andrew's fatal visit to Williamsburg, a young man appeared at the door riding a dark mare from the Springer stables and leading a bay gelding loaded with gear.

"I am Edwin Godwin, for the most part called Ned," he announced with a jerky little bow and a smile. "I am he who was signed on by Master Andrew Rigg for the tutoring of his children."

Aunt Martha summoned her dwindling strength to smile warmly in his direction. Em herself was delighted. Within a month he had Philip puzzling the pages along with his sister. Within two months the lad was contesting against Merit's skill as hotly as he did in feats of strength.

In spite of her fatigue, Em could not help noticing the beauty of that summer. The crops the year before had risen poorly. This season the earth seemed to push the green up. Garden rows elbowed one another. Bees sang daylong along the herb rows. Ned Godwin quoted the overseer as saying that the Indian corn had never stood so high so early in the season. The grapes strained the wood of the arbor, and the melons grew to remarkable size.

It came to Em that Ned would be a great comfort to Philip and Merit if she herself were to be taken from them. Andrew equipped a small frame house for their school, and from it came the comfortable droning of their study. Sometimes Ned cajoled the cook into giving them baskets of breads and sweetmeats for lunch, which they ate in the woods while he taught them the names of birds and flowers. Since the same sun that promised the welcome harvest brought sweltering days, Ned often took the children from their schoolhouse to study in the shade of a walnut tree where Philip's dog lay drowsily beside them.

On the morning of August twelfth, Em was awakened early by the faint tinkle of Aunt Martha's bell. Although only the

166

faintest light illumined the room, Martha sat stiffly upright, her usually amiable face tight with confusion.

"Caroline?" she asked when Em entered.

Em sighed at this evidence of her aunt's wandering mind. Her sister, Caroline, had been dead these fifty years.

"It is I, Emily," she replied, offering her cheek for an embrace.

"A storm is coming," Martha whispered. "Another such storm."

"This is the season for great gusts," Em reminded her.

Martha shook her head. "Like the other," she insisted, "Like the other."

Em soothed her and sent for tea, saddened by this trip back through memory to the great hurricane that had changed the lives of all Martha's family. But indeed the air held great weight, heavier than she could ever remember. Nothing stirred beyond the window, not a blade of grass or a fluttering leaf. At this hour, when the birds generally held riot in the garden and orchard, the world lay still.

When breakfast was finished, Ned rose with a smile. "I will be fortunate to get anything to stick in these two small heads today," he told her. "They are sluggish as hounds gasping for a cooling breath."

"It must get better," Em told him. "This is too sullen a day not to change."

She fought the same lethargy in her own swollen body. She had even taken to her bed for an hour, when Tansey called from the passage.

"Mistress Magda," the girl cried. "You startled me. I did not hear you coming."

Magda's warm laugh was reassuring. "I startle myself," she said, "being abroad on such a day."

Em rose swiftly. Never before had Magda come without notice. Never had she come except when Andrew was upriver, yet there she stood in the passage, the sobriety of her face belying her bantering tone in speaking to Tansey.

Wordlessly Magda drew Em close, even as the first low rumble of thunder began in the distance.

"The storm," Em whispered. "Aunt Martha spoke of storm."

"Let me go to her," Magda said. "You will be needed by the servants."

The fear began with Magda's silent greeting. It mounted as Em passed to the kitchen under the heavy hazy sky. She gave swift directions, sending Chad to the stable to secure the stock and have the slaves called in from the fields. She thanked God fervently that the children were in that secure place, with Ned to soothe their fears.

Halfway down the passage Em realized that Magda was bringing Aunt Martha downstairs. The old woman's cap was askew, but her face was unseamed by concern.

"She is here," Martha told Em brightly. "She promised, and she is here."

"No," Em would have cried, but the sound stopped in her throat. The light was fading even as the clock told noon. Turning to the door, Em stared at the sky. A darkness bubbled along the horizon like a thick sauce, boiling and raging, with tongues of color darting from its great mass. Somewhere a servant began to scream, a high, shrill screech that did not waver but only caught now and then for breath before being torn again from that frantic throat.

"Where is safety?" Em shouted above the sudden clamor of thunder. The windows of the house rattled as stabbing bolts of lightning struck and crackled and hissed.

If Magda answered, Em did not hear her. Magda gently kept Martha moving until she was seated in her familiar chair beside the open Bible. The howling of the wind and tumult of thunder seemed not to affect the old woman. She simply clung to Magda's hand, her face serene.

With the wind came rain, a sweep of giant drops that swelled into a downpour. Within minutes a lake had formed outside the stoop and was rising toward the sill. Slamming the door and wedging carpets against it, Em hastened to the back of the house to stem the tide there.

It was from the back door that she saw the gust of wind catch at the roof of the schoolhouse, lifting it like a lid. Terror tore through her.

"Merit," she screamed. "Philip. Ned."

A single step from the door plunged her into swirling water that dragged at her skirts. Curled against the wind, she forced herself toward the schoolhouse by clinging to a post here, a fence there. Sometimes she found herself dragged down, barely able to find footage again. "Merit," she screamed. "Philip."

She could not breathe, with the pelting rain cutting the very air from her throat. When she finally reached the house, she dragged herself inside.

The schoolhouse was empty.

An overturned stool rose on the water that rushed across the floor. The window was a waterfall. A book she recognized as Merit's skidded across the tilting table to dive into that turgid water. The howl of the wind was like the cry of demons. As she struggled to rise, using the table as a brace, Em saw the uneven line of the roof change and heard a rending sound. The roof wholly lifted and skated from the wall, leaving her fully exposed to the driving force of the rain. Even as she heard that wrenching noise, Emily felt the slice of pain down her own belly. "No," she screamed, struggling against the whirling eddies dragging her down. "No. Please, God. *No*."

It was no use. She was lowered by the power of the child thrusting, thrusting. Twisting in that agony, knowing her screams were lost in the howl of the wind, she heard Aunt Martha's voice speaking of Grandma Bek. "The curse of answered prayers. The curse of answered prayers."

The Shadow

(August 1724)

Man that is born of woman is of a few days, and full of
trouble. He cometh forth like a flower, and is cut down: he
fleeth also as a shadow, and continueth not.
And dost thou open thine eyes upon such an one and
bringest me into judgment with thee?
Who can bring a clean thing out of an unclean? not one.

Job 14:1–4

EM WAS NEVER to know how long she lay swimming with her
dead child in the flood of the wrecked schoolhouse.

Her consciousness came and went through the endless pounding of the storm and the slow ice that seemed to sliver into
her bones. Then she found herself dry, with fiery brandy at
her lips and Magda's dark eyes close to her own.

"Aunt Martha," Em cried, trying to rise. "The children."
Magda's hands were firm, to keep her from rising.

"The children are safe and warm," Magda told her. "Your
aunt will suffer no more."

Em stared at her. "You can't mean that."

Magda's face was puzzled. "I told her I would be here,
Emily. Didn't you realize why I came?"

A shiver passed along Em's spine. Only then did she
remember the baby and pass her hands over her flattened
belly.

"Take this as God's favor to you," Magda said.

Em was fearful of probing the meaning of those words.

"Andrew?" she asked.

"He sent a servant to say he would be here as soon as he could leave his mother."

The sheets of rain against the window were like waves pounding against a seawall. The baby and Aunt Martha. Aunt Martha and the baby.

"She smiled at the end," Magda told her. "She smiled and told me that the last of her lambs must find her own way home. She even closed her own eyes in waiting, Emily. It was her will to die."

Through that long siege of tears that swept over Em, Magda held her. Her flesh smelled of spice. The cold center of Em's bones warmed within the circle of those arms.

But the rain did not cease.

Andrew came, pale and haggard. His words formed a recitation, given flatly, without emotion. The slaves had panicked and left his mother alone. Illness had struck her in the midst of her frantic fear. Abbie's daughter was with her now, along with the overseer's wife. The corn was gone, the tobacco ruined, the piglets drowned in the flood. The house still stood, but a vessel blown inland from the river had torn half the orchard away.

"They tell me that Magda Steele was here," he said, "that it was she who dressed our child for burial along with my cherished aunt."

"You are richly blessed in your kinsmen," Em told him.

He only stared and turned away.

The rain did not cease.

What could not be moved to high ground was lost. Since fires could not be built in the dependencies, the servants ate cold food and slept in the lofts on wet hay.

The rain still did not cease.

On the fifth day Em lay watching her children amuse themselves with darts and a board as the rain sheeted down the windowpanes. Merit noticed the thunder first and sighed in the manner of a person whose patience is wholly exhausted. "There it comes again," she said tiredly.

The delicate warning of distant thunder grew louder as the sky boiled into darkness. What had been spared by the first gust was lost in the second.

When those howling hours were past, Andrew came and sat by his wife, his eyes dark holes in a slack face.

"This was too much for Mother," he told Em. "One side of her has gone stiff now. Her eye droops, and she makes no sensible sounds."

"What does her doctor say?" Em asked. It was Andrew's rueful joke that he knew the best thoroughbred horse in Virginia belonged to his mother's doctor, because he himself had paid the toll for it.

"He says she will live, by the grace of God, but she will never rise again to walk. Nor will she speak."

8

The Wind Passeth

(1724–1730)

Teach us what we shall say unto him; for we cannot order our speech by reason of darkness.
And now men see not the bright light which is in the clouds: but the wind passeth, and cleanseth them.

Job 37:19, 21

FROM THE DECK of the *Lark,* coming out of Plymouth that October of 1716, Andrew Rigg had watched the stars find a second gleaming in the smooth sea as he listened to Captain Robbie Fraser speak of his daughter, Emily.

"An antique virgin," he had called her. "Past the age and softness for marriage. A woman strong in ways not often found in women. I know no man who could take the dictates of her stern God, nor do I know such a man as could come between her and that God.''

Robbie's words were to echo in Andrew's mind over and over in the years following the great gusts of 1724. During the six-score years since Virginia had been planted, hurricanes had often boiled from the sky to lay waste to the land and habitations of these Englishmen. Yet no account had ever come of two such hurricanes' striking within a week of each other. But the work left in the wake of these was always the same: walls to be raised, crops to be cleared from the field and replanted and dead to be buried.

Until the house at Candle Creek was repaired for use, Eleanor Rigg abided with her daughter Sara, alternating between spells of tearful weakness and incoherent rage. By autumn she was installed in her own room at Candle Creek, to be attended by a procession of servants who flew to her at the sound of her bell, and then ran tearfully away from her babbling wrath. Since every morsel must be fed by another's hand, and she took only what she willed, all of her wasted away but her fury. Her once-beautiful face was a parchment skull, her hands such claws that her rings had to be locked away.

When Emily's strength returned after the loss of her child, she proposed to Andrew that their family move into the old home with his mother, so that Em could oversee her care.

''What in the name of God put that in your head?'' Andrew challenged.

''God,'' she replied, her eyes calm on his.

Andrew felt an unaccountable anger rise at the idea. Jason Springer's will had given Martha, his wife, the privilege of bequeathing the Springer plantation to whom she pleased. Having inherited it himself, Andrew saw no cause for Emily to leave a place in which she had lived during the seven years she had cared for his aging aunt. What he should have said of this had gone so long unspoken that it had become unspeakable. How could he tell her now that he had not married her to make her handmaiden and nurse to the aging and ill of his clan?

''I'll be damned if I will see you martyred to one who has treated you so ill.''

Did he imagine the tug of a grin at her mouth?

"No, Andrew," she corrected him. "It is I who will be damned if I don't."

In the end, of course, the move was made. Captain Robbie Fraser had been more accurate about Emily than Andrew had thought him. Strong she was, and in ways that went beyond womanliness. And no man lived, Andrew was convinced, who could stand between her and her stern God. During those years, there were times that he couldn't bear to look at her face for fear that the fatigue written there would break his heart. But their differences held his comforting hand from hers at the same time that he privately suffered agonies of grief and remorse.

Yet no shadow of her trials fell on the children. They were so cheerful and had such zest that Andrew had to fight his immodest pride in Merit's charm and Philip's prowess. The new schoolhouse droned with the voices of Abbie's young as well as his own children and a few from neighboring plantations. With Ned Godwin's indenture past, he was master of this school, which became a credit to his name as well as Andrew's.

By 1730 Andrew and Em's uneasy truce following the hurricanes had sufficiently mended Andrew's old wounds that he could look at Emily with something akin to wonder. She had made of his banished servant, Gil the Toad, an overseer of the Fraser operations in Norfolk, a man of property, respected by the community. She had welded with his Romany cousin, Magda, an intimacy so great that they seemed able to converse without stirring the air with words. Over the great obstacle of his brother-in-law Nat's pride, she had managed to keep his sister Abbie's daughters properly fed and clothed, and had even seen that their minds were developed more than was common for women.

If Em knew that it had been Abbie, in her desire to curry favor with his mother, who had told Eleanor Rigg that the misnaming of the child Merit was purposeful, there was never a sign of it in her treatment of her sister-in-law.

Yet all this Andrew had seen without having the slightest notion of what thought moved behind the eyes still watchful on his own.

The assembly was summoned to two sessions in the spring of 1730. The second one extended from the end of May into

the second week of July. Andrew could not remember a
session that had raised higher hopes in his heart. Not only had
Governor Gooch been able to forge a Tobacco Act, providing
for warehousing and inspection, that would cut back on fraud
and give the planters some chance to control supply, but the
group had even pressed through a policy making it illegal for
a profit-making office-holder to sit in the assembly.

He returned to Candle Creek on the tenth of July with an
easy heart. Standing quietly, a man could almost hear the
Indian corn rustle as it grew. Oxen lowed in contentment; the
orchard trees leaned on their braces, heavy with bounty.
Philip's dog had filled the stable with a squirming nest of
rolling pups.

Only Andrew's mother seemed frailer, her flesh translucent.

"I am long overdue to see to the affairs upriver," he told
Em with hesitation. "I need to be gone a fortnight at least."

"Your mother has failed before, only to rally with the turn
of a moon," she reminded him. It had been six years since
his mother had been trapped in her prison of rebellious silence.
The passage of that great a time span had toughened him to
her predicament.

Yet as he passed upriver in high anticipation of being on
that land he had learned to love so well, he wondered, as
always, where Emily's mind could go to find such sweet
release.

Emily's move to Candle Creek had not been an easy step.
She knew she was unwelcome there, no matter what gift of
service she brought by coming. Eleanor Rigg's attitude toward any gift from her hand was already there for any eye to
see. The single crowded shelf by the hearth held all the gifts
that Emily had ever brought or sent. This mute and dusty
testament of Eleanor Rigg's rejection of her was as clear as
her refusal to take a spoon from Emily's hand.

And having undertaken the duty with disheartened obedience to what she felt was God's will, Emily was astonished to
be rewarded with a new and glorious door's opening into her
life. She became familiar with Candle Creek, which made its
way to the James River through a grove of graceful trees,
sheltered a limpid pond and turned the wheel of the old mill.
The words in Bek Lyon's journal came alive for her in a new
way as she watched the dragonflies hover above the water and

saw the seasons change as generations of wild things interwove their lives in that place. The pain of Martha Springer's death was eased by frequenting the haunts Martha had loved as a child.

For in her simple, hand-written will, made while her sight was still with her, Martha had left the Lyon journals to Emily Fraser Rigg, with the admonition that when it was time for her to pass them on, she should consider, not blood alone, but also the spirit of the new owner. Perhaps it was this that had led Emily to search her own heart and find in it her responsibility to the pitiful creature who watched her come and go with baleful eyes.

And she drew comfort from Magda, whose quick eyes had noted the shelf of Emily's gifts on her first visit.

"What an elegant store," she said, rising on tiptoe to study them carefully. "Why, this legend is in your hand!"

"Aye," Emily said, without looking up from her work.

"All of them are writ in your hand," Magda continued, turning to her. "Even these that have become damnified by age."

"Aye," Emily agreed, nipping a thread with her teeth. As it did so often, Bruce Rigg's comment on loving and giving came back to her mind, but she said nothing.

"Spite is a knife that only cuts the hand of its possessor," Magda commented, finding a seat by Emily.

"In time that is true," Emily agreed. "But only after a long time."

Andrew had been gone from home for four days when his mother's illness took the turn. She seemed to lose all need for sleep, refused food from any hand and shook her head fiercely at whatever anyone said. The babbling attempt at talk, which had dwindled with the years, returned tenfold. Tears leaped to Em's eyes to see the desperation with which the pitiful old woman was trying to communicate with all of them.

Feeding her had always been the most difficult chore, since the old woman had only to seal her lips. There was nothing left but to lay violent hands upon her and force-feed her, as was done to the slaves in the middle passage. Emily would not permit this violence to the old woman's person, which led to endless cajoling and a patient persistence until hunger overwhelmed Eleanor Rigg's resistance.

On the sixth day of Andrew's absence, Emily's mother-in-law had gone two days and a night without sustenance. Darkness was settling in the room as the unhappy servant offered, first tea, then soft wheat bread with butter and finally a dish of fresh, sugared berries. Eleanor reacted with a tight-lipped shaking of her head and furious eyes on Emily's face.

"She wants you," the girl said at last.

Emily drew near with hesitation, only to have that claw of a hand seize her apron urgently. Em offered the tea, with the same response. When she held out the bread, such a frantic babbling ensued that Emily frowned with confusion.

"Do you want more butter?" she asked. Tears coursed down the old woman's cheeks as she shook her head.

"Do you want a sweet on your bread?"

To Emily's astonishment, the old woman nodded frantically and jerked on her apron.

"Could she want some sweet of your making, mistress?" the girl asked from the growing darkness behind Em.

Em turned to stare at her.

"From that shelf that Cook calls Emily Fraser's shelf," the girl explained.

When Eleanor Rigg's frantic nodding affirmed the girl's guess, the girl flew from the room and down the stairs, to return with a crock of Emily's own pear honey.

A wave of emotion shuddered the length of Em's body as she spread the amber sweetness on the bread and held it forth. The old woman's lips tugged at it with a pitiful eagerness. All the while those eyes, the one wide and rheumy and the other half-lidded, stared up at Em as if in supplication.

"Do you want to tell me something?" Em whispered.

When she nodded, Emily sighed. "Oh, I do wish that I could read your desire in your eyes."

The movement of Eleanor Rigg's hand off the coverlet was so irregular that it caught the edge of the tray, sending the cup of warm tea into a dark fan over the white linen. But the hand jerked to Em's cheek for a momentary caress before it fell back.

There was no way that the tears could be stayed. Emily

leaned and caught Eleanor Rigg's face in her hands and pressed her own cheek against that bony one, holding it there for a long tender moment.

"It might have been by chance," Emily told Sara with humility, "it must have been by chance that her spirit left her even as we embraced. I only know that when I drew away, there was no sight left in her eyes, and she had ceased to breathe."

Sara wept inconsolably. "How much easier it would be if we had parted friends. I tried. God in heaven knows I tried, but at last I could not be party to her schemes, hold silent at her treatment of you and Andrew and continue to face my God. I had no choice but to abandon her, Emily. I had no choice." Then she paused. "Andrew must be told. Let me send—"

"No," Emily interrupted firmly. "I shall tell Andrew myself."

"But he's upriver," Sara protested.

"I can reach him as quickly as any other messenger," Emily reminded her, stilling her protests with a shake of her head. "All the arrangements here can be done best by you and Abbie. What I have to say to Andrew can come from me alone."

Emily, who had been close to the sea all her life, still found it remarkable that the same great tide that carried men to the wide world could be tamed to the banks of the James River for all these miles. No forests could be more beautiful than those that lined these shores, no habitations appear more warmly inviting than those that rose beyond their lawns and gardens and wharves along her way. The river gradually narrowed from the seven-mile width at its mouth to less than a mile, garnished with outcroppings of rocks and islands crowned by trees.

The falls, which had been only a word to her, were cascades of light and thunder chiming against the melody of racing water. Only past the falls did Emily's heart tighten within her. It was one thing to know that this duty was hers. It was another and different task to know how it need be done.

As the craft veered from the channel, she eyed the shore warily. This was no extension of the wilderness she had passed. A mill wheel sent out shattered prisms of light as it ground busily by its dormered millhouse. The gardens and fields spoke of loving husbandry. A lazy column of smoke rose from one house, while from another came the clamor of hammer against anvil. This might be a village, were it not for the great space in the center, where a half-grown crop of Indian corn moved restlessly in the wind.

When the craft touched the wharf, the work ceased in the nearest field. A man stepped from the millhouse to shade his eyes with his hand for a better view of who approached.

She watched him walk toward her. So warm was the day that no thread of her clothing was free of dampness, yet her hands, woven one into the other, had the feel of ice. Perhaps he too was conscious of those myriad eyes that watched from field and garden and cooperage. In any event, he took her hand and leaned over it gallantly in greeting.

"You come on no common errand," he suggested.

At her nod, he tucked her hand in under his arm, guiding her to the millhouse he had come from.

"Then relieve me at once," he said, his eyes on the path ahead.

Magda's words came back to her, the words with which she had announced the loss of Aunt Martha.

"Your mother suffers no more pain."

He stopped still in the path. "At peace with God?"

"And man," Emily added after a moment.

He turned and stared at her. "And what of woman?"

She nodded, suddenly so weak as to be near to tears. He supported her until they were inside the privacy of the millhouse. Then she rested against his chest as his hand moved tentatively to her hair.

"What a stern God you serve, wife of mine," he said softly. "How dearly he must love you to make your path so hard."

"For all that I have given, I have received," she told him.

He was very still against her. Then, pulling away, he brought wine and poured a glass for each of them.

"Is our quarrel between your God and mine or the styles of our service?" he asked thoughtfully.

"The God is the same, I think," she finally decided. "And who is to be blamed if we read his words from a differing angle of light?"

179

"You have dragged me nearer your altar by your stubbornness than all the exhorters in the world could have done," he admitted.

To have his voice gentle to her, in this quiet room with none to hear, to feel the warmth of the wine after the feared arrival, these were such wonders that Em found herself laughing softly.

"And you have drawn me nearer to the love of life in these few minutes than all the bishops in the world could have persuaded me."

He sat down by her, his hand warm on hers.

"It is this place, this new Eden."

She shook her head. "There is no bower."

"The woman would have bowers." He laughed, rising to his feet. "Come and show me where the bower should be placed, and I will show you your error."

The wheel turned beside them as she spoke, the droplets chiming from it into that deep pool. The field of corn had changed color with the tinging of sunset.

"There," she said, pointing. "It should stand there, with the angle half against the setting sun. It must be of brick—brick of whatever clay this land yields, with two full stories, trimmed by windows here and there. The doorway will be one in which four can pass abreast. Now, at the ends of the house, on both sides, set back a few yards—"

"Stop at once," he ordered, laughing. "You might lose your inspiration before it can be trapped on paper." Then he turned serious. "You would live with me in harmony in this new Eden?"

The time would come when she must make the confession. Through all that had passed between them, she had yet to break that pledge of honesty. This was a poor time to hold back truth.

"I have been readying for a different existence for ever so long," she told him.

He studied her. "A different existence? Have you loved life so little, Emily, my wife?"

Her words faltered. Pressed against her mind were images, Merit's voice raised in song, Philip's lusty laughter, Magda's eyes warm with mystery, the shores of the James River and the secret humming world of Candle Creek, Andrew's own face half lit by candle as he pored over a book, the rumble of frogs and the high, peeping shrill of their cousins.

She nodded. "But is it possible that on my way to death I have learned to love life?"

His smile was indulgent. "That could be everyman's story."

The overseer's wife, solicitous because of their great loss and extravagant with apologies for the fare she served, brought them a meal to share privately in Andrew's quarters in the millhouse. Emily could not remember such delicious food ever passing her lips. Neither had she remembered how delightful it was to have Andrew's warm bulk beside her shoulder during evening prayer.

She had not forgotten how her heart leaped to him when he turned to her in tenderness.

Later she lay in the dark listening to the cry of a night bird, savoring Andrew's even, deep breathing at her side and the weight of his leg across her own.

What had Magda promised her all those years ago?

A son who would be a great healer. From this night such a son could be born.

Without reason her mind wandered to her Aunt Martha's last words to Magda, and she frowned in the darkness.

Who had been Martha's last lamb, herself or Eleanor Rigg?

PART FOUR

The Time of Singing
(1730–1753)

For, lo, the winter is past, the rain is over and gone;
The flowers appear on the earth; the time of the singing
birds is come, and the voice of the turtle is heard in our
land.

Song of Solomon 2:11–12

Will you allow that I have as much spirit of prophecy as
the swans? For they, when they perceive that they must
die, having sung all their lives long, do then sing more
lustily than ever, rejoicing in the thought that they are
going to the god they serve.

Plato, *Phaedo*

---— • 1 •—---

Slumberings

(1724–1730)

In a dream, in a vision of the night, when deep sleep
falleth upon men, in slumberings upon the bed;
Then he openeth the ears of men, and sealeth their
instruction.

Job 33:15–16

THE NIGHTMARE THAT haunted Merit Rigg after the hurricanes
of 1724 always began with a slow rumbling that could be
heard over the howling of wind. Then she was running.
Philip's hand was cold in her own. Rain needled her face,
mingling with her tears. Chests aching and legs trembling,
they seemed to run forever before the schoolmaster found
them refuge and held her and Philip in his lean arms until the
howling ceased.

She had been six that summer. The terror in her throat had
exploded in a soundless scream. When the dream returned,
the scream was the worst part, tearing at her throat until she
fell into an exhausted sleep.

Other horrors of that season haunted her waking mind.
They had returned home through incredible disorder. The
white kitten with the buff spot lay stiff and stringy beside the
well. A melon's gaping red mouth was filled with rain, like
something wounded and drowning. Bird nests were everywhere,
twigs and fluff fouled with shell and golden wet yolk.

A different disorder prevailed inside the house. Aunt Martha lay with closed eyes and crossed hands. Her mother was bleached of color, like towels whipped in the sun.

Merit had clung desperately to Philip, only to have him wrenched away when, later that year, their household goods were carted to Grandma Rigg's house. Philip was given a separate room, with the nurse's alcove between them. They couldn't whisper together after prayers any more and Merit couldn't fly from the terror of her dreams to fit her body against Philip's grumbling warmth. Merit learned to choke back her tears in silence, while the house crickets echoed the staccato of her heartbeat.

She hated her Grandmother Rigg's house. The air smelled different, and along with the melodies of songbirds came the lonely cries of water fowl. Fear rustled along the passage to her grandmother's room. The kitchen maids complained among themselves, unlike Aunt Martha's amiable servants. Night music from the dependency houses made her throat ache, and the man her father called Uncle Paul terrified her.

She never saw him smile. He stood immobile in the orchard or woods, his eyes glittering between heavy brows and a great bushy beard.

"He means no harm," her father insisted. "He is a man troubled by his convictions."

At least Aunt Magda still came from Williamsburg to visit Merit's mother and smile in that bewitching way.

Even after the color returned to her mother's face, she seldom smiled. Her voice lacked its old richness. She seemed like a guest in her own body, emptied of everything but waiting. Merit withdrew from this shell bleakly, clinging even closer to Philip, who alone was unchanged.

And of course Rascal the dog was the same. She delivered a litter of pups that cavorted in the garden. And school was almost the same once they arrived at its doors.

The schoolhouse was rebuilt on its old site, with two new rooms added and quarters for the master. That next spring, twelve students came besides Philip and Merit and Aunt Abbie's daughters. Joseph, Aunt Sara's son, came briefly. Since Joseph's father forbid the master to punish his son and the master wouldn't submit to Joseph's disobedience, he was sent away.

At first Chad drove Philip and Merit to school in the

chaise, returning for them at twilight. When Merit was ten and Philip nine, they cantered their ponies along the lane, with a servant following discreetly.

Merit was weak with relief when her parents decided to let Philip remain with her instead of preparing for Oxford at the College of William and Mary. She didn't dislike her cousins; rather, she felt bleak and fragile when she was away from Philip.

Together she and Philip built a fort in the grove, crouching behind its palisades to watch for pirates. They mimicked the cries of the boatmen and fished the stream for gray tadpoles, which stared at them from their watery prisons. Only when they practiced shooting and Merit's aim proved steadier than Philip's, did he ever behave roughly to her.

In the summer of 1730, Merit turned twelve.

"She is almost a woman," her Aunt Sara commented.

"No," Merit cried. Her aunt was right, of course. Merit was conscious of the narrowing of her waist and how hard it was to breathe in last year's dresses. But she didn't like the fact that she was changing.

Once she had thought the river fogs exciting. She and Philip crept through the mists to surprise lurking enemies. Now that wavering cloudiness brought hot tears behind her eyes. She found herself interested in the romantic whisperings of her cousins. Instead of stirring martial poetry, she preferred tales of love and painful sacrifice.

"Is it, then, so painful to be a woman?" her aunt teased.

Merit saw her mother's eyes curious on her face. Honesty could only hurt her mother, whose face was empty of joy. Like a mummer's mask, Merit thought, her mother's face was smooth and secret. Who would want to be like that? She sensed no tenderness between her parents. She knew they slept in separate rooms. Such loneliness seemed very like to pain.

Fortunately a servant interrupted. "The mistress is carrying on again," the girl announced timidly.

Emily rose and followed the girl from the room.

"My poor mother," Aunt Sara sighed.

"My poor mother," Merit echoed in her heart.

For Merit's birthday her father had a stockade built near the stable and brought two dappled fawns to be penned there. They cowered together in terror, their eyes watchful on Merit.

How slow they were to win to friendship. At Aunt Magda's suggestion, Merit moved a stool into the enclosure and sat quietly for hours each day. After a week they drew near with twitching noses, trembling with readiness to flee. Aunt Magda had instructed Merit to rub her hands with salt. By July the fawns bounded to greet her, pressing their necks against her, scrubbing the salt from her hands with rough tongues. Their eyes were serene at last.

Merit was with her fawns the afternoon her grandmother died. She saw the servants passing from the kitchen to the house with unusual swiftness. When Chad set off in the chaise, his face tight, her curiosity drew her to the kitchen house. The servants were crying, and the cook was praying in a frantic wordless monotone.

At the sight of her, the praying changed to a shriek.

"Dead!" the cook cried. "Your grandmother is dead."

Merit froze, remembering death, her Aunt Martha with folded hands, the kitten stiff by the well house. Joy and revulsion leaped in her chest.

"You don't understand," the cook screeched. "Mistress Rigg is dead. Dead." She repeated the word as if trying to force something from Merit.

"You hated her too," Merit wanted to remind her. "You hated and feared her as I did. Your grief is ugly and false."

As she turned to find her mother, a sudden hope flared in her chest.

When her Aunt Martha died, her mother had been emptied of spirit. What if her grandmother's death would make her mother warm again, and able to listen with her heart, as she had used to?

Her mother caught her close, holding her while she directed a servant who was folding garments into a trunk.

"I am going to your father," she explained.

"But you've never gone upriver."

Her mother studied her with thoughtful eyes. "I know, my dear. I know."

Before her mother was gone, the house had begun to fill with people. Her aunts came with their children, including Joseph, who was taller and heavier but no less rude and obnoxious. Her mother's friend Cece came with two daughters. Merit clung to Philip's side until her parents arrived for the funeral.

Uncle Paul, his dark suit in need of a brushing, stood at the graveside after everyone else left.

"Come, child," Aunt Sara urged as Merit stared back at him.

"What is he waiting for?" Merit asked. His figure above the mounded earth brought her old shiver of childish terror.

"Horses," her aunt said crossly. "Horses of many colors."

Aunt Abbie exploded in swift rebuke as Merit hurried to catch up with her mother and father, who walked ahead, arm in arm.

Merit's guilty hope seemed to be realized with her mother's return. Her face glowed with life, and her eyes shone. Even her voice had regained its old mystifying richness.

Only with time did Merit realize that this new Emily was as lost to her as the old one had been. Her parents seemed to have found a private place that shut her and Philip out. Their eyes, which had seldom met, now clung. Her father's hand was always reaching out for his wife. They laughed secretly together.

Merit stood very stiffly and watched them, so stiffly that her back sometimes ached and her neck hurt when she turned her head. Neither of them noticed; they only sought each other's eyes and reached out, even without hands.

Merit had forgotten the sound of her mother's laughter. She had never heard her sing before. The first time she heard that melody from the orchard, she went to the window, incredulous that such sweetness could fall from her mother's lips. When her father came up behind her, Merit stiffened herself against his touch. He didn't even notice. She turned to find his face damp with tears.

"There was in her voice a ripple that stilled birds in trees," he whispered aloud.

At Merit's confused look, he pressed her shoulder. "I was quoting your grandfather Robbie Fraser. Em's voice is the living echo of her mother's."

"What song is that?" Merit asked.

He shook his head. "It bears no name for me but Em's joy. How good it is to hear it after all this time."

---·2·---

The Hand of the Fowler

(1730–1731)

Thou art snared with the words of thy mouth, thou art
taken with the words of thy mouth.
Give not sleep to thine eyes, nor slumber to thine eyelids.
Deliver thyself as a roe from the hand of the hunter, And
as a bird from the hand of the fowler.

Proverbs 6:2, 4–5

WHEN HER FATHER went upriver, taking only Philip along,
Merit felt the pain of being a woman.

"Why not take me?" she challenged.

"My love," Andrew said coaxingly. "You are a girl.
Philip and I go to do men's work."

"I can do anything Philip can," she said angrily as Philip
waved triumphantly from the boat.

"But Philip can't do everything you can," her mother
replied. "You need to help me plan the house Father will be
building."

"We have more house here than we need."

Em grinned at her. "You know how long Andrew has
dreamed of moving up there. Now we will go, all five of
us."

"Five?" Merit echoed.

"God willing," her mother said, resting a hand on her
thickening waist.

August glowed along the river, gilding the boatloads of materials traveling to the plantation beyond the fall line. Philip and Andrew returned from each trip high with excitement. Andrew talked of the fine progress of the house. Philip talked of the forests and Matthew Billings.

Every sentence Philip spoke began with, "My friend Matt Billings . . ."

Matt Billings could turn a twig into a flute with stops for all your fingers. Matt Billings could catch a fish without a line and drop a bird with a single shot. He could outrun even Andrew's fastest horses.

"If you say one more such thing about Matt Billings, I'll stop talking to you," Merit warned.

Magda laughed at Philip's astonishment. "You must realize, Philip, that your friend sounds like a giant."

Philip grinned. "He's not a giant, but he's no dwarf, either."

"I suppose he has a head of fine dark hair and eyes like a summer sky."

Em frowned at Merit's biting tone.

"Actually, Matt's hair is red and his eyes are green," Philip told her.

"He sounds loathsome."

"Every man to his taste." Philip shrugged, pulling on his coat.

"What are you off to?" his mother asked.

"To work with Rascal's new pups," Philip replied. "Matt Billings tells me that if I—"

Merit sighed loudly.

"Come, Merry," he protested. "He told me how to train them."

"Don't repeat it to me," Merit interrupted. Philip shrugged again and went out.

"Who is this red-haired giant?" Magda asked.

"The son of a neighbor up there," Em explained. "He's a little older than Philip, but such a great fellow. Andrew says Philip could do worse in choosing a hero."

Merit broke her thread in mid-seam.

"Come, Merit," her mother coaxed. "It's a lovely day. Go be with Philip while you can."

Merit fought hot tears behind her eyes. It had always been just herself and Philip. One day he would leave for England

191

and be gone for a long time. Why did this odious Matt Billings have to come between them like the third horse in the shafts of a cart?

From outside came the yelping of the pups. "From the sound of that, Philip needs your help." Magda laughed.

"While I can," Merit thought numbly as she laid her work aside. "While I can."

Andrew Rigg announced that Matthew Billings would attend Merit and Philip's school on the Springer plantation.

"That's too far to travel," Merit protested.

"If he went back and forth, it surely would be," her father agreed. "He'll stay with us, at my invitation."

Merit felt the familiar pain begin in her neck, and escaped to her room as soon as possible. "I won't go to school," she stormed to her empty room. "I won't even leave this room if he comes here." Not even her tears could drown out her mother's words. "While you can." What good was time with Philip if Matt Billings was to share it too?

Em rested a lot because of her coming child. When Philip was upriver, Merit often stayed with her Aunt Sara, who was lonely, with Joseph off to school and Sally far away. It was glorious to be the center of her aunt's attention even though she only half listened to her aunt's continual chatter. Sometimes, however, her aunt said remarkable things.

"You and Philip must remind your mother of her own childhood," she commented. "She and her brother were remarkably fond of each other."

"But wasn't he lost to pirates a long time ago?" Merit asked.

Her aunt nodded. "But he was near twenty, and your mother fifteen. They had all those years together, just as you and Philip have."

"Philip and I are just beginning," Merit told her.

Her aunt shook her head. "I thought that when your father and I were young. Then he went away and came back a man."

"Philip won't be gone that long."

"He'll still come back a man," her aunt insisted. "Andrew left as a hot-tempered, playful boy and came back a hot-tempered playful man."

"I don't see him like that at all," Merit admitted.

"None of us see Philip as you do either. Men work hard to conceal the boy hidden inside them."

"Philip won't ever change," Merit insisted, suddenly fearful.

"That is true." Her aunt nodded. "But he will seem changed, so in the end it will be the same."

Merit returned from her aunt's and inspected all her favorite places. She petted her fawns and wrestled with Rascal's pups before looking for her cat, which was expecting a new litter of kittens.

When she found the cat in none of her favorite haunts, Merit went to the barn, standing a moment so her eyes would adjust to the dimness. A mingled scent of horseflesh and hay filled her nose as she called softly, "Kit, kit."

The cat appeared above her in the loft, staring greenly down at her. When Merit reached the top of the ladder, the cat pressed flat sides against her.

"You've had your kittens, then?" she cried. "Show them to me."

The kittens writhed in their nest, rearing blindly toward the unseen light. Even Merit's finger seemed too large to stroke such tiny heads.

"They are beautiful," Merit assured her nervous pet, lifting them one at a time into her palm to examine them.

The noise began suddenly, freezing them both into silent listening.

Men's voices, the whinny of a horse, the rattle of a harness. Then Philip spoke. "Ah, good. The stall is ready."

With the terrified cat struggling in her arms, Merit watched from the loft. The young man in the doorway stood no taller than herself. His hair gleamed in the sunlight, with his face still in shadow. His reply to Philip was only a rumbling soft sound.

"Merry's somewhere," Philip went on. "You must meet her at once. As I told you, she's nothing like other girls."

The boy's laughter was indulgent. "I almost dread this meeting, Phil. Do I need a girl who outshoots, outstudies and outwits me at everything?"

"Of course you do." Philip laughed. "You two will get along famously. Let's go find her."

The horses stamped restlessly as Merit released the cat, who rushed to bathe her kittens with fierce protectiveness.

Tears smarted in Merit's eyes. So this was the Matt Billings whom she had hated so fiercely. Why, he was only a slender lad, to whom Philip had boasted of her even as he had boasted of Matt to herself.

As she climbed down the ladder, she echoed Matt's question, only a little changed. "Do I need a boy filled with such unreasonable expectations of me?"

Merit had never known anyone like Matt Billings. His eyes were level with her own, yet she felt him to be larger than herself in every way.

"Matthew is a different young man," her mother said musingly to Magda.

"Matthew is blessed with a personal peace," Magda replied.

Em laughed. "What does that mean?"

Magda shrugged. "He has somehow woven a dam to shut off the world's confusion, leaving him free to be himself."

"You mean something like a beaver dam," Em replied, "with a twig here and a limb there, until nothing can pass."

Magda nodded.

Merit squatted in the grove until the beavers forgot her coming. She watched their dark noses break the water as they bore another twig, another limb to use in their weaving. She could not admit even to herself how much she liked Matt Billings. She told herself it was only because he was Philip's friend, Philip's hero.

Her feelings for Matt made her unpredictable. When she was away from him, she was sad and listless. When they were together, she fluttered with silliness. She worked feverishly to excell him in the classroom, only to suffer anguish when her mark excelled his. The more she yearned for his approval, the more certain she was that he loathed her.

And there was the matter of marksmanship. Philip couldn't wait to show off her shooting ability to Matt.

"I know of few women really skilled with a gun," Matt said.

Philip was astonished that he knew any such women at all.

"On the frontier," Matt explained, "women work alongside their men, handling guns and tools with ease."

Merit felt her color rise. She knew such women. They were poor gaunt creatures, with faces darkened and ridged by the sun. Along with their vanity, their pride had fled, leaving no visible ornament in its place.

"I don't want to shoot," she told Philip.

Matt was astonished. "Oh, please. I've really looked forward to this, after all Philip has said." He paused, his tone thoughtful. "If I insulted you by talking about frontier women, I'm sorry. I meant no insult in that. Only a bold woman would choose such a life, in combat with Indians and wild animals. I admire them more than I can say."

"Another time perhaps," Merit said, turning away. He had done it again—he had made her hate herself. She couldn't stand to think of herself as being anything like those dowdy creatures, yet Matt clearly thought them splendid. She felt miserable that she did out of pride what they did only for their life's sake.

She finally gave in to Philip's pleading. Her annoyance at herself steadied her hand. Over and over she came nearer the mark than either of the boys. Matthew's effort twisted his face into a frown. Merit changed her aim a little so that her shot went awry.

Philip cried triumphantly and ran to inspect the target. Matt set his gun by his side and looked at her.

"What's the matter?" she asked, suddenly uncomfortable.

"You shouldn't do that," he said. "Not ever, for any reason."

"Miss the mark? Sooner or later everyone misses."

"Accidents are different," he replied, leaving them to put his gun away. Philip was never able to persuade him to shoot with them again.

Em's baby was born in late January. When Philip and Merit and Matthew returned from school, the house was filled with people.

Andrew's face was radiant with joy. "Such a brother your mother has given to you, Merry, my girl," he said, drawing her close.

Merit had thought her cousins' newborn babies oddly colored and a little repellent. This child was different. He studied her soberly. Spiky hair tufted his head, and the sight of him made her heart ache with love.

"James," her father whispered. "His name is James."

"Oh, James," she breathed. "You are beautiful."

195

Her father chuckled. "Ah, Merry, you have turned to woman. Only a woman could see beauty in such as this." Then, at her look, he added swiftly, "And a father, of course."

If she had wondered why God had designed her body as it was, James answered that question. His head fitted the hollow of her neck. His body curved sweetly against her breast. Against the limberness of his back, her widespread fingers found new use. Her mother, watching, smiled.

"What will he be like?" Merit asked her. "Like Philip? Like me?"

"Now you talk of miracles," her mother replied. "He'll be like each of you, with his own mysterious differences."

"The blood of a family is a river," her Aunt Magda said dreamily. "It runs through time, and forgotten traits rise like strange fish to glint in new lives."

Merit studied her. "And what if those traits don't go well together? What if they battle, as strange fish would?"

Her mother and aunt both laughed.

"Most certainly they will," Em said. "Your father's temper is always at war with his gentleness. But like you and Philip, James will find a way to live in peace with himself."

Peace. That seemed a colorless goal.

Yet she thought often of that conversation. Sometimes she saw her mother's solemnity in James's eyes. When crossed, he flamed with his father's great fury. He smiled like Philip.

And, as everything did, James made her think of Matt Billings.

If this were her own child and Matthew had sired him, he would be a combination of herself and Matthew. How would her stubborn angry pride ever find peace mingled with Matt's confident thoughtfulness?

"I wished you had named him Robbie," Merit said.

"That was my father's name," Em said, her mouth suddenly tender.

"I shall name my son Robbie Fraser, after your father," Merit told her. Her mother's arms were quick and warm about her.

But she really wished she hadn't tried to imagine her own and Matt's child. The thought of it made her cry. It was wrong for her to love Matt Billings. Not only was she taller than he by a whole inch, but he never even met her eyes.

And how could he be expected to love anyone as prickly and stiff and secretive as she was? She even doubted that her mother loved her, or Philip.

3

The Unsearchable

(March 1731)

It is the glory of God to conceal a thing: but the honour of kings is to search out a matter.
The heaven for height, and the earth for depth, and the heart of kings is unsearchable.

Proverbs 25:2–3

ANDREW HEARD THE slip of oars before the craft was visible through the mist. The cries of the water birds came muted in air that a man might more easily drink than breathe.

His stare was idle. He expected the sound to fade and die as the boat passed his wharf. Instead a general darkening showed the craft nearing. With the creak of wood against wood, a lad leaped from the mist to stand uncertainly, with the boat's rope trailing from his hand.

He was a square-faced boy in his mid-teens, and he stood as if at attention, making no move to secure the boat.

Andrew hailed him. "Have you business here?"

The boy nodded, as if to free his voice. "My father," he began. "My father has business with Mistress Emily Rigg."

"With Mistress Rigg, then," Andrew challenged, peering at the shadowy figure seated in the craft and making no move to disembark.

Wind parted the mist as Andrew stepped nearer to face the staring eyes of Guillam the Toad. He stepped back involuntarily from this symbol of the misery of the early years of his marriage. Toad himself sat calmly, his grayed hair pulled back in a queue. A network of lines had traced the years on that Welsh face, but the eyes still gleamed green and luminous.

Old memories warred against new. Such mists had trailed along the Thames when Andrew had been a lad with Toad at his side, shouting ribald songs in a gin-soaked voice. Friend and companion, viper and sneak.

Andrew had turned away wordlessly, when Toad spoke.

"I come on Mistress Rigg's Norfolk business."

Andrew addressed the boy.

"Tell your father that Mistress Rigg is fresh from childbed, with no interest in business."

Did he imagine amusement in Toad's tone?

"I bring no ordinary tidings. The *Good Anne* is missing, along with her captain, Bruce Forrester."

Andrew knew himself to be the fool who had sawed off the limb onto which he had climbed. "Some manager there can surely relieve a frail woman of decisions."

"Such decisions as the construction of a new ship must come from Mistress Rigg herself as sole owner."

Andrew felt the windows watching. His churlishness had cut off any retreat, and he hailed a servant.

"Tell your mistress that a messenger is here from Norfolk."

In the awkward silence the boy stared into the mist, winding and unwinding the rope around his square fist. Em finally approached, bundled against the chill. Her look of confusion faded as Guillam rose to greet her in his rocking boat.

If she had dared to smile, Andrew would have turned to flame. Her silent acceptance of this ridiculous situation was equally irritating.

Andrew stood aside as she greeted Guillam and listened to his account of the loss of the *Good Anne*.

"It was boarded by the Spanish revenue boats in the islands," he explained, "crippled by a shot across the bow and then boarded. What's come of either ship or captain we can't discover."

Andrew thought of Bruce Forrester rising from his chair by Robbie Fraser's fireside all those years ago.

"Then we have no recourse?" she asked.

Toad shook his head. "That was a chance we knowingly took."

"God forgive us, that Bruce was lost," she said dully.

They spoke of the new ship and its dimensions, of Em's loving message to the widow and her family. She smiled at the lad and told him his good fortune in resembling his mother, Mollie Plum. She didn't move until the boat disappeared into the mist.

"So you're involved in smuggling?" Andrew challenged.

Her glance was curious. "You must have realized that."

He bridled a bit. "God in heaven, Em. You're a British subject. What will our sons think, to learn you deal in illegal commerce against your own crown?"

"God set governments among men to deal as fathers do with children, using mercy and understanding. Does the injured son of a brutish man fail to heal himself by what medicine he can find?" Her steps quickened as she spoke. "Rule upon regulation, act upon act, the crown has forced us to invent our own medicine."

"But smuggling, Em, for God's sake."

"Don't play saintly games with me, Andrew Rigg. Tell me that no tobacco left this wharf on Dutch ships when that was unlawful. A sailing master mends his own hide. A planter does the same."

There was no refuting her charge. He overtook her and drew her arm close. "The sight of his face still enrages me," he told her. "I grieve both for Forrester and my own childish rage."

She smiled up at him. "A lesser fire would cause a cooler flame," she replied.

"I still wish I had taken the step to make peace."

"It's never too late," Em assured him. "That commerce will go to Philip. If you went to Norfolk with him to visit Bruce's widow, the rift could be mended. Bruce's son, Asa, is very little older than Merit."

Andrew nodded, pleased at the idea.

"He might even be gentleman enough to ask you out of your boat," she added brightly.

"Wench," he whispered, digging her ribs in as they entered the passage. Then, glancing up, Andrew cursed silently. Merit stood watching them in that stiff way. Why did she so disapprove of her parents? Why should she grow colder as she ripened into womanhood?

"Your mother has been behaving very badly," he told Merit sternly.

Em grinned. "He means that I have disagreed with him."

He touched Merit's shoulder. "Tell me, Merry, child. Are you a proper subject of your king or a renegade colonial, like your mother?"

She was startled into softness. "A proper subject of my king, of course."

Em would have pulled away, but Andrew held her firm.

"And what is your opinion of pirates, Merry?"

"Oh, I hate and fear them even to their death," Merit said.

"You see." Andrew laughed. "She is fairly our child, with the loyalty of the English and the ferocity of the Scot."

Philip shrugged when Merit told him this exchange.

"That's mostly a joke with them, but it stings of truth. No better English patriot lives than Father, while Mother is Presbyterian and Scot first."

"What about you, Philip?" she asked.

"Good God, Merit." He stared at her. "You insult me with the question."

4

Secret Things

(1732)

The secret things belong unto the Lord our God: but those things which are revealed belong unto us and our children for ever.

Deuteronomy 29:29

BETWEEN THEMSELVES, Merit and Philip bewailed their father's passion for family gatherings. Not only on festive occasions, but for no reason at all, Andrew invited everyone in the family for long, hospitable parties.

Merit thought herself the worse used because she always ended up with her cousins Dorothy and Lucinda, whom she saw quite enough at school. Lucinda was an amiable, overweight girl with a pleasant open manner. Dorothy was quite the contrary, sharp-witted, with a tongue to match.

"She's a reservoir of gossip that never dries up," Merit complained to her mother, not adding how careless Dorothy was about the truth in her reports.

Merit usually stayed silent in Dorothy's company, to avoid being misquoted. That morning as the three of them played with James on a blanket on the grass, she broke her own rule.

"It is May already," Dorothy said wistfully.

"And summer is coming," Lucinda added.

"Then your young man will go west and leave you grieving," Dorothy told Merit archly.

Merit stared at her, hoping her embarrassment wasn't evident. "Philip?" she asked. "He'll be back and forth as usual."

Dorothy's laugh was brittle. "Don't keep secrets, Merit. Everyone sees you watching that sober little Matthew Billings."

Merit forced herself to meet her cousin's eyes. "Indeed I'll miss Matthew Billings," she said firmly. "We're all used to having him around the house. We'll all miss him."

"But you will in a different way," Dorothy insisted.

Merit sighed with exasperation. "I warn you that I don't like such talk, and you had better stop it."

Lucinda rolled over. "Dorothy's always carrying on about your great crush on that boy."

"Great crush indeed," Merit exploded. "Dorothy, if you have been passing this nonsense around . . ."

"Nonsense," Dorothy scoffed. "You watch him all the time. You're as tongue-tied as a slave when he speaks to you. It seems a shame you can't be as silly about someone proper."

"Proper," Merit challenged. "What does that mean?"

Dorothy shrugged. "Oh, stop that, Merit. He's too tiny for such a girl as you. But even if he were full-sized, he's not a match for a Rigg—a third son, with only one measly plantation."

Merit almost reached for Dorothy's fine pale hair. "Tall, rich. God in heaven, Dorothy is that a way to select friends?"

"Not friends, husbands," Dorothy corrected her.

Without thinking, Merit slapped her cousin sharply across the cheek, knocking her down in the grass. James set up an instant howl as Dorothy crawled backwards, yelling, "Get away, leave me alone."

"I'll leave you alone," Merit said, catching James under her arm and jerking the blanket from under both of them. "I want no more from your foul mouth, now or ever."

"The truth always hurts," Dorothy shouted after her, one hand pressed to her flaming face.

"So do spiteful gossips," Merit shouted back, slamming into the house.

Em was passing and stopped. "Trouble in paradise?" she asked.

"Dorothy is a mean, spiteful gossip," Merit told her.

"No one listens to a gossip," Em assured her.

Leaving James with his nurse, Merit fled to her room.

Please God, let her mother be right. No one must listen to Dorothy. Never mind that Matt was shorter than herself, never mind that he would never be rich; he was too fine to be fouled by such a clattering mouth.

"I love him," she whispered into her pillow. "I love him, for all the good it will ever do." She wept bitterly until she drifted to sleep.

She sensed the nightmare coming but couldn't force herself awake. The howling began, the thunder and the terrified flight.

Only the dream's ending changed.

Instead of the schoolmaster's, the arms around her were Matthew's. She was warm and safe, with his voice muffled in her hair. She wakened and rocked herself in her own arms in agony until a servant called to insist that she come downstairs to be with her father's guests.

That spring Matthew's father could no longer afford the fee for the schoolmaster. Andrew took Matt on as an apprentice, eventually to become an overseer for the Candle Creek plantation. "We must leave capable hands here when we move upriver."

"That place needs a name," Philip protested. "Upriver hardly does it justice."

"Gilead," Em said quietly.

"A place of spices, myrrh and balm," Andrew said thoughtfully.

"And the refuge of David the king," Em reminded him.

"What do you think, Merit?" Philip pressed her.

"That's fine," she stammered, "lovely." What did it matter what the place was called? What did anything matter? Dorothy's ugly words echoed in her mind, "Even if he were full-sized . . . a third son . . . one measly plantation."

James cried in the nursery upstairs, and Merit was on her feet.

"I'll see to him," she said, grateful to escape.

Baby James had staggered onto his feet early that spring. Discouragement was unknown to him. He fell and rose again with such stubbornness that by June he was everywhere. He wakened at a run and collapsed to sleep in the same position. The servant who tagged his progress was delighted to yield his care to his devoted sister.

Merit's birthday dress was a deep blue, which glistened to green in the folds. She turned under Magda's watchful eye.

"It's too long." Magda nodded. "Every year I add an inch. You stopped growing, without telling me."

"Have I really stopped growing?" Merit asked, openly delighted.

"Does it matter so much?" Magda asked.

Merit bit her lip. "It matters," she said fervently.

"In dancing, no one notices if you are taller," Magda said, pinning the hem up.

"I don't care a fig for dancing," Merit said. "The same boys grin and trod on me every year."

"All girls say that." Magda laughed.

"But they care nothing for me. They look for the dower they can get from Father. I shall stay unmarried like you, Auntie Mag."

"With me it's different."

Seizing her skirt in her hands, Merit knelt by Magda.

"You are different, Auntie Mag. Oh, please, can you tell me about my life?"

Magda shook her head. "That is against your faith. It's an abomination."

"Not if we do it in fun. As a game."

Magda continued to shake her head. "Please don't ask me."

Merit sat back on her heels obediently. "You're right. You'd tell me that Philip was going away, and I would want to cry."

Magda reached for her hand. "Maybe we can think of more pleasant things."

"Children?" Merit asked.

"Four," Magda told her. "Three boys and a girl."

Merit's eyes glistened. "Boys like James and Philip."

"Perhaps even like your husband," Magda suggested. "Did I remember to tell you about a long, perilous journey? That's always a part of such games. Now, shall we fit this dress or play games all evening?"

"Fit the dress." Merit giggled. "I might need it for my journey."

Her Aunt Mag was strangely silent for the rest of the

fitting, and left with an unaccustomed darkness behind her eyes.

Within a month of Merit's birthday, letters came from three young men in the neighborhood. Andrew received these letters with the poorest possible grace.

"You are Robbie Fraser all over again," Em teased him.

"And Merit is Emily Fraser," he replied. "She thinks as little of these offers as I do. Let her wait for love, as we did."

"What if she has already lost her heart?" Em asked.

"Do you know something I don't?" he asked.

Em shrugged. "She keeps her own counsel from me, but sometimes she has the look of a woman in love."

Andrew was instantly on his feet. "I'll ask her," he said, leaving Em's protest to hang in the air.

To his astonishment, his question brought a flood of tears.

"Merit," he pleaded. "If you have fixed your affection on some lad, his father and I could talk of arrangements."

Her tears flowed even more freely. "He loathes me," she sobbed. "He would not have me as a gift."

"Then he's mad," Andrew said angrily. "He is a madman, and undeserving of those tears."

Her voice echoed his own anger. "Don't you dare to speak like that of the one I love," she cried, rising and flouncing from the room.

"It is just as I suspected," Andrew told Em. "She's only a child with silly ideas. Who could loathe a creature like Merry?"

"She's a strong woman," Em reminded him.

"Worthwhile men prefer strong women," he replied.

She giggled and drew his head down for a long, silent embrace.

• 5 •

Many Waters

(Summer 1732)

Many waters cannot quench love, neither can the floods
drown it: if a man offered for love all the wealth of his
house, it would be utterly scorned.

Song of Solomon 8:7

MERIT'S SINGLENESS was a small cloud on that summer of
1732. Andrew's new house, called Gilead, was almost
completed. His artisans had managed to catch in wood and
brick the magical sense of splendor that Em's hand had drawn
in the air above the trembling Indian corn. This was Em's
house and his own. Even its empty rooms managed to suggest
Emily's grace and bearing.

And this house was Em's in more than style. Virginia's
depression had lasted nine years. The last good tobacco price
had been for such crops as survived in the year of the
hurricanes. In good years there was much risk in transit as well
as the taxes and marketing costs, which could come to eigh-
teen or nineteen pounds sterling above the hogshead price.
Only the steady income from the Fraser firm in Norfolk had
enabled Andrew to complete the house and set aside money
for Philip's education in England.

It bothered Andrew a little that this solvency was the result
of violating the king's laws, but it was clear that the monarch
failed to realize the difficulties of a colony with an Indian war

seething on its western boundary. Indeed, Andrew would have delayed moving his family to Gilead were it not for the line of frontiersmen who lay to the west between him and the French.

But Merit was a cloud that darkened with time. She drew thin and pale over the summer, an unsmiling shadow of herself.

"She needs her own husband and child," Andrew complained. "The love she lavishes on Jamie should be spent on her own."

"She will marry only for love," Em reminded him.

"She won't fall in love staring at the floor," Andrew told her. "Did she give young Asa Forrester a bit of a chance?"

Em could only agree that she had not.

After Philip and Andrew's first visit to Norfolk to make peace with Guillam the Toad, the visits had been frequent. After only a few visits, Asa Forrester had pleaded to make suit to Merit.

"I've no interest in him," Merit told Andrew.

"Give him a chance. He's no callow horse-racer, but a man of the sea, like your grandfather Robbie Fraser."

"I've no interest in him," she repeated stubbornly.

"The girl is mad," Andrew told Em. "She's under some spell. Oh, that I knew what man has bewitched her. He's a blackguard, for all her defense of him."

"Yet you want to talk to him of marrying Merit?" Em asked.

"I want to see him hung," Andrew growled. "What kind of a mother doesn't know her own daughter's yearnings?"

Em's laughter caught him off guard. "What kind of father would hang the man his daughter pines for?" she countered.

The summer was cool and wet. Such conditions were as healthy for the crops as they were dangerous to the people. The flux took a painful toll of the young and the infirm old. The housemaid's son died the first week of August. Poor old Chad, who had been with Em since she was a child, died, as quietly as he had lived.

Philip and Matt worked that summer at Gilead, but Andrew came often downriver, driven by his concern for James. The child had lived safely through his first dangerous summer but was still too young to bear the wrack of cholera. He and Em prayed incessantly for the child's safety, counting the weeks until the first frost, when the scourge would pass.

The frost was too slow in coming.

James slowed to torpor overnight. Refusing food, he buried his head in Merit's breast, too weakened to express his pain. He left her arms only during the seizures of fierce diarrhea, when his sturdy body melted before their terrified eyes.

Em clung to Magda's prediction.

"A son who would be a great physician," she had said.

"Don't you see, Andrew, she was talking of James. He will survive to fill that destiny."

Andrew didn't even remind her that such belief was a sin against her faith.

Servants passed them on the stairs, carrying hot applications. Bark, snake root, and rhubarb quickly resulted in violent retching. Only tincture of opium and sips of brandy soothed the exhausted child in Merit's arms.

When, like a miracle, James began to accept nourishment, Merit began her own perilous descent. The physician was hopeful. "Be of good cheer," he told Andrew and Em. "She is young and well nourished. No creature has a better chance than such as she."

Magda arrived on the first day of Merit's illness. She stayed when the doctor left, bathing Merit's fevered flesh with cooling cloths. When Merit seemed to rally after five days, Em and Andrew collapsed with relief. Magda stayed at her side.

Merit's screams brought Em out of a deep sleep. When she passed a servant carrying a pan filled with rice water flecked with blood, she turned to Andrew in despair.

All time moved with the fateful rhythm of Merit's pain. At last came silence. Too weak to breathe, her lashes lay on sunken caverns. Her flesh was clammy with sweat. Andrew, unable to bear Merit's torture, strode from stable to orchard to grove, screaming at the sky and whipping fence and tree and stone in violent fury.

"Pray," Em begged him. "For Merit's sake, pray. Don't offend God further with your mindless fury."

Andrew turned haggard eyes on her. "Have you no crisis of faith?" he challenged. "That stern God you serve, how does he now serve you, that he lays the pain of hell on an innocent child? Pray for both of us if you will, Em, but leave me to my resources, lest I offend both your God and mine by hypocrisy.''

Even in fever, Merit's mind was clear. Magda leaned close to catch the words. "Auntie Mag," she whispered. "Tell me about my journey."

Em had never seen Magda so distraught. "A game, love," Magda told her. "It was only a game."

"And my children?" Merit pressed, her eyes closed. "My sons and my daughter?"

"A game," Magda insisted, "only a game."

Merit's effort brought fresh moisture to her face. "No," she cried desperately. "It was not a game. Tell me. Tell me."

Magda sighed and laid her hand on Merit's shoulder. Her voice changed. The words came clearly, as if from a new and farther place. "It is no game," she said gently. "This is the journey, Merit, and I take it with you. Whatever comes, don't leave me. Cling to me. Hold to me. If you release me, even for a moment, the rest will not come to pass."

Merit sighed. "A game," she said. "I'm so tired."

As her face went slack, Magda rose and pulled her up to slap her face sharply.

"Waken," she ordered. "Stay with me. Don't leave me here alone." Turning to Em, Magda hissed, "Cold water. Brandy. Quickly. She must not sink into a coma now."

Em was halfway down the stairs when the door slammed open. Matthew Billings, his clothing disheveled and his eyes wild, stared up at her.

"Where is she?" he asked. "Where's Merit?"

As Em hesitated, he leaped up the stairs and seized her arm.

Andrew, in the passage below, stared up in astonishment.

"They told me," Matt stammered. "Where is Merit?"

Before Em could reply, Merit's anguished cry came from above. Matthew was past her and up the stairs within an instant.

"Why is he here? What's all this?" Andrew demanded. Em shook her head and dispatched a servant for cold water and brandy. Then, emptied of strength, she leaned against Andrew's chest.

"Pray that it is Matthew," she pleaded. "Pray."

"Of course it's Matthew," he said crossly, "though how he got here and why, I've no idea."

"No, no," Em whispered. "You saw the passion in his face. Pray that it is Matthew whom Merit has mourned for."

As Andrew and Em reached the door of Merit's room, Magda stepped aside. Without hesitation, Matthew lifted Merit into his arms. Her head rolled against his neck.

"No," Matthew ordered. "You cannot die, you must not die." He was shaking her. "Live," he shouted, "for the love of God, live."

A vague attempt at a smile changed Merit's face. "Matthew," she murmured. "Matthew Billings." Her words ended in a choking cough.

Magda was whispering fiercely. "Hold her. Keep her awake."

Matthew didn't seem to hear her. He held Merit, stroking her sodden hair and whispering over and over, "You cannot leave my life."

Merit opened her eyes to shake her head clumsily. "No," she whispered. "It is I who love you." Her head fell against his shoulder.

He forced her head up, shouting at her. "Waken, Merit," he insisted. "Waken for our lives."

The silence in the room was absolute as a change came over Merit's face. Her sweating stopped, her eyelids rose and fell, and she sighed.

Magda leaned over to touch her arm. "She warms," Magda whispered. "God be thanked, her flesh warms again."

When Merit stirred in Matthew's arms and moaned a little, Magda signaled Matt to lay her onto her pillows. Only then did he see Andrew and Em staring from the doorway. He would have fled except that Merit's hand was on his arm. Matthew flushed under Andrew's gaze. "Forgive me," he stammered.

"Forgive you?" Andrew asked. "Thank God for you, Matthew Billings. But what was all this about a journey, Magda? Is her crisis past?"

"In a coma, she would have died," Magda said. "Now there is hope."

"But what of the journey?"

"It was a game," Magda said meekly.

"It was not a game," Merit corrected, her eyes still closed, "no game at all."

When Merit drifted into a shallow sleep, Magda sent them away. Matthew told of the news coming upriver that the "master's daughter is like to die." "I had to come," Matthew explained, unable to meet Andrew's eyes.

"It took you long enough," Andrew grumbled. "She wasted her strength grieving that you hated her."

"Hate?" Matthew cried. "There was never a day I didn't worship her like my life. But I am unfit."

"In what way?" Andrew challenged. "Land and station? God, what a fool you are, Matt Billings. Where there is love, all else can be added on."

"I'd no right," Matt stammered.

"You had no right to let her suffer."

"But I bring her nothing."

"You bring all Merit yearns for," Em said. "Why were we so blind?"

"She's strong," Matthew said proudly. "She carries her own burdens. Not even on the frontier are there stronger women than Merit."

Magda was calling. "Matthew, please come. Merry insists that your coming was only a dream."

Matthew's expression changed to one of pure terror. "What shall I say to her?" he asked Em.

Em chuckled and patted his hand. "After all that, you can think of nothing to say?"

He grinned back at her as he mounted the stairs.

6

Two for a Farthing

(Summer 1733)

Are not two sparrows sold for a farthing? and one of them
shall not fall on the ground without your Father.

Matthew 10:29

ONLY BECAUSE PHILIP was leaving for Oxford in August of
1733 did Andrew and Em agree to the marriage of Matthew
and Merit, who was still not back to her usual strength.

"I can't marry without Philip at my side," Merit insisted.

"She's right," Philip agreed. "This marriage is wholly my
doing. You might never have unloaded this great spinster
without my cleverness."

"And your modesty," Merit teased.

"Modesty would be out of place. Who else has turned his
best friend into his brother?"

"But there's so much to do," Em wailed.

Andrew laughed. "So many weddings have taken place
here that the kitchen could make the feast without servants.
But there are other things—like the wedding contract."

"What is that?" Merit asked.

"It is nothing for you to fret over," Andrew assured her,
"just a document to insure that your property stays in your
hands."

"But father, Matt and I will be man and wife."

212

Andrew nodded. "Don't be upset. I'm not insulting Matt. But the family land must stay with the blood."

"It is too insulting," Merit decided. "Don't you think it hurts Matt enough to come with nothing? Mother, Philip, please make him see that."

Em shook her head. "Your father signed such a contract, that the Fraser property might stay with me."

"And look at Uncle Paul," Philip added. "He has Uncle Amos's land only for his lifetime. Because he has no heirs, it will go to his cousins and their children."

"He could give it away," Merit suggested.

Andrew shook his head. "No, he can't. And neither must Candle Creek leave the hands of Lyon descendents."

"What of you, Philip and James?"

Andrew smiled. "One of the joys of this colony is that the law does not decree how a father must leave his land. Philip wants land west of Gilead, and since James will grow up at Gilead, that plantation should be his."

"But what of Matthew's feelings?" Merit wailed.

"Matthew's feelings are not for your property, you little goose." Philip laughed. "If they were, you would have no use for him."

The news of Merit's betrothal found Dorothy visiting her mother. She looked up from the child at her breast in triumph. "I told you," she reminded her mother and sister, "when we were in school, I told you that Merit was smitten with Matthew Billings. You didn't believe me."

Abbie shook her head. "A poor lad like that, with no property?"

"Merit loves him," Lucinda said.

Abbie shot her youngest child a reproving glance. "Love never filled stew pots. Andrew is not using his God-given sense. He could marry Merit to any fortune in Virginia."

"There is still Philip coming on, and James," Dorothy reminded her.

"Anyway, Merit loves Matthew," Lucinda murmured.

"If love holds such magic, maybe you can make it dress us for that fancy wedding," Abbie told Lucinda.

"No one looks at anyone but the bride anyway," Lucinda replied.

"Towering above her husband in this case." Dorothy laughed.

Abbie turned away as the girls began chattering about ribbons and slippers. How long had Em and Andrew been married? Almost sixteen years. How passionately her mother had hated Emily Fraser. What would have happened if Emily had returned Eleanor Rigg's attitude with answering coldness instead of heaping coals of guilt on her mother-in-law with her unremitting goodness? Guilt on guilt layered through time.

Guilt was a pain that Abbie knew too well. Nat had approved of her ever-increasing devotion through the years. How could he know that she went to her knees to ask forgiveness for the hatred she felt toward Emily Rigg?

While Andrew was still abroad, Abbie had begun to curry her mother's favor, even if she had to shade the truth to do it. But the children came so fast and Nat's pay was so small, and no other help was forthcoming. Emily had whipped her mother's pride into a storm of fury. After her coming, Abbie feared to argue with any cruel thing her mother said. A single slip of the tongue would have brought greater want to her family.

But only once had she spoken an outright lie, the same lie twice, just like the denial of Christ.

Eleanor's questions had come so fast, so bitterly, into Abbie's weakness.

"And the child was born near death?"

"And Emily Fraser was like to die too?"

"Did you see the child?"

"Did you know the child was a girl?"

"Did Emily Fraser know the child was a girl when she spoke the name Merritt?"

The temptation had been too great. She had whispered "yes," only to have her mother repeat the question.

Once spoken, it was too late. Twice spoken, she was eternally damned.

Andrew knew. She saw it in his eyes. Did Emily know? If Emily knew, she had rubbed the salt of her generosity into that wound for all these years, with food from the Fraser ships, dresses and linens that showed no wear, hams that Emily claimed to be excessive to their needs. All this was salt to Abbie's conscience, even with the schooling for the girls and their handsome wedding gifts. All were spoiled by coming from a wronged and generous hand.

The floor scraped at Abbie's knees. She knew her heart to be a seething display of the deadliest sins—pride, envy, malice—yet how many of these had Emily's generosity fostered in her?

When she slid between sheets worn thin since Em sent them at a time of sickness, a sudden thought brought her upright.

The marriage gift. Custom dictated that the bride's family give the minister's wife a gift in appreciation for his services. Abbie smiled, suddenly warmed. Lucinda, poor goose, was enamored of a poor boy in the parish. Surely Emily's gift would be generous enough to provide the poor girl a paltry dower.

She lay down smiling, eased of one more nagging concern.

Em enjoyed every detail of Merit's wedding arrangements. Memories of Andrew's courtship misted her eyes as she studied fabrics and ordered tables built to be set on the lawn.

But even as Merit's feast would be shadowed by summer foliage, Em dreaded the changes of the season ahead.

She would miss Philip, of course, but, young as he was, he was so independent of spirit as to be more man than boy. She released him confidently to his future, which he alone would choose, with no counsel from her or anyone.

Candle Creek was different. She knew from the journal how much it had been weakened with time. When Bek was young, the mill was busy, the pond kept clear of debris and the path beaten smooth. Now the creek ran sluggishly, the mill wheel only spoke at the turn of the tide and the path was overgrown.

Would that candle of sunlight still remember God in the clearing, when no prayers were spoken there?

And she worried about Abbie. The trip upriver to Gilead was a greater journey than Abbie and Nat would undertake. Who would stop by with a brace of fat hens or freshly ground flour to lighten their load? The best she could do was make the marriage gift to Abbie generous enough to be helpful for a long time.

Magda was making a sapphire-blue velvet suit for James. The road to Williamsburg was bright, with James beside his mother. Em's own joy as she carried him seemed to have set a constant song in his heart. He sang as they traveled, his voice rising and falling with the rhythm of the wheels of the Berlin, laughing when a dove rose thrumming from their path.

"A time for singing," she thought, with the words of Solomon in her mind. Such blessings—Andrew's renewed love, Merit's happiness, and James closer to her in spirit than her older children had ever been.

When the fitting was finished, Magda lifted James down and led them both back to the kitchen house, where a girl, not unlike Mollie Plum, smiled at them under a crisp cap.

"Betsy," Magda told her, "Master James has come to have tea by your fire. You should sit with him and rest."

The girl dimpled solemnly as she shook James's hand. Even her apron failed to conceal the promise of a coming child.

Back on the path, Em teased Magda. "Virginia grows tobacco and Carolina grows rice. Only Magda grows young widows with tender young. After Mollie Plum there was Doris, with the bandy-legged child."

"And happily married she is, to a cooper." Magda smiled.

"And Betsy?" Em asked.

"One of the seamen spends a lot of time by that fire when he is in port," she replied.

"You aren't helping my understanding at all."

Magda laid out an assortment of fine gloves. "It isn't enough that God hears sparrows fall," she said. "There must be hands outstretched to catch them."

Em would have pondered the words longer if the gloves had not been so beautiful. After choosing a pair for Merit and one for herself, she laid aside a third pair. "These look like Abbie's size. Naturally I will give her a gift of money, but she so seldom gets pretty new things."

Magda's eyes were unreadable. "I have a special box for you to present them in." Em studied the carved box with the delicate brush strokes outlining the design.

"I have never seen such a gift box," she exclaimed.

"Nor have I ever seen such a giver as you," Magda replied.

Em felt herself flush. "I could remind you of your words about sparrows."

Magda shook her head. "It is not the same. The sparrow that hurls himself against the hard glass is his own enemy."

Only later did Em think of what she should have told Magda. "A bird can only fly in the manner that it is taught in the nest."

She was folding the gloves into the box when the idea came. She went to her chest where she kept the gold coins that were brought her from the island commerce. In a world where money came as slips of paper promising tobacco, hard gold coins had great value. One at a time she slipped a gold florin into each finger and thumb of both gloves.

"Even if the sparrows fall from hurling themselves against life, there must be hands to help them rise," she told herself.

7

Times and Seasons

(1733–1740)

And He changeth the times and the seasons: he removeth kings, and setteth up kings: he giveth wisdom unto the wise, and knowledge to them that know understanding.

Daniel 2:21

EM'S FIRST REAL understanding of Virginia had come with the trip upriver after Eleanor Rigg's death. The land beyond the fall line seemed to open this world to vast horizons of life and promise.

Later she was to think of that summer of 1733 as the fall

217

line in her own life. Her years of contention were past. She and Andrew lived in jovial peace, and James thrived like Indian corn. Her early trials seemed oddly unreal, like history scanned but poorly remembered.

During the move, she had gone to the rooms above the mill where Andrew had spent so many nights. Dust danced in the sunlight, and a fly butted for freedom against the windowpanes, making a metallic sound. She was opening the window to free him when Andrew came.

"This place has served its purpose," he told her.

When she protested, he grinned at her. "Am I still confined to this tree house from that grand bower of yours?"

"Take your desk if you will, and what books you need, but leave these rooms for us."

"As refuge?" he asked.

"A citadel," she replied.

"You are a strange and wonderful creature." He laughed.

"It is strange and wonderful to have a second life."

"And one so joyful," he agreed, holding her close.

That Merit and Matt's life was joyful her parents had no doubt, but the style of their marriage was so sober and mirthless as to send Andrew and Em into guilty gales of laughter.

Before the birth of their first child, named Robbie Fraser, to Em's delight, Matt had been elected a burgess. When Matt voted with the others to repeal the Tobacco Act of 1730, Andrew stared at him with amazement.

"Good God, Matt," he exploded. "That act was the great hope of all tobacco planters."

"And a windfall to every cleric in Virginia," Matt replied.

"That's defiance for its own sake," Andrew protested. "Any act that helps a Virginia planter is a good law."

"Any act that is healthy for England is a good act," Matt suggested. "Your own son Philip would agree with me."

"Philip?" Andrew said. "Then you have fresh news of him?"

Merit flushed. "He's a good correspondent." She seemed reluctant to hand the letter to her father, before she turned back to her work.

By the end of the first page, Andrew was frowning. He

handed the letter back with a scowl. "Who is this Caroline he rants on about? And where did he get such peculiar notions about his own land—all that silly business about the great strain our Indian wars are laying on the Englishmen?"

"I would say he is in love with this Caroline," Merit said quietly. "She is the sister of his great friend Gordon Farwell."

"You don't think he will marry in England?" Em asked.

"That can be repaired by an ocean crossing. How fine it would be to have him home again." Merit's tone was wistful.

"And clear his head of his silly notions," Andrew grumbled.

"At least we got Father and Matthew to stop discussing the Tobacco Act," Merit told Em, as the men's talk drifted to other things. "I have small fondness for men of the cloth or their families myself."

"Such as your Aunt Abbie?" Em asked.

Merit nodded. "And Uncle Paul and his strange friends. Did something happen between you and my aunt at my wedding, Mother? When we wanted little Robbie baptized, Uncle Nat came alone."

Em shook her head. She tried not to think of the scene when she had presented the wedding gift to Abbie. After all this time it brought a sudden chill along her spine.

Lucinda had been in the carriage with her mother when Em handed her the carved box.

"With love and thanks," Em had said as Abbie took it and clutched it close.

"Open it," Lucinda had begged. "Let me see."

Abbie had lifted the lid, only to have her smile freeze on her face.

"Oh, Mother," Lucinda breathed. "May I try one on?"

Abbie had slammed the box shut. "No. I shall keep them for myself . . . to remember your Aunt Emily by." Her face was so dark with hatred that Em could barely catch her breath as the carriage moved away.

She had assured herself that, once home, Abbie would find the gold, and great joy with it. Instead, three years had passed without her seeing Abbie's face. When she and Andrew invited them to Gilead, they pleaded previous engagements. When poor dear Sara was buried, Abbie came veiled, and turned away at Em's approach.

Em was suddenly conscious of Merit's glance curious on her face.

"And Uncle Paul too?" Em asked lamely.

Merit groaned. "He travels here and there, seeking those preachers who talk of hell and damnation above all else. He travels to Georgia and Charleston and lets his house go to shambles. Now he has three young prophets eating at his board and accosting me in the grove about the eternal fires of hell."

Em struggled not to laugh. "Whatever did you tell them?"

"To go home and leave my salvation to God," Merit told her. "I wanted to tell them they would better serve God by harrowing Uncle Paul's fields than my ears, but I hadn't the courage."

Em laughed and rose. "They must be harmless, or the governor would not give them permits to preach."

"Philip says they would not be so gently treated at home in England."

The word home echoed strangely in Em's ears, but she said nothing.

While a student in England, Andrew Rigg had developed the habit of faithful correspondence with his absent family. He fell easily back into that pattern when Philip left home. The move to Gilead had filled him with a new rush of vigor. Poring over blueprints, he began the development of the plantation that Philip would return to. He found it strange that Philip never responded to his reports but rather confined his comments to reports on his visits to the Farwell estate and complaints about the economy in England.

When Merit's son Bruce was born in 1740, Andrew sent Em down to Candle Creek alone to visit the new mother.

"It is hard enough to swallow Philip's letters constantly railing at how Virginia is letting her king down by not supplying more men for this Indian war, without listening to Matthew beat the same drum."

"Be fair, Andrew," Em chided. "We have sent nothing to aid our countrymen except convicts and other undesirables."

"England called them men when she sent them to us," he reminded her. "We give them back in the same disguise."

By the time Em returned to Gilead, Governor Gooch had put the colony on a war footing. She left her daughter sunk in such a dismal melancholy that she would have stayed if she were urged.

"Isn't it common for a mother to suffer sadness when a child has just come?" Andrew asked her.

Em nodded. "Merit's sadness comes from a more particular cause, I fear. Her last letter from Philip bears bad news for all of us."

"He wrote me of nothing more dire than usual," Andrew protested.

"I think he dreads to tell you," Em admitted. "His banns were being cried for marriage to Caroline Farwell. He is caught on the horns of a great dilemma, Andrew. He cannot imagine life without Caroline, and Caroline cannot imagine life in what she calls 'the wilderness' of Virginia."

"Silly little goose," Andrew exploded, then nodded to himself. "It is only a matter of time. We will finish the buildings and start construction of a house. Andrew is a Lyon and a native Virginian. Once married, his head will clear, and he will hunger for home. You'll see, Em, you'll see."

· 8 ·

Ninety and Nine

(1744)

How think ye? if a man have an hundred sheep, and one of
them be gone astray, doth he not leave the ninety and nine,
and goeth into the mountains, and seeketh that which is
gone astray?

Matthew 18:12

THE YEARS FLUTTERED by like pages of a journal stirred by the
wind. By 1741, when Philip wed his Caroline, Merit had
added a son, Bruce, and a daughter, Honor, to her family. By
the time her son Rigg was born in 1744, Philip had fathered a
son named Alexander. Philip's letters never mentioned coming home.

Em felt as if the war on the western frontier had dragged on
forever. "Your father believes that our new treaty with the
six Indian nations will help us win against the French," she
told Merit.

Merit smiled. "A full nursery makes politics a distant
business. Didn't you find it so?"

Em frowned. When her nursery was full, her life had been
too painful to leave room for anything else. "Guillam the
Toad's son has gone to war," she replied absently.

"What a thing to say, with a son at my breast," Merit
protested. "God willing, there will be no wars when these
boys are men."

"Once we have overcome the French, who could we war with?" Em asked, to reassure her.

As if in answer to Em's question, Andrew Rigg found himself waging an inner war that same year. It was time for James to proceed with his education. What if he sent another son to Oxford, only to lose him forever, as he seemed to have lost Philip? The outbreak of smallpox in England eased him of his problem.

"There's no cause to expose him needlessly," he explained to Em, knowing that she too had dreaded the boy's absence from home.

Indeed, Williamsburg seemed fully far enough from the quiet of Gilead. The taverns throbbed with music and talk of the war, which had changed from the War of Jenkins's Ear to King George's War. Revels were held nightly, and Andrew's finest mare was a winner in the races during the week that he spent there with James.

Although he left the capital in high spirits, Andrew arrived home in a thoughtful mood, brought on by the *Virginia Gazette* he had studied on the trip home.

"I would be a poor wife not to notice your thoughtful mood," Em told him.

He grinned at her. "And I a poor husband if I didn't try to explain it."

She watched him spread a map on the table, held down by candles at each corner. "See that mark? That is Balcony Falls, in Rockbridge County. The militia fought a battle there with the Iroquois. Among the losses was a man named Joel Lyon."

"Joel Lyon," she repeated. "Uncle Amos's lost son?"

"More probably a grandson. The *Gazette* lists him as coming from the Northern Neck of the colony."

Em nodded. "It was there that the first Joel went as a servant."

"I have to go and search that family out," Andrew said bluntly. "Like the trip I made to meet Uncle Younger when I came back to Virginia, it is something I have to do. I tell myself it is to locate the heirs who will own Uncle Paul's land, but it is more than that. Do you understand?"

Emily sighed. "I understand well enough, but winter is coming on."

"I will proceed slowly," he promised, "and will stop for rest and bad weather."

She was half sleep that night when he spoke from his pillow.

"As a brash youth, I was puffed up with promises. I think of myself then when I read Bacon. He says that those who begin with certainty will end with doubt. I was too certain by half, Em."

He rose on his elbow to lean over her. "You taught me that God must be the first master. Younger taught me that love is the necessary parent of duplicity. Time has taught me that families are not welded by a single man's will. Yet I must still try, Em."

"With my blessing, Andrew," she whispered. "With my wholehearted blessing."

Andrew had hoped to reach Fredericksburg in four days. A lamed horse and the swollen North Anna River slowed his progress. Late on the fifth day he began his inquiries in Fredericksburg.

"There are a passel of Lyons around Dumfries," an old man in a tavern volunteered.

"Not so many in Dumfries as in Colchester," his companion argued. "And that's two days travel at best."

In the heated argument that ensued, Andrew made his escape. That the family was known of was encouragement enough for one night.

After ferrying the Rappahannock into the Northern Neck, Andrew and his man stayed with a gentleman in Stafford County. Andrew's host not only recognized the Lyon name but recalled his father's speaking highly of Master Joel as the finest tutor the neighborhood had seen.

"There was some story about him," his host mused, puffing on his pipe as if to warm his memory, "that he was from quality, for all that he came here indentured."

"He was the son of Amos of Lyon's Hundred," Andrew explained. "His father was swallowed by debt, as many have been in this place."

The old man nodded. "And this dead lad would be his grandson, like as not. There was a Morgan Lyon around Colchester who was married to Nellie Dunkley. Both are dead now, I believe."

224

Andrew felt the man was holding something back. At their parting the next morning, his host held Andrew's bridle a long moment.

"Never mind that these people seem plain," he cautioned. "The best fall on hard times and are yet honored by all who know them. The Lyons are proud people and close to God."

Through Dumfries and over the Occoquan River was a twenty-mile ride. The town, which Andrew and his companion reached at twilight, was a plain enough place, as was the only tavern lit against the darkness.

Andrew's question drew a startled look from the innkeeper. "There's Thomas Lyon himself, if you're of a mind to speak to him."

The man who looked up at Andrew's approach wore the Lyon blood in the arch of his brows and his great size. His eyes were wary as Andrew introduced himself.

Thomas Lyon studied him without a change of expression. "And your business, Andrew Rigg?" There was less hostility than coldness in his tone.

"To bring the family condolences on the loss of Joel Lyon in battle with the Iroquois," Andrew said carefully.

A murmuring passed through the room, and Thomas Lyon rose.

"Let us go home then," he said, no less coldly. "You might say this to Belle."

It was difficult to ride abreast with this silent man. Andrew guessed he was in his late thirties, having seen more years of labor than rest.

"We claim no family in Virginia," Thomas said at last.

"But blood is blood," Andrew told him. "And land waits there for your grandfather's heirs."

"Charity from the grave is dusty business," Thomas said, turning in at a gate and dismounting to drop his reins on barren sod beside a sagging porch.

Andrew was prepared for plainness by the outside of the single-room house. He was not prepared for the stark utility of the room. A young woman rose, distaff in hand, to question his companion with her eyes.

"This is Andrew Rigg of the tidewater," he announced without ceremony. "My sister Belle."

Fleetingly she reminded Andrew of his Aunt Martha. She

225

was taller, but her eyes were the same, with those remarkable brows. Her clothing was as drably useful as the room, and the hand he took was rough and dry. Thomas offered red Virginia wine and Irish usquebaugh in rough mugs. Belle sat very straight, as his Aunt Martha always had, hearing him out silently.

"We never saw our grandfather's face," she told him at last. "He died when Father was a child. The Lyon men are given to early death."

"It's pride that they have in abundance," Thomas put in. His level glance made Andrew's errand seem pointless and affected.

"I wish my wife were here," Andrew admitted. "She's studied the family journals until she knows each life like an acquaintance. The land I speak of was an original headright that Amos Lyon took in the earliest days. It belongs to your grandfather's heirs when Paul Lyon is through with it."

"Paul has no heirs?" Belle asked.

"It doesn't matter," Thomas told her. "He can give it or sell it by act of that assembly. That's how those planters run this place."

"That's been tried," Andrew told him. "The act was refused. The land goes to Joel Lyon's heirs."

"Not while I live," Thomas said. "Our grandfather tried to shake the dust of the tidewater from his feet, only to have it turn to a chain around his feet. We need none of that."

Andrew was not so much encouraged as emboldened by Belle's level glance.

"There are just the two of you now?" he asked.

"Abraham is dead from the iron furnaces. Joel fell to Indians. There's only Belle and me and the two boys, Alexander and Will, both in Indian trading.

"That's all there is for a man with no land," Thomas went on bitterly. "The mills, the militia or Indian trading."

"But there is land," Andrew insisted. "Tillable fields with orchards, the old house and a mill."

"Charity from the grave is a dusty business," Thomas repeated with finality as he rose. "I'd be no kinsman not to offer you what comfort this house affords. Be welcome if you wish."

To accept would clearly disturb the meager comforts of this crowded room. Not to accept would be to define a contrast already made too obvious by Andrew's clothes and the horse and servant waiting outside.

"I am always grateful for the hospitality of a kinsman," Andrew replied, meeting his eyes squarely.

He was haunted by Belle Lyon all the way home. Inside that rough shell dwelt a gentlewoman. No one told her story, but he had pieced it out through the evening. Morgan had indeed died young, and the passel of children had been his widow's responsibility. When she failed, Belle had stepped in, taking care of, first an invalid mother, then four brothers, the youngest just turning twenty.

Judging by the cough that racked Thomas all night, Belle would soon have only two brothers. Andrew pledged himself to hold Paul's land for this plain woman with the level eyes of Aunt Martha Springer.

Less than a year after that journey, Andrew sought out Em who was in the millhouse with a cat curled around her ankles and the Lyon journal on her knees.

"Let me read you this letter to prove that an old reformed gambler can still win on a long shot."

She cocked her head with curiosity as he took a place beside her on the bench. "Before I left the house of Thomas Lyon in Colchester, I left my name and where I could be reached with Belle Lyon. This came from her just now."

"My thanks to Father Stephen Brockman, who writes this for me. Greetings and God's blessing on your family. Thomas, my brother, departed life this Tuesday last from the sickness of his chest. I am betrothed to Jethro Sommers, who will care for me. Alexander and Will, by the Grace of God, still deal in western trade. God's blessing. Isabelle Lyon."

"You must write her," Em said.

Andrew nodded. "And that parish priest. He needs to know that a kinsman, even this distant, is watchful of her welfare."

9

The Sons of Men

(1746–1747)

For man also knoweth not his time: as the fishes that are taken in an evil net, and as the birds that are caught in the snare; so are the sons of men snared in an evil time, when it falleth suddenly upon them.

Ecclesiastes 9:12

WHEN JAMES CAME home from college for the Christmas of 1746, he did not come alone.

"I invited myself," Magda explained. "And James was too gallant to protest."

"We are delighted," Em told her. "Merit and her family divide their time between Matt's parents and us. We'll have many chances to visit."

As Magda laughed with Andrew by the fire, Em studied her. For almost thirty years Magda had been her closest friend. As little as she understood this bright, fey woman, she could sense the tremors from Magda's secret world even when no words were spoken. She knew from the shadow behind Magda's eyes that more than a Christmas feast had drawn her to Gilead. She also knew that she would be informed only when Magda was ready.

Through all those festive days, Magda was a child among the children. Robbie at twelve was as tall as she was, and almost as light-footed. Bruce and Honor were a fair match, while Rigg, a bulky, teething two-year-old, clapped and drooled from Merit's lap.

But between the games and the laughter and the feasting, Em caught that wistfulness in Magda's eyes and waited.

At twilight of the last day, with everything already packed for the return to Williamsburg, Magda rose and took Em's hand.

"Em and I are going to go to the millhouse, if you gentlemen will excuse us."

"There's nothing there but the old Lyon journal and a spoiled cat." Andrew laughed.

"That's all we need," Magda told him. "It's been too long since I've touched those hallowed pages."

With the journal in her lap, Magda turned to Em almost shyly. "Do you know why I brought you here?"

"To tell me something," Em replied, "though I've no idea what it might be."

"My mother was Romany," Magda reminded her. "I know her gifts and mine fly against your faith, even the king's laws, but I am sorely troubled, Em."

She raised her strange eyes to Em's. "I see three shadows on a line."

Em waited, not understanding.

"If we were all at peace with one another, I would keep my silence," Magda went on. "But there is enmity in our blood. I thought—I even hoped—"

"Who are these shadows?" Em asked, her own blood chilling at Magda's words.

"I only know they are of my own blood, all three of them. I needed to tell you."

Em caught Magda's slender hands and held them tightly.

"I don't like your vision, Magda, but I respect it. What can I do?"

Magda smiled. "You see? I feel better already. You must just do what you've always done, Em, pick up sparrows, forgive the unforgivable and have faith in time."

"That is hopelessly enigmatic," Em protested.

Magda rose and set the journal on the table. "You are also obliged to put more into this book than dates and numbers. Let's go back to our gentlemen. That was all I had to say."

• • •

Friday, January 30, 1746

James Rigg had risen in darkness for 6:00 prayers in the cold chapel. Following a hasty breakfast, he was fighting sleep in his classroom as the morning light brightened the windows.

He was suddenly fully awake at the pounding of feet along the hall outside and shouts drowning out his classmates' droning.

"Fire," the voices shouted. *"The Capitol is on fire."*

Duke of Gloucester Street between seven and eight o'clock on a January morning usually held no more than some hurrying servants and tradesmen gossiping in their doorways. That morning the whole street, from the college all the way to its end, was crowded with people running wigless and hatless toward the smoke rising from the top of the Capitol building.

Even moving in the street was difficult. Travelers poured from tavern doors; horses reared above servants scurrying for buckets and water. By the time James had walked down the street, the blackened shingles had sent forth a burst of flame that licked up the cupola and blackened the air with smoke. All attempts to battle the blaze were handicapped by the swarming crowd. Coughing from the dense smoke and slapping at falling embers on their clothing, James and his schoolmates helped to pile the state records and portraits of the royal family onto carts to haul to safety.

Even without the confusion of wailing women and shouting men, the crackling of the blazing building was thunderous. When the fire finally subsided, leaving nothing but bare brick walls, James turned his blazing face back toward the college.

Only a healthy respect for his master's rod kept him from stopping into his Aunt Magda's for the welcome that always awaited him. With this thought in mind he was startled to hear his name called. He turned to see his aunt's maid, Nancy, heavy with child, running awkwardly after him and wailing his name. The tears streaking her blackened face fell like ink on her white apron.

As she reached him, her voice rose to a scream.

"Master James. Oh, my God, my God."

"What is it, Nan?" he pressed, as his friends crowded around them.

"The mistress," she wailed, covering her face with both hands and weaving back and forth, weeping helplessly.

"Come," James said, taking her hand and pulling her along. "Let us go see."

With the stench of fire everywhere, he noticed nothing amiss until she dragged him past the still-closed shop to the lane that led to the kitchen house. James stopped aghast. That kitchen where he had played as a child and visited so often since, was reduced to smoking ashes in a yawning chimney.

"Aunt Mag?" he cried, turning to Nancy, now hopelessly wailing.

"God help me!" was all she cried. "God help me."

James himself found her and pried up the fallen timber that had pinned her down. Her charred garments clung to his arms as he lifted her small blackened body from its prison.

"Mother," he heard himself repeating. "My God, my mother."

The confusion of those hours was past all later recall. It was small comfort to be told that her end had been swift and painless. It was even less comfort to know that he, among the others, had failed to notice one more fire in the excitement of the blazing torch of the capitol. He kept seeing her strange bright eyes fully on his own and that smile that brought a dimple to her cheek.

Em and Andrew left for Williamsburg upon the arrival of James's servant. Em's hand, tight inside Andrew's, was the only part of her that had not turned to stone. The shock and grief battered her chest in physical waves of pain.

And fear.

She heard Magda's voice against the purring of the cat in the room above the mill. "Three shadows on a line . . . of my own blood."

Tradesmen, townspeople and servants crowded the airless space in Bruton Parish Church and stood bareheaded as the casket was driven away to the burial ground at Candle Creek.

Em saw James's puzzled eyes glance around the mourners at the graveside. Guillam the Toad and his Mollie. A cooper and his wife, Doris, with their fair crippled daughter. A seaman with Betsy weeping on his arm.

And Nancy, her face bloated with tears, and her body by the child that puffed her apron. Em left Andrew's side to stand by Magda's weeping servant. All the way from

Williamsburg she had cried inconsolably, repeating her story over and over.

"Nothing spilt or nothing," she insisted. "It was like fire had dropped from heaven and set the roof ablaze, falling everywhere. She drove me out for the child, you see. I should have stayed even if I died. Oh God, what am I to do? I should have stayed."

When the mourners were warming themselves at Merit's fire, Gil the Toad and his Mollie approached Em quietly.

"Could we have a word with you, mistress?" Toad asked.

In the quiet of an upstairs room, Em finally understood why Mollie twisted her own hands to such a painful whiteness.

"We need to talk about Nan," Toad stammered. "Somewhat must be done with her."

"Of course," Em said. "Surely you can find her a good situation."

Mollie's eyes were pleading on Toad's face. Em had forgotten how painfully Toad stammered when he was under strain.

"She's not just any girl," he began. Then, "Not just everybody would . . ."

Em studied them thoughtfully, then took Mollie's hand.

"Please explain all this," she asked.

"She's no widow," Mollie blurted almost hysterically. "No more than I was, or Doris, or any of them. We was all damaged girls, mistress, damaged with child, each of us."

At Em's stunned expression, Gil turned defensive.

"Wimmin isn't always coddled like yourself and Mistress Merit, you know. They's taken advantage of and out on their own. Masters sometimes, or friends, or strangers even. What's to come of them? Hang them in pillory for the crime of trusting? Brand their babes with shame for a weakness for some sweet talking?"

"Ah," Em said, fighting hot tears behind her eyes. Magda. Magda and her sparrows. "But my God, Gil, how did she find them all?"

Mollie replied, her smile wry. "How does the bitch fox find the warm cave and the wounded bird a nest?"

"We'd take her ourselves but for the maid we have now."

"With a boy just up on his feet," Mollie added pointedly.

Em wanted to gather the two of them into her arms. Instead she nodded briskly.

"My friend and neighbor Mary Dunbar up by Gilead is carrying a child at too great an age. She and Sam will need a wet nurse for that baby as desperately as Nancy needs a good home."

"God bless you, Mistress Em," Mollie breathed.

"And Mistress Magda," Toad added.

Struck anew by the magnitude of her loss, Em turned away in tears.

The grass grew green and tender on Magda Steele's grave. In April, wild flowers bloomed around her headstone. In May, Em and Andrew were wakened after midnight by Sam Dunbar pounding on their door.

"Sam?" Em cried, urging him inside. "Does Mary need me?"

Sam's face twisted, and his great shoulders heaved as if under a massive weight. "God help me if I have sinned. There was only slaves there, and it happened all at once."

Andrew pressed a glass of brandy into his hand.

"We lost the child," he finally stammered. "Mary's babe came dead, and the girl Nancy couldn't be saved."

His eyes pleaded with Em. "Tell me I didn't sin. Mary herself don't know. When she woke I put the babe in her arms, Nancy's babe, a little girl.

"It was like God sent her," he continued, addressing himself to Andrew.

"Or you," Andrew corrected him. "Perhaps God sent you to save Mary and the child." He touched his own glass to the one trembling in San Dunbar's hand. "Let us drink to the health of the living, the peace of the dead and the mysterious wisdom of God."

When Em and Andrew received word of the hurricane that swept the tidewater in October of 1749, they couldn't rest until they were assured that Merit and her family were safe. Miraculously, Candle Creek suffered only small crop damage. Around Williamsburg, the storm hit harder, carrying away houses. One entire family was killed.

In the aftermath of that storm, smallpox, the scourge of England, struck Virginia. When Andrew was called to the deathbed of his sister Abbie, he went in fear and self-loathing. Although he carefully hid his failing strength from Em, he did not know if he was sturdy enough to survive that plague. His self-loathing came from his long lack of contact with this bitter unpleasant sister for causes that now seemed frail and distant.

Em insisted that she go along.

When Nat opened the door, Andrew knew they had come too late. From the sounds in the room beyond, it was plain that Nat's parishioners and his daughters had already assembled. Lucinda embraced her aunt and uncle; the others nodded coldly from afar.

Only with the funeral over and the house emptied did Em and Andrew sit down with Nat and his two younger daughters.

Nat, even in grief, attempted the ritual of social conversation.

"We hear that James plans to be a physician."

Em nodded. "He is studying in Maryland to that end."

"My mother had no doctor, for want of money," Dorothy said.

Nat winced and broke in with a question about Philip.

Knowing Andrew's tenderness about his absent son, Em spoke again. "He continues in England. His dear friend Gordon was lost to the pox, leaving no heir to manage the estate but Philip's wife, Caroline."

"It is a fortunate man who married such ready money," Dorothy put in.

"And dear Merit?" Nat asked.

This time Andrew spoke. "She and her family are well, for which we thank God."

Lucinda, seeing her father's discomfort, spoke up in an obvious attempt to lighten the air. "Do you know, Auntie Em, I don't think Mother ever used those beautiful gloves you gave her at Merit's wedding. She cherished them too much even to wear them."

Dorothy stiffened with annoyance and began to sniffle, but Em straightened in her chair.

"Never wore them?" she asked. "But she must have at least tried them on."

Lucinda shook her head. "She never took them from the box, that I know of. She came from the wedding, set them in her chest, and that was that."

Dorothy burst into a furious wail. "How can you behave so? My mother lies lifeless and you chatter of weddings and frippery."

234

Andrew would have spoken, but Em's order came too swiftly. Only when she was in the grip of a strong emotion did he ever notice the Scottish burr still clinging to her tongue.

"Go get the gloves, Lucinda," she ordered.

The startled girl looked a question at her father before skittering from the room. Dorothy's anger had boiled into fury. She rose and prodded the fire like an enemy. She stood with the blackened poker in her hand when Lucinda returned to set the carved box beside Em.

"Please open the box and look at the gloves, Nat," Em said firmly.

"Emily," Andrew protested.

"Just lift one glove out," Em told Nat, ignoring Andrew.

Nat rose and crossed the room. His hand trembled as he laid back the light paper. He frowned as he lifted the glove and slid his hand along the length of the fingers. "My God, Em," he said in astonishment.

Dorothy frowned and Lucinda gaped, as their father lifted the gloves, one after the other, and spilled the shower of gold coins onto the table.

Nat shook his head. "Can you forgive her, Emily? Poor creature that she was."

Em reached for his hand, and he lifted hers to his lips. Once before she had needed these words, and they hadn't come. Now they came, but she could not say them aloud.

Indeed, sparrows can only fly as they are taught in the nest.

The heat of the room spun in Em's head as she leaned back in her chair. Three shadows in a line. Magda herself, now Abbie. She turned to find Andrew's eyes gentle on her face, and she breathed deeply to ward off tears.

"We have all seen too little of one another for kinsmen," she said. "Please join us, Nat, for Christmas. We'll have such an old-fashioned Christmas as Grandma Bek describes in the family journal. A Yule log, candles, and fragrant green boughs."

· 10 ·

Some in Chariots, Some in Horses

(1747–1753)

Now I know that the Lord saveth his annointed; He will
hear him from his holy heaven with the saving strength of
his right hand.
Some trust in chariots, and some in horses: but we will
remember the name of the Lord our God.

Psalms 20:6–7

WHEN SHE AND Andrew had been young, making extravagant
promises to each other, Em had never thought about birthdays. But the years kept bringing them. Andrew was fifty-
seven the first year that they celebrated an old-fashioned
Christmas at Gilead. Nat Horne had come with Lucinda, and
Merit and Matthew with their marvelous, almost grown-up
children.

By the next year Andrew had given up traveling farther
from home than to the hearth of some neighbor like Sam
Dunbar with whom he could sit and argue the state of the
colony.

In 1752, Em almost didn't have the heart to hang the
garlands. Merit would come, of course. It was clear that she
meant to do everything just as Matt had done it. But Matt
himself, halfway through the summer, had been struck by a
great agony in his belly that not even opium could touch. He

died in a matter of hours, putting out the light behind Merit's eyes.

That same year, by order of the Crown, even time was changed. The old calendar, with its New Year's Day on the twenty-fifth of March, was gone. The new calendar would begin on the first of January, when all the earth slept in a small death called winter. Em was glad that she didn't believe in omens.

On Christmas day, 1753, James was expected. So eager was Em to see him that she went to the window again and again, pretending to adjust a wreath as she peered into the gathering twilight. She suddenly paused, thinking she saw a figure at the edge of the garden, a woman's figure weeping, with her hands before her face. Without even a shawl, Em ran out to her. Em was only a few steps from the door when the figure, so indistinct in the light, raised her arms to point to the roof of Gilead. Em turned to see the darkness lit by an explosive pillar of flame bursting from beside the west chimney.

"Andrew," she cried, turning to the house in panic. "Andrew, my God, Andrew."

He had come to the top of the stairs at her call. Even as he answered, the flames burst from a door and sped along the carpet toward the polished wood of the curved handrail. Once out of the house he worked relentlessly, directing the bucket brigade back and forth to the river, ordering the removal of what treasures could be saved without risk to anyone.

By the time James arrived with Merit and her family, the fire was totally beyond control. Em kept watching the garden for a sign of the woman who had warned her, the woman scarcely taller than a child, no bigger than Magda.

The Billings family offered hospitality to all at their nearby plantation. Only Em and Andrew refused.

"The millhouse was saved," Andrew reminded them. "Em and I will sleep where we spent our first night together at this place."

James examined them soberly before departing with the others. When they were alone, Em brewed tea over the hearth and they finished a tin of biscuits over the complaints of Em's cat, who thought they belonged only to her.

"Our children had faces longer than dray horses tonight,"

Em mused, staring at the fire. "I hated to tell them it was only a house."

"Only a house. God in heaven, woman. I have been building this place ever since I can remember."

"And you had no more than set the last brick before you started planning another one," she reminded him. No longer did they refer to the west plantation house as Philip's. That dream was too long dead. "Can't we move there now? The buildings are all finished and the land cleared. There is only the matter of a house."

"Emily," he rebuked her. "Gilead was our dream."

She leaned toward him, tracing the line of his jaw with her finger. "Come, my love. Dreams don't burn. No lives were lost. Not even a servant was injured. Be Presbyterian for a minute. That was meant to be, or it would not have taken place. What rises from dust returns to dust. And Gilead gave us James."

As Andrew pulled her close, she thought of the woman who had warned her. No larger than a child really, like Magda.

PART FIVE

A Feast of Wild Grapes

(1753–1764)

My well beloved hath a vineyard in a very fruitful hill:
And he fenced it, and gathered out the stones thereof, and
planted it with the choicest vine, and built a tower in the
midst of it, and also made a winepress therein: And he
looked that it should bring forth grapes, and it brought
forth wild grapes.

Isaiah 5:1–2

In the middle of the journey of our life I came to myself in
a dark wood, where the straight way was lost.

Dante Alighieri, Divine Comedy
"Inferno," Canto I, lines 1–3

---- • 1 • ----

Rock and Fortress

(1753)

For thou art my rock and my fortress; therefore for thy
name's sake lead me, and guide me.

Psalms 31:3

AFTER SLEEPING LITTLE, James Rigg wakened in an unfamiliar
room. The Billings house was already astir. He dressed, his
thoughts bleak, and stopped to stare dumbly at nothing. Now
twenty-two, he had been working for five years with Maryland's
finest doctor. He had treated fever and dropsy, gout and
tumors. He had also seen men with the symptoms his father
had shown on the night just past. His memory set him at war
with himself.

He knew what his master would do. With needle in hand
he would bleed Andrew Rigg to a whiteness. How many men
had James seen fade into death wondering whether the blood
gathering in the pan was cure or curse?

He jerked on his stockings roughly. Would to God that the
truth of His word were more clearly written. It was there.
Hadn't men searched the sky to find the astounding order of
that universe? Hadn't the nervous light been tamed with the
name of electricity? Where was God's truth on the order of
his creature's body? He must enlist his mother's quiet strength.
Together they would win or lose this battle for Andrew
Rigg's life. God willing, they would win.

News of the fire had spread. The Billings house was filling with hams and puddings to replace the feast blowing in the ashes of Gilead.

"We're sending a chaise to fetch your parents," Mr. Billings told James.

James shook his head. "Please give me the joy of driving them here myself."

His mother was laughing as he mounted the millhouse stairs.

"We are ragamuffins, dressed in tatters and rags," she told him. "Are you sure you wish to be seen with us?"

"Are you sure you feel well enough for this day?" he countered. "Everyone would understand your need to rest." His mother's eyes were terrified and pleading in spite of her determined smile. His father rose heavily, like a man sodden with drink.

"Miss Christmas with the children?" Andrew asked. "Not on your life, son, not on your life."

"Then you'll be the king and queen of ragamuffins," James teased, taking his father's arm firmly to descend the stairs.

It was past midday before James was able to draw his mother aside.

It was unlike her to refuse to meet his eyes. "Out with it, James," she ordered. "Why are you so suddenly so secretive?"

"Don't tell me you don't know."

"The fire was a great shock," she began. "He worked so hard. He needs a little rest."

"Do you see how he holds his arm useless against his side? Have his words ever come so slurred before?"

She would have wept but for his arms around her. "Listen to me," he whispered. "He must have rest and light food. He must be kept cool without becoming chilled. He is desperately ill, and no surgeon's skill can help him."

"But he is a stubborn man," she reminded him.

James leaned down and kissed her hair. "You will manage him, Mother. You always have."

The sun still rode high when Em turned apologetically to Mrs. Billings. "Please forgive me, but I have no choice. Would you excuse me if I retire early? James could drive me home."

"And leave me here?" Andrew protested, his face suddenly tight with concern for her. Then he forced a laugh. "I can't imagine this high-stepping filly slowing to a walk, but I'll be gentleman enough to stay by her."

What a clever schemer, James thought as Andrew watched Em with concern and accepted James's advice without a murmur.

"The overseer will send your breakfast. Don't come back into all that fray until midday at least."

"Don't worry, son," Andrew replied. "I'll have Em rested and well very soon."

Each morning James looked for some improvement in his father's condition. Each morning he was disappointed. Had he been wrong? Should he have forced such treatment on him as another man would have used? Men had been bled for centuries. Who was he to risk his father's life because he disagreed?

"I am a man of science," he shouted at the studded sky as he drove back to the Billings'. "Where are my tools for life? Where is the truth of my father's need?"

That great network of stars seemed to be flying from him even as he spoke, receding into darkness even as his father was moving toward that other darkness.

"God. God. God," he screamed. "Heal thy servant."

The stars continued to fade.

Em was to cherish the memory of that week forever. She and Andrew shared lazy breakfasts and laughing suppers in the millhouse, spending only the middle of each day with the family. A brush of snow past the windows was glazed by sun. A slow rain cleared the earth as Merit began packing to return her family to Candle Creek and James readied to go to Maryland.

That night Em wakened to a change in Andrew's breathing. She rose on an elbow, and he raised his good hand to her cheek.

"Shall we talk about the new house?" he asked in that heavy tone that deadened her hopes. Even the vague light from the hearth showed the pain in his face. She felt death curled in the corners of the room, and the immensity of her love for him thundered in her chest. How could she please him? What did he want in these last hours: fresh protestation of a love that was long past being doubted? Promises of a future he couldn't share?

The jesting note in his voice was forced. "Where's my old Em? What ridiculous ideas do you have about the new house?"

She drew a pained breath and looped her arms about her knees to grin down at him.

"Ridiculous indeed! It will be Georgian, with perfect symmetry, one side with the other. Deep windows clear to the earth."

How often had she heard him rant about that style?

"Boxes on boxes in the German style, eh? Long windows for the rain to paint with mud?" His laughter ended in a groan.

She held him so as not to see the pain in his face. His grasp was like iron as she whispered fiercely of her love. He tightened, trembled and then softened in her arms. Her own silent tears began to flow.

By morning, when James came, the hearth held only a winking ash. Em stared at her son from the circle of Andrew's arms. She yielded to James's hand, and stood apart as he covered his father's face.

"There was nothing you could do," James told her. "Nothing in God's world that anyone could do."

She sat silent a long time. When she looked up, her face was almost childlike.

"He died with laughter on his lips, James. Will he waken to our next world in that same joyous condition?"

Mottled clouds hung over the mourners at Andrew Rigg's grave. Gray river and gray sky and mourners as barren of life as the bare-branched trees. Gil the Toad was bent and balding, and Mollie was past her bloom. The years that had thickened Asa Forrester had patterned his face with seams. The shaft of watery light found its way through the clouds as Nat Horne droned the service to a close.

Merit, watching her mother, saw her lips move and leaned forward to catch the words.

"The sun always shines for Andrew," Em was saying, not even noticing her daughter's attention. Merit felt her grief sharpened by a nameless anger.

The crowd moved toward the house, the wind whipping

Nat's cloak. Only Merit and her Uncle Paul remained, the old man staring at the mounded earth with streaming eyes.

"God be merciful," Paul pleaded, his voice rising. "Be gentle to this heinous sinner. Cool the fires of fire around his guilty feet. Hold him from the grasp of demons."

Merit was frozen to the spot. Crows jeered from the naked grove. She needed to scream, to ask by what right he condemned Andrew Rigg.

"Unrepentant sinner," Paul moaned. "Grievous sinner."

Then James was back, his hand on her arm.

"Leave me alone," she hissed, her eyes baleful on the gaunt old man.

"Come," he insisted, his grasp imperious on her arm.

"Why?" she challenged him. "To warm my body for this little time? Let it be cold like Father's, cold and in the earth and done with for a madman to jeer at."

"Walk with me," James insisted.

She was trembling uncontrollably, so that she stumbled against him.

"Our father will never die as long as his anger flames in you, Merit. Who are you fighting? Surely not that pitiful old man."

She shook his hand away. "It's all so unfair. Too many dreams died with Father. His house is in ashes, his firstborn son a stranger."

"For every loss there was a gain," James told her. "Your children carry his dreams forward, as you and I do. What of your own dreams, my dear? First Matthew, then Father. How will it go with Mother in your house?"

She felt her anger sway toward the foolishness of his question. What choice did she have? Where else could Em go? West to the new plantation, even as Governor Dinwiddie was warning of fresh Indian danger?

"I love Mother," she told him, "but I very seldom like her."

"Don't take any blame for that. She's a fortress on a hill, more terrible than an army with banners."

She was startled by her sudden tears. "I'm afraid of her. I'm not strong, as she is." Now the tears were past her control. "James, don't you see? All I have left of Matthew is the dreams we had for the children. You can't imagine how many dreams we spun. I must see them all come true for him.

245

Mother always infects me with doubt. I know I can bring our dreams to pass if I'm left alone. If Mother weakens me with doubt, I'm not sure I can."

Her tears stopped when James pulled her close. She had not rested her head against a man's broad chest since Matthew died. The feel of James's arms robbed her of breath.

"God, God," she moaned. "I'm not sure I can do it."

"I'm sure you can," he said, his voice muffled in her hair. "Mother was long apprenticed to other women's houses. You saw her back there. She was more conscious of Father's life than his death. She will live with him in memory from now on."

When she lifted her face, he wiped the tears from her wet cheeks. "But remember, Merry," he cautioned. "You can only dream for yourself and Matthew. Father learned this from Philip. Your children will pursue their own dreams, and you must free them to that."

With the turn of the tide, the boat was readied for Norfolk. Asa Forrester planted himself before Merit with a twisted face.

"I've been coming up this river a long time," he said.

When she nodded, he reddened and went on. "My reasons haven't changed, you know."

She would have replied except that she feared her own words.

"I'm here, just as I've always been, Merit," he stammered. "In sickness, in health, that way, you know."

He pressed her hand and fled for the ship under Honor's thoughtful gaze.

"Isn't he a marvelous old man?" Honor asked softly.

Merit bridled. "He's hardly old—only a year older than I." Then, embarrassed by her defense of him, she turned away. "As for marvelous, if God set out to design an ugly man, he would use Asa Forrester as a pattern."

She felt Honor's confused glance on her back.

— • 2 • —

Messengers

He that sendeth a message by the hand of a fool cutteth off
the feet, and drinketh damage.
Where no wood is there, the fire goeth out: so where there
is no talebearer, the strife ceaseth.

Proverbs 26:6, 20

MERIT WAS TO remember James's words with wonder in the
weeks following. "Mother was long apprenticed to other
women's houses." Certainly Em slipped into her own household without disturbing its peace. She was able to amuse
herself endlessly. By the time Em had dispatched the last
letters to friends and kinsmen telling of Andrew's death, she
was busy corresponding with her neighbors near Gilead.

Merit was sitting with her mother and Honor when Em
received the letter from the Northern Neck. "Look at this,"
she cried with delight. "Belle Lyon Sommers has answered
my letter about Andrew." Then, after a moment: "Listen to
this. She has a child, a girl named Alice, who will soon be
six. Her brothers have signed on to fight in the French and
Indian war. For this they have been promised land of their
own."

Merit nodded, knowing that many had signed for such
land, only to earn earth six feet below for their pains.

"I hope they come back safely," Em mused. "Your Uncle
Paul's land is rightfully theirs. They needn't take such a
risk."

"Father said they wanted nothing from the tidewater."

"That was the oldest brother, Thomas. Andrew felt that Belle might be more open-minded. For now I can only make sure I keep in touch."

"Father would be pleased," Merit told her, knowing that this was what her mother most liked to hear.

With great tact, Em managed to be "resting" or busy with her journal when Merit entertained guests. She was in her room the first time Jared Soames visited Candle Creek. Philip's letters, which preceded the visit, had praised the man so highly that even the children were curious to meet this friend of their Uncle Philip's.

Even so, Honor came to her grandmother's room almost at once, in a fit of giggles.

"You can't believe what a peacock he is," she reported. "He has a great belly under a bright vest, and all of his chins are buried in a nest of ruffles that would hide a hen."

"And this is your Uncle Philip's friend?" Em asked.

Honor grinned. "Mother is trying valiantly to get news of Uncle Philip and his family, but Mr. Soames insists on regaling her with tales of the court. I think he's showing off for her."

"That is too bad," Em said. "Because he is Philip's friend, Merit hoped he would be like your father."

Honor laughed. "My father wouldn't sit still for such tales as this man tells." She leaned forward and whispered. "He told Mother about the death of the queen. He said King George wept, and Queen Caroline, knowing that she was dying, urged him to marry again. The king cried out that he wouldn't, but would only have mistresses."

Em's astonishment turned into helpless laughter.

"I wish I could see your mother's face," she admitted.

"Poor Mother doesn't know how to act. He called the king a blockhead even as Mother was deciding that he was the same."

To Em's amazement, Merit received Mr. Soames a second time. Em sat and listened to him telling how great a hatred the king felt toward his son Frederick, who had been killed by a blow on the head by a cricket ball. "All these Hanoverian kings hate their sons," he said, accepting a second glass of Madeira wine.

"That strikes us as very strange," Merit put in. "To us our sons are our greatest treasure and concern."

Mr. Soames dropped his voice sympathetically. "My friend Philip speaks of this great concern of yours, your loneliness with such responsibility."

"Philip doesn't know my sons," Merit reminded him. "Robbie manages his grandfather's and my estates with rare skill."

Soames's manner turned almost simpering. "He must be scarce more than a lad, to be your son, mistress."

Em had to hide her smile as Merit stiffened almost belligerently to meet her guest's eyes. "Robbie is nineteen, the same age his father was when we wed. Robbie is no more a lad than his father was, both being full-grown men."

When Mr. Soames called for the third time, Merit pleaded indisposition and did not receive him. Within days of this attempt Asa Forrester came upriver saying he needed to confer with Em about the shipping business. After the briefest time, he sought Merit in her garden.

"What's this I hear of your marrying an Englishman?" he challenged her.

She rose to stare at him. "My God, Asa, what tale will the gossips make up next?"

"They name a name, they do," he said angrily. "Some Soames from Sussex, sent by your brother to take Matthew's place."

"Sent by my brother indeed," Merit said angrily. Then she paused. "And what is it to you if I marry or not?"

He flushed scarlet and fell silent. She grinned at him as she regarded his rugged face, with his wig askew. She laid her hand on his arm.

"Come, now, Asa, I was teasing you. You know the manner of my life. My mother ages in my house. My uncle rages madly beyond the grove. My daughter fancies herself in love and weeps and laughs by silly turns. Do I have time to fool with a court dandy for husband? Go back to your ships and forget these tattles."

He grinned back, visibly relaxing. "You didn't even mention the Fraser company," he reminded her.

"That is my mother's concern."

"For now, perhaps, but Guillam Jones ages in body and

spirit. My own birthdays make a lively tally. Who will be ship master next?"

She turned thoughtful. "Philip has sons."

"Your sons are here."

She shook her head. "Robbie is a planter, and Bruce trains for the law."

"Rigg is coming on," he suggested.

"He's but a boy of ten," she protested.

"Tadpoles turn into frogs," Asa reminded her. "It's something you need to be thinking of."

As they turned toward the house, he stammered that same halting phrase he had spoken at her father's funeral.

"If your mind was to change, I'm here, the same as always. In sickness and health, richer, poorer, all that. Don't be forgetting that."

• 3 •

Sparks Flying Upward

(1754)

Although affliction comes not forth of the dust, neither doth trouble spring out of the ground. Yet man is born unto trouble, as the sparks fly upward.

Job 5:6–7

MERIT WAS WAKENED in the chill of dawn by the distant sound of an animal in distress. Only slowly did she fix the cry in her mind as that of a cow lowing. Bundling herself against the chill, she stood at her window staring toward the barnyard. No calf was expected, and there had been no illness among the beasts; yet the sound, coming now fainter, now stronger, certainly indicated a beast in pain.

Only when she was dressed and let herself out into the heavy wet air did she realize that the sound came from across the creek, at her Uncle Paul's place. Wrapping a shawl about her against the wet chill, she set off through the grove. A clattering of crows rose in protest at her passing, and the furtive sound in the pool advertised the flight of a night visitor.

Only at her Uncle Paul's was there no sign of life. Merit picked her way through the rubble in the barnyard to reach the cow that was bawling frantically as it banged itself against the wooden sides of its stall.

Once released, the crazed animal sped past Merit to the water trough. As it drank feverishly, Merit drew another bucket, her anger rising.

God in heaven. It was one thing to be slovenly about hanging gates and rusting tools, but to let a dumb beast suffer for want of water was a sin against God's creation.

She left the beast still gasping at the trough, in order to march to the door and bang on it with her fists. There had to be someone there. Since her uncle had joined forces with these wandering preachers, there had been a parade of young men at his table, young men of strange faith and violent words. When no answer came, she shoved the door ajar. The stench of the place drove her back for a moment into the sweet air.

"Uncle Paul," she shouted into the musty silence. A mouse skittered along a table, only to flee. After calling his name over and over, Merit made her way through the house and upstairs.

She thought at first that he was dead. He had slipped from the bed to the floor, where he lay in his own filth. Throwing open the window to clear the air, she knelt and felt for a pulse at his wrist. Only after bringing fresh water and bathing his fevered face for a long time did his eyes flutter open.

"Woe," Paul cried hoarsely. "Woe to the poor sinner."

"What happened?" Merit asked.

"Woe," he repeated, his voice rising into hysteria. "God in His mercy, God in His strength." His hands were claws on her arms.

251

"Help," she stammered, gulping against her own nausea. "Let me bring help."

Even as Merit fled back through the woods to fulfill this promise, she was flooded with guilt.

Why had she paid so little attention to this old kinsman with no closer family of his own? It was true that she had been much concerned about the betrothal of her daughter, Honor. The stubbornness of the child had caught her off guard.

"Your father and I had planned for you to delay marriage until you were of a sounder age," she told Honor.

"But I love him and he loves me," Honor wept miserably. "This concerns our lives, not yours and father's. He is going north to school in Princeton. We shall die if we're apart."

"Many have wished to but few have died of love," Merit told her briskly. Fortunately, Peter Tucker's parents were of the same mind. The betrothal was to be announced, with no date set for the marriage. And meanwhile she had let the lovestruck children blind her to conditions as close as the next plantation.

As if to make up for that lost time, she immediately sent servants to take over Uncle Paul and his house, and dispatched a summons to Williamsburg for a physician.

"I would to God that James were nearer," she told her mother. "Uncle Paul is clearly out of his mind, and his bones are barely covered by flesh. How could those men call themselves Christians and leave an old man destitute there?"

"They go where their God sends them," Em replied. "They feel themselves called to be fishers of men."

"How do you know that?" Merit challenged.

"Paul said this of himself when he left for that trek to Georgia to hear the man Whitefield preach."

Merit studied her mother thoughtfully. "How patient you are to sit and listen to his ravings."

"He is a lonely man made what he is by an empty life. Even as a child he saw harsh things in an embittered house. A child is clay that carries the potter's hand."

It was the journal, Merit realized. Em's hours with the old family journal had made her more Lyon than one of the blood.

• • •

The physician came from Paul's bed with a somber face.

"He has a tumor," he told Merit, holding her eyes as if to convey the word that neither of them wished spoken. "He'll need much nursing, good food and clean dressings. Later he will need opium to deaden his pain."

The tears were involuntary. Why did such tears flow for a man she had feared all her life and never loved? When she gained control of her voice, she asked how long he would have to suffer.

"The spirit chooses its own time, but from this moment he moves only toward his maker, not toward this life."

"Am I a hypocrite?" Merit asked her mother. "All my life I have dreaded his very aspect. At some times I have even hated him. Yet his plight cuts to my soul as if we had been the tenderest of friends. Even his God is stranger to me yet I mourn him as my own."

Em raised a hand to Merit's cheek. "His God is the same as ours. Only understandings have kept you apart. Be glad for him that he lives in this place where different faiths are tolerated. In England it would not have gone so easy for him."

Merit moved away. Philip had often suggested in his letters that part of the problem with Virginia was that she had no bishop closer than London to remind the people that the church and the state were one and the same. And surely these years saw strange preachers on Virginia's roads. The rector of St. Paul's in Hanover had even opened his pulpit to a preacher of this new and frightening faith. Indeed such things wouldn't happen in England, but Virginia could only be the worse for it.

"I must locate a housekeeper to care for Uncle Paul," she told her mother. "With his strange beliefs, he will not let a slave serve him."

"I know," Em said, not meeting her eyes. "And I must write again to Belle Sommers. She should know that the time is nearing when she and her brothers must make a decision about their birthright."

When the servant left for Williamsburg to place an advertisement in the *Virginia Gazette*, he carried Em's letter to post in the capital.

4

Directed Steps

(1755)

A man deviseth his way: but the Lord directeth his steps.
Proverbs 16:9

THE WELCOME RAIN had begun the night before and continued through the morning. Robbie, penned in the millhouse at Gilead with the plantation's books, rose now and then to stare through clouded windows at the swollen river.

Under his mother's tutelage he had begun managing the Candle Creek plantation when his father died. With the loss of his grandfather, his duties had been stretched to include the Springer plantation near Williamsburg as well as Gilead, the little Simms place and the land first bought for Philip in the west.

Spending time at Gilead had made Robbie realize the spell this land had cast on Andrew. A sense of virgin wildness remained in the air that had been lost along the lower reaches of the James River. Robbie had grown close, not only to his father's family, the Billingses, but to the other neighbors and friends who had brightened his grandfather's last years.

Hearing a shout from below, he wiped the mist from his window with his sleeve. A small carriage, its wheels deeply mired, had drawn to the opposite side of the river.

As he watched, a bundled figure marched through the mud

to wave at his servant below. By the time Robbie had come down the stairs, the visitor's voice was overpowering even the pelting of the rain.

To his astonishment, the face under the dark hood was that of Barbara Dunbar, a neighbor's young daughter.

"Thank God," she called as he emerged. "That lout of yours won't send me a boat."

"The current is too swift to cross," his man grumbled. "Tell her to go home."

"I heard that," she challenged him. "Surely even you have wit enough to throw across a tow rope."

"She's right." Robbie laughed and sent his man to fetch what he needed.

With the weighted rope secure, Robbie himself rowed across, amused at Barbara's imperious manner.

"Now, what is important enough for you to mire that rig and risk drowning in the river for?" he asked her.

Her childish face was sleek with rain but amiable. "Kinsmen of yours," she explained. "They were seeking your grandmother, so I brought them here."

He glanced at the carriage, whose curtains were drawn against the rain.

"A woman and her daughter," Barbara explained, her back to the carriage. "They walked from Colchester."

"Walked," Robbie echoed in disbelief.

She nodded, a sudden elfish grin on her face. "And drowned rats they were when they reached our place. But they're fed and dried out now, and I thought to keep them so if I could. Dad and I tried every way to get them to linger with us until the weather cleared, but Mrs. Sommers—"

"Sommers," Robbie echoed. "Belle Sommers?"

Barbara's glance on his face was bright. "You know her, then? Isn't she fine?"

He shook his head. "I only know her from my grandparents' talk. How good of you to shelter her. And a child?"

"A precious little girl, but lame, and they walked all that way. But come, I confess I am afraid I might mire the rig. If you could just get them across to a dry place . . ."

Robbie was ill-prepared for his kinswoman Belle Sommers. She was plainly dressed, with her hair pulled severely back from an open, sun-browned face. Her grasp on his hand held the strength of a man.

He was even less prepared for Barbara's farewell to this woman and child. She acted like a woman herself instead of a mere child. She took Belle's face in her hands and kissed both cheeks tenderly. "Once for yourself, dear lady," she told Belle Sommers, "and once for Mistress Emily with my love."

As he rowed his guests across the river, Robbie saw the driver painfully extricate the carriage wheels from the mire. Barbara leaned from the window into the rain to wave cheerily.

"What a remarkable girl," he said musingly.

Belle Sommers, her arm around her fair daughter, smiled.

"They treated Alice and me like royalty," she told him. "There must be some magic in your grandmother's name."

Robbie looked at the lines of that open face and at the remarkable eyes beneath winged brows. They had walked all the way from Colchester, had they? And then thought their welcome rested on a neighbor's name?

"I would guess the magic lies in your own noble face, Aunt Belle," he told her.

The overseer's wife found space for Belle and the child that night. Come morning, Robbie would travel downriver to take them to his grandmother at Candle Creek. The rain stopped at twilight, but the eaves chimed against the roar of the river as he prepared for bed.

A sense of excitement brought him back to the desk in nightshirt and slippers. The coming of Belle Sommers and Alice was exciting, more than that was stimulating him. He had watched Barbara Dunbar grow up over the past years, dressed in ruffles and seated at the table, demure and unreachable in chapel. The girl standing on the muddy bank shouting insults at his servant was a different and much more compelling creature, more woman than child. She had clearly seen past common clothing and obvious need to the spirit of Belle Sommers. And by God, she was beautiful there, with the rain sheeting down her face, not beautiful in any classical way, but with a pert strength that clung to his mind, the shape of her fine small head as she lifted it to embrace Belle Sommers.

"My dear Barbara," his letter began. "On the morrow I will take Mistress Sommers and Alice to Candle Creek. I take this opportunity to add to the thanks I so awkwardly expressed. Upon my return, I would like to call and more adequately express my gratitude for your kindness to my kinswomen."

256

He hesitated a long time over the closing before writing simply, "With deepest regards, Robbie Fraser Billings."

Merit was returning from her morning check on Uncle Paul and his household. Mist hung along the river, and the sea birds she had hated as a child now called as friends from that fused light. Life hummed around her in the grove. The tadpoles she and Philip had trapped as children darkened the rim of the pool. To go from Paul's house to this place was to go from death to life. When the humming of the grove stopped, she looked up to see Robbie on the path. It was clear from his face that no ordinary errand had brought him downriver.

"I'm glad to find you alone," he said, taking her arm.

"Something is wrong?"

He shook his head. "No, something is new. Isabelle Lyon Sommers is here with her daughter, Alice. They walked all the way from Colchester to Sam Dunbar's place, and he had them brought to me at Gilead."

"Why is she here?" Merit asked.

"I only know she undertook that long journey to see Grandmother. I had Cook make them breakfast while I found you."

"What is she like?"

"Silent," he replied. "Plain and strong and silent. The child is lame."

Merit nodded and took his arm. "We'll go make them welcome."

Belle Sommers rose from a bench as Merit entered. She was a tall, seemingly ageless woman with dark brows and a face seamed by sun.

"Welcome, cousin," Merit said swiftly.

Belle nodded. "Your son has been very kind to us."

The child studied Merit over her spoon with solemn eyes.

"You must be Alice," Merit told her.

The child's head disappeared under her mother's arm.

"Sit," Merit urged Belle. "Mother has taken to sleeping late, but she will be down soon."

The mother did not share the child's shyness. Her eyes met Merit's levelly. "Your mother wrote of your uncle's illness," she said quietly. "I thought you would need practiced hands for his care."

Merit stared at her in disbelief. This woman couldn't know the endless agonies of trying to keep help in that somber house without resorting to slaves, which Paul would not permit. Yet she said nothing about the land or about her obvious need; she was simply offering her help.

"But cousin," Merit stammered.

Belle Sommers smiled tenderly. "The letter came within a week of my husband's burial. It seemed almost a sign."

Merit was struggling for words, but Belle shook her head.

"Taking care of people has been the whole of my life," she explained. "My hands are restless at other tasks. There were many children when my father died. After my mother's health failed, I claimed that I raised them for her. I was ten, you see, when young Will was born."

"But you owe us nothing," Merit protested. "Not us, not Uncle Paul. I am delighted to have you here but—"

"I have nothing better to do," Belle told her firmly.

Only Em greeted Belle Sommers without surprise. She took her close and held her with delight. "You are exactly as Andrew described you, like Aunt Martha Springer. Oh, Belle Lyon, how welcome you are."

"She says she has come to care for Uncle Paul," Merit said.

Em smiled. "She has come to be a candle in a dark corner, as a gift from God. But Belle, it isn't an easy corner to light. He battles death with the same violence with which he warred against life."

Belle nodded. "Better that than a spiritless slipping away."

Belle was more than a candle in the darkness; she was a godsend. She changed the sick man's room from a reeking hellhole to a place of tranquility. She threw open windows and removed all the clutter that could be spared. Within a week even the stench of his illness was tempered by great armsful of green herbs that she kept in pitchers and changed daily. Her gentle patience seemed to tame Paul's raving terror. His eyes followed her in peace.

But it was difficult for Merit to think of Belle as a kinswoman. The plainness of her speech and the poverty of her dress brought her a secret shame when friends and neighbors stopped in.

And the memory of Matthew pressed back in spite of

herself. The three of them, Philip, Matthew and Merit, standing in the sunny yard talking about marksmanship. Matthew had compared her skill to that of frontier women, and she had taken quick offense. Belle was such a woman as he had praised. Could she have walked all those miles in rain and sun with a lame child, slept in groves and eaten from a bundle to serve a stranger she had never seen?

"I had nothing better to do."

Quickly enough Merit learned that Belle's husband's burial had left her penniless. It didn't matter that Belle needed them as much as they needed her. The point was that she had come, drawn by the power of kinship to do an unpleasant task.

And still Merit could not sit with her in comfort, for the jealousy that rose in her heart.

Although Alice had a cot in Paul's house, she spent most of her time with Honor.

"She isn't a doll," Merit teased Honor as her daughter brushed and plaited the child's long fair hair.

"Of course you're a doll, aren't you, Alice?" Honor teased, smiling into the child's face.

"Dolls can't read," Alice protested.

"Neither can you, you little fraud." Honor laughed. "You only guess the story from the pictures. But I am going to teach you to read properly, from letters."

"Only if my mother thinks it's all right," Alice corrected her.

"Your mother will be delighted," Merit assured her, turning away.

She had seen Belle prepare herbs and soft foods for Paul. She had seen her take a tool and perform strange wonders without giving them a second thought. But Belle could not read the letters of her own name or make any other mark than an X.

Yet Merit felt her soft, pale hands were an offense, compared to the veined dark efficiency of Belle's.

All the way back to Gilead, Robbie amused himself by thinking about Barbara Dunbar planted in the mire shouting furiously at his servant. What a little feist she had seemed that day, and yet she'd been so tender with Belle Sommers.

His Grandma Em, after hearing the story, supplied him

with a gift of fine lace from the shop Aunt Magda had operated in Williamsburg. Only as Sam Dunbar greeted him at the door with a hearty handclasp did Robbie's courage fail him.

"If it isn't Robbie," Sam said warmly, drawing him in.

Barbara Dunbar had been seated on a stool by the fire. She rose stiffly as he entered. This, then, was the test. For this was the Barbara Dunbar he remembered from earlier meetings, childish, prim and self-effacing, hair curled and clothing ruffled, with eyes turned carefully away.

As he greeted the housekeeper, he challenged Barbara's apparent shyness.

"And a good day to you, Mistress Barbara. I bring you a gift of thanks from my grandmother."

"A gift? For doing what any neighbor would do?" Sam asked.

"In such a downpour?" Robbie challenged with a grin.

"With the drought we have all suffered, we are our most genial when it rains," Sam Dunbar told him.

Barbara curtsied as he set the package in her hands. Her soft words of thanks would have been lost if the yellow cat by the hearth had been purring any louder.

"Come, Barbara," the housekeeper urged. "Let's see what dear Mistress Rigg has so thoughtfully sent you."

Even Barbara looked up as the length of lace was lifted from its wrappings. "My goodness," Mrs. Cox breathed. "Such lace as I've never seen."

"The only work of this kind I've ever seen was a christening dress that your grandmother had made for our Barbara, here. The vicar vowed he'd seen brides adorned less handsomely."

"My Aunt Magda Steele owned a shop in Williamsburg," Robbie explained. "She had such goods as have seldom been seen in Virginia, according to my mother. She died in a kitchen fire the day the Capitol burned, and Grandmother keeps that stock of hers for . . . special people."

It was astonishing how quickly Sam Dunbar turned the talk to other things, asking Robbie what he knew of the governor's campaign to drive the French from the forks of the Ohio River.

"I know little enough," Robbie admitted. "Colonel Joshua Fry, who was my brother's teacher at the college, set out from Alexandria with one hundred fifty men, who were joined by more forces at Will Creek. I understand that they barely set out before Colonel Fry was thrown from his horse and killed.''

"So that's how young Washington from Mount Vernon was put in command," Sam said musingly. "He'd done well for the governor before. How did it happen that he failed so miserably this time?''

"In their single encounter with the French and the Indians, one warrior escaped. Knowing that Indian would alert a great force, Washington erected a hasty fort of palisades, which he called Fort Necessity.''

Sam laughed ruefully. "It was well named. We Virginians have been palisading this land of such necessity for a hundred and fifty years now.''

"It's generally said that Washington fought that long, bitter battle valiantly, only capitulating after losing a fourth of his force and negotiating honorable terms.''

Dunbar struck his hand with an angry fist. "God help us now that they have smelled our blood.''

"The assembly agrees with you, fortunately," Robbie said, rising. "They have doubled their previous appropriation for defense.''

Robbie saw Dunbar's eyes linger on his daughter as he rose. "We have much to protect here in the west, God willing.''

It was a clear night and cold, as Sam followed Robbie out to his horse.

"Do come again, son," Sam Dunbar urged. "I miss the good company of your parents as well as of my own sons.''

"I haven't the good fortune to know your sons," Robbie reminded him.

Sam nodded. "You wouldn't, I suppose. Both of them are planters to the west of here." Then he laughed. "I always wanted a daughter like my own Mary. When my sons were already well grown, God granted my great desire by giving me Barbara. The child was barely walking when I lost Mary. Barbara's been my own child, you might say. I myself taught her to ride and shoot like one of the lads.''

"She shows no marks of such training." Robbie laughed.

Sam nodded toward the house, "That's Mrs. Cox's doing.

But women are deep pools, showing only what depths they choose to let us see.''

On the way back to the millhouse, Robbie struck his fist thoughtfully on the pommel of his saddle. So Barbara was a deep pool. Very poetic. She was a double-faced creature, that's what she was, half parlor doll and half raving shrew. He grinned. Why should he be more drawn to a girl half-grown than to the handsome young women in Williamsburg whom his mother so pointedly forced on him, he couldn't say. Indeed he would go back to visit Sam Dunbar. He would carry him news until Sam's ears were stuffed. One day he might even surprise that deep pool enough that the real Barbara Dunbar would leap from its depths for him and be the irresistible creature she had seemed that day, with her feet buried in mud and her face glistening with cool rain.

—————— • 5 • ——————

From the Wilderness

(Late summer, 1756)

Who is this that cometh up from the wilderness, leaning on her beloved? I raised thee up under the apple tree: there thy mother brought thee forth: there she brought thee forth that bare thee.

Song of Solomon 8:5

IT WAS A rare morning when Merit did not rise to give fervent thanks for the coming of Belle Sommers and Alice. Not only had Belle lifted the burden of her suffering uncle from her days and eased the progress of his disease, but Alice had made a scholar of restless, dreaming Honor.

Honor even laughed about it. "How can I lecture to her about letters and numbers unless I become a better student myself? Besides, with Peter becoming so wise at Princeton College, I shall have to run to catch up with him."

"Few men value learning in a woman," Merit reminded her.

"Daddy cherished it in you and deferred to you on most things," Honor reminded her.

Merit look at her daughter with astonishment. Who are we in the eyes of our children? she wondered. Matthew deferred to her? The thought had never occurred to her. She thought of Matthew and herself as two streams that God had set flowing for their one-time joining. Their dreams for the children, had they been mutual dreams or only her own, to which Matthew had agreed with his customary gentleness?

Would Matthew know her now? She had been as much a student as Honor since Belle and Alice came. Never had a woman taught her so much as Belle Sommers had. Her strength, her unfailing common sense, made such a mockery of Merit's carefully learned manners that she found herself drawn to Belle's simpler style.

And when Belle raised her fine eyes to smile at Merit in friendship, she felt an exultation. "I would rather be well liked by Belle Sommers than by any lord of the land," she told her mother, only half in jest.

Months had passed without Robbie's having worked up the courage to speak to Sam Dunbar about his daughter. His silence was not wholly due to Barbara's being full young to be betrothed. He was also confused about her. Not once in that year had Barbara shown even a glimpse of the spirit that had livened her that day on the river bank. If he was to settle for a custard of a woman, many were to be had for the dickering, among the girls his mother was fond of. Privately Robbie thought his mother as often wrongheaded as right, and he knew that Honor was cursed with uncommon stubbornness. Still, better such a woman than the pallid, affected dolls who circled, simpering, in his arms at the revels in Williamsburg.

The drought lingered on, laying such depression on the

common people that Robbie found himself heartsore at the end of a day's travel through the countryside. Dust blew in the fields at Candle Creek. Even the hogs on the Simms plantation ran lean from the poorness of their forage. But not even this concerned him as much as the military campaign of the summer past.

Sam Dunbar always expected the latest news when Robbie came to Gilead. How pleased Robbie had been to report that Braddock had arrived in Virginia with two incomplete regiments of British regulars. This force had been strengthened by militiamen from both Virginia and Maryland, together with some light horsemen. New York had contributed two companies under the command of Horatio Gates. More than two thousand men had marched west with Braddock, and George Washington was among that number.

In the heat of summer this army had hacked out a road for the passage of wagons and artillery. Sam had laughed at tales of how the British regulars wilted in the Virginia sun, but there was no thought of less than a complete victory against the French.

But that had been earlier in the summer. In late August Robbie sat in the millhouse with his head in his hands. Perhaps other tongues would have reported Braddock's defeat to Sam Dunbar. Robbie's own blood had run cold at the reports.

The column had been caught just after crossing the Monongahela River in a narrow space. They were surrounded by Indians and French concealed among the trees. Four horses were shot from under Braddock as he tried to form his troops. The regulars were panic-stricken. The only volley they aimed well was at a squad of Virginians emerging from a flank attack.

Sixty-three of the eighty-nine officers fell on the field, with over nine hundred men wounded or dead. Washington had buried Braddock under the road and driven wagons back and forth, that he not be dug up and scalped by his enemies.

Sam Dunbar listened without comment, not even lifting his eyes from the floor. The housekeeper, Mrs. Cox, seemed to flutter around the edge of the room like a tethered bird.

Only when Robbie fell silent did Sam raise his eyes. His voice was broken, the voice of a man suddenly aged. "This marks the end of many things, son," he told Robbie. "Among them is peace. Virginians have always fought against maintaining a standing army. Now we must have one for our lives' sake." He turned to Mrs. Cox. "Bring some wine for our guest and call Barbara."

Mrs. Cox hesitated. "She isn't here."

"Where is she?" her father asked.

"She slipped out after . . ." Mrs. Cox paused. "Maybe she's in the garden." There was doubt in her voice.

"I would like to extend my greeting to her." Robbie said.

Sam Dunbar and the housekeeper exchanged a cryptic glance.

"Do that, son," the old man said. "We'll save the wine for later."

Clouds of grasshoppers rose before Robbie's feet as he walked through the empty garden toward the stable. A man was mending harness in the open door.

"Have you seen Mistress Barbara?" Robbie asked.

The man rose and pointed to the woods. "She took her pony that way," he explained. A barren riding trail wandered under the trees. A dusty scent hung in the air, and no birds sang. Robbie was startled to a stop by the whinny of a horse and the splash of something heavy striking water.

She hadn't heard him coming. She was too intent on venting her fury. With the pony tethered in the shade, Barbara Dunbar, legs braced on the river bank, was picking up great stones and hurling them with all her might into the sluggish stream. "Damn. Damn. Damn," she was whispering fiercely in a voice choked by tears.

The horse whinnied again at Robbie's approach. Barbara wheeled with a stone clutched in each hand. For one horrified moment Robbie considered ducking.

Her face was tight with fury and pain. "How dare you?" she screamed at him. "How dare you come on me like that?" She dropped the stones and ran to her pony, tugging the crop from her saddle.

A gambler's grandson, Robbie decided to take the risk and waited, unmoving. She seized the whip and raised it to strike. When he still didn't flinch, she let it drop at her side and began to sob bitterly.

"Barbara," he said quietly. "I came to share yours and your father's pain, not to gain any more of my own."

"You know, then?" she asked.

"I know that we lost the war, and many fine men with it."

She wilted before his eyes. "Benjy," she whispered. "Did you know my brother Benjy?"

He shook his head.

"He was my favorite among my brothers. He was also my friend." The fire stirred in her eyes, and the crop slashed against the earth. "Like a stupid ox he had to go to war and prove himself a man, though neither Daddy nor I could spare his loss."

"Your brother," Robbie breathed, dumbfounded. "Oh, my God, Barbara. Your father said nothing."

She shook her head helplessly. "He couldn't," she whispered. "Neither of us knows how to grieve. Oh, God, God."

Robbie reached for her, and she fitted into his arms as Honor did when she was pained. He felt the warmth of her tears against his coat and waited for her sobbing to ease.

"Do you know why I always come back, Barbara Dunbar?" he asked finally.

She stiffened against his chest, waiting.

"To see this Barbara, the full-hearted creature who has such a capacity for anger and, God help me, grief."

She sniffled and ducked her head against him. "I have been embarrassed ever since that day at the mill. You must have thought me a shrew."

"I thought you a girl turning woman, Barbara Dunbar," he told her. "The girl I love with no man's permission."

She studied his eyes. "That last part might be arranged," she said gently without leaving his arms. "In time."

Robbie had not returned from Gilead, but he was much on Merit's mind that morning.

"I dread to take the news of Braddock's defeat to Sam Dunbar," he had told her as he readied to leave.

"Will it change so much?" she had asked.

"More than any of us like to admit," he told her, leaning toward her for a farewell embrace.

She was watching the river for his return when the dogs set up a clamor. Merit sat up, shielding her eyes from the glare of the water. A man was being helped out of a boat onto the wharf. Even as she rose, the boat pulled away and continued downriver, leaving the stranger on the wharf.

Even at a distance it was clear that the man was lame. Merit called the dogs away and walked toward the wharf. As she drew near she saw the stump of his leg strapped to a wooden peg. His face was gaunt, half hidden by a brushy beard, and he wore the tattered coat of the militia. The pallor of his flesh and his obvious exhaustion as he leaned on his cane froze her voice in her throat.

"You must be—" she finally stammered. His reply came with a swift, blinding smile.

"Alexander Lyon," he told her. "I seek my sister, Belle, and her child."

"Alexander," Em breathed. "Thank God. Come in. Come in. She's just next door. I'll fetch her."

"Do you think that's best?" he asked, glancing at the folded flap of his breeches.

"I think that will be the easiest way," Merit replied.

Merit saw that he was given a plate of cold meat and fresh bread and mustard and a tankard of cold cider.

"You are nowise what I expected, Merit Billings," he told her quietly. "Belle is long apprenticed to loss."

"No soul ever becomes a master at that," she reminded him.

He studied her in his thoughtful way. "A man among men loses his way with words. You might start by telling her that young Will thrives. She'll be grateful for that." Then he smiled again, that unexpectedly brilliant smile. "It strikes me that the right words are probably waiting inside your own head."

Charming. Belle had not exaggerated when she called her brother Alexander charming. But little did he know that the composure he complimented was owed to the example of his own sister.

Never had the path to the other plantation been so short. Belle, seeing Merit coming, stood in the door for a moment before running down the path toward her.

"What is it, then? What is wrong?"

"Am I so transparent without words?" Merit asked.

"You walk as if to the gallows," Belle replied. "Is something amiss with Auntie Em?"

Merit shook her head and took Belle's hand. "I bring a message," she said, finding it hard to draw her breath.

"Your brother Will is well. Your brother Alexander brings you this news."

Belle's strange eyes held her steadily. She did not seem to be breathing. Her hand was as cold and hard as stone.

"Has he come to live or die?" The question was spoken so flatly that it didn't admit other than an honest answer.

"He has come to see you," Merit said softly. "Even on a peg of wood, he has found his way to you."

The strange eyes widened as the air escaped Belle's lips in a slow hard stream. Then she turned and stared at the river, wordless, for a long time. When she turned again, it was to take Merit's hand.

"Let's go greet my brother." Her tone was warm and normal. When she turned again, it was to call her daughter.

"Come, Alice," she said. "Aunt Merry has a wonderful surprise for us. God be praised. Your Uncle Alexander has come home."

⎯⎯⎯⎯ • 6 • ⎯⎯⎯⎯

The Work of Hands

(1755–1761)

Thy hands have made me and fashioned me: give me
understanding, that I may learn thy commandments.
Let the proud be ashamed; for they dealt perversely with
me without a cause.

Psalms 119: 73, 78

WHEN MERIT HAD been a child, the old calendar had been in
use. New Year's Day had come late in March. New kittens
nestled in the barn loft and buds had begun to swell on
orchard trees. The days were growing longer, so that she and
Philip could run with the dogs in the evening in air that
smelled green and promising.

With the change to the new calendar the year after Matthew
died, the new year came in the depth of winter. Bare branches
raked a curdled sky, and the frozen earth resisted Merit's
footstep.

Life itself seemed to have been changed by the rearrange-
ment of its time. Days, months, even years passed swiftly.
Time went by without bringing any fresh scent of hope. The
depression lingered on the land. Not only along the western
frontier, but in the north, the English battled against French
and Indians, only to accumulate loss after loss.

Thanks in large part to the distraction offered by little
Alice, Honor submitted gracefully to being away from Peter

Tucker. Then, in the autumn after the defeat of Braddock's army, Honor gave the first hint of Robbie's attraction to the Dunbar girl.

"Robbie is easier to talk to since he is in love," she told Merit with a grin.

"In love?" Merit looked up, startled. Robbie had always been popular with other young people, and Merit had even watched hopefully for him to pay attention to one of the eligable neighbor girls. "He has said nothing to me."

"He may not even know it himself," Honor suggested. "But he does mention the Dunbar girl with remarkable frequency."

Merit frowned, remembering how Philip's letters had begun to be full of comments about his Caroline, only to have it end by losing him from the family. "Is that the Dunbars who live a little north and west of Gilead? I thought they had only sons, and one of them was lost with Braddock."

Em's increasing deafness kept her silent through most of such quiet conversations, but this time she spoke up.

"The girl Barbara was given to Sam Dunbar by God when Mary was well along in life. She's full young to be thinking of marriage."

Merit would have pressed the question, but her mother was nodding back into her usual silent withdrawal.

Plagued by the thought that Robbie might be contemplating a less than suitable match, Merit spoke of this when she visited Matthew's parents in November.

"Honor thinks that Robbie is interested in Sam Dunbar's daughter," she told her mother-in-law.

She saw the swift exchange of glances between Mr. and Mrs. Billings and knew from the drawing down of Mrs. Billings's mouth that she was holding back words.

"I thought Sam Dunbar had only sons," Merit added.

"Mary Dunbar was with child late in life," Mr. Billings said. "This girl is from that time—still little more than a child."

"Why do I sense a strangeness when I speak about this girl?" Merit asked, almost annoyed by their sudden withdrawal.

"The family is not of our parish, and we have never known them personally," Mr. Billings said firmly. "It is hardly suitable for us to talk of things of which we know nothing, is it, Mother?"

The question was so pointedly sharp that Merit dropped the issue.

When Robbie finally spoke to her of Barbara, he asked for no counsel but simply assumed that she would approve his betrothal. "You will love Barbara," he told her. "Her manners are so elegant that you would never guess what a strong and vibrant person she really is. We plan to be betrothed at once."

At Merit's hesitation, he laughed. "Now, surely you aren't going to tell me that I am too young, as you did Honor?"

She shook her head. "It is only that your father and I had hoped—"

"What had you hoped?" he challenged when she paused.

"That you would marry here in the neighborhood, where you could assume the responsibilities your father carried in the assembly."

"She is not carrying me away," he told her. "It was my hope to add her to my family. Will you talk to Sam Dunbar?"

After writing a letter to Sam Dunbar, Merit went to her Uncle Nat Horne to discuss her concern over her son's betrothal. Lucinda, still unmarried, still kept house for her father and tended to his wants. That day Dorothy was visiting with her brood of contentious children. Dorothy leaned forward almost hungrily at Merit's announcement.

"What was that strange story that passed about when Barbara Dunbar was born, Father? I know you remember."

"I don't remember any strange story," Nat told her. "I know there was a death in the household at the same time, but death comes commonly enough not to be called strange."

When Nat neither spoke more of this nor permitted Merit any time alone with Dorothy, Merit returned to Candle Creek determined to question her mother, who had been intimate with the family.

"When did you start listening to Dorothy's gossiping tongue?" Em challenged her. "Are you trying to stir up some hornet's nest about your own son's betrothal? That has been done in this family before, only to yield a bitter harvest."

"It's natural for a mother to worry," Merit replied, bristling. "Whatever ghost there is, should be laid to rest."

"You alone can do that," Em told her, "for you alone are raising it."

"I shall ask Sam Dunbar," Merit said firmly.

Em reached for her cane and thumped from the room in a manner that spoke more clearly than any words.

Robbie was west, on the plantation that had been acquired for Philip, when Sam Dunbar went downriver to talk with Merit Billings about the marriage. On his return to Gilead, he rode with a light heart, eager as always to be with Barbara and her father. He arrived at the Dunbar plantation at twilight and was greeted by Sam Dunbar himself. To his amazement, the older man came out into the crisp air and closed the door behind him.

"Hard words are best spoken swiftly," he told Robbie. "There will be no marriage between you and my Barbara."

"But sir," Robbie protested, stunned. "What has happened? What's wrong?"

Sam Dunbar shook his head. "If there were more to say, then I would say it. Since there is not, goodbye to you, Robbie Fraser Billings."

For all that the door was shut quietly, the sound of it was final.

Robbie left for Candle Creek a little before dawn. He knew from his mother's face that she expected him.

"What came about between you and Sam Dunbar?" he challenged her.

"Nothing," she said firmly.

"I gathered that." His tone was acid. "But why? How have you come between me and Barbara?"

"Robbie, I must insist that you use a more civil tone with me. What would your father say, to hear you address me in such a manner?"

"You can't stand behind a dead man for living acts," he told her. "I went to Sam Dunbar's house, to find that door shut against me. How did you come between us?"

"It was the father himself who said that no such marriage could take place."

Robbie studied her. "Sam and I have been long friends. Something changed that. Barbara and I love each other. What went on here?"

"Her father has a right to find you unsuitable."

"Unsuitable," he exploded. "Unsuitable how? Could I become unsuitable in the turn of a moon, with no word between us?"

Robbie saw his mother's eyes move toward the doorway. He hadn't heard the tap of his grandmother's cane, but she stood there, bracing herself against the lintels of the door.

"A man might find this family unsuitable for many reasons, Robbie," she said quietly. "After all, your grandfather Bruce Rigg was an indentured yeoman. Your uncle Benn Elliott was branded a murderer before he escaped to turn pirate. This is a family of such violent passions and overweening pride that a man might think twice before releasing a treasured child into it."

"Mother," Merit gasped. "How dare you say such things?"

Em smiled wryly. "Daring is a quality we have always had in excess, to match our pride."

Robbie stared from his grandmother to his mother.

"Was it for this?" he asked Merit. "Did Sam Dunbar refuse my suit from pride?"

"Aye," his grandmother answered. "Your mother's pride, not his."

"For the love of God, will somebody tell me what went on here?" Robbie shouted. The doorway was empty. His grandmother was gone, and his mother's face was pale with anger . . . or fear.

When he repeated his question, she turned away so that she need not meet his eyes.

"There was a story abroad," she said quietly. "It was said that Sam Dunbar had no daughter, that the child his wife Mary carried lay in the tomb with her. I simply asked him about that."

"Wasn't it enough for you that the girl lives and breathes?" Robbie asked.

Merit shook her head. "No man turns so surly except when prodded by the truth. He was rude, Robbie, positively rude to me, in a way your father would never have permitted. He said he wanted no part of me or my son and that our blood was never to look on his daughter's face again."

Robbie felt a sickness in his guts. Those were such words as Sam Dunbar would have chosen.

"Your father and I had such dreams for you, Robbie," she coaxed. Her hands were reaching out for him as he strode from the room.

He was gone from the wharf within the hour. He passed

Gilead and waited in the darkness outside of the Dunbar house for morning to come.

Sam Dunbar came out, as before, but his face was dark with annoyance.

"Let me speak," Robbie said swiftly. "I am no longer my mother's son. I have no land, no property, no name. I have only so great a love for your daughter that I would be a servant in her house rather than return to where I came from."

"Words come cheap," Sam Dunbar told him.

"It was words that lost me Barbara," Robbie reminded him.

Sam Dunbar stood a long time staring toward the west. Robbie waited, his body damp with the sweat of fear.

"If you can take Barbara as I have done, as a gift from God, she will be yours Robbie Fraser. Hers is not a life to be probed with tongues or shadowed by false pride. Only on such grounds can you stay."

Robbie nodded, unable to find words.

"Then you are welcome, son," Sam said, throwing open the door.

Not until the months continued to pass with no word or sign from Robbie did Merit realize how completely she had lost her son. Not until she tried to replace his services with a series of inept, dishonest and shiftless managers did she realize how much more than a son she had lost. It pained her to hear Robbie's name whispered. It was enough that she had failed Matthew so miserably and lost her firstborn. His very name scalded her mind.

Only Asa Forrester seemed to understand.

As the lonely months went on, he continued to come from Norfolk to discuss the shipping business with Em and shout amiably at her over a cup of tea. Then he and Merit would walk together. On these walks he taught her the uses of silence.

"I can only speak my piece so many times, Merit," he told her. "You know where I am and what I desire from you. I'm waiting."

She looked forward to the rhythm of his bulky shoulder next to hers on the path. She liked the pungent scent of his pipe smoke hanging in her hair after he left. He surely knew when Robbie was elected a burgess, but he said nothing. He must have known of the children that came to Robbie and Barbara, but he never spoke of this. Only when Honor's fiancé, Peter Tucker, graduated from Princeton and was given a vicarage in Pennsylvania did he reply to her complaint.

"You cannot keep the girl from her life, Merit," he told her. "Honor must go where her heart leads her."

"But my grandchildren," Merit wailed.

"They will be her children and Peter's," he reminded her. He knew, as she did, that Robbie and Barbara had two sons in the west, whom she had never seen. The uses of silence.

Even Philip had grandchildren around him. The death bells were barely stilled from the death of King George II before Philip's triumphant letter came. "I cannot help feeling that things will go better for the children of our children, Merry," he wrote. "This George III is English born and bred. He is said to be a gentle man for all that he is backward in manners."

"Let him be backward in setting levies on us and we'll love him dearly," Asa told her.

"All Virginians do is complain against the crown," Merit rebuked him. He did not argue. The uses of silence.

It was her misfortune that Asa was not around to remind her to hold her tongue when Honor received the fateful letter from Peter Tucker. She was curled up by the window, unfolding the letter as she always did, slowly, to make the pleasure last. As she read it her face emptied of color, and she whispered intensely, "No. Please, God, no."

Merit followed her as she fled, hopelessly weeping, up to her room.

"Come, my love," Merit coaxed, "you'll make yourself ill."

"I could die," Honor gasped. "I would that I could die."

"You haven't told me what's wrong," Merit said. "It can't be so dire."

"Oh, can't it?" Honor flared. "He has offered to release me from our engagement. He feels this is no time to marry."

Merit felt a spiral of hope in her chest. What was a broken engagement to one so young? The pain would pass. Honor had many admirers. Another suitor, another betrothal, and she would have the round warmth of Honor's children in her arms, just as she and Matthew had dreamed together.

Her silence betrayed her. Honor looked up and glared at

her. "You'd like that, wouldn't you? You'd like it if I chose a man whose politics were closer to yours and your precious brothers'."

"Politics," Merit said in confusion. Nothing had been further from her mind.

Honor wiped her cheek with the back of her hand and sniffled.

"Only politics keeps us from marrying now," she sobbed. "Peter is much involved with this lawyer who left his practice as the king's advocate general to plead the case against the king's writs of assistance. He thinks we should wait until this ferment settles before starting as a family."

Merit stared at him. "Peter a follower of James Otis? Honor, that is disgraceful. That man Otis pleads the case of smugglers. The king has a perfect right to search out where he is being robbed of his rightful taxes."

"You see," Honor cried. "I knew you opposed Peter's politics."

"Breaking the law is not politics. It is crime."

"Ask your friend Captain Forrester about that," Honor said, flouncing from the room.

"I know I handled her badly," Merit admitted to Asa a few days later.

"But she hasn't broken her engagement?" Asa asked.

Merit shook her head. "She says she will wait for Peter, no matter how long it takes. She said that I should ask you about these king's laws that Otis is so stoutly protesting."

"I hold with him," Asa said.

"You hold with him?" She turned to stare at him. "You hold with smuggling, against the king's law? Philip says—"

He looked at her soberly, shaking his head. "And James Otis maintains that unwarranted searches are against the constitution and thus are no laws at all."

"I can't believe you hold with such people," Merit began, only to have him take her hand firmly. "I have just made politics a forbidden area between us," he said quietly.

"There is a difference between politics and crime."

"To answer you would be to drown out the call of songbirds," he told her, still holding her hand.

Probably because of Asa, Merit did not bring up the subject of James Otis with Honor again. Even so, a new coolness fell between them. Honor, having postponed her wedding, spent more and more time in Williamsburg visiting friends. Alexander Sommers wavered between strength and weakness. Often he became delirious and cried out for his dead brother Thomas and for young Will. Belle seldom left his side.

Merit found herself more and more restless in the quiet house, with only her mother for company, nodding in her chair or reading the old journal to Alice. It became Merit's habit to take a shawl and stand looking at the changing face of the river by the hour.

How had she failed so miserably? One by one she was losing her children. She even feared to reply to Bruce when he came from Williamsburg prating about the whimsey of the king and talking of a committee of correspondence between the colonies.

She would save Rigg at least. He was old enough to send to Norfolk as apprentice to Asa Forrester. The thought brightened her spirits in the same way as Asa himself, with his gentle, amiable smile.

7

Not With Silver

(1764)

Behold, I have refined thee, but not with silver; I have chosen thee in the furnace of affliction.

Isaiah 48:10

DR. JAMES RIGG had told his friends in Maryland that he was going home. Yet, as he stepped onto the wharf at Candle Creek, he felt no sense of belonging. Had he been gone too long? Did ten years loosen a man's roots from his own earth? He blamed some of this sense of alienation on his place in the family. Perhaps the last child of an aging couple was doomed to fall between the stools of the generations, to find himself more sensitive to his brother and sister's children than to his siblings. It was certainly true that he felt closer to Rigg Billings, who had traveled with him from Norfolk, than he did to Merit, who now approached him with open arms.

His mother's flesh felt powdery to his touch, but the pulse that beat behind the pale veins of her temples was steady and strong.

And Honor as a bride was overwhelmingly lovely.

"I had heard that you two intended to wait for the troubles to be over," James commented to Peter Tucker.

The young cleric's smile was rueful. "It began to look as if the end might never come."

James was startled by Honor's nervous glance and the speed with which she turned the talk to other things.

This was not to be the last of such nervous glances, but even this tension was less noticeable than the empty places of those missing from this festive event.

Robbie was gone, of course. And Uncle Paul.

"He was a man in advance of his time," Bruce told James. "These new preachers are everywhere, ranting about hellfire and damnation, promising a personal God who bends to their will like beech trees in a high wind."

Peter smiled. "Most of the parsons in Virginia would settle for a vestry who would bend to the king's will."

Bruce agreed. "Any lawyer can keep his days filled by taking on the suits the clerics are bringing against their parishes."

"And even the other way around," Peter reminded him. "The word passed all around Philadelphia of young Patrick Henry binding a jury with his voice, up in Hanover. He is quite a folk hero, and on everyone's tongue."

Again came Honor's nervous glance and a swift change of subject, to the king's declaration of war against Spain.

"Kings have their reasons," James sighed. "Common men only clean their muskets."

The finest addition to the family was clearly Belle Sommers. James found himself drawn to her again and again, for all that she was an unlikely person to find in his mother's parlor.

"Your daughter has clearly been a godsend to my mother," he told Belle. "How my mother treasures that child."

"Even as Alice treasures your mother," Belle told him. "She never had much family before, and to have Aunt Em act as grandmother has been wonderful for her . . . especially since the loss of her Uncle Alexander."

"I grieve that I never knew your brothers," James told her.

"I can't grieve that Alexander's pain is over, but I sorrow that he did not live to see young Will again."

"Your brother is still west with the army, then?"

She looked confused. "There has been no word for a very long time, but I can only think that he is."

James cursed silently. "No word" too often meant a young body moldering in the swamp, with his scalp adorning some warrior's belt.

"My prayers on his safe return," he told her, not meeting those level, studious eyes.

The notion of time was seldom far from James's mind during those days. He marveled how the passage of time, like that of water, deepened the channels in a human life. Asa Forrester was grown blunter and stronger, Gil the Toad more wide-bellied and amiable. Merit, God help her, was even more filled with restless anger than when she had stood trembling above their father's grave.

The wedding was a model of what such a sacrament should be. James himself gave Honor into Peter's trembling hand. The music was by Handel, and played with grace on the spinet beyond the hearth. The tables boasted such food as Candle Creek was famed for, rich, hard hams and roasted game, great fish swimming in a succulent sauce, with endless breads and puddings.

But there was no jovial ease. The coolness between Merit and the bride was palpable. The nameless tension raised Bruce's voice to an unwonted heartiness and dampened Rigg into sober silence.

The storm broke swiftly. No number of nervous warning glances was able to keep the men from talk of the news in the colony. James saw Merit turn with a frown as Peter Tucker's father raised his voice against the king's closing of settlement in the western lands. "This has been a long war and a weary one," he said bluntly. "And what reward to us? The Treaty of Paris has slammed the door on our rightful expansion west."

"If that were not enough," a neighbor spoke up, "this infernal proposed Stamp Act is hanging over our heads."

"You have a brother in the assembly," Mr. Tucker said, turning to Bruce. "Surely they will take some steps to save us."

Bruce tried to keep his reply low. "There is talk of addressing the crown on the subject."

"Let their words be firm, then," Tucker nodded. "No tax should be laid on a man without his consent. We are free men."

Merit's voice was so vibrant with passion that her guests froze. "Are you free of your king, then, that you challenge his stewardship of you?"

Mr. Tucker's jaw went slack before he swelled a little with

annoyance. "Mistress, I am such a horse as rears when the bit cuts my mouth. As Patrick Henry said at Hanover, when a king behaves like a tyrant, he forfeits the right to his subject's obedience."

"That is not a name that I will permit spoken in my chambers," Merit announced coldly. "Like the crowd in that same court, I call such words by their proper name—treason."

The room was stilled for a breathless moment before, in the way of society, a sudden babble began to fill that void, as if the offending words could be swept away by sound.

Peter's father stood for a frozen moment before nodding to his wife. "Since I insist my own opinion is fair, madam, it is best that I leave your chambers." They were gone before the shock left Merit's face. James took her arm, hoping to lead her apart to compose herself, but she stood firm.

"And you, my brother," she challenged. "Where do you stand on this sedition? Are you a loyal subject still or have you turned to unruly rebel like these Virginians?"

"I am a loyal subject," James told her quietly. "But I stand with the Virginians and all the colonists against this proposed Stamp Act. Come, Merit," he pleaded, "you are tired."

"Tired I am, and bitterly so," she told him, tugging from his grasp to run up the stairs like the girl he remembered. The party was over. He and Honor and Belle saw the guests into their carriages with stiff farewells.

The sun had left the sky and the orchard was gathering darkness when the tide turned.

"Will you be traveling to Norfolk with us, James?" Gil the Toad asked quietly.

James stared bleakly into the upper darkness. "I travel with you," he replied.

Rigg was already sitting in the boat, staring at the water in thoughtful silence. Now and then Gil glanced restlessly toward the house. "Captain Forrester will be taking his last farewells of your mother," he explained to James. "Deep love lies between those two, God bless them both."

James saw the figures of both Captain Forrester and Merit framed in the door against the light. He looked away, remembering Merit's words of ten years before: "All I have left of Matthew is our dreams."

James would have risen to go back to her, but Asa Forrester was striding toward them and the craft was being readied to push off.

Merit, in the room she had shared with Matthew, heard the clatter of her departing guests. A sickness in her soul held her in her own room. Let them gossip and talk once they were free of her house, but let them be gone. How had Honor fallen in with a family filled with such wrongheadedness? Who were these fools to think they had the right to challenge the rights of kings? Treason it had been named, and treason it was.

As the house fell silent she remembered Asa. She was swift on the stair and found him bending to bestow a farewell kiss on Em's cheek. Then she was at the door beside him, as always.

"Don't go, Asa," she begged. "Stay a little. I need to talk. I'm sorry I couldn't hold my tongue."

He looked at her in astonishment. "God in heaven, Merit Billings," he exploded. "It's not your tongue that offends me, but the slavish mind that powers it. How long will you lock yourself away from the truth? How many children and friends and brothers must you lose before you stand face to face with yourself?"

"But Philip always says . . ." she stammered. "Matthew . . ."

He shook his head in disgust and swung the door wide.

"Other men's minds. What did God put a brain in your head for? Don't tell me what your brother or dead husband think. Tell me what you think. You have made yourself a blind, stupid woman with your dependence on other men's opinions."

As he turned away, she saw the same angle of his head that had caught at her heart when he bent to kiss her mother goodbye. A flame like jealousy coursed through her. She wanted to scream, to tear at him with her hands. Instead, her voice came low and strong and mean.

"Go," she said fiercely. "Go, and don't bother coming back for me. You worship my mother's clearheadedness and her strong-minded ways. Come to see my mother, not me. You call me stubborn? She nearly ripped my father to shreds with her stubbornness. She has defied the king's law steadily

282

with that company of hers. What you call stubbornness in me you consider something else in her, something appealing and gracious.''

His anger had carried him halfway down the path, but he turned and spun on his heels at her words. He lunged toward her, his fists red knots at his side. He didn't so much speak the words as spit them out.

"How dare you compare yourself with Emily Fraser? You're not the same size, Merit Billings. And do you know why?"

He was close again, his eyes level on her own. When she tried to turn from his fury, he held her painfully by the upper arms.

"No, no," she told him. "Go away. Go away."

"I'll go when you've heard me out. The case in point is where the counsel comes from. You throw me the words of common men like myself . . . your father, your brother, your dead husband. You call this truth. Truth comes from God alone, Merit Billings. It comes when you are on your knees, not with your nose in the air, furious with pride. The difference between you and your mother is the difference between an idol worshipper and a child of the true living God.''

His hands were gone from her, leaving her flesh tingling. Then even the sound of his footsteps disappeared from the path and the wharf. She stood still, staring at the earth, her flesh burning. When she looked up, there was no sign of his craft, only the wide smooth river flowing its way to the sea.

PART SIX

The Valley of Decision
(1764–1776)

Multitudes, multitudes in the valley of decision: for the day of the Lord is near in the valley of decision.

Joel 3:14

I rejoice that America has resisted. Three millions of people, so dead to all the feelings of liberty, as voluntarily to submit to be slaves, would have been fit instruments to make slaves of the rest.

William Pitt, Earl of Chatham
Speech in the House of Commons, January 14, 1766

That God who gave us life, gave us liberty at the same time.

Thomas Jefferson, Summary View of the
Rights of British America (1774)

Is life so dear, or peace so sweet, as to be purchased at the price of chains and slavery? Forbid it, Almighty God! I know not what course others may take; but as for me, give me liberty, or give me death!

Patrick Henry, Speech in the Virginia
Convention, March 20, 1775

1

Trials

(1764–1765)

The Lord trieth the righteous: but the wicked and him that
loveth violence his soul hateth.

Psalms 11:5

THE WEDDING GUESTS returned to Williamsburg under a moon
so pale that it barely challenged the stars. The coach wheels
struck fire from stones, and the horsemen jested among themselves in the crisp air.

Bruce Billings stayed silent. More than anything he wanted
to lay the crop to his mare and let her measure her length
along the moon-dappled road. His riding companions had
regained their good humor soon enough, but they had not lost
sister, confidante and friend by Honor's marriage. Neither did
they suffer from a mother who had publicly humiliated a
guest with her swift and venomous tongue.

Bruce's friend William cantered up to speak privately to
him. "Come, Bruce. We're all friends here. The hot blood in
your family is too well known for any to take offense."

Bruce cursed silently. It was miserable enough to be branded
as one of a family of hotheads by a close friend. It was
doubly miserable to a man apprenticed to an Englishman of
such stiff and proper manners as Geoffrey Brainard. He had
only the barest hope that the gossip of his mother's rudeness
would not reach the lawyer's ears. Brainard had come from

Sussex and London only a year or two before Bruce went with him. He had spent so much time buying property here and there in the colony that he seemed to have few social contacts in Williamsburg to justify the harsh judgments he made on both the wit and the manners of its citizens.

For Brainard himself, Bruce did not give a fig. Bruce was within months of being ready to take his bar examination. The problem was Janet.

Even the thought of Brainard's daughter loosened Bruce's hands on his reins to ease his horse's pace. Janet. Bruce had been nineteen when he first went to work with her father. Accustomed to a relaxed, bantering relationship with his sister, Honor, Bruce was quick enough to establish a similar friendship with this fair child of twelve. In truth, Janet could not have been more different from Honor. She was small, with wide-set pale-blue eyes and the slowest smile that ever dawned on a face. Unlike Honor and his own mother, Janet's gentle surface seemed to conceal no roiling passion. Her docility toward her father was a living enactment of scriptural admonitions to women. Janet had been a delicious child.

But the same five years that had readied Bruce for the bar had transformed Janet into a glowing woman. Her wrists were as fine as the bones of the fawns at Candle Creek. Her flesh glistened like new apples. Bruce had long ago realized that if he couldn't have Janet Brainard for his wife, life held little appeal.

And she knew this. Bruce read it in her eyes and felt it in her lingering touch on his arm. Only the words remained to be spoken. But first Bruce must be free of his apprenticeship and able to rely on his own resources. Brainard commonly made such brutal assessments of his Williamsburg neighbors that Bruce was wary of his own family's acceptability to the old man. Here Janet's docility would be a handicap instead of a help.

Once in Williamsburg, Bruce accompanied his companions past his own lodgings in what had once been his Aunt Magda's shop, in order to pass the Brainard house. A candle flickered in Janet's window. He stared at it until it split, to dance before his eyes, pale-blue lights as clear and innocent as the ones that shone in her face.

He looked bleakly around his own quarters. Honor and

Peter would be off to their joined lives in Philadelphia. Robbie and his Barbara would be curled in sleep in their houseful of smiling babes that had arrived as regularly as spring robins. He must have Janet for his own.

In a few weeks Robbie would be in Williamsburg for the Assembly. The six-year difference in their age widened or narrowed according to Bruce's need. Perhaps Robbie would counsel him like a father on this business with Janet. If not, he could at least sympathize like an understanding brother.

On the eleventh of January Robbie stood before Bruce's fire with a groan of relief. "A harsh wind blew me all the way here," he told his brother. "Every mile I thought of this fire and of that wine warming on the hob. I'm greatly envied, you know, for having you put me up during these public times. Many a burgess will sleep tonight in a roomful of snoring strangers and foraging vermin."

Only as he accepted a tankard from Bruce did he frown.

"Look at you. I expected fine tales of a joyous wedding and you wear a brooding face. Don't tell me there's bad news from Candle Creek."

Bruce shrugged. "The bride was beautiful and the groom properly terrified, and Mother was in shrewish as usual."

"At the wedding?" Robbie asked, incredulous.

"Politics," Bruce said bitterly, recounting the exchange between Merit and the groom's father. "It was enough to scatter the guests like startled birds."

Robbie sighed. "Poor old thing. When will she learn to attend her own hearth or salt the gossip she hears before she swallows it?"

"I gather you don't take this clamor about Patrick Henry very seriously. Honor's Peter says his fame is even general in the northern colonies."

"We are a war-weary people, Bruce," Robbie said, sitting on a bench. "The king may call it a seven-year war, but we have fought the French and Indians along our borders for nine long years. England has paid in money, and we have paid in blood and exhaustion. This restlessness will pass, and men like Patrick Henry and James Otis with it. Those same wars have made our country the greatest empire since Rome. That matters greatly, or it will when the common people realize it."

Bruce was to remember Robbie's words with some wistfulness as the months passed.

In April the British Parliament passed the Revenue Act, which the colonists called the Sugar Act. Angry voices rose in Raleigh's tavern at the crown's intent to put a vice-admiralty court in Halifax, Nova Scotia.

"An Englishman has the right to be tried by a jury of his peers," people insisted. "To set a man into chains and ship him to a faraway court violates his rights."

"The king has every right to protect his revenue against smugglers," Brainard said with finality. "Any tools he can find are his to employ."

When the currency act eliminated the use of colonial paper money, the shouts rose again in the taverns. "This is only a club to beat Virginians into their own soil."

"The Virginia Assembly should have looked to this day when they issued £440,000 in paper money to pay for their war," Brainard reminded Bruce. "Can a British merchant be expected to accept worthless paper in place of solid goods?"

When Robbie came to the Assembly again in October, Bruce was quick to press him about the town gossip. "They say this assembly will confront the crown about the Sugar Act."

"That's probably true." Robbie nodded.

"Brainard calls this rebellion," Bruce told him.

"Such hot words should be saved for the kitchen or times of war. Bread cannot be made without yeast, and much is being fomented by such hotheads as Patrick Henry and Otis and Sam Adams. They make an evil bread who try to upset the delicate balance we have always had within our country. Let the king wage his wars and run his navy. Let the Parliament be the bookkeeper for colonial goods. This is the Parliament's doing, not the king's. They are only trying to pay for England's wars. The king will see the justice in our complaint. The tempest is in the taverns."

He sighed and stretched his legs. "I shall hear nothing but such talk for days now. Tell me about yourself. Aren't you due for your bar examination by now?"

Bruce nodded. "I have delayed it because of a predicament. Once through, I must choose to practice alone or go into practice with Geoffrey Brainard."

"What do you want to do?" Robbie asked.

"He is a harsh and secretive man," Bruce said. "But I want his daughter for my wife."

Robbie pulled out his pipe and stared. "You have yourself in a box, don't you? You stand to lose both personal and professional independence with a single misstep. What will you do? You can't delay forever."

"I'm praying for a sign." Bruce grinned.

Robbie nodded thoughtfully, then smiled in a way that implied mischief. "Tell me news of Candle Creek."

"Grandma Em changes very little, bless her. She walks or sits with Alice Sommers and reads to the child by the hour. Her hearing fails but her sight remains keen. Captain Forrester still comes and shouts to her about shipping business, but he and mother have lost their fine friendship since Honor's wedding. Oh, yes," he added. "Mother plans to travel to Philadelphia for the birth of Honor's coming child."

"That's good news," Robbie said. "I doubt she has ever been farther from home than Norfolk or Gilead."

"I hope it works well," Bruce said doubtfully. "Her brother Philip keeps her in an uproar, berating this colony in his letters. I doubt that she will swallow northern talk with much grace. We should rather ship her to England and cure her boredom with this place."

"Her boredom may be coming to an end," Robbie said, clearly grinning now. "Do you remember that Aunt Belle's youngest brother went to war when Alexander did, and he hasn't been heard from?"

"Young Will, she called him." Bruce nodded. "She still waits with that serene calm of hers."

"Her waiting is near its end," Robbie said, appearing unaccountably entertained by this news. "A man named Will Lyon, a veteran of the French and Indian campaigns, passed by Barbara's brother's plantation a while back. He was asking the way to Candle Creek."

"My God," Bruce cried. "How marvelous for Belle. What's he like? Alexander was a man to grieve for."

"I didn't see him," Robbie explained. "Barbara's brother only directed him downriver and told me when we next met. This Young Will was traveling on foot, with a pregnant Indian wife and a half-breed child plodding in his wake."

Bruce set down his tankard with a thump and stared at his

brother for a long minute. "Will God never cease to test our mother's pride?"

"She has never failed to have enough," Robbie reminded him.

• 2 •

Rumor Upon Rumor

(1764–1765)

> And lest your heart faint, and ye fear for the rumor that shall be heard in the land; a rumor shall both come one year, and after that in another year shall come a rumor, and violence in the land, ruler against ruler.
>
> Jeremiah 51:46

PERHAPS BECAUSE Belle Sommers always referred to her absent brother as Young Will, Bruce had pictured him as a younger, shorter version of Will's dead brother Alexander. Instead, the man who rose to greet him seemed a giant. He stood taller than Bruce, with thick dark hair drawn back with a leather thong. His shoulders were extremely wide, and his smile was as ample as the hand that clasped Bruce's.

Merit's tension was almost visible. Her words were terse enough. "Belle's brother has come after this long time."

Will's voice was remarkably soft. "You must meet my wife, Nabby," he said. "She'll be down directly."

"Nabby?" Bruce asked. "Is that short for Abigail?"

Will laughed quietly. "It's short for something my tongue can't handle. It's a name I favored so I rechristened her."

"Is she with the children, then?" Bruce asked, finding a seat for himself in Belle's warm kitchen. The silence startled him.

"She lost the baby," Will explained. "We have only our son."

Merit's eyes challenged Bruce for an explanation. "You inquired the way here from my brother's brother-in-law," he elaborated. "He reported your wife was with child."

"The journey was too harsh for her condition," Will said. "We both grieve." Then he frowned. "That would be your brother in the Assembly. I hear they do all they can to talk the king out of this Stamp Act."

Bruce nodded. "They wrote a plea explaining the great burden the tax would impose on us."

His mother rose briskly. "Teaching the king his own law," she commented acidly. "I must be off to see to my mother, if you will excuse me."

Will stared thoughtfully at the closed door. "What did she mean about teaching the king?"

Bruce laughed. "The burgesses reminded him that Englishmen could not be taxed without their consent. Here in Virginia only the burgesses have taxed Virginians all these years."

"Your mother seemed mighty incensed."

"The king little knows what a staunch fighter he has in that woman," Belle remarked indulgently.

"He'll be crying for such friends if this act is pressed," Will said. "There was talk of little else among men we met along the way."

"I would like to hear about your adventures," Bruce asked.

To his astonishment, Will's face seemed to change, his eyes becoming shuttered with privacy. "It began with what no man should endure and ended with what few men can possess."

He had been with Braddock, Bruce remembered. The forces had been routed and the British regulars had fled.

Later Belle would explain that Will had been left for dead. By good fortune he was found by a tribe with whom he had traded as a friend. "They gave back his life and strength," she said. "And also Nabby."

A rustle in the passage brought Will to his feet. The woman in the doorway stood as straight as Bruce's Grandma Em. Her dark face and intent eyes suggested the same sense of privacy. Her cotton dress seemed incongruous under the free-swinging plaits of thick black hair.

"Welcome, cousin," Bruce said.

Her eyes caught the points of light from the candle as she returned his gaze. Then she nodded and smiled at him.

"Nabby is weak in our language," Will explained, making a place for her at his side.

"With such a smile, words are little needed," Bruce told him.

Returning through the quiet grove, Bruce felt sorry for his mother. Clearly Will's arrival was difficult for her. He had been no help, tipping his hand with the question about the baby. Done was done. As for Will, dressed in a gentleman's clothes, he would turn heads anywhere. Nabby was something else. He shuddered to think what Geoffrey Brainard would make of this connection.

He found his mother waiting alone.

"I enjoyed meeting my new cousin," he told her.

She sat without moving, watching her own folded hands on the table. "I summoned you for another reason."

He waited warily. "Honor's child is expected in March. I need you to superintend the plantations while I'm away."

"But you have overseers," he protested.

She looked, visibly annoyed. "Overseers are men who must be watched."

"I know less than nothing of being a planter."

She exhaled sharply. "You know the rhythm of the land. You can set a smithy to his forge, a carpenter to his hammer. A tight hand must be kept on accounts; that is the main thing."

When he didn't instantly reply, she looked at him, her anger palpable. "When your father died, you were only a boy. When your grandfather was taken, we had a man to fill his place. Now there is only you."

He would have spoken of the bar, but she anticipated him.

"Must you make me beg for your help, Bruce? I am alone. What can be keeping you from your natural place at my side?"

"The law," he began, fighting a rising sense of guilt.

Her laugh was dry. "Are you planning to be catapulted from apprentice to high court? My brother James is a doctor but he plants. Young George Washington is a surveyor and manages to plant and bring in harvests at the same time. Do you expect such a flood of clients that you can do nothing else?''

"Forgive me," Bruce said, genuinely contrite. "I've been less than honest, Mother. I have chosen a wife."

Her head rose swiftly.

"She is Geoffrey Brainard's daughter, Janet," he went on. "I tiptoe with Brainard for fear he will refuse my suit."

"Refuse you?" she challenged. "What about the girl? Are you pleasing to her?"

He felt his color rise. "Yes, but Janet is too gentle a woman to go against her father's bidding."

"And how do you propose to earn the father's favor?"

"He has invited me into his law firm."

She sat and turned her hands again in the light. "Perhaps your Mr. Brainard and I should sit down together. He could surely spare a future son to help his mother for a brief time."

Bruce felt the easing of an inner weight. Would she submit so easily to his marriage in exchange for a few months of his help? Or had she learned so much from losing Robbie?

"You would do that?" His voice betrayed his delight.

"I am no tyrant, Bruce," she said quietly. Then, to his astonishment, he saw tears in her eyes. "I grow no younger. I hunger for a grandchild in my arms. Honor needs me. Belle even suggested that her brother Will might take over for me, but I—"

Bruce started at her words. "What a capital idea."

Her anger flamed instantly. "Don't be a fool, Bruce. What makes you think my overseers would work for him?"

The words she didn't speak echoed in Bruce's mind.

It was a rare Englishman who didn't wholly despise a man who took an Indian for a wife. How different had his own question about Brainard been?

This time it was his mother who rose. "I will contact Brainard about you and his daughter at once." Strangely, the gratitude he felt wouldn't pass his lips.

Bruce knew without asking why Merit visited Geoffrey Brainard in Williamsburg rather than inviting him to Candle Creek. The meeting was held in Bruce's lodging, with a bottle of the best Madeira decanted between them.

Brainard accepted Merit's compliments on his daughter and

registered Bruce's protestations without a change of expression. Then, as if on signal, he began his questions.

He asked not only of the plantation at Candle Creek but also of Gilead. He even mentioned the undeveloped western lands and the plantation Andrew had obtained for Philip as well as the Springer and Simms properties.

Bruce felt himself begin to sweat at the precision of his mother's words. "My only property is the plantation at Candle Creek," she reminded him. "You talk of my mother's estate, and I am only one of three living children."

"And there is the Fraser shipping company in Norfolk," Brainard went on relentlessly.

"My mother still lives," Merit repeated.

Only Bruce could know how close the old man brought Merit to the edge of her self control.

"Janet will bring with her only property that is worth half of what your son brings," Brainard told her. "I must be assured that she suffers no loss of comfort in a marriage."

"We must limit our discussion to my own property," Merit insisted. "I have four children, all living."

Brainard stared at her. "Surely you don't include a married daughter or that son who neither claims your name nor darkens your door as he makes mischief in the Assembly?"

Bruce watched his mother open her bag. Instead of the wisp of fine linen that another woman might draw forth, she lifted out a sheet of paper covered with notations.

"It is true that my daughter Honor has taken her dowry with her. All your considerations must be based on one-third of the property described here."

Never had Bruce seen fine wine tasted with less relish.

His mother's comments as she left were acid enough. "Let us hope that the daughter has inherited her mother's soul. For a lawyer, he speaks remarkably like an accountant. Or a pirate," she added with a swish of her skirt.

It didn't matter. Nothing mattered but that Janet would be his own. Unable to settle into bed, Bruce began a letter to Honor.

"When Mother is with you, I beg you to treat her with uncommon gentleness. She has proved today that you and your child are more precious to her than rubies . . . more precious than her pride, if you can believe that."

• • •

Taking over the management of his mother's plantations plunged Bruce back into his family in a way he had not expected. His grandmother Em spoke of his ancestors as if their footfalls echoed from the next room. Will spent long hours with him by the fire, describing the lands to the west in such glowing terms that Bruce could see the giant trees, the lush green valleys and the tumbling rivers come alive in the flames.

"We'll go back, Nabby and I," Will told him. "But first we will put that place into shape for Belle and see Nabby well and strong again. If you ever saw it, Bruce, nothing else would do for you. It's free, wild and fruitful and free."

Bruce was amazed at what Will accomplished in the brief months that he was there to watch him. The mill, long unused, was restored to bring a brisk traffic to the rebuilt wharf. The orchard was pruned, and in the newly mended poultry house Belle had a flock that Bruce insisted yielded two chicks for every egg.

By the time Merit returned, the Stamp Act had been passed, as well as a law demanding that the colonists provide supplies for the British troops quartered in America.

But Bruce was free to plan his marriage and resume the practice of law with Brainard. Everything else faded in comparison to those joys.

In spite of Merit's fierce insistence on division of the property, he and Janet would begin their lives on his Aunt Martha Springer's plantation near Williamsburg. Janet had become a chatterer since their engagement. This nesting talk was like the twittering of spring birds, endless discussions about tapestries and silver, bed coverings and curtains. It was as if a bowl of cream had been whipped by a sudden hurricane. But when Bruce caught her small body against his to bury his face in that cloud of pale hair, he knew that even such determined housewifery couldn't dampen his passion for this delicious woman.

There was little enough time for him to be distracted by such petty things once he was in Brainard's employ. He was conscious of the heated talk about the passage of the Stamp Act principally through Brainard's diatribes against colonial stupidity. This changed when Robbie was with him for the meeting of the Assembly.

On the last night of May Robbie came in late, lurching into

the room, and stumbled against the table. Falling into a chair, he thumped a bottle down on the table with a curse.

"There," he said thickly. "It's the devil's day and the devil's brew, and we'll drink to what's coming."

"If that's a wedding toast, I'd like it rephrased," Bruce told him.

"It's no wedding toast, and pray God it's no funeral toast either," Robbie replied, struggling with the cork.

"You're a bit into the cups already," Bruce reminded him, taking the bottle and opening it.

"The speech," Robbie said. "Have they recited the speech to you yet? Have you heard what passed today in the Assembly?" Bracing himself with one hand, he waved the bottle. "Caesar had his Brutus," he shouted. "Charles the First, his Cromwell—and George the Third—"

"For God's sake, lower your voice," Bruce cried. "Have you gone mad?"

"No, no." Robbie shook his head. "They shouted it was treason over and over. Treason."

"Calm yourself," Bruce said, shaking him. "What in the name of God are you raving about?" He had never seen Robbie so drunken or distraught. When Robbie started to get out of the chair, Bruce pressed him back, holding him there until he became limp.

"You with your talk of weddings and toasts," Robbie jeered. "Your head is turned by petticoats. All hell broke loose in the assembly today. Every man in Virginia is talking of it tonight, and the talk will move like brushfire through the colonies."

"Then tell me," Bruce said. "Those can't have been your words, spoken in such treasonous style."

"My words? Good God, no. I have a wife and children, and no love for British prisons. Would I dare think, much less voice, such words?"

"Henry," Bruce decided aloud. "It must have been Patrick Henry."

"Aye." Robbie nodded, the life suddenly gone from him. "When he spoke on his resolves about the Stamp Act, his tongue was lit by demon fire. No man's brain could survive that heat. We passed his resolves, Bruce, five of his seven resolves. God help us when this comes to the king's ears."

Patrick Henry had a wife and children too, Bruce thought as he loosened Robbie's clothes and guided him to the bed.

Almost at once Robbie was snoring as lustily as he had been shouting. Bruce lit a pipe and sat watching him thoughtfully. Where did Robbie really stand on these difficult questions? How would he have spoken if he did not have Barbara and the children's welfare to consider? Could Patrick Henry be right, or was he only a hotblooded orator carried away by his own soaring words?

Bruce rose, damped his pipe and emptied his glass. These were questions he dared not ask himself. Like Robbie, he had too much to lose. He was a lawyer, thank God, and not a statesman. And soon to be a husband, he reminded himself as he blew out the candle. He had too much to lose.

3

Friend and Brother

(1766)

A friend loveth at all times, and a brother is born for adversity.

Proverbs 17:17

BRUCE WAS NOT immune to the tension rising in the colony. Rather, life was too sweet for him to let it be soured by the furies of other men. He realized that the Stamp Act had managed to achieve what the long, bitter French and Indian war never brought about. The colonies at last were working together by passing circular letters and calling for a Stamp Act meeting in New York.

299

Geoffrey Brainard, his face ashen and his wig askew, had fled to Bruce and Janet's plantation when the mobs cornered the king's stamp agent in Williamsburg. From the day that the agent resigned, business came to a stop. Courts did not function. No actions on public business could be transacted. Virginia ground to a halt.

Brainard, as uncomfortable with Bruce's idleness as with his own, sent his son-in-law on inspection trips to a fine plantation he owned in Hanover and to his warehouses in York, which Bruce had not even known the man possessed.

But mostly Bruce became husband and planter. He spent cold evenings with Janet, now blooming with child. The winter snow melted as here and there, around the colony, men banded together, swearing to protect one another to their death. Bruce pruned his orchard and cleaned the debris from the maze garden and spoke to no one of his concerns.

It couldn't last. When his mother summoned him in early April, she came at once to the point.

"Tell me what you know of the Sons of Liberty."

He frowned. "I have heard differing reports," he began.

She broke in crossly. "Good God, Bruce. Don't dance your words about in that tedious, craven lawyer way."

He chuckled to himself. What a change her briskness was from his Janet's endless submission. "On the surface they appear to be a rabble intent on troublemaking. In truth they are supposed to have a group of solid men who move their strings as if they were puppets . . . men like Sam Adams and James Otis, with John Hancock providing the funds for this work."

"But they are rebels," she said firmly, "all rebels against the crown."

He hesitated. "Let us say that they voice their protests in a way that a gentleman would not."

"They are now in Norfolk, these Sons of Liberty," his mother said bleakly. "Your brother Rigg was in their number when they adopted some resolutions against the king at the courthouse there."

"That boy?" Bruce said in astonishment. "Against the king?"

"Against the king's Stamp Act. Don't tell me that you too are turning rebel."

He shook his head. "Never question my loyalty, Mother, but this act has had an ill effect. Business has stopped. The courts can't function. Even the ships must leave the harbor with only a certificate."

"I swore I would not lean on you again, Bruce, but I have nowhere to turn. Please, my son, go to Norfolk. Talk to Rigg. Persuade him to withdraw his name and allegiance from this rabble before he is numbered among the traitors."

He had called Rigg a boy. Rigg was now a man of twenty-two. He had been living apart from the family for many years, as apprentice to Asa Forrester, in the largest city that Virginia boasted, spending time in its taverns and along its wharves.

One glance at Merit's face, and Bruce didn't have the heart to protest. "I'll talk to Rigg," he promised.

"Persuade him to abandon this indiscretion."

"I can only promise to do my best."

Even the layered smoke of the Norfolk tavern held the salty tang of the sea. Rigg, his fine face glowing with pleasure, leaned toward Bruce across the cluttered table. No boy this, Bruce thought. Rigg's strong muscular body was vibrant with confidence; his hand on the tankard was broad and strong, like his father's had been.

"How wonderful to have you in my own place," Rigg said. "Give me news. I hear of Granny Em from Asa, but little of the rest."

"Honor writes that her son thrives," Bruce told him, "And Robbie claims that his son Fraser grows like new corn."

"And Mother?" Rigg studied him. "She's the reason you came, I wager."

Bruce had long struggled for an easy way to open this conversation. "God has been overgenerous to our mother, Rigg. Most women fall from exhaustion at the day's end. She is cursed with energy to spare."

"The Sons of Liberty," Rigg decided aloud. "She's heard of my work with them. There's always a tongue sharpened for carrying tales." His smile turned wry. "What did she expect of you, Bruce? To slap my hands and tell me to straighten up? Order me to close my ears to what is happening and be a good and dutiful son?"

Bruce sighed. "I'm not a political man, Rigg. I only care for my work and the joy of my family"

Rigg set his tankard down hard. "For God's sake, Bruce, what do you think we want? We're only fighting to keep what's rightfully ours and has always been ours. We don't lightly boycott British goods that we need. It's only to get their attention, to remind them that we're Englishmen, still free Englishmen, with only the sea between us."

"The Stamp Act might yet be repealed," Bruce suggested. Then, conscious of Rigg's angry frown, he changed his tack. "Our family has been British in Virginia for a hundred and fifty years. Mother is distraught at what these rebellions could lead to."

"And well she might be," Rigg replied hotly. "Robbie hides his head in his fields. You let yourself be controlled by your King-loving father-in-law. There's only Honor and me—"

"Honor?" Bruce challenged. "I hear no word of her protesting on courthouse steps."

Rigg laughed. "I understand that Mother always refers to her grandson as Baby James. Has she ever mentioned that his entire name is James Otis Tucker?" He rose. "Asa and I have a ship due in this afternoon. It was pleasant to see you, brother. Tell Mother that I am too much her child to be swayed from my beliefs by soft words."

Bruce was guilty of softening Rigg's own words a little in making his report to Merit. She tightened her lips and thanked him in a surprisingly docile tone. "There is only one thing more," she added. "If the Stamp Act is repealed, will you talk to Rigg again?"

Bruce agreed, not realizing that his promise would take him back to Norfolk within a month. Unfortunately that same month brought Janet so near to term with her child that Bruce resisted his mother's plea at first.

Merit was adamant. "Only get him to listen," she insisted. "Never have I heard such an outpouring of love for our king as has come since he repealed that act. He has heard our cries as a father. Exact a promise from Rigg. Now is the time."

There was no tavern cameraderie between them on this visit. Bracing himself against a mast, Rigg heard Bruce out with a cold face. Gulls dived overhead. The ripeness of rotting fish heads fouled the air. In a chorus of sounds, the shouts of seamen, the rattling of masts and shrouds, only Rigg stayed silent.

When Bruce was through, Rigg drew a gold coin from his pocket and tossed it in his palm.

"The king's repeal was only half a victory, Bruce," Rigg told him. "That same day the king signed an act permitting Parliament to legislate for us in all cases."

Bruce waited out Rigg's forbidding expression.

"We come of gambling men, my brother. I'll wager you that before a year is out, another such insult will cross that water and the king's new act will bind us to it."

The wager had been too intense to permit even a handshake. Not until his craft started upriver toward Candle Creek did Bruce realize the significance of Rigg's last words.

"I stand with my fellows. Tell your mother what you please."

God in heaven, Merit Billings had lost another son.

4

The Eyes of the Blind

(May 1767)

> Say to them that are of a fearful heart, Be strong, fear not: behold, your God will come with vengeance, even God with a recompense; he will come and save you.
> Then the eyes of the blind shall be opened, and the ears of the deaf shall be unstopped.
>
> Isaiah 35:4–5

WITH THE BIRTH of Bruce's son, Chris, a window opened in Merit's life, flooding it with joy and light.

There had not been such a baby since her brother James, she thought. Chris was strong-willed, even as James had been, and had with this spirit a teasing warmth that made Merit a slave to him from the day of his birth.

Secretly Merit had felt small interest in Janet Brainard. Although she was pretty in a pallid way, she seemed to have as little wit as she did spine. But with the birth of the child Janet had turned to Merit for guidance. Almost at once Merit began to understand the fascination of Bruce for his wife. She was like a warm wax in one's hands, worshipful and soft with gratitude for the smallest kindness. Merit was never apart from the child for more than a day except when Brainard sent Bruce off about the colony. At those times, Janet's father moved in with her, making the girl wholly her father's child.

Merit would have been welcome even during those times, but she so loathed Geoffrey Brainard, considering him a ruthless, small-minded tyrant, that she avoided Bruce's home when Janet's father was in residence.

The coming of the child inspired her in a myriad of small ways. She labored over christening clothes made from Magda Steele's fine stock. For Chris's first birthday she had a foal bred from the racing stock that had been the pride of Candle Creek since her grandfather's time. Astonishingly, when the boy's birthday came, Brainard himself was off in England.

"Whatever for?" Merit asked Bruce.

Bruce shrugged. "He plays his cards very near his chest. Checking on property there in Sussex, I imagine. Perhaps he was only homesick for old friends, old places."

During Brainard's absence, Merit gloried in her time with the child, but she found her mind dwelling on this trip. His journey fired her with a secret guilty dream. She wondered why she hadn't thought of it before. To be in England would be to see Philip and know his family. His sons now had sons of their own. And in England she would be free of the grumbling talk and the inconvenience of boycotts, which only half worked anyway.

Only her aging mother kept her here. Her mother and the child Chris. With his face raised to hers, she knew herself both loved and loving, a rare sweetness flowing in the drought of her lonely life.

Brainard returned as he had left, without explanation. He brought with him a young man named Harvey Kriswell, whom he described vaguely as a manager. By the time he had settled Kriswell into his warehouse in Yorktown, Bruce was off again on his travels around Virginia in Brainard's stead.

When Chris turned one in the fall of 1768, he was already promising to reach the great height of the Rigg men. Asa Forrester came for the celebration, bringing Chris a three-masted ship so well carved that it would sail in the pool in the grove. He also brought a stranger, whom he introduced as Jonathan Rye.

Instead of his usual brief conversation with Merit's mother about the Fraser company, Asa was closeted with Em and his friend for a long time, with the door firmly closed. In the late afternoon Asa summoned Merit to come to sign a document as a witness.

She stared at the quill in his hand. "A will?" she challenged. "But you made such a testament years ago."

"Those same years have outdated it," her mother explained. "This time I deed the Fraser company to Rigg alone. Asa says it is time."

"But what of the others?"

"Planters and lawyers and housewives?" Em challenged. "Robbie has seen to his own fortune. Honor is wed and in no short shrift. As for Bruce, who can that old vulture leave his property to but Janet and the child?"

"But Rigg is a wild and unsettled boy," Merit protested.

"If you don't want to sign, I can send for the overseer," Em said. "Rigg is a man who knows ships and seamanship and his own true mind."

As tempted as she was to turn away, Merit lifted the pen. She watched her name flow onto the paper in ink that seemed a world away. She had lost. Over and over and over she had lost. Robbie, then Rigg. Honor had named her second son Patrick Henry Tucker. The young fools had even moved to Boston, where the fever was the worst. The dreams she and Matthew had spun by the hearth had faded with the smoke from its embers. She looked up to see Asa watching her. Could he still be waiting? They were old now, both of them, but sometimes she still saw that shy, hopeful question in his eyes.

She turned away briskly. God willing, she would see England and leave the memories of her bitter losses on the shores of this miserable river.

• • •

In the spring of 1769 Chris fell victim to whooping cough. Merit and Janet nursed the child in spells, battling his fever and praying by his bedside as his strength failed. There seemed to be no world outside that draped room, no cause for concern past the child's next painful breath.

Only as he began to regain his strength enough to be carried out to sun in a chair, did Bruce mention to his mother what had been going on during those lost weeks.

"Life will change now for all of us," he warned. "The governor dissolved the Assembly rather than let them send their address to the king about the Townshend Acts."

"He had the right to do so," she reminded him.

"But the burgesses held a meeting later in Raleigh Tavern. There will be no more English goods brought in after September, and no more slaves after November."

"They tried a boycott before. It was more a nuisance than anything else."

"This will be different. This will be enforced."

"That's ridiculous. What do you propose to wear for clothing? How would you replace a broken dish? Will tea suddenly sprout in tobacco fields?"

She saw his rising color. "I am making no political statement, Mother." He lowered his voice, that it not carry beyond the two of them. "I only say that you should watch your tongue and be careful of what you say. The people have an ugly spirit concerning all this."

She stared at him. "I don't believe my own ears. How have you turned so craven? Have you bent and leaned for old Brainard until you have no spine of your own left? God help me that I see the day when a son of Matthew's asks me to conceal my loyalty to my king. I have never yielded to tavern-roistering rabble and I never shall."

Even as she spoke, Merit was secretly conscious of how few of her old friends ever came by or sent for her own company. How many heads had turned away on the streets of Williamsburg as she passed?

She rose and would have left the room, but his urgent tone made her pause.

"George Mason," he recited. "Peyton Randolph, Thomas Jefferson. Are these men who can be named tavern-roisterers?"

Merit wanted to know if her oldest son was in this rebel number, but she could not—or dared not—put the question into words.

5

The Light of the Candle

(August–September 1769)

Moreover I will take from them the voice of mirth, and
the voice of gladness, and the voice of the bridegroom,
and the voice of the bride, the sound of the millstones, and
the light of the candle.

Jeremiah 25:10

WITH A SINKING heart, Bruce looked at the itinerary his father-
in-law had set up for him. Even if each of his stops could be
managed with the utmost speed, he would be absent from his
family for a full month. With any delay at all, he would not
see his wife or child for six or seven weeks. Brainard was
watching with a closed face.

"Is there something amiss?" Brainard asked.

"Not amiss," Bruce replied. "I only notice that I will be
away for the celebration of Chris's birthday."

"It is the nature of a child to have such a celebration every
year."

"With his health so newly restored, we'd hoped to make
this birthday one of special thanksgiving."

"What better way than to work at securing the child's
coming estate?" Brainard challenged. Bruce was startled into
silence, this being the first time he had ever heard the old
man mention Chris's inheritance, even in passing.

He realized at once that it had been foolish to expect any support from Janet on his resistance to the trip.

"Father never plans without good reason," she assured him. Why had he considered this obedience to her father as such a fine thing in a wife? Yet when she sought his eyes, his annoyance always melted.

"If your father hadn't sired such an irresistible daughter, I wouldn't complain of these great trips."

She smiled and slipped into his arms, her hair soft against his face. He was astonished to feel the sudden warmth of tears through his blouse.

"It isn't like you to cry," he whispered, holding her very close. She caught his arms in an almost painful grip.

"We've never parted this way before," she told him.

He couldn't remember her lips being so soft and yielding as they were when he bid her farewell.

With the August sun punishing their backs, Bruce and Brainard's servant Roger rode to West Point by evening of the first day and crossed over into King and Queen County, where Brainard had a plantation of some nine hundred acres.

The overseer, Benjamin Porter, greeted Bruce in a manner that seemed a little strained. Only after they had ridden the land and gone over the books together as usual, did Porter come out with his question.

"Will you be making this trip again then?" he asked.

Bruce was startled. "As far as I know."

Porter shrugged. "I just wondered, the instructions being different this time. Brainard said these reports would go to a certain Harvey Kriswell at Yorktown."

"Ah." Bruce nodded. "Kriswell. That's the new man that Brainard brought back with him from England. He manages the warehouses in Yorktown for Brainard."

"And such places as this too?" Porter asked.

"Brainard said nothing to me," Bruce admitted, "but then, he's not a man to bandy words."

Porter added more wine to Bruce's glass. "A man would starve with such clams for food," he said with a grin.

Predictably, not all the stops could be managed with dispatch. By the time Bruce was finished with Brainard's business in Caroline County and was riding toward Germanna, he was not only hopelessly behind schedule but totally confused.

Every stop brought new questions. The Rappahanock plantation had been sold, with the promissory note to be delivered to Kriswell in Yorktown. What was the old man up to? In all honesty, Bruce would feel himself lucky to be relieved of these tedious trips of Brainard's properties. Strange pillows only increased his fondness for home, for Janet's pale flesh under his hand, for the grinning mischief of little Chris.

By the night of Chris's birthday, Bruce was on the Potomac River. He had hoped that a letter might await him from Janet. When none was waiting him, he drank deeply until bedtime, angry at her, and angrier at Brainard for sending him on this miserable trip. Heated by wine and restless of spirit, he walked outside along the river by himself. A night bird sang, and the slip of fish was curiously soothing. Only as he turned to go in did he see the star. It had come from the east and rose slowly, trailing a great tail of fire that stretched like a giant eel upward toward the southwest. He stared at it for a long time, heavy of heart for no reason he could name.

At the door of the tavern a man stepped from the shadows.

"It's been coming like that for two days now. God knows what it portends."

Bruce muttered something reassuring. He couldn't expect a tavern idler to know what maps of the sky had been drawn these last years. Such blazing planets had been read as omens since time began, and plain men would find it hard to give up such superstitions. Why had God set such delicate order in the skies if he meant to put it into disarray for the death of a king or the small problems of man?

Yet each night the rest of that week Bruce watched the planet trail its tortuous path across the sky, plagued by apprehension.

By the first of September there was no sign of it left, though he searched for it a long time in the star-sprinkled sky.

On Thursday the seventh of September, Bruce reached Yorktown. He dismounted at the tavern under a dark, mottled sky. The ships in the harbor rode low, as if burdened by the weight of the heavy air. Although he wanted nothing so much as a draft of cold ale and a cool pillow, Bruce knew that two long hours' of work lay between himself and Kriswell. Having secured a room for himself and his man, he looked for Kriswell at the warehouse.

"He's out for the evening," the clerk explained. "There's friends of his on the ship just in from England."

"Then I'll have my mail and see him first thing in the morning," Bruce decided.

After a frowning inspection, the clerk shook his head. "There's nothing here for you this time."

"That's impossible," Bruce argued. "There must be something there from my wife."

The clerk shook his head again. "Not from her or from Brainard. Haven't had a line from him for a week or more, maybe two." Then he smiled. "Your mistress is probably too busy keeping the boy happy, with you gone and all."

Bruce smiled weakly. Chris could certainly keep her occupied, but Janet might have stirred herself to write a few lines at least. That nothing had come from Brainard was equally amazing. For a man so careful with words, he was a dedicated paper scratcher. Tomorrow, Bruce promised himself. He would be home tomorrow if he had to teach his mare to fly.

After supper, he walked along the wharf, stretching the miles from his bowed legs. The air was still. Occasional snatches of music and muffled laughter came from the English ship whose hospitality Kriswell was enjoying.

"Tomorrow," he promised himself, "tomorrow I will be home."

The rattling of the shutters wakened Bruce a little before dawn. The servant groaned as Bruce rose to the window. An occasional ribbon of jagged light showed the trees outside bent from the urgency of the rain driving along the street.

"Get up," he ordered his servant. "Up and dressed. There's a storm coming in."

His man was still grumbling as they made their way downstairs, but no man was sleeping. The innkeeper, barelegged and in his nightcap, was overseeing the securing of his windows and doors against a gale.

"There's nothing to do," he shouted at Bruce. "We've always stood, and we always will. What God starts, he can likewise stop."

The wind was still howling at dawn. By midmorning four ships had been driven ashore. Only the cutting of her mainmast had left the English ship still safely riding at her anchor.

Over the protests of the innkeeper, Bruce let himself out to seek out Kriswell.

The bowsprit of a schooner was imbedded in one of the

warehouses, and the top of Brainard's warehouse had been blown cleanly away.

"Any word from Williamsburg?" Bruce shouted at Kriswell, who was desperately trying to protect his merchandise.

"You'll be lucky if it still stands," Kriswell replied. "God curse this heathen climate of yours anyway. They say that the rain forced through fourteen-inch walls farther up the bay."

"I'm off to home, then," Bruce told him. "I'll come back for what meeting we need."

"Don't be a fool," Kriswell barked. "There's nothing to go for and less than a road to follow there."

"I've no choice," Bruce replied.

"God loves a fool." Kriswell shrugged, turning again to his labors.

How many times had Bruce ridden from Yorktown to Williamsburg in a brief three hours? Not in this gale. His horse slid in mire, picked her way past fallen trees, and circled tobacco houses ripped from their foundations. The wind still blew. If Bruce had shouted the prayers he was whispering, they still would have been torn from his lips by the force of the storm.

He passed Williamsburg without a curious glance. Only at the gate of the Springer plantation did he draw to a halt. Uprooted trees rested on the hedges of the maze garden. The cooperage had lost its roof, and pools of yellow mud swirled in the stableyard. The front door of his house hung open, banging uselessly against its frame.

His shouting finally brought a servant from the nearest field.

"Gone," the man told him. "They're all gone."

At Bruce's question, the man pointed to the fields.

Bruce turned away. No doubt the slaves had sought refuge in the fields. He had no time for them now. He must find Janet and Chris, God keep them safe.

But he paused. Janet and Chris would be in Williamsburg with Brainard. He was too near Candle Creek not to check on his mother and Grandma Em. And as he had feared, the damage was even more extensive as he neared the river. Only by dismounting and leading his horse could he pass from the land road to the house. But felled trees and flattened sheds seemed like nothing once he saw Merit's reassuring face.

"No lives lost, thanks to Young Will," she told him. "As

always, the crops are gone. But tell me, how did the dear ones fare?''

''Apparently they are with Brainard in Williamsburg. The house is empty and the servants have fled. How has she been?''

''I never see them when you're gone, you know that. I did stop by a couple of times but only to find her gone.'' Her eyes darkened. ''Do go to them, Bruce. Poor Chris must be in terror.''

With the lessening of the wind, the rain increased its force. Wet and chilled to bone, Bruce retraced his steps.

Brainard's house was locked and silent. The darkened windows started the first spiraling of Bruce's panic. The office, he thought. There would be a message at the office. His key was stubborn against the lock, and his hand trembled at the lighting of the lamp. As the room sprang into light, Bruce stood staring stupidly. It was clean, clean of papers and books and the leather stand that had stood inside the door. The light slid off the polished top of Brainard's desk.

Frantically Bruce tugged at the drawers, one after another, seeking some sign. Empty, all empty. Even as he slammed the last one back into place, old Jim opened the door, broom in hand.

''They're gone,'' Jim said, ''and have been for nearly two weeks now.''

''What do you mean, gone?'' Bruce challenged him.

Jim shifted from one leg to the other, ducking his head against the anger in Bruce's voice. ''Packed and gone,'' he chanted. ''By cart to Yorktown, and from there to the sea. So they say.''

''To the sea,'' Bruce whispered numbly. My God, then where were Janet and the child?

''To England on the *Merry Hart*,'' Jim went on. ''That's how it's told. Him along with the young ones. The *Merry Hart*.''

Bruce felt the life leak from his limbs. Dropping to Brainard's chair, he stared at Jim, who wavered strangely in his sight. ''England. Janet and Chris.''

''Aye,'' Jim replied. ''On the *Merry Hart*.''

The candle wavered and darted as Jim closed the door behind himself.

Of course. God in heaven, why hadn't he realized? Brainard

312

had plotted to leave the Virginia that he increasingly detested. And Janet, weakling that she was, had obediently trailed along with him, taking their son. Bruce himself had carried the contracts for the plantations Brainard had so carefully sold. Bruce himself had laid Brainard's remaining property under Kriswell's management.

"Bastard," Bruce howled in the empty room. "Bastard. May God strike him dead!" Dead, dead, dead, echoed hollowly around the deserted room.

He could almost hear Janet's voice, feel the warmth of her tears against his chest.

"Father never plans without good reason."

"We've never parted this way before."

Where was the fury of his mother's blood? His pain went past fury to nausea. The candle sputtered quietly as he sat resting his thundering head in his arms.

It was night when he carried his candle through the Springer house. Nothing was gone but Janet's own possessions. The ship Asa Forrester had carved for Chris lay on its side in the boy's room, but the cupboards were emptied of his clothing. Bruce turned his horse toward Candle Creek with blinded eyes.

Somehow Asa Forrester had gotten there already, to check on Grandma Em. From the passage Bruce could hear him shouting the news to his deaf grandmother.

"As well as could be hoped for," he was saying. "God be praised no lives was lost."

Asa was sitting with his back to the door, leaning toward Grandma Em's chair. He was still shouting when Merit raised her eyes to Bruce's face.

"Not all were so blessed," Asa was shouting. "They fear for a ship bound for Gravesend out of Yorktown. A rig called the *Merry Hart*."

Something in Bruce's chest turned and bolted, to land painfully against his gut.

God in heaven! The *Merry Hart*.

He turned. Setting one foot carefully in front of the other, he left the house. The lawn was sodden and littered with refuse. Cattle, released by the uprooting of their fences, grazed in his mother's garden. The face of the river was scarred by floating timber. On one of these, a bedraggled rooster crouched, its neck buried in its folded wings. Beyond lay the sea.

· 6 ·

The Wanderer

(Autumn 1769–1773)

He taketh away the heart of the chief of the people of the earth, and causeth them to wander in a wilderness where there is no way.
They grope in the dark without light, and he maketh them to stagger like a drunken man.

Job 12:24–25

IT WAS CLEAR at once that Bruce could not stay in the haunted rooms of the Springer plantation. Only when he had arranged for its management and returned to Williamsburg did he realize that the specter he was trying to escape walked within himself.

He was unable to keep his mind on a topic for more than a few scattered moments. No chair was comfortable, and no bed fitted his frame. He ordered meals brought, only to lose his appetite before they were set in front of him.

He went to see Rigg in Norfolk.

His brother considered his words for a long time before replying. "A man doesn't lightly undertake an ocean crossing. Once begun, there is no turning back. Once arrived, you will need to make the decision a second time."

"But I have to know the truth," Bruce insisted.

Rigg sighed. "Truth isn't delivered in a barrel labeled with its contents. Truth comes out slowly, one fragment and then the other, until the shape is exposed. And it comes in its own time.''

"But the *Merry Hart*—'' Bruce began.

"What can you learn?'' Rigg asked. "A small ship saw her in distress in the path of the gale. No word has yet come of her arrival in Gravesend. What can you learn by following her there?''

"I have to know.''

"Granny Em had to know too when our grandfather's ship was sighted under a black flag. In time she knew. You will too.''

"You're telling me that Janet and Chris are lost.''

"I'm saying that the *Merry Hart* was not a homemade smuggling craft slipping from cove to cove under cover of night. She went registered from Yorktown, and if, or when, she arrives at Gravesend, that too will be a matter of public record. All of that takes time.''

"It will be too late.''

"It was too late when your wife chose the stronger of her two masters.''

Bruce inhaled sharply. "If you were not my brother, I would challenge you for those words.''

Rigg's expression turned rueful. "And if you were not my brother, I would not be trying so hard to stiffen you to face reality. A man stands to lose more by action in such cases than by default.''

Bruce chose to act. "You could go with me,'' he told his mother. "It would be an easy way to see your brother Philip after all these years.''

Strangely, her eyes did not shine at that. "It's too late,'' she told him. "Everything is too late.'' The light that had come into her life with Chris had died with him, taking all other fires with it.

Bruce sailed for Gravesend in February, six months after the storm. He was three weeks in passage and a month in London, breathing the stink of coal smoke. He sought and asked and pleaded. In return he got more platitudes than fact. The *Merry Hart* had been sighted in distress in the midst of a gale. She had never arrived in port.

Brainard's land in Sussex had fallen to a nephew who mumbled of God's mysterious ways. Bruce stared at the

315

fields and lanes where Chris would have been brought. So young and dear a life, so pointlessly taken.

Every Londoner he met wanted to talk of the colonial situation. People told him of blood in the streets of Boston, in America, of a mob attacking British soldiers. He shrugged away their questions.

His Uncle Philip Rigg rose cordially to greet him. His face, which was seamed with time, grew damp as he took Bruce's hands.

"Merit's son," he kept repeating. "And Matthew's."

His Aunt Caroline explained her poor health to him at elaborate length, while her hands stayed busy with the butter spreader. Her pale fat fingers, heavy with rings, left more of an impression on him than the lines of her aging face.

"Merit's letters touch me deeply," Philip told him when Caroline had withdrawn. "I have prayed a great deal over her difficulties with her other children." He sighed. "Old skeletons, old bones. I realize now that it was harder for Merit than for me to have parents more interested in their private wars than in our welfare."

Taking no notice of Bruce's amazement, he passed on, like the London strangers, to questions about America under Lord North's administration. "You must have heard that the Townshend Acts have been repealed except for the one on tea," he told Bruce. "Will that finally settle this rebellion among the colonists? What do those Americans want anyway?"

"I have paid small notice to politics," Bruce admitted.

"Of course," his uncle said, as if just remembering the reason for Bruce's presence in England. "You surely know that in your son, Merit lost the only person she ever loved deeply besides Matthew and me."

Again his uncle ignored Bruce's astonished expression, as his tone turned confidential. "I must tell you that I constantly press Merit to join us here. Caroline would welcome her as much as I. She would be among her own."

"Perhaps the great age of Granny Em keeps her there."

"Oh, surely not," Philip protested. "I can't imagine that Mother greatly cares whether Merit stays or goes."

"Those are hard words for me to understand," Bruce told him.

"They would have been hard for me to say once," Philip replied. "I had to become a man before I understood our childhoods, Merit's and mine, for what they were. I left in time; Merit did not. She deserves better than life has given her. You see, our mother lived for her god and our father, in that order. There was little love left over for us.''

Bruce returned to find his mother much changed. She was thinner than he had ever seen her. Her eyes were shadowy and her voice subdued. Even her anger seemed to have fled.

"Tell me about her," he asked Belle Sommers.

"You can see from the condition of the plantation," she replied.

"Is it an illness? Has she had the fever?"

Belle shook her head. "She lost her love for life with your son."

"But she can't go on like this," Bruce protested.

"It is common for lives to outlast hope," she told him.

Bruce might have moved back to Candle Creek if she had asked him to. The courts were at a standstill, leaving no work for him. Instead he simply took over the management of the family properties. Merit barely seemed to notice.

Using his house in Williamsburg as a base, he began those long rounds of inspection that had led Robbie to Barbara Dunbar. His chronic restlessness welcomed those same long hours in the saddle that had so plagued him when Janet and Chris still lived.

"What do Americans want anyway?" his uncle had asked. Bruce had left the question hanging in the air. He continued to do so, but the great comet that had traversed the sky before the hurricane obsessed him.

Brainard had not been alone in shaking the dust of the troubled colony from his life. From a scholar returning to England, Bruce bought a telescope to study the stars. He began to keep a diary of temperatures and barometer readings. The Indian war continued to rage along the western border. Rebels were defeated in North Carolina by the governor's forces. From the disorder of the society around him, Bruce turned increasingly to the order of the heavens and the rhythm of the seasons.

In the summer of 1772 Sam Dunbar died.

Only a fingernail-paring of a moon silvered Dunbar's fields when Robbie staggered from Sam's deathbed into the crisp air.

Certainly he was no stranger to death—his own father, his grandfather, Barbara wielding her whip in fury over the loss of her brother. He was painfully conscious of the hollowness of Bruce and his mother's lives since the deaths of Janet and Chris. And Sam Dunbar's death had come as no surprise. The old man had been a veined whiteness against his pillow since the turn of the year.

The surprise was that Sam, surrounded by his blood relatives had asked that Robbie alone stay with him during those last pained hours.

His strength ebbed and flowed like the river tide. And like that tide it flowed both salty and sweet.

"You are my son, Robbie Fraser Billings, even as Barbara is my daughter, by the grace of God."

"Through you I have been privileged to have two fathers," Robbie told him.

"That is a debt that runs two ways," Sam said. "You live in strange times, my son. We are in a calm between storms. The next gale will tear the timbers from many lives."

When Robbie didn't speak out of confusion, Sam raised his head to stare at him sternly.

"Hear me, Robbie. During calms you mend fences. When the storm comes again you must meet it bravely, putting away fear."

Before Robbie could probe the meaning of his words, the old man sighed and was gone.

Barbara, strange, strong Barbara moved slowly from her predictable fury to acceptance. "At least he died as he lived," she told Robbie at last. "With dignity and grace."

"And as a father," Robbie told her. "His last words to me were admonitions."

"About what?" she asked.

"I confess I'm not sure." As he repeated Sam's words, she listened soberly, then drew him close. "Sometimes his mind was not the clearest, there at the last," she reminded him.

Robbie, in Williamsburg for the assembly of 1772, leaned against the hearth and talked to Bruce of his father-in-law. "Sometimes I think that Sam Dunbar was a prophet. We have indeed had a calm between the storms. Now this Gaspee has been destroyed and the governments are at it again.

"This occurrence hardly seems large enough to constitute a

storm," Robbie went on. "But I often think about prophecy—Aunt Magda and her special gifts. What wouldn't a man give to know the truth about what is coming."

The truth. Bruce looked at Robbie but heard Rigg's voice. Rigg had been right. Somehow, during these restless years, he had accepted the loss of Janet and Chris, accepted it gingerly, like a scar that must be touched once in a while with a tentative finger. But the restlessness had stayed. A calm between two storms?

"You've left me," Robbie teased. "You're a thousand leagues away at least."

"Make that years," Bruce told him, leaning forward to fill his glass. "Granny Em still reads a lot to Alice from that old Lyon journal. I find myself listening almost compulsively.

"When Sir Francis Drake stopped in Virginia to check on the men whom Grenville had left there in 1585, a storm blew in from the southwest. It was a hurricane gale that drove Drake's ships into disarray. The terrified Englishmen, our ancestor Bennett Lyon among them, waded to the ships in such panic that Harriot's records were lost in the swirling tides. All these years we have been conditioned by experience to watch for such storms. We are poorly warned of such storms as come from the north."

In October of 1773 Will Lyon came home from his journey west. Nabby's new son walked toward him on uncertain legs.

"Some of Daniel Boone's party have returned too," Will told Bruce. "Those that survived the Shawnees."

"Are you going back?" Bruce asked.

"I would in a minute if I were a man alone," Will told him. "Having Nabby and the boys, it is different."

When the tea shipments arrived that November, New York and Philadelphia turned them around and sent them back. Charleston stored the tea in damp cellars to rot. In Boston, the Sons of Liberty boarded the ships in disguise and dumped the tea into the harbor.

Bruce listened to the merchants celebrating this act of daring in Raleigh Tavern, and he thought of Will's words.

"I am a man alone," he told himself, wondering why his restlessless hadn't abated after five long years.

7

Season and Purpose

(1773–1775)

To every thing there is a season, and a time to every
purpose under the heaven:
A time to be born, and a time to die; a time to plant, and a
time to pluck up that which is planted.

Ecclesiastes 3:1–2

IN THE OLD days, when Merit had still cared about the life of
the colony, she had warned of a fateful day.

"They will go too far," she insisted. "These rebels will
one day snap the king's patience. Then they will taste the
cutting edge of a sovereign's fury."

Her words turned to prophecy after the spilling of the tea in
Boston harbor. The city was boycotted, its people to be
starved into submission for the rashness of a few. Strangely,
although Robbie was among the planters donating grain to
send to the beleaguered city, it was neither the Intolerable
Acts nor the governor's dissolution of the Assembly that
turned him patriot at last. Bruce listened to his brother's story
without surprise. In his heart he must have known that it was
only a matter of time.

That summer elections had been held all over the colony.
Many counties chose delegates to a Virginia Convention as
well as to the governor's Assembly. Robbie declined his
neighbors' urging to attend this convention.

"I am subject to the king," he told them, and added, in honesty, that concern for the welfare of his family dictated his course.

Fraser, his son, turned cold eyes on him at this report. "If I were of proper age I would take your place."

"You don't understand," Robbie told him. "This convention is openly designed to plan to battle against the king's laws. Think of your future."

Barbara answered for her son. "We have thought, Robbie, and we have prayed on this together, Fraser and I. You can be forgiven much for your upbringing, there in the tidewater among slaves. Fraser and I see slavery not as a matter of color but as one of condition. We see little difference between being shackled in iron or living with laws designed as chains."

"I was being wholly our mother's child on this," Robbie told Bruce. "I was denying the truth of the present to protect a safety that was already past. Thank God for Barbara, for her homespun clothing and sassafras tea."

At the Virginia Convention, Patrick Henry rose to twist men's hearts with his eloquent words. Plans were formed for volunteer companies in every county, and Fraser Billings was among the first to volunteer and the youngest to be accepted.

By this time, Bruce had become sufficiently concerned over Merit's health to write to her brother James in Maryland. Dr. James Rigg read Bruce's letter until he knew it by heart before he reached Norfolk.

"I fear for Mother," Bruce had written.

She is as slender as a girl and barely touches food. She seems unconscious of pain. Her friends have long ago abandoned her for her unpopular views on the king. She seldom leaves her room. When torches thrown by patriots from the river set the wharf on fire, she didn't even watch the servants fighting the blaze. She is emptied of life. Is there some elixir for such grief?

"She's enough to break your heart," Asa Forrester told James. "I only doubt that it comes from grief."

"How would you name the problem?" James asked.

"You're the physician," Asa reminded him. "I'll only tell you that she'd never have made a sailor if she was a man. It takes imagination to set out like that. You have to see your-

321

self on that wide ocean, on those strange shores. Why, she's never even been able to imagine a new life since Matthew's death. She can't conceive what a different life we would have without the weight of the crown's pressure on us. She can't even imagine her heart being stirred again since the loss of young Chris.''

"Then what can we do for her?" James questioned.

"Send her to England," Asa said flatly. "England is the past. It's Virginia's past and Merit's own, in the form of her precious brother Philip. Better she should stir the ashes of an old fire than die of the chill.''

James stepped onto the wharf at Candle Creek with a heavy heart. The great old double rows of cedars that had been planted and replanted for over a century had been half burned away. The wharf was charred. In the orchard, the limbs of unpruned trees drooped like tired birds.

The same bleakness was echoed in Merit's greeting.

"Aren't you even going to ask why I'm here?" James teased.

"Some sons visit their mothers," she replied. There was not even the glint of sarcasm in her tone.

"And brothers visit their sisters," he reminded her.

When she only shrugged, he studied her a moment.

"Do you know that this colony has raised arms against the king?''

"Fools pick nettles for their own beds," she told him.

"I'm talking about war, Merit," he said firmly. "The colonists had a pitched battle against the British at Concord and Lexington in Massachusetts. Your own governor's wife and family have taken refuge on a ship at Yorktown.''

"Why are you telling me all this?" she asked.

"I think you should leave. I think you should go to England and visit Philip until this trouble is past.''

"And what of Mother?"

"What can you do for her that Belle and Alice would not be happy to do in your place?''

"There was a time when I might have gone," she admitted.

"The time is now," he insisted. "This trouble cannot last forever. Go, and return if you wish, but go. Would you want to die without seeing Philip again?''

Her gasp was almost imperceptible. Her eyes widened, and

she rose unsteadily to stand with her back to him. He hoped that she might be weeping, anything to break through that spiritless shell.

She turned to him, dry-eyed.

"It's too late," she said with finality. "It's altogether too late."

Before James arrived back home in Maryland, the Continental Congress had rejected Joseph Galloway's conciliatory proposal, and three more generals had been sent from England to support Gage against the colonial forces.

By August, when King George III proclaimed the colonies in rebellion and called on all loyal subjects to help suppress this uprising, James Rigg had been commissioned in the Continental Army under Commander in Chief George Washington.

Merit's nightmare began as they always did, a slow rumbling and the rising howl of wind as rain lashed against the windows. Then she was running. She had been running all her life in this same frantic way, clinging to Philip's hand and running. She felt the silent scream rise in her throat and could feel the jagged red lines of terror coursing across her brain.

This time hands were laid on her. She screamed and fought, only to have Bruce shout at her desperately, "For God's sake, Mother. Come." He was wrapping a blanket around her even as he tugged her toward the door.

This was wrong. The dream was to end with Philip and herself shielded in the schoolmaster's arms. She fought the alteration of her dream.

"No," she kept screaming at Bruce. "Leave me be."

There was no resisting Bruce. She was terrified that he would force her outside. She knew what stench hung in that air. The rain had begun five days before, and pelted steadily, until the barnyard swirled with yellow filth and the corn lay level with the ground. The very air would smell like an open grave.

"Let me be," she shouted, "For God's sake, leave me be."

But her mother was there too, and Alice, clutching the old Lyon journal, and Belle with Nabby and the half-Indian children. Bruce was gone with Will Lyon, shouting. Snatches of his words were carried to her on the howling wind.

The storms of her life fused together in that reeking darkness. The wind, the rain, the lights of hell written jagged in the sky, and death. Aunt Martha with folded hands. The cat by the well house. Chris swallowed by the sea in the *Merry Hart*. Nabby's children were crying as Merit had wept as a child. Only her mother stayed serene, walled from the horror of the storm's screams by the mercy of deafness.

"No," Merit kept repeating quietly to herself. As long as she kept making that promise to herself, she wouldn't scream, she wouldn't lose control. "No. No. No."

When the wind lessened and the rain abated, Merit rose and went silently to her own room. The air was so heavy with moisture that she had to stop now and then to rest from her labors. She lifted her garments and folded them carefully. The servant who brought the tray stared curiously at the open trunks. Merit glared at her so fiercely that she set down the tray and went away wordless.

Merit had already been brought more news than she wished to know. Early that week Bruce had returned from the western plantations to shout the news to Em—of the Second Virginia Convention and the two regiments it had established, one under Patrick Henry and the other under William Woodford. James had called it war. The governor's family had fled. The coming of the hurricane had stripped Merit as it had the native trees. The pain of her loss was fresh again in all its torment— the memory of Chris's warm, loving arms and the *Merry Hart* diving into the dark maw of the sea.

Had she expected questions?

There were none.

Asa Forrester looked around Merit's cabin, fretting about her provisions. The ship was crowded with other Englishmen fleeing home. Only as she studied Asa's face did Merit feel the beginning of doubt.

"My children," she told him. "I am leaving my children."

"You have no children," he reminded her. "You have sons and a daughter." His eyes were gentle in the old way.

"But how can I leave my mother like this?"

"Your mother would far rather die apart from you than

have you live with such pain." He paused and covered her hand with his. "And I feel the same, Merit. I feel the same."

She couldn't meet his eyes. "I know you hoped," she stammered. "I'm sorry, Asa."

He shook his head. "There is nothing to be sorry for. I had dreams that didn't come to pass. You had the same. It's the way of life."

"I'm not running away," she insisted suddenly.

"And even if you were," he replied, "who would love you so little that they would hold you to a land you no longer loved? To children who have flown to strange roosts?" He smiled and leaned to press his lips against her cheek.

"Godspeed, Merit. Go to Philip and home."

8

Everything Beautiful

(Winter 1775–1776)

> He hath made every thing beautiful in his time: also he hath set the world in their heart, so that no man can find out the work that God maketh from the beginning to the end.
>
> Ecclesiastes 3:11

MERIT BILLINGS HAD been gone from Virginia for less than a month when Dunmore took the war to Norfolk. He seized the town, only to lose it again to the Virginians on the fifteenth of December.

The idea for the New Year's party came from Asa Forrester,

who slipped upriver by night bearing fresh fruit, sugar, and fine rum from the islands. "Such a celebration is an old tradition in this house," he reminded Belle Sommers. "If only Mistress Em's patriot sons and grandsons were to come, there'd be a host to feed."

"It's not likely many of them will be here," Belle mused, her mind already in the poultry yard.

"In body, perhaps not," Asa agreed. "But in spirit, there's no doubt that they will."

The preparations brought fine old perfumes to the kitchen house, sage and onion, the salty sweetness of Candle Creek ham. Asa claimed that the smell of the pudding alone was enough to bring on an attack of gout.

Rigg, in Williamsburg conferring with the Fourth Virginia Convention about the establishment of a Virginia Navy, came with a group of friends too far from home to have a place to celebrate. Robbie and Barbara and their children crossed the threshold for the first time since their marriage. The house rang with young voices talking and laughing. Alice was pressed by Bruce to play the spinet, and gave them a more rollicking tune than even Belle knew she could handle.

But not even the clamor of youth could drown out the distant thunder of cannonades, which began early in the day and went on until the evening without stopping. From the wharf, puffs of smoke could sometimes be seen rising from the air in the direction of Norfolk.

"As long as the cannons continue to fire, our forces are holding their own," Rigg assured Belle.

Emily Fraser sat in the midst of them, as Asa said, "The queen bee of an unruly hive." When there were many people in a room like this, turning their faces one way and another in conversation, Em became confused. She had learned to watch a speaker's lips and was able to understand most of what was said. But groups like this were impossible for her. The lateness of the hour and the blue haze of tobacco smoke must be the cause of a certain smudging of her vision, she thought. She saw young Will Sommers talking to a friend of Rigg's about the West. Even as he spoke, she remembered her Andrew describing the West to her. Her mouth tightened at the memory of the pungent grapes he had brought from the wild vines at Gilead.

Only Asa Forrester noticed when she rose, and was instantly at her side, his hand under her elbow.

"My shawl," she whispered, not wanting to disturb anyone.

"Let me come with you," he begged.

She shook her head, smiling. "I need the air," she explained.

The sudden chill of the winter twilight took a moment to get used to. High in the double row of cedars, dead limbs still hung from the hurricane that had been one too many for Merit to endure. Em knew that the wind that stirred those dry limbs sang of winter.

Her cane had long ago cut pockets in the path across the lawn and through the orchard to the grove by Candle Creek. The scent of cider hung among the trees, where reddened crisps of windfall went unharvested. She felt the girl Alice following her, and smiled. Alice would come, not because she should, but because she wanted to.

She had come through the orchard to the edge of the grove when she saw the figure among the trees.

She stopped and felt Alice's hand warm on her arm. Em hadn't seen Magda since the night she had come to stand before Gilead and warn them of its passing. Magda was unchanged by time. Slender as a child and not much taller, she stood among the trees, with the branches shadowing her dark clothing.

What had Andrew said? "We are all children in the school of God's universe. The lessons never cease. That your faith and mine and Magda's magic are all part of one God doesn't astound me."

The astounding thing was the sudden rise of faraway flame and billowing smoke in the distance beyond the trees. Will had spoken of Dunmore's firing cannons into Norfolk earlier in the day.

Em felt a shudder and knew with a certainty what she was watching. How clearly she remembered that house that her father had built for his long-awaited bride. She could trace the flaw in a certain brick of the hearth facing, the step that creaked, three down from the top, the sound of Robbie Fraser's footfall in the passage and the gruff rise of his voice calling her name.

"It's burning," she told Alice. "My home is burning."

By looking away for that moment she had lost Magda. When she turned back, the grove was empty of life.

"It is burning," she told Alice calmly. "That light you see above the trees is my old home burning."

A strange sense of exaltation filled her. Andrew often said that Gilead had been the one true home of his life. The burning of it had released him from all life. She was ready. Only God knew how ready she was.

"Andrew," she whispered, clutching at Alice as waves of giddiness battered her. A leaf, she thought with surprise. I crumple like a blazing leaf.

It was fully dark when Belle, having looked for them in the crowded rooms, came outside with Asa and a lantern.

"The grove," Belle suggested. "I can't believe she would go anywhere but to Candle Creek."

He didn't answer but stood staring at the sky.

"What is it?" she asked, following his gaze.

"I would say that Norfolk is turning to ashes."

"But my God, who would do such a thing? That fine port, that great city."

He was already moving toward the grove, along the familiar path. "We'd even burn it ourselves to keep Dumore from having it," he told her.

Without the lantern, they might have stumbled on Alice and Emily Fraser Rigg. Alice sat in the clutter of darkened leaves with Em's frail body cradled in her arms.

"My God," Belle cried softly. "Oh, Alice, my dear. What happened?"

The girl's face shone silver from her silent tears. "She saw her home burning over there. Then she smiled and called her husband's name and died."

"And you stayed with her," Asa said gently, leaning to lift his friend from her arms.

"I knew someone would come," Alice explained. "I didn't want to leave her all alone."

The lantern cast long shadows back and forth like the clapper of some giant silent bell, illuminating now the naked orchard, now the singing cedars. Em's white cap bobbed companionably against Asa's shoulder as he carried her home.

EPILOGUE

Pillars of Smoke

(January 1776)

And also upon the servants and upon the handmaids in
those days will I pour out my spirit.
And I will shew wonders in the heavens and in the earth,
blood, and fire, and pillars of smoke.

—Joel 2:29–30

To Mistress Peter Tucker
Boston, Massachusetts

My dearly beloved Honor,

How many times have I lifted this quill from ink to
write of my return to Candle Creek for the celebration of
this new Year, only to have it turn into a time of mourning.

It would be easy to blame the tardiness of this letter on
the ferment of our times, but that would be neither fair
nor honest. Instead, as brother and friend, I confess that
writing these words is more difficult than the journey.

The long years of my growing differences with Mother
pressed in on me as I approached that familiar door. It
was festooned with patriot ribands, Honor, that house
that was so long a bastion of stubborn loyalty to the king.

The air was like cider, from windfall, as always. The
bitch that came clamoring from the stable bore the spots
of her ancestor, Rascal.

Aunt Belle met me at the door. I had forgotten the clearness of her eyes and the strength of those remarkable hands. Her son was there with his Indian wife and their bright-eyed sons, and Alice of the beautiful soul.

I know that others have written of how Granny Em died there in the grove, with Alice at her side. Alice insists, and I believe her, that even though Granny spoke of her old home burning, she left life as happily as she lived it.

I remember scenes from that precious day, only scenes. That famous ham of Candle Creek curling from the knife like the petals of some exotic flower. Asa Forrester, his face bearing a new shadow since Mother is gone from our world. Robbie and his Barbara with their wordless communication that after all these years would light a candle in a dark corner.

The most important thing is that as we sat at supper and I looked around at our family, I thought of Mother in a strange new way. What I long considered her stubborn blindness might just be a loyalty that passes my understanding. The men of her life, Grandfather, our father and Uncle Philip, either died or still live still loyal to that crown. How can we claim to battle for freedom without giving her the freedom of her own conviction without blame or rancor? And she had the strength to give up all of us, excepting Bruce of course, and even him in the end, for the sake of that belief.

I guess what I most wanted to say was that we are blessed, Honor, in the woman we have sprung from.

May God's guidance be constant with you and yours. Your loving brother,

Rigg Billing
Captain, The Virginia Navy

Forgive me, but a postscript follows. . . .

One thing more came from my visit, a tale so strange that I thought to keep it to myself but find that I cannot. As a communicant of the Church of England and disbeliever in the superstitions of the past, I hold small credence in such tales. Yet my own peace of mind demands its telling.

You will recall that at the moment of her death, Granny

Em looked at the fiery sky and told Alice her home was burning.

She was right, Honor. At that same hour, the very streets that she played on as a child were being set to the torch. Some say that patriots did it to prevent the town falling into Dunmore's hands. Others claim it was malicious mischief done by our own troops, who were badly garrisoned and poorly fed and exhausted from their labors, holding the town against the British.

Whatever the real story, the house that had been Captain Robbie Fraser's and later the home of Guillam Jones, called Toad, flamed against the sky.

God only knows what brought this blazing vision to a dying woman's eyes, but it was not a story that I could leave untold, locked in my heart.

Again my love to you and Peter, James Otis and young Patrick.

Rigg

Turn back the pages of history...
and discover

Romance!

as it once was!

_____	05470-4	**CRYSTAL HEART** Lisa Gregory	$2.95
_____	07100-5	**THE WAYWARD HEART** Jill Gregory	$3.50
_____	07071-8	**A GLORIOUS PASSION** Stephanie Blake	$3.50
_____	04628-0	**THE FIFTH JADE OF HEAVEN** Marilyn Granbeck	$2.95
_____	867-21205-5	**CAPTIVE DESIRE** Kathleen Victor	$2.95
_____	04729-5	**PRAIRIE FLAME** Jessica Howard	$2.95
_____	06045-3	**RENEGADE LADY** Kathryn Atwood	$3.25
_____	04756-2	**A SHARE OF EARTH AND GLORY** Katherine Giles	$3.50
_____	05908-0	**TOUCH ME WITH FIRE** Patricia Phillips	$3.50
_____	07251-6	**MARIE FLEUR** Patricia Phillips	$3.50